# THE LOOK OF LOVE

Judy Astley

BLACK SWAN

TRANSWORLD PUBLISHERS
61–63 Uxbridge Road, London W5 5SA
A Random House Group Company
www.transworldbooks.co.uk

THE LOOK OF LOVE
A BLACK SWAN BOOK: 9780552773294

First published in Great Britain
in 2011 by Bantam Press
an imprint of Transworld Publishers
Black Swan edition published 2012



A CIP catalogue record for this book
is available from the British Library.



Addresses for Random House Group Ltd companies outside the UK
can be found at: www.randomhouse.co.uk
The Random House Group Ltd Reg. No. 954009

Typeset in 11/16pt Giovanni Book by Falcon Oast Graphic Art Ltd.

4 6 8 10 9 7 5

The Random House Group Limited supports The Forest Stewardship Council® (FSC®), the leading international forest-certification organisation. Our books carrying the FSC label are printed on FSC®-certified paper. FSC is the only forest-certification scheme supported by the leading environmental organisations, including Greenpeace. Our paper procurement policy can be found at
www.randomhouse.co.uk/environment

Printed and bound in Great Britain by Clays Ltd, St Ives plc

*For every woman who has had that heartsink moment while trying on clothes in front of a multi-angled mirror.*

# ONE

'One day, you'll look back at this and laugh!'

At 5.30 a.m., weak with the desperate exhaustion of the unslept, Bella murmured this familiar homily to her overlit reflection in the hotel's bathroom mirror. She was trying the words on for size, reminding herself firmly, seven floors up in New York, that this was the traditional ha-ha British way of coping with all manner of things going wrong, from granny tumbling into the wedding cake right through to full-scale bath-crashing-through-ceiling disaster. Were the annoyingly bouncy optimists who said this always right?

Bella reckoned that in this particular case, absolutely *not*. Surely it added up to something permanently *not* amusing when the highlight of a romantic weekend, a whole continent and a great big ocean away, was the bit when you raced out of the sleek boutique hotel and into a taxi, desperate to be on the plane home? Alone, that is. Alone because the one essential ingredient to *that* kind of weekend, the so-called lover, was in another room way down the corridor, cosied up in bed with the wife he'd somehow forgotten to mention. Terrific. Dis-bloody-aster. Bella wished on Rick the kind of nightmares that would make him wake up screaming, quaking and committing himself to a lifetime of desperately miserable celibacy.

Bella was counting slow seconds to the end of the long lonely night, when she could get the hell out of this city that was wrongly supposed never to sleep. Looking at her face in the mirror (skin a disturbing shade of lemon: she had to trust that was a trick of the peculiar eco-light), she had the impression that the opposite was true – that she was the only one awake. Furiously, she scrubbed at a blob of toothpaste that had found its inevitable Sod's Law way on to the front of her black Joseph jacket. Ha! Black! According to Rick's wife Carole, she shouldn't even be wearing black at all. She would now forever have doubts about at least half the contents of her wardrobe. Thanks, Carole, for that.

'Black just piles on the years, honey,' this pin-thin spike-nailed woman had sneered, leaning angular and elegant against the door frame of room 703, then adding, with one perfectly groomed eyebrow raised, and slight Botox-cracking smirk of the mouth, 'or perhaps you really *are* that old?'

Wow and ouch! How to respond to a comment like that? What to say when you were all glammed up in your slinkiest black silk strappy number, about to go out for a lush dinner with a man who had insisted, back in the UK, that he was safely long, long divorced from his wife? A wife who he'd also claimed (and goodness, how he'd lied here too, with bells on) was far more a moose than a minx. If so, there must be a whole lot of very cute mooses (meese?) out there in the good ol' US of A. The essential stinger retort-quip that had eluded Bella at the time would surely come to her three days too late, when she was lying in the bath back at home still seething about the insult and concocting the perfect phrase she hadn't had the instant wit to fling back. Wasn't it always the way? Even for Bella-the-writer (novelist, journalist), never usually short on words, the perfect phrase just had to go missing when it was most needed. And in truth it was Rick, the lying, cheating, two-timing slimeball, who deserved the whiplash words the most, not his stunning, immaculate wife. Oh how very, very swiftly after he'd been hunted down had he scurried around repacking his belongings and trailing Carole down the corridor like a naughty puppy. And he hadn't even had the grace – or possibly nerve – to look back at Bella once. Three months, she now reflected bitterly, three months of him in determined pursuit, all that passion in London, obliterated in three swift I-win minutes in New York by this stray's keeper, the moment he was on her home patch.

On the street way below Bella's window the city was at last waking up. Early office workers power-walked like cheetahs on a hunger mission, utterly unselfconscious in their sharp suits teamed unattractively with clumpy trainers and clutching skinny lattes and carb-lite pastries from the diner opposite the hotel. Bella, on the other hand, hadn't actually slept at all and, aching with jet lag, tiredness and crushing disappointment, she longed and longed to be on the plane, snuggling into seat 16K, a professionally smiling steward asking if she'd like tea, a *Daily Telegraph* and a nice cosy blanket. Oh, the comfort of small rituals. And yet she almost hoped no-one would be *too* kind to her, for surely one word of concern, one casual, well-meant 'And how are *we* today?' could set the floods off and she'd be weeping blotchily all the way to the Heathrow baggage carousel.

Five thirty. The phone rang and a morning-eager voice told Bella her cab was outside and that she was to Have A Safe Trip, Now. Thank goodness – time to get out of here. Bella took one last look round the small but perfectly formed hotel room to check for left-behind items. She hoped the room maid would find a happier home for the scarlet lace underwear that she'd left lying on the bed – tissue-wrapped, unworn, labels still on – which Rick had planned to see on Bella. She should have seen the warning light with that particular little gift . . . should have listened to her doubts about Rick being the kind of man who considered red underwear sexy. Red just . . . *isn't*, was Bella's opinion, or at least not on anyone who is no longer a girl of twenty. On anyone who came firmly under the heading of 'woman', it either looked plain trashy or as if it was being worn with a joky Santa seduction in mind. Even worse, the knickers were thong-style. Bella didn't *do* thongs as – regrettably – Rick already knew well. She'd be willing to bet serious money that Rick's wife didn't wear them either. Nice to think the two of them had something in common.

Bella wrestled with the handle of her blue leather Bric case (bought specially for this weekend – could she send Rick the bill?) and towed it after her into the corridor. Now, which room was Rick and Carole's? She tried to remember, as she walked towards the lift . . . oh yes, 712. Definitely. Almost definitely. Worth a guess anyway. She stopped outside it, kicked the room door viciously and repeatedly, thumping the trusty Bric against it for good measure, and yelled, 'Have a crap life, you lousy rotten bastard!' Then walked on as calmly as she could and pressed the elevator call button. As she stepped into the lift, she caught sight of the door of 712 opening. A small, bald old man in purple satin pyjamas peered, blinking, into the corridor, staring at her with a puzzled and decidedly half-asleep expression. As well he might. He certainly wasn't Rick. And he *definitely* wasn't Carole. Damn, Bella thought, giving the poor man a feeble, apologetic wave. Can't even get the parting gesture right.

'I dunno, it just feels a bit like . . . wrong?' Giles shrugged. Molly gazed at him, trying to guess where 'wrong' came into this. OK, it was Sunday. And maybe this was more of a Saturday-night sort of event – but Giles wasn't a churchgoer, so the idea of being scrutinized by God wasn't likely to be the problem. She couldn't help thinking Giles looked a bit like a lopsided shop dummy in oversized clothes. He was quite skinny but had lovely straight wide shoulders and they looked weird scrunched up like that, as if someone had snapped them and tried to fold them away, untidily. His hands were so firmly wedged in the pockets of his jeans that Molly was convinced he was keeping them safe from her, perhaps fearing that if she took hold of him, pulled him on to the bed, he would surely just die or dissolve into gloop or something. And there she'd been, thinking that the bed-thing was *exactly* what he wanted. He'd *said* he did. Hardly ever stopped saying it. What was not to believe? They'd planned this together, hours of whispering down the phone, texting, emailing, getting all geed up – it wasn't just some instant crazy plan she'd suddenly come up with.

Molly sighed lightly and prettily but felt like punching a big jagged hole through the huge mottled old mirror that had leaned against her mother's bedroom wall for so long that the carpet behind it was now a darker shade of blue and fluffier than in the rest of the room. What was the point of a boyfriend with a conscience? Conscience hadn't exactly been part of the scene all those times Giles had been trying – and failing – to persuade her to have sex with him under heaps of coats at parties, or in the ferns on the common, or that night at his place in the garage, in the back of the Range Rover when his mum had suddenly climbed in with the car keys and driven off to get petrol, without a clue that Giles and Molly were on the back seats, trying not to sneeze or giggle under the hairy, smelly blanket the dogs usually lay on.

She'd had this evening so perfectly organized; *everything* was working so far. She was one of the last in her school year group to offload her virginity and she wanted it to be a night to cherish, not a night to shudder about years later over bottles of wine in one of those 'how bad was it for you?' competitive conversations that she'd overheard shrieky women having in the pub. Mum was off in New York with that creepy, smiley American having whatever passed for a good time among Old People (details best not thought about). Alex was in Scotland visiting Dad. Her alibi plea – 'I *can't* miss Carly's party! It's the last one of the holidays!' – had, after a bit of a struggle ('A party on a Sunday? Strange day . . .' her mum had reasonably quibbled) and some convincing wailing, been accepted all round. Right now Bella would probably be picturing her innocently giggling on Carly's bed with lots of their classmates, in a scene like the sleepover from *High School Musical*, all trying on make-up and dancing around to popcorn music, drinking innocent Coke, getting ready for their so-fun evening. Yeah, right – like they were twelve or something.

Instead, Molly had slid back home from Carly's with Giles, creeping in over the back fence and keeping only the security lights on so as not to alert Jules from across the road who'd been coming in to feed the cat. She was now wondering why this boy she'd been seeing for four months and who claimed she'd been doing him serious damage by making him stay on the safe side of her underwear, had suddenly gone all reluctant on her. Perhaps a bit more vodka would help. Or not. She didn't know how much had the wrong kind of effect on boys. So far tonight they hadn't drunk much of it – neither of them liked it much with Tropicana orange and there wasn't anything else in the fridge apart from some milk that could have been there ages. You wouldn't want to risk sniffing at it. Why was her mum such a useless shopper?

Molly came up close to Giles and whispered into his long soft hair. It smelled of Bedhead serum, sweet, delicious. 'Don't you love me any more?'

She didn't touch him, just kept her body close to his and waited to see if those hands would stay crammed in the pockets. They didn't for long. She felt them slide round her back and he pressed her close against him, breathing hard in her ear. The bed was just falling-distance away. She wanted to lie on it and roll with him on the soft duvet. She wanted to be *under* the duvet, giggling with him, excited, a bit scared, skin against skin.

'Course I do! It's just . . . here . . . your mum's bedroom. There's all her stuff around. That dress hanging on the wardrobe door, it's like she's inside it. I can smell her perfume and it's like freakin' me?'

Molly, relieved that this was something simple she could fix, opened the wardrobe door and hurled the dress inside, then came back close to him.

'There. She's gone, vanished, and besides, the real *her* is on the far side of the Atlantic. Thing is, this is the only available proper grown-up big bed in the house. The guest-room one's covered in stuff for Oxfam, Mum's got her office in the littlest one with papers all over the sofa bed, Alex's is disgusting and boy-gnarly and my bed's just *child-size*.'

And it had her old soft polar bear on it, and an embroidered cushion that spelled out 'Princess Molly' and her cosy flowery PJs stuffed into a cloth poodle. These were things he didn't need to know about. He might smile and say, 'Ah, cute,' but it would also turn her back into some kind of infant. Also, on the big pin-board on the wall there were silly photos of all her mates and she'd think they were all watching her and Giles, especially Aimee who, even in the happiest pic, looked as if she knew it all and everyone else knew nothing. In Molly's case she was too close to right about that. She could just imagine Aimee, sneery and jeering, 'You're like *soooo* crap at that, Molly Duncan.' Also on the board was her brother Alex, who also really thought she was at Carly's and would mind that she hadn't trusted him enough to let him in on the truth; and then there was her grandmother Shirley who would definitely tell her – very loudly and preferably in embarrassing company – that 'you're only young twice!' and that free love wasn't anything new, darling, just *enjoy*.

Giles still looked unsure. His eyes had gone big and worried.

'OK, look it's no problem.' She stepped back from

him and looked at him, giving him one last chance. He smiled, hesitant and still, waiting to see what she wanted to do.

'Let's just go back downstairs and watch a DVD. It's all right. I just feel a bit sad . . .' She felt like a complete fool, actually, and close to tears. Like she'd made all the running and in the end had turned out not to be good enough for him. What did he want? A slapper like Aimee who'd done it with half of St Mart's sixth form? Yes, he probably did. Didn't they all? She made a move towards the door, but he caught her hand suddenly and pulled her back.

'No – it's fine. I'm over it,' Giles said. 'Come here, you.'

Home! Oh, how much more reliable were bricks and mortar than flesh and bones and the unfathomable so-called brains of stupid, stupid men! Now this, *this* really *was* like being reunited with a favourite lover, Bella thought as she trundled the Bric up the path. Never had she been so happy to see her mad turrets-and-gables Edwardian villa as she was tonight. The minicab squealed off down the road as Bella plonked her case on the step. Like a pope on airport tarmac, she kissed the front door's flaking Farrow & Ball Hague Blue paint-work before she put the key in the lock and whispered fondly, 'Oh house I love-love-love you!'

Thank goodness Molly and Alex weren't around to

witness this ignominious swift return. She wished Molly a fun time at Carly's, and hoped that Alex was putting up with James's finicky kitchen tidiness in the Edinburgh flat without completely exploding when he was reminded to clean the sink for the fifth time that day. James had taken to providing rubber gloves (new pack each time) for all house guests, laying them out on the beds along with towels. 'Dad's getting more loony by the bloody minute,' Molly had grumbled, the last time she and Alex had gone up to stay with him. You couldn't argue with that.

Bella was a bit surprised to see Molly's favourite black jacket hanging over the post at the bottom of the stairs, but assumed she'd simply forgotten to take it to Carly's with her. The jacket was still quite new and could barely be prised off the girl. She wore it with everything, but then that was, she remembered, the way with teenagers: they wore something to death for a couple of weeks, then it was abandoned for ever, or at least till you put it in the jumble bag, at which point they suddenly had a hissy fit about how *dare* you think it was OK to chuck it out, merely because it had been lying forgotten on a dusty floor for two years.

But it wasn't just the jacket. Bella switched on the kitchen light and had a confused moment when she wondered how it could be possible that she'd had a last-minute drink of vodka and orange – two things that she considered should never be mixed – before leaving for the airport at seven a.m. only thirty-six hours previously. Of course she hadn't. She wasn't even that nervy a flyer – why would she *not* have had her usual English Breakfast tea? Maybe Jules, in to feed the cat, had had a crafty nip? After all, it was now only Sunday night. She wasn't expecting Bella back till Tuesday morning. She'd just put it back in the fridge and forget . . . Music. *Music?* From upstairs. Oh-oh, just who *was* here? Jules was keen on Gilbert and Sullivan, not the Kings of Leon – Molly's current favourite – which was the sound echoing round the stairwell . . .

So. It had to be Molly. Telling herself she was lucky not to come home and find three hundred Internet-summoned teenagers rampaging through the house, uprooting roses in the garden and throwing up on the sofas, she tiptoed as silently as she could up the stairs. Then, having had a gruesome second-thought premonition about what she really *didn't* want to see, she retraced her near-silent steps and bounced back up the stairs noisily, shouting, 'Molly, is that you up there?'

There was a scuffling sound. Bella waited a moment before warily pushing open the door to Molly's room, but no one was there. Only the grubby white polar bear stared back at her. With a sigh that carried in it all the despair of the last couple of days, and with a dreadful foreboding about the inevitable, Bella went into her own bedroom and almost tripped over the scattered tangle of clothes and shoes on the floor.

'Mum! Hi! You're, like, not supposed to be here?' Molly's voice was high and scared and falsely bright.

''Lo Mrs Duncan.' Giles, in bed beside Molly, gave her his best lop-sided smile and waved a limp hand. Horribly, Bella couldn't help wondering about the rest of him . . . the part that was sure not to have been that limp. Alongside her seventeen-year-old daughter. Oh, terrific.

Molly pulled the duvet up further towards her chin. A bit of a pointless gesture at this stage, Bella thought.

'*I'm* not supposed to be here? Shouldn't I be saying that to you? What happened to "I *have* to be at Carly's"?' Bella snapped back.

'Um . . .' Molly's face went into a contorted-puzzled expression, as if she didn't really understand the question. Admittedly it was quite a daft one. Why on earth would she be at Carly's when she could be in a conveniently empty house, in bed with her completely delicious boyfriend? Lucky bloody her, Bella thought bitterly, her mind going back to what, if all had gone to plan, she herself could be doing right now. The Kings of Leon rocked on in the background, something about Sex on Fire. *Shut up*, Bella thought.

'Oh . . . aaaagh! Get dressed, Molly. And you . . .' She could hardly look at Giles. Those naked, skinny yet broad shoulders. Bare, male skin. It was all too much to face right now. 'Just . . . go home, Giles. Please.'

Bella left them to get sorted, went back to the kitchen, shakily poured the last of the vodka into a tumbler and added the orange. As she glugged down the oversweet repulsive drink she caught sight of the best-before date on the carton. It was way past its prime. 'It's not the bloody only one,' she said, swigging down the rest of it.

# TWO

'And he stayed on in the *hotel*? The same hotel as *you*? With his *wife*?' If Jules's disbelieving eyes got any wider they'd surely drop right out of her face. It was also obvious to Bella that Jules was trying very, very hard not to laugh. Her eyes were glittering with squashed-down mirth and her mouth was doing that involuntary twitching thing. All her little laughter lines, half obscured beneath the frondy wisps of her ginger-and-scarlet fringe, were trembling, desperate to crinkle into outright hilarity. Aha – so that's how the old saying worked; what the pundits *actually* meant was, 'Some day you'll look back on this and *everyone else* will laugh.' Well of course they would.

'I know, I know,' Bella groaned. 'If it wasn't me it had happened to, I'd think it was pretty damn funny too. A classic. It's like a *Family Fortunes* question, isn't it?

"What's the worst thing that could go wrong on a romantic weekend away with your lover?" The top answer would have to be: "A wife he's sworn he doesn't have turns up to reclaim him and he scurries off after her without a backward glance." OK, not the snappiest trip-off-the-tongue phrasing, but that's about the up and down of it.'

Bella yawned, still exhausted from sleep that had been full of strange primary-coloured dreams of scarlet aircraft and yellow cabs and a dozen naked, writhing teenagers having sex in the wrong beds. How come only one night in a far time zone could cause as much jet lag as being away for a whole month? Or was it a result of feeling just plain old misery and hopelessness? Jules had dropped in to feed the cat, letting herself in with the spare key and getting a shock to find the place occupied and smelling of coffee. She'd expected Bella to be away for another forty-eight hours. Now she was settling in comfortably, filling the kettle, helping herself to Bella's heap of honeyed toast, wanting the full story and determined not to leave without it. That was what you got from people you'd been friends with since day one at secondary school. If they were still hanging in there, still part of your life when you were into middle age, they were sisters by default and weren't going to let you get away with waffling through bitter truths. You couldn't hide much from a woman who'd clocked you stuffing your trainer bra with tissues when you were changing after hockey practice.

'But to a room only a few along from the one he was supposed to be in with *you*?' Jules took another mouthful of toast. 'Insensitive or *what*? Why couldn't they go somewhere else? It's not as if New York is exactly short of hotels, is it? Or why didn't she just drag him back home, wherever that is?'

'Well, quite. My thoughts exactly at the time – turns out she's only from somewhere out on Long Island, not the far side of the continent. Ridiculous, isn't it? Unbloody-believable how far some people will go to make a point. I mean, it was hardly my fault – I really, honestly, thought the "wife" aspect of her had the word "ex" in front of it. You see, Rick and I were just about to go out for dinner . . .'

'Wait, wait . . . start at the beginning, I need to know all! You'd arrived in New York late morning-ish on Saturday, right? He came and met you at the airport?'

'He did.' Bella didn't want this to make her smile, not now, but she couldn't help herself. Even though it had ended disastrously, she was going to hang on to the few memories that were worth stashing away for old-age reminiscence. It was like keeping a photo album – some shots would always give you a bit of a lift, whatever the story each side of the picture. 'It was quite romantic actually. That bit, anyway. He'd brought all these beautiful pink roses with him, a huge bouquet of gorgeously scented blowsy ones, not like the tightly furled-up sterile sorts you get in the roadside buckets by the Chiswick roundabout. It was like something out of a Richard Curtis movie, all bliss and feel-good. There were people around us going "aaah, *cute*" as if we were teenage lovers instead of a pair of mid-life idiots who'd been round this particular block more than once in the past. He was going to show me New York, he'd promised. I did even wonder if he was going to . . . er . . . um . . .' She hesitated, because what she'd been going to say was something obviously only *she* of the two of them had considered. It had involved the words 'marry' and 'me' being said together in the same sentence. As a question. And by Rick. Well she'd got that bit wrong, one hundred per cent.

'He was going to ask you to be wife number three, wasn't he?' Jules read her mind. 'Or at least . . . I assume you thought he was because I remember you dropped some comment in your "Week Moment" column a few Sundays ago, about how diamonds weren't your idea of a best friend. What was the theme? "I Really Don't Get . . . Engagement Rings". I love that "I Don't Get" thing you write! Sometimes you're *sooo* cross! Brill to have an outlet for all your gripes like that, *and* get paid. Sure beats teaching yoga to the Mortlake-mummy mafia. I have to be so *nice* and so *beatific* all the time! I should have got them on to karate . . .' Jules's eyes gleamed suddenly. '. . . or fencing!'

'Huh!' Bella spluttered. 'Well that'll teach me, won't it? That's the trouble with a weekly column, especially in the Sunday press. You end up so desperate for material that your own life has to be trawled to its muddiest depths for every possible space-filler. And to be honest, at the time I was just dropping in a general opinion on gemstones, not hinting at all. I've done marriage. James was more than enough for me in the husband department, thanks.'

Jules smiled, looking as if she didn't believe her. 'No really,' Bella protested. 'Even if Rick *had* asked me, I'd have had to do something like laugh girlishly and somehow shake off the whole idea, kind of "Oh but, how sweet of you to think of it!" and fluff on about how we're fine as we are, aren't we, and how I'm not that keen on hats and cake.'

'Oh come on now, Bella – everyone likes hats and cake. *And* you've got a big gullible romantic streak in you; you must have, to have seen marriage material in James.'

Bella let that one pass. 'But anyway, what happened next? Did you go straight to the hotel? Did you . . .' Jules leaned forward, blatantly eager for salacious detail. Bella was almost sorry to disappoint her.

'Not quite – it was pretty early; we dropped the bags off at the hotel then he took me for a teensy bit of lunch at the Oyster Bar at Grand Central Station. We just had . . . well, oysters, and Chablis. Flying blunts your appetite – well, it does mine anyway.'

'It does, doesn't it?' Jules agreed, using a finger-end to scoop up the last toast crumbs from round the edge of Bella's plate. 'But only for food! So after that . . . *then* you went back to the hotel?'

'Still no, in fact.' Bella sipped her tea and thought for a moment. 'Thinking about it now, he seemed a bit nervous by then, actually. First we got a cab and had a quick lightning tour down Madison and over to Fifth Avenue and stopped off at Barney's because he thought it was my kind of store. He slid off and picked up a present for me while I wandered around in a bit of a daze, feeling that as I was in New York some kind of shopping was almost compulsory. But really I just wanted to have a bath and lie down in a darkened room for a while with my eyes closed. They had a pool table in the menswear department where I was vaguely looking for a present for Alex and I got playing with that because, you know, I was tired and I can shop any old time in London – it isn't actually my idea of a *treat*. He found me there on his way back from buying fancy underwear and almost dragged me away, looking really embarrassed as if he thought I'd rip the surface of the table or hold the wrong end of the cue or something. I suppose that was a bit of a clue. I mean, I'm really good at pool . . . comes of a misspent student life. In retrospect, I think the kind of man I need in my life would have put the shopping down and challenged me to a proper game, right there in the store. Rick didn't really *do* fun, not unless it was something you had to get tickets for so he could show off that he'd got special ones, Access All Areas or a box at Covent Garden, anything that would *impress*. He's a bit . . . proper.'

Jules frowned. '*Proper?* Are you mad? Bella, do the words "maybe he's a tosser" mean anything to you? You've always been useless at picking boys. Remember that dork when we were Molly's age – the one who pretended he was Simon Le Bon's brother? You fell for it, no problem. Even though he had a Glasgow accent and Simon's a bit Surrey.'

Bella laughed. 'Yeah, yeah, you're right! But generally, kind of on the whole . . . Rick was good to be with in so many ways. And he was . . . *there*, you know? I mean, how many available men are out there, of the right age, own teeth, own hair and . . .'

'Own platinum Amex? Not that I'm saying money was an attraction . . .' Jules backtracked hastily.

'No, it wasn't!' Bella protested. 'I earn my own, pay my way. Always have. Except for the house . . . this is still half James's, I suppose, technically.' She looked at the kitchen units as if she was slightly surprised to see a full set of them still on the premises. James . . . she knew that if he were still in residence he'd be scrubbing every smear and fingerprint from the drawer handles. They *were* looking a bit dulled, it was true. Dulled and dated, like the rest of the kitchen. It used to be such a pretty room, very big, being part of an outsize glass extension, built twenty years ago all across the back of the house, unusual enough at the time to have featured in three home-style magazines.

The space itself still looked contemporary (dark walnut floor, pale walls, all the glass), but the units were all reclaimed pitch pine and oversized lamp-black hinges and handles which just looked . . . clapped out was the term that came to Bella's mind. More than slightly embarrassed to exist in the twenty-first century. It was all far too farmhouse for south-west London, especially in a room that had twenty feet of slideable plate glass as a back wall. It had been installed in the days when stencilling was every city woman's weekend hobby and the design statement *du jour* was country-feel strings of dried hops. The hops (looped above the Aga like leftover Christmas streamers) had gone the minute James had noticed their dust-gathering capacity, the stencilling was long since painted over, but the rest would have to be lived with till the lottery gods smiled on Bella.

'So did you and Rick . . .' Jules persisted with unashamed nosiness.

'Didn't get the chance!' Bella laughed. 'Got to our room, which was lovely but not exactly enormous, as per usual, apparently, in New York, and he gave me the present. Er . . . red underwear . . .'

Both women grimaced and giggled. 'I know,' Bella said. 'Another warning sign. It was *hugely* expensive – he'd left the Amex receipt in the bag, which I now think was accidentally on purpose, to impress me. Anyway, I just said, "Oh how lovely," because what else could I say, but I made the excuse that my black dress needed sleek smooth underwear, not lacy stuff, though I said it in a way that made him think I'd try it out for him later. I had a shower and got all dressed up. Funny . . .' She drifted off and watched a squirrel stealing from the bird feeder, hanging upside down, looking as if it was showing off. It saw her, flicked its tail at her impudently and stared at her as it munched a pawful of peanuts.

'What? Tell me!'

'Nothing really, except that he did seem to get more and more nervous. I couldn't understand what was bugging him; we've stayed in hotels together before. There was the one in Devon with the cows outside the window and another in Dublin . . . But hey, over now.' Bella got up and put her plate in the dishwasher, then rinsed her fingers under the tap, noting briefly that the butler's sink was looking even more crazed than usual. It probably wasn't the only one; her post-flight skin felt like a cracked old leather sofa. 'Maybe he had a premonition about what was coming. I got all togged up in my dress, the sheeny Joseph one, and when he opened the door for us to leave for dinner . . . there was the wife, leaning on the door frame with this awful "gotcha!" look on her face. I've always hated surprises. And skinny as she was, that was a bloody giant-sized one.'

'Bastard.' Jules sighed, looking deeply satisfied with the story.

'Exactly. Bastard.'

'Mum hates surprises,' Alex reminded his father as they waited for their luggage to make an appearance at the Heathrow baggage carousel. 'You should have called her before we left.'

'Rubbish! She'll be fine with this,' James insisted. 'She'll soon get the hang of me being back in the area. I've missed more than enough of your and Molly's teenage years, and there are a few outstanding things Bella and I need to touch base about. It's great timing, the new office opening in London, and the flat I've rented is brand new . . . no-one else's bugs and grubbiness. So all in all, it couldn't be better. Ugh! Which is more than you can say about this place. Look at the state of this!' He hauled his suitcase off the carousel and on to the baggage trolley, then pulled out a perfectly folded white handkerchief from the inside pocket of his jacket and wiped a greasy smear off the case's side. 'Horrors!' He shuddered. 'The filth these bags must have been in! And all the germs too; you could catch anything . . .'

Alex watched as James rolled the handkerchief into a ball and stuffed it into a small polythene freezer bag that he'd pulled from his pocket. He then took an antiseptic wipe from a travel-size pack and cleaned any last trace of residual grime off his already immaculate fingers. Alex, who more than once had been late-night hungry enough to rescue a slice of thrown-away pizza from the kitchen bin, had one of many moments of wondering if James really was his father.

'Dad . . . do you ever think, you know, that you're a little bit . . . ?'

'A bit what?' James looked at him, puzzled. Alex shrugged and gave up. It didn't matter, really. The world was full of people even madder than this Mr Clean.

'Nuffin', Dad, no worries. Let's go. Buses are this way.'

'Taxi, boy, a taxi!' James looked pained. 'We've had enough public transport for today: we'll be coughing and sneezing by Wednesday. Thank goodness for echinacea, that's all I can say. Come on, we need to be out of here. We'll pick up a nice bunch of roses for Bella on the way – that's one surprise she *will* like! Women always do!'

'I Really Don't Get . . . *Weekends in New York*' Bella, now revived enough to think about work and revenge in the same satisfying sentence, briskly typed into her MacBook. Well, not that I exactly even had a *weekend*, she thought, waiting to see if the perfect opening paragraph would suggest itself to her instantly and inspiringly. An entire neat and complete seven-hundred-word article should, in an ideal world, transcribe itself effortlessly and elegantly on to the page. Her fingers almost went into auto-writing mode as she tried to assemble a sequence of events in such a way that would neither make her look a total fool nor really give away enough to have anyone calling up and suing her for libel. Some of her best work had come out of genuine fury, so she might as well allude to what *could* have happened, throw in some extra thoughts and get a column out of it – not to mention her fee – while it was all still fresh.

She'd write about how so many people (OK, mostly women) treat the three-day transatlantic dash as a huge thrill, so glamorous, so full, full, full of shopping and shows and shoes and (if you're luckier than she was) shagging, and yet really there wasn't much, frock/shoe/bag-wise, that you couldn't get in Selfridges; the jet lag was vile and the rushing around exhausting, and in the time between handing over your credit card and the monthly statement dropping on to the doormat, something *calamitous* would have happened to the exchange rate. She would write that to be cost-effective you have to fly cattle class among the hen parties, and you need to overcome any fear of plummeting to earth from 37,000 feet above the Atlantic while watching – on a titchy, badly lit screen – a movie you've seen only the week before. You get a stomach upset from inflight food and a hangover before you land and . . .

Oh God, I do moan on, don't I? Bella thought as she typed the flow of vitriol. But that was what this job required: for her to deconstruct those things that most folks took for granted as being universally wonderful. She'd covered so many things in her 'I Really Don't Get . . .' column over the past year: skiing (scary, cold, and yes your bum DOES look big in that), George Clooney (the thinking woman's estate agent), giant shopping malls (hideous, manipulative, soporific air con), farmers' markets (tomatoes at about 50p EACH? And what kind of farm grows falafels?) and elaborate pubic topiary decorated with Swarovski crystals. She'd had a lot of emails about that one . . . too many of which invited her to sample the process in premises alone with the kind of strange man her mother had warned her about.

A fast hour passed while Bella tapped away at the Mac, getting up enough speed and momentum for the piece to be written almost as stream of consciousness. It was now past midday but there was no sign of Molly, who was still upstairs in her room, either sleeping or sulking. With teenagers, it was often hard to tell the difference. The night before, Bella had been too exhausted to have the mother-and-daughter conversation that needed to be had about entertaining boys in the household beds, and now, still enfeebled by travel and trauma, she was quite glad that the teen need for long hours of shut-eye meant the inevitable confrontation was a bit delayed.

It was probably one of her best 'I Really Don't Get' pieces. The spontaneity of it had given her a sharp and elegant turn of phrase. Feeling rather pleased with herself, Bella checked through for accurate spelling, grammar and blips of punctuation, sent a quick email to the features editor, attached her work and pressed send, now very much revived. She would take the rest of the day off, do the kind of satisfyingly large supermarket shop that would give her the illusion of being a Proper Domestic Woman. She might, she thought, even make a batch of bread – or was that taking the domestic thing too far? Or maybe roast a luscious lemony chicken and do some Molly-bonding. Perhaps invite Giles too? She liked Molly's boyfriend, and he'd had many a supper in the house with them in the past few months . . . but somehow all she could see in her head when she thought of him was his slim naked body, those broad but bony shoulders leaning against *her* pillows, in *her* bed. No, maybe he was best absent from their house today. It would be early pasta, a Molly chat which would be more sympathetic and friendly than the girl was probably anticipating. Then Bella would try to catch up on sleep, maybe watch *Frock Shock* on her bedroom TV, find out if the makeover-guru couple had any suggestions for women like her who'd blithely yet wrongly always assumed they looked pretty hot in black.

She had another quick look at the emails, checking for any acknowledgement from her editor that the piece had arrived safely. Charlotte usually said a quick hello and thanks. And yes, there was one. Bella clicked on the message and was surprised to see it was a lot longer than the usual 'Hi, thanks for that!' sentence.

*'Bella, hello . . . we've just crossed in the ether. Thanks so much for sending in your latest piece – wonderful, as ever, and I think we'll just about be able to squeeze it in . . .'*

What? 'Squeeze it in?' Bella swallowed and sat down to concentrate properly, having a horrible gut feeling that the rest of the email wasn't going to make comfortable reading. She skimmed through quickly, eyes half shut, taking in the key phrases . . . *'Revamping the "Week*

*Moment" page', 'Updating the layout', 'Guest contributors', 'Keeping it fresh'* and the final insult, *'Valued your input'.* Fired. Well, not exactly – was it more or less hurtful that she wasn't actually being sacked but her column reduced to one week in four? Would it have been better to be properly sacked and leave it looking possible that she'd jumped rather than been pushed? She'd think about that later. For now, it was tough enough that a good regular monthly cheque – so rare and so precious in the freelance journalism world – was to be reduced by 75 per cent. And she knew why.

'Fuck!' Furiously, Bella threw her empty mug very hard at the wall behind the sink. There was a delicious shattering sound and pieces of pottery tumbled into the sink. 'Bugger, bollocks and crap!' She cursed on. Well, whatever else did she expect? When bad luck turns up at your personal party, it rarely comes on its own.

'Mum? Like why are you throwing things around?' Molly, sleepy-eyed and hair like blonde candyfloss, was in the doorway.

'Been pretty much bloody *fired*. Bloody *Rick*!' Bella seethed, still staring at the email, checking that she hadn't read it all wrong. No, she hadn't.

'What's Rick got to do with it?' Molly asked, scratching her tangled hair with one hand and rummaging in the bread bin with the other.

'He's on the board of that group of newspapers,'

Bella told her. 'Bloody quick work. I bet his wife . . .'

'*Wife?*' Molly suddenly became wide awake, staring at her mother in horror. 'You were going out with someone *married*? And you were furious with *me* just for sleeping with *Giles*? At least he's . . . God, you're *gross*. *Married*. That's . . . like . . .'

'I know what it is, thank you Moll. At least I do now. Why do you think I came home two days early? Please don't give me a morality lecture. I've lost, in the past twenty-four hours, a conveniently comfortable boyfriend, most of my job and . . .'

Although Bella hadn't thrown anything else, there was a follow-up sound of ceramic clattering from the sink area and Molly laughed suddenly. Oh, the mysteries, Bella thought, of changeable teenage moods. 'I know what else you've lost,' Molly said, picking up some pieces of pottery from the sink. She held them out to Bella. 'Wall tiles.'

Bella looked at the wall behind the tap. Molly was right. Three of the large hand-glazed pink tiles, in a shade specially mixed to complement the hint of raspberry tone in the worktop, lay in shards in the sink – loosened, presumably, by the mug's impact.

Oh sod it, Bella thought, what else can go wrong today? Anything else that's All My Fault? She heard a key turn in the front door, heavy male footsteps approaching.

'Hi Mum, I'm home!' Alex came into the kitchen, looking a bit shifty.

*Alex?* God, what now? Bella thought. He (like her) wasn't due home for another two days. He hadn't said anything about an early arrival when she'd texted him to say she'd returned last night. Had he been arrested? Could you get deported from Scotland? There was someone with him. Please, she thought, don't let it be the police. But oh Lordy . . . There was that shuffling sound, the old familiar one – James taking off his shoes by the front door in the interests of a pristine carpet. He padded into the kitchen, clutching a bunch of clench-budded roadside roses.

Oh terrific. Her ex-husband. Well, no real surprise there – didn't they say bad luck always came in threes?

# THREE

'Oh! You've broken the tiles!' James looked at Bella nervously, his eyes fast-flickering towards her hand and then back to her face as if he was checking she wasn't preloaded with more dangerous missiles.

'You weren't here. How did you know Mum did it?' Molly asked quickly.

'Just a lucky guess,' he shrugged, picking bits of tile out of the sink and stacking them up carefully on the worktop. He was still clutching his flowers and he'd trailed in a suit-case on wheels which stood to attention by the table. Bella wondered if she should introduce it to her unpacked Bric . . . perhaps they would breed, the way wire hangers seemed to in a wardrobe. She had a fanciful vision of a row of cute handbags, little leather offspring.

'And hello to you too, James,' Bella said. 'How come you're here?'

'Oh nice welcome!' He turned and smiled at her, a glint of sarcasm in his eyes. 'So glad you're pleased to see me!'

'Well, a bit of warning would have been good. I'm not even supposed . . .' She stopped. He didn't need to know about her failed New York trip.

Alex looked slightly puzzled but seemed not quite concerned enough to ask immediate questions. That was Alex all over, bless him. Vague, other-worldly. It would probably be several hours before he finally put two and two together and came out with, 'So what happened to New York then?'

'Sorry! You're right,' James conceded. 'Alex warned me you didn't like surprises. But I brought you these.' He handed the roses over to Bella and tentatively kissed her quickly on the cheek before backing away, sharpish. He kissed Molly even more nervously, as if scared that all teenage girls snap like terriers. 'You'd better put the flowers in water before they start shedding petals everywhere.' James opened a cupboard and peered inside, looking for a vase.

'Did you know you've put a great big three-litre Le Creuset on top of an earthenware dish in here?' he said, rummaging among cookware. 'It'll get all scratched. Shall I move it? This cupboard needs a thorough sort-out.'

Bella bit her lip to stop herself snapping at him.

James hadn't lived here for ten years now, since he'd gone off to live with a dental nurse who'd appealed to his inner clean-freak – what right did he have to rearrange her casserole dishes? She peeled the paper off the flowers and started slicing the ends off the stems. The petals were so tightly furled they didn't look as if they'd open this side of the twenty-second century, let alone start dropping off at random. She couldn't help thinking of the so-lush roses that Rick had given her. She hoped the room maid had taken them with her, given them a good home along with the underwear.

James's back end was now sticking out of the cupboard under the sink, reminding her of the rear half of a pantomime horse. He had rather womanly hips, she noticed. Was this new? It was a good many years since she'd seen him unclothed (an experience she had no desire to repeat), but even so . . . did men get beamy over the years, like women? As it looked as if she was heading for a rest-of-her-life in celibacy, these were the kind of observations she could make quite dispassionately and with purely writerly interest. Perhaps she could write something about it. If anyone wanted to employ her, of course.

'James, please just leave it all alone, will you? You're looking in the wrong place; I keep vases in the cupboard in the sitting room. Alex – would you go and fetch the tall glass one, please?'

Alex ambled away, texting into his phone as he walked. 'Er . . . I'll go with him.' Molly trailed after her brother, closing the door firmly behind her and leaving James and Bella alone.

'So! What's with the surprise visit?' Bella asked him, making an effort to sound upbeat and cheerful. Apart from the beaminess he was looking good, she'd give him that. He'd never been the kind of man that women turned to gaze at in the street but somehow, in his middle years, he'd managed to keep a sharp jawline and plentiful dark hair, only lightly scattered with recent grey. And it was on his head, a bit Paul McCartneyish in quantity and style – though not that weird aubergine colour – and not sprouting from his ears or meeting over his nose like one big eyebrow.

'Well – it's not exactly a visit. Thing is, Bella, I'm moving back to London.' He glanced at his watch. 'Look, it's lunchtime and all they had on the plane were limp sandwiches.' He shuddered slightly. 'And you know . . . So – is that Italian place round the corner still going? That was always reliable. Why don't I take us all there for a nice family lunch? I've got a couple of things to discuss, items to run up the flagpole, give you a helicopter view of my state of play at this moment in time.'

Bella – once she'd roughly construed James's jargon – managed not to comment that it had been a long, long time since the four of them had constituted A Nice Family. After all, it was a kind offer and there was no need to take her current sourness out on him. It wasn't James's fault that she was feeling bad-tempered and miserable. And soon to be a bit on the cash-strapped side to boot. Free lunch. And from her habitually miserly ex, too . . . Bring it on.

Several miles away in Surrey, Bella's mother Shirley was deciding between the Nicole Farhi dress and the DKNY one. She didn't buy a lot of clothes, being a lifelong believer in quality rather than quantity so when she did, it was important to get the purchase just right.

'Are you looking for anything special today?' Shirley felt pleased to be approached by this young, eager-looking assistant. The promise of good service was rare and welcome. Usually in this big, impersonal department store the staff preferred to loiter out of range in far corners, chatting to each other behind rails of clothing. This one, she assumed, must be new. Good.

'One is always looking for something special when it comes to elegant clothing,' Shirley said, diluting what could have sounded rather harsh with her best smile. At seventy-four she was far more accustomed to being ignored, as if being over twenty-five rendered her invisible. Maybe the attention she had attracted today was something to do with the soft, suede, biscuit-coloured

Joseph jacket she was wearing and her stark white, crisply angular haircut (no cauliflower perms for Shirley). And there was the extra-broad Tiffany silver bracelet, the bold silver hoop earrings. Statement jewellery gave even the most average clothes that extra edge. The girl probably scented money and (if they still had such things these days) a good sales commission. She was wrong about the money, as it happened. Shirley was lucky to be comfortable enough financially, but not lavishly so. She was simply a natural at style.

'I really can't decide . . .' Shirley considered for a long moment, holding the Donna Karan dress against her and looking into the full-length wall-mirror. The lighting was terrible. This colour (slaty deep grey, with almost a bluish sheen to it) was a well-loved one, very much a favourite in her wardrobe, but her skin looked slightly grey against it. That couldn't be right.

'Shall I take it to the changing room for you?' the girl offered. 'Or . . . ?' That was something they did a lot of these days, Shirley thought . . . leaving 'or' hovering in the air without supplying the necessary alternative. She'd noticed it on the plane back from Nice after the cruise the week before, when the flight attendant approached each row of seats with 'Tea, coffee, or?' Being of a rather literal frame of mind, Shirley half expected 'ore' as in a plateful of small gold nuggets, looking like Ferrero Rocher.

'Er . . . yes please, dear.' Shirley handed over the dress. It would be worth trying on, at least. 'And this one too.' She gave the girl the Nicole Farhi. It had a bit of a pattern to it, which she didn't usually go for, but it was a subtle smudgy floral design in perfect shades of taupe and cream, and really quite lovely. 'Nothing to lose by trying them both, is there?'

The changing area wasn't busy. In the middle of a warm early September day, few people were in the mood for thinking about buying autumn clothes. The gaudy rejected remnants of the summer sale lingered on a few overcrowded and highly untempting rails, ready to be shipped out as soon as more seasonal stock arrived.

'I'll be just out here if you need anything. Just pop your head out and give me a call.' The salesgirl hung the dresses up carefully and backed out, swishing the curtain closed behind her.

Shirley peeled off her black linen skirt (Jigsaw, a useful wrapover style), her jacket and her white shirt and hung them neatly over the back of the green velvet button-back chair. She tried the Nicole Farhi first. The sleeves were a flattering bracelet length (good slender wrists were one body part that didn't deteriorate with age), the neckline a fairly low V, but neither so deep that the dress couldn't be worn without a camisole nor so high that a little cashmere polo top wouldn't look amiss in winter. Either dress would work for any season, with the right accessories. Pound per wear, they would both be terrific value, excellent quality and eternal style, without being over-quirky or of a definable moment.

'Are you all right? Do you need any help, or . . . ?' The assistant was so close to the curtain Shirley could hear her breathing.

'I'm fine, thank you, though actually . . .' Shirley pulled back the curtain and stepped out, almost on top of the girl. 'I wouldn't mind a better view. More distance,' she said, spotting a much bigger mirror at the end of the row of cubicles. She studied her reflection, checking the skirt length, thinking the dress would look as good with boots as with heels.

'Oh that looks lovely! It really suits you!' The comment was too spontaneous to be sales-calculated. It had an element of surprise in it, and Shirley understood: the girl had assumed the dress was meant for a much younger market. If she stayed in the job, customers like Shirley would be part of her learning curve. Good style doesn't stop with the age of thirty. In most cases it didn't even start till then. Shirley beamed at the girl, pleased. She knew she looked good in the dress; it had that This Is Me quality about it and made her feel quite thrilled, but it was always flattering to have third-party reassurance. Dennis would like it too, assuming he'd meant it about meeting up in the UK. It was one of the first things he'd said to her, that he admired her taste. She could see him now, beside her at the ship's rail smoking an after-dinner Gitanes and watching Venice slide out of sight in the distance. And the young thought they were the only ones who had holiday romances. If only they knew . . .

'Yes . . . I do love it. But I must try the other one as well. Otherwise, if I take this one, I'll still be wondering, won't I?'

Shirley took off the Nicole Farhi and put it back on its hanger. The slate DKNY again had bracelet-length sleeves and a V-neck, but with a broad tie sash that wrapped round more than once, cinching in her middle. Shirley was lucky – she was tall and slim and hadn't gone apple-shaped with age, and still had a well-defined waist. This dress, too, flattered her body and skimmed to just below knee-length. Again, she could see herself wearing it over many years (should she be lucky enough to have them, you had to think about that at her age), another many-season, versatile staple.

But on balance, no, it had to be the Farhi. She had plenty of slaty clothes already, and there was a slightly off-the-wall feel to the smudged-grey flower pattern that appealed to her. She put her jacket back on and left the changing room, carrying the chosen dress. 'I'll take this one,' she said to the waiting assistant and followed her to the till. 'You do take American Express, don't you?'

It was about fifteen minutes later that Shirley left the store. She went by way of the shoe department on the ground floor to have a quick look at the first of the season's boots that were just coming in. She didn't really need any – her black Prada sale ones would probably see her out and she'd picked up some perfect brown suede pull-ons in Tesco, of all places, the winter before, breaking her own rule about cheap clothing because they were such a plain, classic, comfortable style. As she walked out of the store and into the town's mall, she was wondering whether green tights and her necklace of large emerald-coloured stones would go well with the new dress and her mushroom-coloured Gina shoes. An alarm beeped behind her as she went. Probably, she thought vaguely, another customer wanting, as she had, to see what something looked like in better light. They really should do something about that . . . Or that bunch of teenagers, joshing about and shouting . . . had they stolen something?

'Excuse me . . . would you come this way with me please?'

Shirley, at the top of the escalator, felt as if the man standing too close to her was some kind of octopus. His arms were everywhere, blocking off her escape as she tried to sidestep him. She considered screaming, half guessing she was being mugged by someone with excellent manners, but this was a smart, suited young man in his mid-thirties. He carried a walkie-talkie which crackled and muttered in his hand.

'OK, fish landed. Coming in,' he murmured into it now as he put a firm hand under Shirley's elbow and turned her round, back in the direction of the department store.

'Will you stop *manhandling* me?' she demanded, starting to pull away. Struggling was unseemly, but she shook his arm off her as hard as she could. People were slowing, beginning to scent a scene. She *hated* that sort of thing and glared around her, embarrassed and furious.

'We'll do this the easy way, in private,' he said quietly. 'But you'll have to come to Security with me, right now, please. I have reason to believe that you have removed an item from this store without paying for it.'

Shirley felt relieved. 'Oh but I did! I have the receipt! Look, it's right here!' She opened her bag, pulling out her wallet.

'Er, yes, I know you paid for the one item,' he said. 'It's the other one we're concerned about.'

'Sorry?' Shirley didn't understand. All the same, she walked alongside the man, who, thank goodness for her dignity, seemed to have decided she wasn't about to do a runner (hardly – at her age and in ballet flats) and didn't continue to hang on to her. She smoothed her skirt down . . . and suddenly felt sick. This was *not* her Jigsaw wrapover. It was the DKNY dress. Where, for heaven's sake, had her mind escaped to for those last minutes in that changing room? Moments surely didn't come much more senior than this.

'Ah! Bella, ma bella!' Luigi kissed Bella effusively, shook James's hand with full-strength Italian energy and ushered the two of them towards the best table in the restaurant. There was a view of the little street of cute shops and the small square where the winos liked to get together on the benches outside the tapas bar to sing old blues songs on summer evenings.

Bella looked around to see who was in – this was her favourite local eaterie, popular and busy, and she usually knew one or two of the clientele at any given time. It was her default venue to take friends, work colleagues, the occasional date. She'd been there only a couple of weeks before with Rick, and it had been at this table that he'd invited her, seemingly on a spontaneous, romantic whim, to visit him in New York. All in the past now, she told herself briskly, no point looking back. Now instead of her-and-Rick, it was just her and James, Alex and Molly having decided that sudden emergency Facebooking was preferable to the Nice Family Lunch James had offered.

'Bella! Hi!' At a table in the corner, half hidden by a

large potted orange tree, two women were waving across to her.

'Who are they?' James asked as she smiled and waved back.

'They're two of our local writers' group,' Bella told him. 'We meet up every fortnight at the River Fox in Richmond, just to chat and grumble, you know. Mutual support, all that.'

'Ah, a chance for the demon drink. You always did like a drop, didn't you?' James smirked.

'Hardly,' Bella retorted, 'And please don't criticize how I live. I barely drink at all, as it happens – I've usually got the car with me. And you can hardly grudge me getting together with other writers – it's a lonely old job being a freelance.'

What was it about James that always put her on the defensive? Maybe it was that he was always on the attack. He'd been such good fun at the beginning too, in spite of his cleanliness obsession.

'He's barking, you know,' Bella's mother Shirley had warned her, only a month before the wedding twenty-one years before. 'He went through my larder and washed all the tops of the jars. Some of them were things we hadn't used in years. I'd think carefully, darling, before saying "I do" to a man who's going to see germs on every damn surface. I hate to think what he's like in bed . . .' This last comment had been made very loudly over lunch with a selection of aunts, two of whom came firmly under the heading of 'maiden'. Bella had only been twenty-two at the time, caught up in the heady whirl of wedding preparations, and had blithely taken no notice – Shirley had a knack of dropping in some sexual reference whenever the opportunity arose, somehow convinced that she had to show off that it was a subject she knew all about, as if nobody else possibly could.

As it happened, that was the one area where James had been content to get down and dirty . . . or at least at first. Was it after Alex was born? Or was it after Molly when he'd suddenly decided that the warm, slow moments immediately after sex weren't a time for post-coital snuggling but were just perfect for getting into the hottest bearable shower, lathering vigorously and scrubbing his nails with insulting thoroughness? Their sex life stalled and faltered after that. After all, who wants to make love with a man who would clearly prefer to wear protective gloves rather than risk skin-on-skin contact? In the end, Bella wouldn't have been surprised if he'd approached her wearing an all-over anti-radiation suit. Borderline obsessive-compulsive, that was James. Unfortunately he was not quite bad enough for anyone to tell him he should consider seeking help with it. He got by OK. Just.

As Bella studied the menu she wondered idly who the

man was with the writer women across the room. Another author? Friend? Lover? Those two were younger than Bella, in their thirties. Chloe and Zoe – Bella could never remember which was which because they were very much of A Look, very neat and Boden-mummy, though she knew one wrote for a teenage vampire series and the other was trying to break into the spicier end of the Mills and Boon range. Both were looking summer-chic in strappy little tops beneath toning cardigans with arty jewellery, and both were beaming lip-glossed smiles at their companion. He was older than them, older than Bella too, and the white of his linen shirt fairly zinged against his tanned skin. Good hair too, mid-brown, sun-streaked and attractively overgrown, the ends forming tiny corkscrew curls. If she wasn't firmly out of the man market (the words Never Again were her first waking thought that morning, and she suspected this wasn't a conviction that was going away soon), she wouldn't have ruled him out if he'd chatted her up at a party. Which one of the women was he actually *with*, she wondered idly as she skimmed a look at the menu; both of them (married as they were) seemed pretty keen, giggling and hair-flicking like a couple of flirty teenagers. Whoever he was, he'd certainly made an impact on the Zoe-Chloe twosome.

'You're doing that thing that you always do, Bella,' James commented, following her gaze to the far table.

'You're miles away across the floor with those women, tuning in.'

Bella laughed. 'I'm just wondering what the score is, that's all! It's what all writers do, checking out the what-if and the maybe . . . you never know when it might come in useful.'

'Or you could just call it damn rude, poking your nose in. Look, can we just order, fast as possible?' James snapped his menu shut and glanced around for a waiter. Bella remembered how he'd always been like this when hungry; impatient, bordering on the hostile till the first mouthfuls had made an impact on his stomach. Thank goodness the service in here was reliably swift. James told her sketchy details about his new job (financial services, sorting out the feckless and reckless, with whom she was sure he had very little sympathy), but he didn't ask about hers. She was rather relieved. On either work or personal front she had nothing but failure to report, and would rather not admit this, not to James, anyway.

'Is there somewhere you have to be?' Bella asked, as James bolted his food in record time. 'You seem very tense.'

James kept looking at his watch and didn't appear any more relaxed, even with a glass of wine and half a hefty portion of lasagne inside him. 'Yes, actually. I've got an appointment pretty soon. And that's connected with what I wanted to talk to you about. I'm coming to live in London again. Just over at Kew. I'm meeting the agent to pick up the keys.'

'You said at the house that you were coming back . . . so no more Scotland?' Bella asked. 'But you've been there years now. I thought you were well settled. And what about what's-her-name?'

'Fenella. Don't pretend you don't know.' James grinned. 'Be careful, you might have me thinking you cared.'

'OK, Fenella. Does she want to move too? Or . . .'

' "Or" is it. We're over, as it happens. As from about three months ago, actually, but I didn't want to say anything in case, well in case we weren't, quite. But no, we definitely are. All over. Definitely.'

'Oh – I'm sorry.' And she was – Fenella had seemed to keep him happy enough for several years. Bella had only met her once, at the wedding of James's niece, where Molly had been a bridesmaid. Bella had been impressed by Fenella's hat – a high toque in purple satin with what looked like a gold sovereign pinned to the front of it. A bold choice among a traditional mix of pastel and straw.

'Don't be,' he said, looking a bit mistily distant, all the same. 'She's gone to live with an old hippy weaver in a croft.' He shuddered. 'A woman, as it happens. And with no running water!'

Bella hardly knew what to say, either about the woman or the water situation. She wondered which of these appalled James more. Her money was on the water thing.

Across the room came the trilling of girlish ripply laughter from Chloe-Zoe. Good for them, Bella thought. In an hour from now they'd be outside the primary school, back to being someone's mother, then later someone's wife. For now, she was glad they were having some time to be *themselves*.

'Anyway . . . about the house,' James continued.

'Hmm? The house? What about it?' Bella said, her attention slowly returning to him.

'Well, it's time we sorted it properly, isn't it? I mean, for me renting is fine for a while, till I find somewhere I like to buy, but prices are higher than Scotland. So the thing is, I could do with releasing some of the equity now I'm going to be living down here. And now the children are grown up . . .'

Luigi took the plates away and took their order for espressos, which appeared in seconds. James was quiet for a moment, checking the edge of his cup for marks. There wouldn't be any, Bella knew that, but it didn't stop him running the edge of his napkin around the cup's rim before he dropped a couple of chunks of sugar in.

Bella felt confused. 'Wait a minute . . . what are you talking about, James? What equity?'

'The house, Annabelle. That bricks-and-mortar place you and our offspring occupy. The one I still half own, that we never got round to splitting when it came to assets and custody. Remember?'

Her attention had snapped to full alert now. 'So what do you want to do?' She laughed suddenly. '*Sell* it?'

He didn't look as if there was any joke involved. Oh surely, surely not?

James frowned. 'Well, yes – that's what I had in mind. Unless you can buy me out? Of course now Alex and Molly . . .'

'But Alex and Molly still *live* in the house! As I do, in case you'd forgotten!' Bella protested.

'For now, yes. That's why I'm mentioning it *now*. But we've got to do some blue-sky thinking here. Alex is already away at university and Molly's got only months till she leaves school. I mean, you must have known this was coming one day. You've had years . . .'

'Oh. Right. So that's it, is it?' Bella felt weary and defeated. 'Yes, I've had years. I've had years of scraping by in a hugely precarious job, raising *our* children single-handedly with barely any input from *you* because *you* claimed that because I'd got the house your contribution stopped *right there*! And that if I sold it at any point during that time, I'd have only half the cash with which to get something else! So thanks, James, thanks for reminding me how little I actually have to call my own. Thanks a whole *bunch*!'

The eyes of white-linen man across the room met hers as she looked away from James. He half smiled, raised his glass. Chloe-Zoe grinned at her, both with the same 'look what we're having lunch with' expression. She tried to smile back at them but her mouth got all twisted up somehow, and her vision had gone swimmy.

James's BlackBerry beeped and he glanced at his watch. 'Look, I have to go. Got to meet the agent to pick up the keys to the flat. We'll continue this another time, shall we? Get all the ducks set out in a row? Sorry and that,' he said, pushing back his chair and looking eager to be out of Bella's orbit. 'We'll touch base again soon: I'll give you the new address and so on. And er . . .'

'Oh just go, James. Just *go*.' And he did, scuttling out fast to avoid having to deal with emotion, something else he'd always considered messy and unpleasant. Bella finished her coffee and sat for a moment, trying to feel calm. She still had half a glass of wine and she downed most of it in one go. So . . . the score so far this week? No boyfriend, no job (well a quarter of one, nothing much to speak of), and soon no home. Just great.

There was chair-scraping and signs of imminent departure from across the room. Chloe and Zoe were on their way out and stopped by Bella's table on the way. 'Hi Bella, are you coming to the Fox tomorrow? Hope so!'

'Er . . . yes, probably!' Bella smiled brightly, amazed she still had the power of speech.

'Great! See you there – got to dash, school-time! Ciao!' The two women were on their way out, their lunch companion left behind, dealing with the bill and talking to Luigi. Bella finished the rest of her wine, feeling numb and as if she couldn't move. She put her hands over her face and felt warm tears on her cheeks. Oh, great.

'Are you all right?' She opened her eyes and found she was disturbingly close to crotch-level denim, property of the Chloe-Zoe man. She scuffed at her face with the napkin, realizing too late that it was smeared with Amatriciano sauce.

He sat down in James's seat and leaned across. 'Here, let me; you've got an orange nose,' he smiled, smudging a thumb down her cheek. His skin felt warm. She wanted to nuzzle her face into his hand the way a cat does, craving maximum comfort from his small, tender gesture.

'Chloe said you were a journalist, gave me your name. I'm a great admirer of your "Week Moments" pieces, especially the "I Really Don't Get" ones. Very caustic!' He then added, 'I'm Saul Barrett. I was picking their brains for a TV series we're about to do. Fashion – a different take on the makeover lark. I'm coming to their writers' group thing tomorrow and they said you'd probably be there. You might be interested in the programme, actually, as a journalist.'

Bella smiled. 'Yes, I'll be there. It's a good group, they're a fun bunch.'

He stood up. 'Great . . . well, I'll look forward to it. Bye! And . . . whatever it is that's upset you . . . well, I hope . . .' His words fizzled out – she didn't blame him. Sympathy to a crying woman only tends to make things more waterlogged. He must be married, she thought, as he waved goodbye to her through the restaurant window. That much empathy, it takes years of practice. She collected her bag and jacket, went off to the loo and used cool damp paper towel to try to make her face look more presentable.

It was only as she was halfway out of the door that Luigi caught up with her. 'Bella, sorry – but your bill . . . is not . . .' He looked apologetic.

'You mean James just left without paying . . . ? I'm so sorry, Luigi.' She delved into her bag and pulled out her credit cards. Maybe after today she should cut them all up, get used to a new and necessary thrift. Not that she'd been exactly chucking her money around over the years. Bloody James. Bloody everything.

# FOUR

Bella sat on the end of Molly's bed and picked up the old toy polar bear. The poor grubby thing was flattened from years of being slept on. Having a sudden fast-forward, Bella imagined herself tucking this soft toy into Molly's bed when the girl was away on gap-year travels. With Alex already away at university most of the time, this was going to be a lonely echoing house a year or so from now.

'The thing is, Molly . . .' Bella began, as Molly had been dreading since the Giles incident. This was not a discussion either of them wanted to have, but both had known it had to happen. Molly had been playing a crafty game of avoidance ever since Bella had walked in on her and Giles, but now, cornered on her own territory, there was no escape. She sat cross-legged on top of her pillows, as effortlessly supple as only the under-twenties can be, computer balanced across her flat-down thighs and a trapped expression on her face. She looked swiftly at the door the moment her mother sat down, considering the hopeless logistics of making a run for it.

'OK, OK, Mum, I *know*! Please – we really don't have to go there!'

Before Bella could say anything more, Molly put her hands over her ears and closed her eyes. Her hands had the skinny sleeves of her pink top pulled over them, so her finger-ends poked out like little stubs. A current fashion thing, Bella recognized, the same way Moll and her friends all seemed to have their hair parted a mere few centimetres over their left ears and mussed up to a straight-from-bed look, though in Molly's case it often was exactly that, no effort required. Bella had a flashback to Molly as an underweight baby, so delicately tiny at less than five pounds that everything she wore during the early months had sleeves that swamped her twiggy arms and she'd be constantly punching fists at fabric, battling to get her hands out into the air. Why did it seem like only ten minutes ago that Bella wondered if Molly would ever outgrow her wicker cradle? How did she so quickly become this long, leggy teenager who was all huge grey eyes and pout? And hormones . . .

'No, I think we *have* to go there, Molly. You know I'm pretty liberal – Giles is welcome to stay overnight here whenever you like. Obviously I wouldn't be happy if you were bringing home boy after boy . . . *but* . . .'

'Mum! Just *stop*! This is like *sooooo* embarrassing?' Molly was giggling, but she was blushing as well.

Bella could feel her own mouth twitching too. The mother–daughter having the boys-staying-over talk – it was a classic toe-curler, though on the plus side Molly wasn't that far off eighteen and generally pretty sensible. Far worse would be having this conversation with an easily exploited sixteen-year-old.

'Yes, it is a bit, isn't it?' Bella couldn't disagree. 'But let me just say one thing . . . It wasn't what you were doing with Giles, you know that. You're old enough to make your own decisions there.'

'I know, I know . . . It was the *your bed* thing.' Molly groaned into her hands that now covered her pink face. 'I've already apologized for that. *And* I've washed and ironed all the sheets and things and put them all away.'

'Well actually it wasn't really that either,' Bella continued. 'Not entirely. Obviously I wasn't exactly delighted, being completely travel-whacked and bloody amazed to see you at all. I do think my private space should be respected, so please don't do it again. But I mean, really if you want to sleep with Giles, fine. Your sex life is your own business. He's a lovely boy and so long as you're careful . . .' (More groans from Molly. Bella was almost beginning to think this was fun. How to torture your teen . . .) 'No, what upset me was that you'd lied to me. Simple as that. You said you couldn't go to stay with your father in Edinburgh because you were going to a party at Carly's and you would be staying there. But that wasn't true, was it? I really need to be able to trust you, Moll.'

Molly emerged from behind her hands. 'Oh God, now you're doing "disappointed". I knew you would – you *know* that's the one that gets to me.' Her eyes started to look wet. 'Why can't you be like other mums and just say Giles is banned from the house and that I'm grounded or something?'

'Is that what they'd say? Really? But you're almost a legal adult.' Bella felt puzzled. *Was* she too lenient? She wasn't quite on a level with her own mother, who had made it perfectly clear (gleefully so) from the day Bella turned sixteen that the safest place for her daughter to have sex was in her own home. As parents went, Shirley was a bit of a one-off in that respect, because even in the easy-going 1980s, everyone else's parents had seemed to be reliably old-fashioned in quite a comforting way: boyfriends in the house were to be kept to public family spaces at all times. Some daughters even had to be in by midnight, after which the doors to hell opened and late-night sinners would hurtle straight to damnation.

Bella remembered telling Jules on the school bus that she was allowed to have boys to stay overnight if she wanted to, and both had recoiled into horrified giggles at the very idea. All their friends had thought the idea completely gross too. No teenager wanted to have the parental seal of approval on their sex life. It would ruin the whole thing. Where was the thrilling secrecy? The rebellion?

The overly liberal attitude completely put Bella off taking any boy up to her room, even for an innocent conversation with them, knowing Shirley would be just the other side of the wall. She would be sure to be listening in and barely able to stop herself barging in before any possible action, with an exotic condom selection on a tray and then with tea and brandy only seconds after all was over. And imagine, as she and Jules had, breakfast the next morning. Shirley asking if they'd slept well . . . What a disappointment Bella must have been, boyfriends kept forever on the pavement side of the front gate; no devious questioning answered, no contraception advice sought. Her mother's determined liberalism had surely been a factor in keeping Bella a virgin till she was nearly twenty. Or maybe that had been the idea – in which case, what a neat and sneaky double bluff.

'But I *did* go to Carly's. I was going back to stay there too, um . . . later . . . and it's not as if . . . I mean you did come back *a bit early*.'

'OK . . . look, it's all right. We'll leave it there.' Bella propped the bear up against the end bars of the bed. He flopped down, exposing a ragged back foot where Molly had sucked it nightly when she'd been a toddler. 'Just – honesty, that's all I ask, Moll.'

'Er . . . and that works both ways?' Molly, safely off the hook, rallied quickly with something to say.

'Of course it does. Why? I haven't told you any lies.'

'Right. So what about that Rick bloke? You said he was divorced and he like, wasn't? Did you know? Truly?'

'Molly, trust me, the first I knew of his wife still being on the scene was when she was standing outside the hotel room telling me I looked rubbish in black, OK?'

Molly smiled. Bella felt touched – it looked like womanly sympathy.

'Poor Mum – what a cow!' Molly said. 'But you know, she might have a point. Black's a bit harsh on you . . . Oooowwww!' The bear hit her on her left ear and her shrieky giggle was joined by the sound of the doorbell downstairs.

'I'll go – it's probably Alex, forgetting his key,' Bella said.

Shirley looked worryingly wrong, somehow, very much not herself, standing on Bella's doorstep clutching her vintage crocodile bag in one hand and a small suitcase on wheels (another one – was this house becoming a Terminal Five outpost?) in the other. She looked smaller, older. Her hair seemed wildly wispy and uncombed instead of the usual immaculate blow-dry, her blue patent shoes were scuffed and her orange paisley silk scarf definitely didn't go with her flouncy red cotton coat. Was she ill?

'Mum – come on in! Did you phone earlier? I didn't know you were coming. Was there a message I missed?'

'No, well, I didn't know I was coming either, not till just earlier when I decided it was for the best.' Shirley bustled into the hallway, parked the case at the bottom of the stairs and clicked its handle down with one well-practised flick of the wrist. She then strode briskly into the big kitchen and flopped with unusual inelegance on to the old leather sofa, her legs at don't-care angles. Bella felt worried. Shirley's posture was habitually of the finishing-school type. On a low sofa such as Bella's saggy kitchen one, that should mean knees together with ankles crossed and slanting prettily to the left.

'It was a spur-of-the-moment thing. I needed to get away. Tea, darling, please? Or possibly something stronger?' Shirley's fingers twitched at the fringe of the old plaid throw on the sofa arm. Fidgeting was something else she didn't normally do.

'Er . . . well . . .' Bella looked at the cuckoo clock over the Aga. It was doing its preparatory whirring, ready to spring out and tell them it was ten o'clock. Morning not evening, though it would be a very special plastic cuckoo that could tell the difference.

'I suppose it's never too early for a Bloody Mary,' Bella murmured, opening the fridge, snatching out of her memory a drink that she could faintly justify at such a time. Her late father had been a drinker. Shirley had divorced him when Bella was nine and he'd reached the stage when he needed Scotch before breakfast to steady the trembling. That sort of memory made you wary of odd-hours alcohol.

'No, no, not vodka! Nasty sly stuff. I like something you can taste, then you know you've had it. Pour a slug of brandy into a coffee for me, please darling. That'll hit the spot.'

'OK,' Bella started as soon as her mother was a few sips into the brandy-laced coffee, 'but why is there a spot that needs an alcohol hit at this time of the morning? You look a bit as if you've seen a whole castleful of ghosts.'

Shirley began to seem somewhat revived as the coffee and brandy kicked in. She patted her hair into place, her hand hesitant as if suddenly realizing she'd forgotten to comb it. This, Bella was worried to recognize, was probably true.

'What must I look like?' Shirley murmured. 'I just wondered, Bella, if it would be all right for me to come and stay for a week or so. Just till . . . Well, just till.'

'Till what? What's happened? Is there something wrong with your flat? Have you got the men in again?'

Shirley was a great one for redecoration and her apartment – in a smart enclave purpose-built for well-off retirees – was forever being painted in some newly fashionable shade from a range of whites and neutrals. The changes were often so subtle that Bella really couldn't tell the difference between the pre- and post-painting stage. 'No wonder your wardrobe is such a hit and miss botch-up of colour,' Shirley had said, the last time Bella failed to comment on the hallway's colour change from Dairy to String. 'You have no instinct for the tonal nuance at all!'

'No. No decorators, not just now. I've . . . er . . . the thing is I've been – oh this is so silly!' Shirley laughed lightly, finishing her coffee in one swift gulp. Bella topped it up from the pot and added another – but smaller – slug of brandy. She wondered if she should have one as well – this was going to be bad news, she could tell.

'I've been arrested.' Shirley managed to get the words out at last.

'*Arrested*? Good grief, whatever *for*?'

'Who's been arrested?' Molly strolled into the kitchen carrying an armful of her laundry. She dropped items as she headed for the utility room, leaving tiny, bright knickers strewn across the walnut floor like collapsed bunting on a yacht's deck.

'I have,' Shirley admitted. 'For shoplifting.'

'Wow! Will you get an ASBO? Cool!'

Shirley laughed, cheered by her granddaughter's admiring approval.

'But . . . how come you were shoplifting?' Bella asked, mystified. She was trying to work out whether it would be a better thing if this was a deliberate turning to crime or an accidental lapse of memory. For the sake of her mother's sanity, she found herself coming down firmly in favour of the first option. Please, she thought, let it just be a new but short-lived hobby.

'Oh it was all just a stupid mistake!' Shirley looked a lot better now, almost as if she were enjoying herself. Bella suspected she probably was. 'I tried on two dresses, bought one, and accidentally walked out of the store wearing the second one. That's all. I simply forgot to change back into my own clothes. But they made me so cross! There was this *ridiculous* bossy woman in the security office, wearing one of those badges that make people feel important. She kept asking me if it was *my age*. If it was a *lapse*. *And* she kept calling me "my dear" as if I was some frail old thing in my dotage. I told her I was *not* her "dear". And I absolutely *didn't* have *lapses*. I was insistent on that! So then the police came and I've been charged with theft.'

'Aaagh! Mum! Didn't you think maybe she was trying to help you get off the hook? If you'd played the slightly forgetful card you would have been able to hand the dress back and simply go home.'

'Bella! Are you mad? When you get to my age you'll understand. Don't you realize I'd rather be banged up in Holloway with a bunch of tarts and junkies than even *pretend* I'm going senile? It would be tempting fate.'

'Good on you, Gran. Don't let them push you into old-age madness.' Molly plonked herself heavily down on the sofa next to Shirley. A small cloud of dust and cat fur flew up around them, brightly lit in the sun's rays through the sloped glass roof.

'But the price of not being pushed into dementia is that you'll have to go to court and go through a trial and all the trauma that goes with it. Wouldn't it have been worth playing the part to get away with it? I mean, it's not as if you meant to steal it.' Bella truly hoped not, anyway. Maybe next time she went over to Shirley's she'd sneak a look in that massive triple wardrobe she had. Possibly there'd be any number of designer frocks in there, labels still on, security tags attached.

'Oh, it won't be that bad,' Shirley laughed. 'I'm pleading guilty. So much easier. I'll tell them I absolutely didn't intend to steal, but clearly I did it and I'll apologize and let them do their worst. So you see, Bella, I just wanted to get away for a few days . . . well, it'll be in the local paper this week and I decided I could do without the whole neighbourhood clacking around my door. Small-town Surrey doesn't have a lot of excitement. Even the resident rock stars spend all their time on the golf courses. I know what it'll be like; people will be dropping in to "sympathize". I'll have Lois Dobbs from opposite, knocking on the door with a Victoria sponge and a demand to *confide*. Well, I don't want to.' Shirley's gung-ho mood suddenly evaporated, and she glanced out of the window at the garden as if already anticipating missing green outdoor spaces from a bleak prison cell.

'Look – I don't know a lot about the law,' Bella said. 'But I do know that if you plead guilty to shoplifting, you're saying you absolutely *did* intend to do it. Premeditated, all that.'

'That's right, Gran. We did it at school,' Molly chipped in. 'You have to have meant *to permanently deprive* the shop of the goods. And you didn't. So you have to say not guilty.'

'No!' Shirley was adamant. 'If I say it was unintentional, it'll drag on for months. And . . . and . . .' She looked down at the rug fringe that she was playing with again and almost whispered, 'There'll be . . . medical reports.'

There was silence for a while, then Shirley said, 'When you get to my age, you'll understand that whatever the cost, you'd rather be found bad than mad.'

* * *

Oh, the relief of getting away for an evening's respite from the problems that were collecting inside the house like a slowly gathering swarm. Bella went out just after eight, leaving Molly and Shirley exchanging opinions about padded bras as they finished supper together. Shirley was of the view that Molly should 'maximize her assets', as she put it, and Molly was saying she couldn't be doing with underwiring and having a cleavage to flaunt. 'I like my male friends to look at my face when they talk to me,' she said, reasonably enough.

'Ah, but what about the ones you'd like to be *more than friends* with?' was Shirley's argument. Bella, leaning on the bus shelter and fishing her Oyster card out of her bag, wondered if her mother was really suitable company for Molly. She'd have the girl looking at the Myla website within minutes of Bella's absence, and be offering her nipple tassels and a feather-handled riding crop for her eighteenth birthday.

The River Fox garden wasn't busy for a warm September weeknight. Some of the writers were already there and had dragged three of the long outdoor tables together in a row, bagging plenty of space for the group. The Thames – at mid-tide – was moving sluggishly and with a faint late-summer sheen of blue algae on it. A posse of Canada geese wandered on the garden's grass, boldly demanding crisps from customers who were more scared of the birds than of the Please

Don't Feed The Geese notice that was up on the fence.

Jules – whose frequent poetry-competition wins well qualified her for the group – was there with Dina and Phyllida. Phyl wrote hugely successful historical thrillers under two different names and Dina taught creative writing at the local adult education college, was undertaking a very slow PhD in the subject, and had had a novel (ground-breaking, according to Dina) on the go for a good three years. Bella tended to avoid Dina, as any conversation usually ended with Dina denouncing all popular contemporary fiction as 'mindless rubbish', and with Bella pointing out that as writing was a full-time career for some people, it could be useful to write what people actually like to read.

'I didn't know you were coming tonight; you should have called, I'd have given you a lift.' Jules broke away from the beginnings of an argument about the role of literary agents. She was sitting at the table with a glass of lemonade and a bag of pork scratchings. 'I saw your mother arrive at your place earlier and thought you must be staying in with her. Or possibly going out with her.'

'I wasn't sure I was coming either, but once I decided, I definitely didn't want to bring the car. I *so* need this drink.' Bella climbed on to the bench seat beside Jules, getting a sharp splinter in her calf and spilling the top inch of her glass of wine in the process. ('Small or medium?' the barman had asked. 'Large,' Bella had snapped, before apologizing. It wasn't his fault that she could soon be borderline bankrupt and homeless.) 'These stupid tables,' she murmured, pulling the wood out and dabbing at the tiny spot of blood that was left. 'But . . . sometimes you just have to get away. It's been a tricky few days. James has turned up and wants us to sell the house.'

'Bleed'n' 'ell!' Jules spluttered her lemonade. 'Has he not noticed that you live in it? Can he force you to sell?'

'I don't know. I've lived there on my own with the kids for over ten years since he left . . . but it seems that might count for nothing, because on paper it's still half his. He hasn't contributed at all though, so I'll have to find out where I stand legally.' Bella sipped her drink. 'I suppose I should have seen it coming. This week, I'm feeling I should have seen a lot of things coming.' She smiled at Marcus, who was joining the table with his wife Sally; the two of them were scriptwriters, working together on a follow-up to a successful sitcom series. Both had short floppy fair hair with overlong fringes and wore striped tops – Sally's a Boden Breton, Marcus's a cheery pink and white – with jeans. Was that what happened when you worked, lived and raised your children so very closely together, Bella wondered, the same way dogs and their owners start to look alike?

'Things not going well?' Phyllida chipped in. 'Is it deadline hell for you right now?'

'No – I finished a book a while back, thanks Phyl. I'm halfway through the next one. No, it's just . . . well, home stuff. Everything going wrong at once.'

Phyl chinked her glass against Bella's. 'Well, you're away from it tonight, my darling. Out among friends – you can leave all that stuff behind. And well done on the deadline thing. I live in constant battle with it.'

'Goodness, don't you churn them out! You and Phyllida both!' Dina exclaimed. 'Isn't that more than one a year? But then of course . . .'

'Yes, two a year,' Bella told her. 'But my Orchard Girls books are for a series, which makes it easier as I already know the characters. And it's not as if I have to do much of the creating. For these big series, the plot decisions are made at editorial level and we writers just do a form of colouring in.'

'Of course, you're writing for the *young*. Remind me, what's the age group you're aiming at? And it's essentially *romance*, isn't it?'

'About eleven to whatever age, really. There is an element of romance, but it's very tame and safe. Girls get to that love-curiosity stage at such a wide age range,' Bella explained, thinking at the same time about the word Dina had used: 'churn'. Hard work, churning. The word reminded her of Tess of the D'Urbervilles as a milkmaid. Making butter would have given her wonderfully muscly arms.

'So I suppose for them you're a kind of jump-off point, leading them on to the chick-lit and bodice-ripper stage later!' Dina laughed. Bella didn't.

'Oh come on now, Dina, surely anything that gets them reading has to be good?' Phyl interrupted.

'Well, within reason. But by eleven, of course, there's C. S. Lewis and any amount of *quality* literature. I swear by *Treasure Island*, myself. Now that *is* adventure,' Dina half conceded. 'But don't get me wrong! I do admire you, Bella – you do all that and the journalism too.' Somehow Bella didn't feel remotely admired. Dina was looking at her as if she was from another planet. Planet Chav, at a guess. So, she wrote about feisty adventurous young teens. So, when you put it like that, did Jacqueline Wilson. And J. K. Rowling. Both responsible for getting a whole generation of children absolutely besotted by books. It couldn't be bad.

'So how about you, Dina?' Bella asked brightly. 'Thesis all done?'

'Gosh no!' Dina laughed. 'It's a painstaking process! And of course *the novel* is only part of it. I'm at the stage of battling with the demons of character purity. It's all terribly Chekhovian. My mentor has hinted about the Costa prize, but of course that's way in the future!' Dina pushed back her long mane of hennaed frizz and took off her glasses, rubbing the lenses vigorously on her long purple skirt. 'I don't expect to get a *final* draft worked in under another couple of years.'

'Is your editor OK with that?' Jules asked. 'And what does your agent say?'

'Ah . . . well I haven't actually chosen an agent yet,' Dina admitted. 'My mentor feels one should be absolutely *ready*. I tell my students the same – the essence of creative writing is about *the voice*. And of course you can't expect to find *the voice* until you've studied those of the great and good. Otherwise, to think one can write borders on *impertinence*. And of course there's all the research. I may have to move to Moscow.'

Phyl leaned forward. 'Dina, sweetie, you're writing a novel, not changing the world. Just *make it up*.'

Bella bit her lip to stop herself laughing. Luckily, she was distracted by the arrival of Chloe and Zoe, who were picking their way across the goose-crap grass carefully, carrying drinks and bringing Saul between them like a prize.

'Hello everyone!' Zoe said cheerfully. (It had to be – Bella noticed the gold Z on a chain round her neck.) 'I've brought someone to meet you all! This is Saul Barrett and he's got an exciting proposition for us!'

Saul caught sight of Bella and smiled. She hoped she looked better than when he'd last seen her, all blotchy and sauce-smeared. For a second, she remembered the gentle touch of his thumb on her skin, and could feel her face going pink. She suddenly realized Zoe was in full flow and tried to concentrate.

'. . . Anyway, Saul's production company needs a group of people so they can each be made over: dress, hair, make-up, the lot. Colour counselling, you name it. He thinks we writers could be just the thing. If anyone's up for it, that is! I mean, think of the publicity!'

'Oh, the great media machine,' Dina sniffed. 'Shouldn't one's work speak for itself?'

'Trinny and Susannah already did that group thing,' Sally pointed out. 'I saw the one about the dog-breeders, and wondered why they put them into bright satin frocks and stilettos. You can't jog a spaniel round the park in that get-up. Plain silly.'

'Ah, but this is a bit different,' Saul told her. 'It's about the group bonding, living together for a short while and helping each other find their own solutions, rather than being lectured at by those who don't properly understand how they live on a day-to-day level. It'll be far more about the group than the presenters. They'll be just the enablers, the catalysts. Which is why I thought *writers*. Articulate by definition, always got something to say. It should make great TV.'

'What's it called?' Dina asked.

Saul hesitated. 'Er . . . *Fashion Victims*. But don't let that put you off. This is absolutely *not* about ritual humiliation by 360-degree mirror and big pants, I promise. It's more about mutual support and so on.'

'It's a pilot then?' Marcus asked, one media professional to another.

'Yes, a pilot. Hopefully part one of six; we'll see how it goes. I really want to start with a bang, so when Zoe suggested this group I thought we could talk it through, if enough of you are interested.'

'Living together?' Phyl asked. 'Where, exactly? Because if it's the Savoy, count me in!'

'Well – that's where TV magic comes in. The idea is to take a largeish house, have it look as if the whole group are staying there for the duration – in reality it'll only be about ten days. And you won't, I promise, have to live on the premises. It won't take up anywhere near as much time as the programme will make out. Actually, I'm still trying to find the perfect location.' Saul looked a bit worried at this point. 'We did have an excellent one but it was suddenly sold and it all fell through . . . so if anyone knows a detached house with a fair bit of character, some good-sized rooms, ideally having one of those very large family-room set-ups, just let me know. Anyway,' he said, finishing his beer, 'um, that's it really. I'll . . . er wander off home now and leave you all to discuss it, because I feel I've interrupted your evening for long enough. If it's a yes, and I hope it is, just give Zoe any questions you want answered and I'll do my best to help. And there's a pretty hefty location fee if anyone knows of a suitable venue . . .'

Oh is there? Bella thought, some cogs in her brain starting to whir. Now there's an idea.

# FIVE

'I *hate* the first day of the school year.' Molly grumbled to Carly, who was driving them to school in her mum's old Polo. There was an ominous clunking sound every time Carly changed gear, which Molly suspected might not be the car's fault. 'Day one is always so *false* – everyone hugging people they'll hardly talk to again and saying how *brilliant* to see each other. Like those who *are* actually friends haven't been hanging out together for the whole holidays anyway?'

'And then you get the ones who've spent six weeks at their dad's bank-robber villa in Spain.' Carly giggled.

'Too right. So that'll be Tania then! How many clothes will she *not* be wearing today to show off her tan and her new bling? And do you think she'll do that thing she did after Easter, "accidentally" dropping in the odd Spanish word?' They were going down the high street now, slow in the school-run traffic. Molly caught sight of a sign in a pub window urging those who wanted Christmas office parties to book early. She immediately felt as if half the term was already over – and this was only September's first week. She had a sense of time racing; her mum said that's what happens when you get old. That couldn't be right – she wasn't even eighteen yet.

'She will, she will,' Carly agreed, applying lip gloss while waiting for the traffic lights to change. 'It's always good to rely on Tan. She's a natural-born WAG. But it's cute watching all the shy little year sevens on their first day, isn't it? Now we're really old, I think ah, how sweet they are. Only eleven and so scared of the first day at Big School.'

'Careful, Carls, you're going all nostalgic on me. And watch that bus, it's pulling out!' Molly gripped the sides of her seat and shut her eyes. Carly's driving was still of the essentials-only variety. Sometimes she drove as if the car should be the one making the effort and Carly was still just a passenger.

'Oops – sorry!' Carly waved and smiled at the bus driver, even though there was no chance he could see her. 'We should be really happy,' she said to Molly, turning her head to catch the new autumn clothes display in Jigsaw's window. 'This time next year we'll be *not* going to school. Ever, ever again. Can't wait!'

Molly frowned, feeling the time-passing shiver again.

'But don't you think that's a scary thought? I mean, school's been *what we do* the whole time from when we were, like, four? And then as soon as our As are done, we're out of there. It's like being a big ship that's being built and it's all snug on its thingy in the shipyard, and then whoooosh! Clunk goes the champagne bottle and it's out into the freezing sea.'

'It's a ship. That's what they do! And are you mad? OK, I'll miss school *slightly*. But only for . . .' Carly thought for a moment. 'Twenty minutes, tops.'

'I think I quite like knowing what I'm going to be doing and where I'll be. Otherwise I get all twitchy. Really, I'm like *so* boring. I'm going to look like a total numpty on the UCAS form, aren't I? This'll be my personal statement: "I will not be building schools in tropical rainforests in my gap year. Or doing work experience on a major movie in the Gobi desert or joining a polar trek. I will probably work in the garden centre like I already do on Saturdays and then go for a nice fortnight in Crete where I'll lie on the beach and read fun books and only go sightseeing the history stuff if I'm forced to." Lazy, would you say?'

'"With my devoted boyfriend, Giles." Don't forget to add that bit. They'll want to know, at your uni of choice.'

And there he was. As the car trundled up the school drive to the car park, Giles was sitting on the front steps, waiting for Molly.

'He's pretty hot, you know, Moll. Have you . . . ?'

'No. *Still* not – well not quite . . . I told you about Mum coming home early. Haven't had a chance since. I think I'm doomed. Doomed to be still shagless when I leave school. Another adventure I won't have had.'

'Could be worse,' Carly said, as she had her third go at backing into a space. 'You could have ended up like the Terrible Example. Think of Pram-face Lisa – up the duff at fourteen.'

'I know, I know. But at least . . .' Molly hesitated and looked towards Giles. He'd seen them, was coming over to meet them.

'At least what?' Carly switched off the ignition and gathered her bag and books together.

'Lisa knows what she's doing with her life. And yes I know it's cos she's got no choice. But right now, I don't know if our house is going to be sold, if my gran's going to prison or if I'll die a virgin like some Victorian old maid.'

Molly climbed out of the car and Giles wrapped his arms around her. 'Hi babe,' he murmured into her hair.

'I think I can probably answer one of those for you!' Carly laughed as she locked the car door. 'Guess which!'

It had taken only minutes of discussion before the general consensus of the group at the River Fox came down in favour of giving Saul's programme idea a whirl.

'So who's up for million-viewer humiliation and having their dress sense trashed by some skinny teenage tart?' Jules asked as soon as Saul's cute little Mercedes pulled out of the pub car park.

'Why don't you put it a bit more bluntly, Jules?' Zoe commented, but all the same she, Bella, Jules, Phyl and Dina volunteered without so much as a second's hesitation, even before the magic words 'think of the publicity' had been uttered. The others opted out as being too shy or too busy. Dina scorned the publicity angle and preferred the argument that taking part could be 'useful research'. Bella wasn't too bothered about the clothes aspect – though the chance to find out exactly where she'd been going wrong with black wasn't to be passed up – but she did think there was a good opportunity here to write a well-paid feature on the inside story of being a makeover victim. To show there were no hard feelings (or at least to *pretend* there were none for the sake of her bank balance), she would even run the idea past Charlotte at the *Sunday Review* first. She and Charlotte had always got on well enough, professionally speaking . . . till now, anyway. Maybe if there was a teeny sliver of sympathy somewhere in Charlotte's psyche, she'd at least give the idea some consideration.

Having thought about it long and hard during a night that had involved much 2 a.m. tea-drinking and back-of-an-envelope sums, Bella got Saul's number from Zoe and called him to see if his production company would consider her house as a possible location for the shoot. Not only would there be useful cash in this (last year Jules had gone to see her sister in Australia on the proceeds of renting out her front garden, just the path really, gate-to-door, for an advert), but it would buy some time in which Bella could do some thinking about the fast-accumulating uncertainties for her future. For one thing, James could hardly put the house on the market if there was a film crew on the premises. She could just imagine some young, keen estate agent showing potential buyers around. 'And here's the kitchen . . . and . . . oh, as a special feature here's a smiley bossy camp chap telling a size-22 woman that she *must* minx it up in swagged lime satin and eight-inch stilettos.'

Saul had sounded charmingly delighted by Bella's offer and was now due within minutes to give the place his professional once-over. Trying to see the place through his eyes, she took a good last look round the house and could – of course – only see faults. The hallway needed painting – there were greyish fingermarks all over the front door, which were now so ingrained that it would take a lot more than a rub with Cif and a J-cloth to shift them. The stair carpet's colour had been listed as 'Rich Coffee', but when Alex had spilled a cup of the real stuff two years before, the resulting splashy stain had been, still was and forever would be, a good couple of shades darker. And would Saul's inspection be so thorough that he'd discover (and be put off by) the wispy spider nests in the back folds of the cream curtains in the sitting room? Bella never had the heart to move them, imagining (probably wrongly) trails of tragic spider families, desperately seeking new premises. Given her own uncertain position, it could be tempting fate to evict them right now.

As Saul had said, it was really just the one big family room he would be needing, Bella had concentrated the best of her efforts in the kitchen. She had cleaned and polished every surface, nagged Molly and Alex into moving the various abandoned shoes, CDs, books, electronic toys and sundry plastic bags of God-knows-what to their rooms. She'd crammed every gadget including the Magimix, juicer and toaster into the cupboards, and was now clearing the last of her own paperwork pile from the worktop. Devoid of its usual random clutter, the room looked even bigger. The sunlight streamed in on the treacly walnut floor and the whole place was so meticulously scrubbed that even if James dropped by for a crafty spot check and ran a critical finger over every surface, he'd have trouble finding one mote of muck.

The leather sofa's decrepitude was disguised under a velvety purple throw that had been disinterred from the vintage trunk in the hallway, and there was a tall vase of the longest possible branches of pinky-mauve hydrangea from the garden on the table. This looked a bit precarious. The oversized flower heads were heavy and so carefully counterbalanced against each other that it would only take one careless flick of a cat's paw for the whole lot to go crashing down. Not that the cat was allowed on the table – but who could trust an attention-seeking feline when there is a house visitor and thus an opportunity to push its luck?

Bella had even included her own outfit in the overall look and, so as not to provide colourful distraction, was wearing a simple loose white linen shirt over a skimpy vest top and black linen trousers. New York Carole's 'You shouldn't wear black' niggled slightly, as Bella knew it forever would, but right now she merely wanted to look unobtrusive. And black – well, everyone knew it made you look slimmer. Body-wise, Bella was the kind of medium height, medium weight that could, with a bit of clever underwear, look good enough in most things, but even she, realizing that cameras add a good ten pounds, was now considering making herself a temporary no-carbs zone.

There was still one small (or not so small) unsolved problem, if Saul *did* want to use the house. Where would they all live for the duration of the project? Alex would be all right – he would be going back to Oxford in a few weeks and before that was heading down to

Biarritz in a van with a crew of his surf-crazy mates. But Molly would have serious schoolwork to do, and was entitled to her own premises and enough peace to get on with it. And then there was Shirley, too . . . how long did she really intend staying? She'd said it would be just a few days but now she'd settled into the spare bedroom, unpacked a massive array of cosmetics in the tiny en suite bathroom, she seemed perfectly content and had just left for lunch at the Royal Academy with 'a gentleman friend' as she coyly put it, whom she'd met on her most recent cruise. 'And I'm wearing the dress I *didn't* steal!' she'd called as she was leaving.

When the doorbell rang, Bella was staring at the gap behind the sink where the tiles had fallen down. That was possibly the most obvious of many defects Saul would find. Too late now, though. Swiftly, she glanced around the room and could see, in spite of the effort she'd put in, it still looked decidedly shabby. How much magic could a props organizer (or whatever the term was) really work? Possibly none, in this case. One look and it would be 'thanks, but . . . er, no thanks', there'd be a pitying smile and it would be back to harassing the regular locations companies for something a lot more suitably glam. This was a crazy idea. Even if he liked the place, the potential disruption would be hell and the money nowhere near compensation for the upheaval. And how would the neighbours feel about a row of TV-company trucks parked outside, generators blasting?

'. . . And this is Fliss,' Saul said as he came into the house, introducing a tiny waif of a girl with long auburn hair piled up messily and jeans so tight her legs looked as if they belonged to a baby stork. 'Fliss is *work experience*,' Saul went on, his eyes glinting at Bella over the top of the lethal-looking purple spike that inefficiently held Fliss's untidy mass of hair in place. Bella smiled, hoping to convey that she understood whatever subtle hidden message he was trying to give her. She didn't, quite: did he mean that the girl was free labour and therefore pleasingly cheap? Or that she was a burdensome observer who didn't have a clue about the job? And what job? Was she the fashion side or production?

Fliss hadn't said anything, not even hello, but was smiling in a vague and distant way while focused on something in the middle distance, as if only she could see an interesting resident spectre. Bella quickly looked to see if she had iPod earplugs in, but she didn't. Perhaps she was simply the dreamy sort.

'Hi Fliss!' Bella said in too-bright a way which she thought made her sound as if she was talking to a toddler. 'Would you both like coffee?'

'Please, yes.' Saul accepted eagerly on behalf of the two of them.

'Fliss is also my stepdaughter,' he told Bella as they went through to the kitchen. 'She got this gig on a shameless *who you know* basis but I intend to make her work her arse off on the project, see if that'll put her off going into the media,' he explained.

Bella, nervous, filled the kettle and hauled the cafetière out from its new hiding place in the dresser cupboard. She'd stashed it behind the blender and it was awkward to retrieve. Why on earth hadn't she put the one thing she was most likely to use within easy distance? Rootling about in the cupboard made her all hot and she could feel the shirt starting to crumple and flop, as linen will. She pictured James tutting at her inefficiency and felt as if everything she touched, every part of this room slightly failed at being on best behaviour under inspection. She told herself it really didn't matter that much – it wouldn't be the end of the world if Saul said no. She'd just have to go back to thinking of other income options.

Keith the cat strolled through from the hallway and stopped to take a look at the three of them before flicking his tail impolitely and ambling out through the open glass doors to the garden. Bella had folded these all the way back so the kitchen-to-garden space was as close as possible to being seamless. The air outside was hot and almost completely still. It was one of those beautiful, almost breath-free, early autumn days, as if the end of the summer could stay captured that way for months, and only the scent wafting in from the pair of urns planted with a mass of pinks showed that the air had any movement in it at all.

'Nice cat. Is it Siamese?' Fliss suddenly said. Bella jumped and Saul laughed. He had a good laugh, she noticed, slightly too loud but that was OK; it was spontaneous, unforced.

'Yes, it does speak now and then!' Saul said, then added, 'I meant Fliss, not the cat. Obviously.'

'It's OK, I realized. And no, Keith is a Burmese, a chocolate one.' Bella told Fliss. 'They look a bit like very dark Siamese, but they're a lot less noisy.'

'Like Fliss,' Saul teased the girl. 'Looks like a teenager but a lot less noisy. Win–win, both girl and cat, I'd say.'

'Well it's a very cute cat. And Saul, I'm like twenty-three?'

Saul pulled a that's-telling-me face at Bella as Fliss went back to looking prettily distant, staring out down the garden towards the plum trees against the far wall. Given her earlier imaginings about the cat and the hydrangeas, Bella was glad to see Keith was now happily many yards away, sitting in hope under the bird feeder that hung at a safe height from the mimosa along the side fence.

Bella opened her Princess Diana biscuit tin to find that the supply of Shirley's flapjacks that she'd baked the day before had been seriously diminished. Molly must have scoffed about twelve of the things. She piled what was left on to a plate and put them on the table. 'Sorry – there were loads more than this yesterday. Some teenage mouse has been down in the night and raided them.'

'Well I'm not surprised,' Saul commented through a mouthful of syrupy oats, 'they're completely delicious.' Fliss eyed them as if they were going to bite her, not the other way round. 'Go on Fliss,' Saul teased, 'just try one. You might like it.'

'Carbs,' Fliss murmured fondly, taking a flapjack and licking the edge of it. 'Mmmmm.'

Bella eyed her enviously – she had the kind of all-bones little body that shouldn't even need to know a word such as carbohydrate.

'So . . . er, what do you think, Saul?' Bella asked. 'Now you're here in my house you probably wonder why I wasted your time. I know it's a bit tatty round the edges and the kitchen's dated and . . . do you need to look at the rest of it? Probably not . . .'

'No, no it's great!' Saul interrupted. 'It's just . . .'

'What? You *do* hate it!' Bella laughed, covering a mood-plummet of disappointment. 'You're just trying to find a polite way of telling me!'

'That's right,' he said, looking serious. 'I want to hang out here and eat all the rest of the flapjacks and have some more of this delicious coffee and *then* put the boot in. I'm like that, aren't I Fliss?'

'Hmm? I don't really know,' she said, still gazing at the garden. Were there fairies down there that she was watching?

'No – you probably don't actually . . .' he conceded, looking a bit downcast for a second. Bella was puzzled. If this was his stepdaughter, presumably they knew each other really quite well? She was enormously curious but (unfortunately) not ill-mannered enough to ask.

'So it's "just" what?' Bella persisted, pouring more coffee into Saul's mug. Her brain whizzed through the 'it's just' possibilities. The space wasn't big enough, the garden could do with as much of a makeover as the fashion victims, the house frontage didn't have space enough for whatever vehicles would be needed, there'd be parking issues, neighbour problems . . .

'It's just that we need to get in here from *next week*. How would that suit you? Too short notice or would you be all right with that? Because if you'd need time to think about it, then I'm afraid I just don't have it. Shooting is another ten days away but the time to get this place styled up to look the way we want it . . . well, that kind of starts now.'

Bella gulped. 'Wow. What would you have done if I hadn't volunteered? You surely couldn't have scrapped the show?'

'No, no – I had a studio space on stand-by, but it would have been a lot more hassle building the whole thing from scratch. There's nothing quite like an authentic home when you're using "real" people, if you see what I mean. A studio mock-up never has quite the atmosphere. This is so much more natural and everyone involved will relax more. I want to use exterior shots a lot too, so I had a good look at the front of the house on the way in. I *love* the turrets on the corners and the pattern of the roof tiles, the overgrown clematis. The whole place has a slightly crazy mock-Gothic feel to it.'

Bella tried to take this all in. He liked it, he wanted it. The money would buy her some serious breathing time (not to mention eating and bill-paying time) till the payment on release of her next Orchard Girls book. The only downside was how little hope she had of losing ten pounds in the time without resorting to amputating her head. Oh well.

'Apparently this weather's supposed to hold for a few weeks, so we should . . .' Saul crossed his fingers and tapped on the wooden tabletop, 'be lucky. It's just a matter of whether you'll be up for the disruption. The props guys will sort the details – it's no big deal to give it a swift update, paint the walls, revamp cupboards and so on . . .' Bella listened, smiling. His arms were all over the place, gestures ever bigger as his enthusiasm and ideas took off. 'That tiling can go . . . and we'll rent in a huge sofa . . . make it a one-room-living kind of thing. And this is one *big* room – even the one I'd originally picked wasn't as massive as this one.'

Saul slowed at last, grinned at Bella and said, 'Sorry – I do get a bit carried away. Will you be all right with this? Please don't think I'm being critical of your decor – it's only about what looks good to a camera. We can put everything back exactly the way it was after, obviously.'

'Hmm – what happens if I don't want any of it put back?' she murmured, thinking any alteration, however superficial, could only be an improvement. 'A revamp for this room is long, long overdue, as you can see.'

'We can negotiate on that,' Saul told her. 'That's in the devilish detail. Fliss, have you made any notes?'

Fliss seemed to be texting. 'I have,' she assured him, without looking up. 'That's what I'm doing right now.'

'Excellent!' Saul's conspiratorial smile to Bella expressed a certain amount of surprise at this. Bella smiled back, wondering how much of the Fliss employment was as a favour to . . . well, his wife, presumably. She imagined Saul in a home setting, fancifully giving him a far more minimalist and stylish place than her own. It *had* to be all cream sofas and feature walls and something signature-mad like a fabulous Vivienne Westwood rug. The wife would be a still-slender sort who looked wonderful padding around barefoot in ancient jeans and a silky floaty top. Bella pictured her with long brown caramel-streaked hair, and a knack of looking utterly shaggable with it loosely tied up. Tendrils would escape and he'd move them from the back of her neck when he went to kiss her as she stirred something succulent and aromatic at a massive halogen hob . . .

'You're miles away.' Saul broke into Bella's mad fancies, jolting her back to earth. Whatever was she thinking of? Whyever did she even begin to think of him kissing someone? She'd almost felt envious there for a second, though whether at the imagined fabulously stylish house or the imagined ongoing hot romance, she couldn't be sure. Almost certainly the house, she told herself. Saul and Mrs Saul wouldn't have coffee stains on *their* stair carpet and piles of Oxfam-bound cast-offs languishing in Waitrose bags at the top of the stairs. Oh no . . . But she would concede that she was thinking about the other thing too, just a little bit. Not that she fancied Saul, it was just that – still dented from the abrupt ending of the Rick relationship – she couldn't help thinking that the chances of one day sharing a home with some lovable, trustable, desirable man were even slimmer than Saul's imagined wife.

'Sorry. I was just . . .'

'. . . imagining the chaos to come,' Saul supplied for

her. 'Don't worry, honestly. The props boys will sort it all for you. You won't have to do a thing except be here for the shoot. But before even that, you and the rest of the victims have to meet Dominic and Daisy. They're your makeover team. She's frocks and a bit overwhelming, he's finishings and very rarely gets a word in.'

'Finishings' is hair, make-up, accessories,' Fliss explained, suddenly coming to life. 'That's actually my field of interest. I want to be a fashion journalist really.'

'Oh . . . right. So this is . . . ?' Bella asked.

'Filling in time and getting to know people, like networking?' Fliss told her. 'And making a list of Essential Tips to maximize one's *look*.'

'Got any tips going spare?' Bella laughed as she cleared the coffee mugs and stashed them in the dishwasher.

'Hmmm.' Fliss scrutinized her thoroughly and thought for a moment, her thin little face contorted in concentration. Eventually this smoothed out into a broad smile. 'OK. Never wear a shade of white that's lighter than your teeth.'

'Er . . . Right. Thanks for that,' Bella said. Bummer, she told herself, instantly vowing she'd never wear this once-favourite linen shirt again. She'd file this moment under 'questions better left unasked'.

* * *

Shirley was glad she hadn't worn the mauve shoes. Their heels weren't particularly high but were quite spindly, and she'd forgotten how the floors of the Royal Academy had these annoying metal grids here and there. Given her recent luck, she would be sure to trap her foot in one and break an ankle. *Not* the thing you want on a first date. Or did this count as the first? On the cruise, she and Dennis had spent so much of their time together from the moment they met in the corridor, being shown to their respective cabins, only two away from each other. 'We'll be able to wave to each other from our balconies,' he'd joked as the ship's smiley stewards simultaneously unlocked their doors.

Shirley, who would have sworn solemn and repeated oaths that she was *not* looking for a man, had nevertheless been rather skittishly delighted that Dennis was also travelling alone and over dinner that night, as the ship pulled away from the French coast, the two of them bonded as experienced and confident lone voyagers, outdoing each other with tales of Ships I Have Known. And when the ship docked at its various destinations, it somehow seemed quite natural that Dennis and Shirley should quietly avoid the organized tours and venture ashore together. After several trips to Barcelona with groups of mostly female shipboard companions, it felt a lot more grown-up to be having leisurely tapas with one thoroughly civilized man at a backstreet bar off Las Ramblas than to find herself resigned to a lunch choice of the group majority, just to keep the peace. Frankly, you could have enough of herded widows.

'Did you enjoy Venice best? Or maybe Barcelona?' Dennis asked as they made their way slowly through the Byzantium exhibition.

'Oh I couldn't choose! Both were so wonderful, in spite of the crowds and the heat. It's amazing to think of the historic connections with all this . . .' she said, indicating the exhibition's treasures. 'Coins, icons, fabrics, pieces of sculpture, fragments of building and mosaics, so many of these from those places. When you're there you can *feel* the link to this history.'

'Well it's all around you, isn't it?' he agreed. 'Though I have to say, now we've seen all this, I'm honestly not sure I can take much more of it.'

Shirley laughed. 'Oh I always get that! Exhibition overload! We could get some tea, perhaps?'

'No – I can do better than that,' Dennis told her. 'I've booked us a table for lunch at the Wolseley. If that's all right with you?' He took her hand as they approached the stairs. As Shirley felt the warmth of his skin, the slight roughness of his palm against her soft one, she recognized that the extra thumping in her heart was of elated delight, not something to phone NHS Direct about. It had been a long, long time since she had felt like this about someone. And better yet, it was clearly reciprocated.

There were, Shirley thought several hours later, as she lay in bed beside Dennis in the Ritz hotel sipping Veuve Clicquot and deciding between a miniature coffee eclair and a raspberry millefeuille, just enough advantages to being older to make one's increasing age bearable. The best one was how the rest of the world perceived you. If you were lucky enough to have a sexual encounter – especially a spontaneous, out-of-the-blue one like this – it was absolutely nobody's business but your own. When she left this famous building, she would have no sense of the Walk of Shame, as she'd heard it described. For who would imagine that two people of her and Dennis's age would have spent an afternoon making such passionate love? It didn't all have to end with the menopause.

'Happy?' Dennis asked, leaning across to top up her glass.

'Oh, very much so,' Shirley told him.

'You haven't stopped smiling since . . .'

'Since they brought the cakes?' she teased.

'No . . . since the moment we got into bed,' he said, stealing her eclair and taking a sly bite.

'That's more than happiness,' she assured him. 'It's relief. That I can still do it, that you wanted to, that *you* can still do it . . . that it was *so* good, all sorts of things. And there's another secret delight too.' She giggled, feeling ridiculously bad-girlish.

'And that is?' he asked.

'That when I go back to my daughter's house later, she'll assume I've simply had a good widow-woman type of day, taking in an exhibition, having a light and sensible lunch, possibly browsing in Harvey Nicks or Hatchards, that kind of thing. I'll tell her yes, thank you, I had a lovely day. But inside here,' she tapped her head, 'I'll have my secret knowledge of *this*.' She looked around Dennis's chintzy room with its heavily over-swagged curtains, yet palely delicate furniture. Understated opulence, she would say. You didn't get a lot of that in Walton on Thames. You didn't get many men who habitually stayed in hotels like this, either.

'Or you could just tell her,' he suggested wryly.

'*Tell* her? Heavens no! She'd be terribly shocked. Young people, they have no idea.'

'Poor things!' Dennis laughed, gently biting her naked shoulder.

'Exactly. Poor things!'

# SIX

Three precisely two-second rings on the doorbell made Bella feel instantly irritated. Absolutely classic James. Always three rings. What made him think one wasn't nearly enough?

'I thought you might like to give some of these a bit of perusal,' James announced, thrusting a pile of documents into Bella's hand and striding past her into the house the moment she opened the door. A blast of too much aftershave filled the air, as if he had learned over the years that women like something 'tangy', but he was still experimenting with how much was likely to make them swoon at his feet. Bella wondered if it would be a kindness to let him know that appealing as the scent was, he'd gone way past the optimum amount. Newly attuned to current style, by way of more than usually close scrutiny of all the weekend papers' fashion features along with a sinfully expensive selection of the glossies (tax-deductible, thank goodness, in the interests of research), Bella also privately thought he was mistaken to be wearing a yellow and pink Pringle-diamond cardigan. On a skinny twenty-something, floppy-haired catwalk boy it looked edgily louche and cutely ironic. On portly James it gave the impression of a huge Battenberg cake. He couldn't even claim golf-playing as an excuse.

'"Hello Bella and how are you?" might be a good way to start a visit if there's something you want me to do for you, James,' Bella told him, giving the top one of the bundle of papers a quick shufti to make sure it wasn't an eviction order. Estate-agent bumf. Well, he didn't waste any time, did he? She didn't close the door but waited to see if he'd notice that she was holding her handbag and keys and was clearly about to go out. He didn't and was now halfway across the hallway, so reluctantly she pushed the door shut and followed him into the kitchen, where he was already switching on the kettle and searching through the tea-bag selection in the cupboard. She dumped the pile of papers on the table.

'James, look I'm sorry but I've got to be somewhere. This *really* isn't a good time.' She was going to be late. She was off for lunch with Charlotte to talk about exactly how much of her freelance work was likely to be acceptable to the *Sunday Review* in future. After more than three years at this, and with such short notice of the cut in her column, Bella felt entitled to some degree of clarification as to where she stood. If she were to be phased out completely, she'd have to make serious new career plans, and fast.

'But I've brought you a heap of house details! I've been checking out a few local estate agents for you,' James declared cheerfully, spooning sugar into a mug, utterly oblivious to Bella's impatience. 'Because, you see, I completely understand that you're rather reluctant to initiate proceedings, so I've been doing some pre-searching into downsizing the peripherals for you, like we talked about!' He looked so pleased with himself, so sure she wouldn't be anything less than delighted.

'No, *you* talked about it, James. It came as a huge surprise to me, remember? Look, think about it; how can I inflict a house move on Molly while she's in the middle of her A levels? Be reasonable, for heaven's sake! And, please, don't get settled,' she added as he opened the fridge and took out a new bottle of milk. 'I really do have to leave, *right now*.'

Feeling angry that James was treating her kitchen as familiarly as if he actually still lived in the house, she swiped the mug from beside him and poured the unbrewed tea down the sink. He stared at her and then at the empty mug, as if he didn't quite understand what she'd done.

'Sorry, I don't mean to be hostile but you have to go – *now*. OK?' she insisted. 'I'm meeting someone and I *really* can't be late. I'm having lunch with the *Sunday Review* features editor in Soho.'

He looked puzzled. 'But you can go, I don't mind. I can just stay here and have my tea. I mean, it is . . .'

'Yes I know, *half your house*.' How infuriating he was. 'But only on paper, not in reality for years and years. And besides, I'll be double-locking the door, which would mean you couldn't get out. I want to set the burglar alarm too.'

'I think you'll find that *on paper* still counts for something in law, Bella my darling. I can lock up for you if you give me the alarm code. Why don't you just tell me where the spare keys are? Better still, why don't you let me have one, now I'm back?'

Bella could feel her blood pressure soaring. If she wasn't in such a hurry she'd pick a full-sized argument about this. 'Because you might be "back" in the area but you're not "back" in my life or my house. You don't live here, James. You haven't since the day you packed your belongings, left me and the children and took off with Miss Dental Hygiene all those years ago. You can't just invade my space like this. What would you call it in your corporate-speak? Try to think of this as *negative territory*.' James seemed confused; she must have used the term wrongly, not that it really meant a lot whichever way you used it.

'I tell you what: if you really want to talk to me about this,' she conceded, 'you can give me a lift down to the station and then maybe, just *maybe*, I'll think about looking at your house-detail selection.' Well, it was true – she would. But only because it was always fun to see who was selling what and to look at pictures of other people's domestic interiors.

Like a small boy promised an ice cream, James looked visibly cheered, and Bella managed to whoosh him out of the house, lock up swiftly and get him into his shiny new company Lexus.

'You'd find it much easier to manage, being in a smaller place,' James began as soon as the car pulled out of the driveway. 'Lower bills, less space to heat, minimal upkeep.' He turned to face her at the traffic lights and actually wagged an admonishing finger, telling her with deep seriousness as if discussing imminent death, 'Because we're not getting any younger, are we? Forward planning is the thing. You need to be considering a downstairs shower, a staircase broad enough for a stair-lift, that kind of arrangement. It all needs some 360-degree thinking. Get the right choice and you might never have to move again.'

Bella couldn't help laughing. 'James, stop it! I haven't even got to my mid-forties yet. Give me a break, will you? Next thing you'll be herding me off to a south-coast retirement bungalow.' James looked so serious, so pleased with himself for having all the answers to questions she hadn't even thought of asking. 'And don't you think all this *forward planning* – which incidentally is a mad term, because what other sort is there? – all this *planning* is like wishing time away? I don't intend to think about stairlifts and walk-in baths for years and years yet, please God. When I leave this house I might want to live in a loft apartment in Soho till I hit my dotage – or even during it – or over a funky shop on the Portobello Road.'

James carefully made a right turn into the station forecourt, tucking the car in neatly behind a convertible Golf in which a young and pretty couple were kissing frantically. Bella looked away; what she had seen of the boy looked a bit like Alex, whose love life was so closely guarded a mystery that she only assumed he had one from the swift goodbyes as he left the house at night muttering something like 'seeing Manda/Ellie/Caro'. A recent spate of Henri/Charlie/George had had her wondering if he'd gone gay till Molly had put her right about their full – female – names.

'You'd find both those options would be terribly noisy, you know.'

Bella didn't respond to that but counted to ten, out loud. He seemed to get the message.

'OK.' James gave in, switching off the engine. 'I'm not asking for instant decisions. But we need to take an ideas shower about who owns what. No need to involve solicitors, I'd have thought; don't you agree?'

'Yes James, I do agree. For several reasons: first, I'd have thought you'd know that the months before Christmas aren't a good time to sell. For another thing, I've got a TV show being filmed in the house over the next few weeks, and for another, I'm not planning to go *anywhere* just yet. Apart from lunch with Charlotte, right now.' She leaned over and gave him a brief kiss on his overscented cheek. 'But, hey, thanks for the lift.'

'Bella darling! *Lovely* to see you!' Charlotte hugged Bella and airkissed a loud 'mwah' alongside her left ear. Bella inhaled a delicious scent of Chanel 19 mixed with expensive hair products.

'Charlotte – you're looking fantastic, as ever.' And it couldn't be denied, however much Bella would have loved it if this woman who was responsible for scything her income had turned up looking like a dowdy crone. Charlotte always looked wonderful, and her shoes became ever more eccentric as she got older. Today's were lavender faux snakeskin with pink and purple straps twining halfway up her calves. Bella also guessed she was carrying the kind of handbag that was more expensive than a pedigree show dog and probably involved a two-year waiting list. Bella thought she'd keep her own Top Shop bag (stylish in its way) well out of Charlotte's line of vision.

Both women had a swift look round the restaurant as they were shown to their seats. The clientele at the Quo Vadis looked very media: women had haircuts that were either expensively mussed up or sleekly angled. Far more men than the national average for their pre-fifties age group were bald. Style-wise, Bella's newly sharpened radar for clothes noted a typically London-safe preponderance of black, even though the September day was scorching, but that set off the abstract art selection on the walls rather well. Thorough observation was a bit thwarted here, as diners were obviously sitting down and you couldn't get much clue about *a look* when it was only from the waist up. Beneath the heavy white tablecloths, the otherwise black-clad could be almost to a woman (and possibly to a man) wearing tartan, or floor-length citrus brights, or glistening satin in sugared-almond shades.

Dotted about were faces that Bella thought she almost recognized but couldn't quite name. They were probably *not* famous, but as with any place that you'd read about in the chic magazines, you couldn't help feeling that they *should* be. Bella could see that all the women sitting nearest to her had perfect make-up and very sleek and well-tamed eyebrows that were clearly accustomed to professional attention. On the pretext of moving her fringe out of her eyes, Bella ran a finger over her left one. When had she last plucked hers? When did she last really look at them for spikes and stragglers? She couldn't remember. And did it really matter that much, or would anyone with any style take one look at her and recognize a woman whose personal grooming could – at the most generous – be described as slightly chaotic?

They ordered food and relaxed with a glass of champagne each (Bella crossing her fingers that Charlotte was going to pick up the bill on behalf of the *Sunday Review*), and after a few minutes asking after each other's families and with Charlotte rather pointedly *not* asking about Rick, the serious business of the meeting had to be faced.

'I'm so sorry, Bella,' Charlotte began when she was comfortably a third of the way down her champagne glass. 'It absolutely wasn't my idea to change the "Week Moment" page. Not *at all*. There are editorial changes all round, honestly. You should see what they're doing to the garden section: in line with straitened times, there's a movement against the purely decorative and it's to be all guest vegetable experts from now on. The only flowers are going to be something called "companion planting".' She giggled. 'It makes me think of organizing a shallow grave after a big row with your partner! But,' and she turned serious as their food arrived, 'there have been other changes too . . . at management level, I mean.' She hesitated and then said, 'You know Rick has gone as well, I assume? I mean, of course I knew you and he were . . . um . . . friends.'

Bella wished Charlotte hadn't mentioned him; the remembered vision of his sneering wife Carole looking her up and down in that hotel doorway was in danger of putting her off her crab tagliatelle.

'I didn't know that, actually,' Bella told her. 'So has he quit? That was sudden.' She wondered if it had involved a degree of foot-stamping from Carole's dainty size 4s.

'Ooh, well he's gone over to the US side of things, apparently. For good,' Charlotte went on. 'No further contact with the UK sector as from this week. Didn't he say anything to you?'

Charlotte was looking at her expectantly, a forkful of sea bass halfway to her mouth.

Bella smiled. 'I'm not seeing him any more. Bastard turned out to be still married and . . . well, it just wasn't going to work.' Work? Ha! Understatement. Three months they'd been together and he hadn't even, after the final debacle, had the manners to be in touch to apologize. Not so much as an email. Even 'Sorry' on Twitter would have been something (an insultingly small something, but still. . .) but he'd vanished from the site.

'*Really?* I assumed he was divorced! Strange, he was kind of half based over here for two years and he'd never mentioned a wife. I mean, as far as I know, not to *anybody*. But what if he hadn't been married? Would you two have . . .'

'Even if he hadn't been, it wouldn't have lasted. There were clues we were never going to be long-term – I should have listened to my own head. God knows it's old enough by now to know a thing or two about men.'

Rick wasn't the first mistake since James had left, she reflected. There'd been the literary agent who constantly (and sometimes wrongly) corrected her grammar; the accountant who still lived with his mum and who had brought his laundry round to Bella's when his mother went away for a week. When she'd asked him why, exactly, he expected her to deal with it, he'd seemed not to understand the question. And then there was the rather sweet burly one who was evasive about the nature of his job but assured Bella he had friends who'd 'look after' her if she ever felt unsafe. But Rick had been a real wine-and-dine grown-up; the one she'd least expected to be a mistake. Just shows, she thought now.

'Oh, I'm not sure we ever learn,' Charlotte laughed. 'Look at me, divorced and child-free, yet still I assume there's a soulmate out there with my name on him. I'd blush to tell you how many frogs I've kissed in the past two years. And when I say "kissed", I – well I don't have to spell it out. Let's have more wine.' She smiled at the nearest waiter, who came over immediately. 'We'll toast all men to hell! *And,* do tell me what you're doing, work-wise. You know we're still going to be able to use bigger freelance pieces from you. This revamp might even be a good thing for you, in some ways. Of course there won't be that comforting regular cheque, but . . .'

'Well – I've still got the teen books. That's a regular, two a year, though not madly profitable income. But . . . er, while I'm here, there's one thing I'd like to pitch here and now.' Bella sipped her wine, then took a deep breath, feeling this was *the* important moment of the meeting. 'Don't know if you'll like the sound of it though.' She heard herself laughing nervously and wished she wasn't such a wuss.

'Now let me stop you *right there,*' Charlotte interrupted, her perfectly manicured *Rouge Noir* nails on Bella's wrist. Oh no, Bella thought, all remaining confidence sliding away; she really doesn't want to hear.

'Always pitch positive!' Charlotte laughed. 'You've just told me I'm not going to like it – chances are I'll agree if you can't be 100 per cent *go, go, go*! OK, now start again! Sell to me!'

'Makeovers. TV. Programme called *Fashion Victims*.'

'Old hat, darling,' Charlotte cut in, frowning. 'In fact, old hat, old shoes, old dress. Done to death.'

'What happened to positive?' Bella felt cross at being so immediately slapped down. 'I know there've been years of *What Not to Wear* and *Ten Years Younger*, but it's *me* who's one of the Victims. I can do the personal angle. The production company are using my house too, and there are some people called Daisy and . . .'

'Not Daisy and Dominic?' Charlotte squealed.

'Well yes, as it happens. Why? Who are they?' Bella was mystified by Charlotte's reaction.

'Oh-my-god, Bella! Have you never *heard* of them? They are *major* fashion players!' Charlotte had gone quite shrieky and people were looking – most were sending condemnatory *uncool* judgement vibes, but three pouty young women on the next table swivelled round to do some brazen listening in.

'Well . . . er, no. Who are they? I look at *Vogue* in the hairdressers, for the pictures only and to go "wow" at things I can't afford. And I generally keep up with celeb gossip, obviously, because of work, but whoever these two are they've missed my radar.'

'Well no, maybe you wouldn't know of them. Fashion isn't really your thing, is it?'

Bella smiled, but inside experienced a distinct ouchy nettle-sting moment and wondered if Charlotte had intended it to be one.

'They are just *so* amazing,' Charlotte gushed. 'I'd heard they were going to do something – there was a press release a while back, but we were to put it on hold so nothing's been announced yet. Daisy and Dominic are personal stylists who dress *everybody* who's anybody, but nobody really knows all about the who-and-what because they're sworn to discretion. After all, celebrities don't want it widely known that they can barely match their bra to their knickers. Without proper guidance they'd have Primark and Prada all mixed up – most of them not being what you'd call *pedigree*. Anyway, according to the press statement, this is their first go at a TV thing, something about sharing the star-treatment secrets, filtering down to the plebs. Though it'll be all Daisy, believe me. Dominic is well known for hardly saying *a word*. He's a tad spooky with the silence thing but the perfect foil for *her*. So – how on earth did you get this? And why *you*?'

Another sting – closer to wasp than nettle this time. Bella could feel Charlotte's eyes taking in her appearance, as if she hadn't really noticed her before. She felt conscious of her too-low neckline showcasing her unevenly sun-scorched cleavage on which perched the wrong necklace (years-old Tiffany heart on a chain), because she couldn't find the red and cream beads that *would* have gone with her slightly too girlish floral dress. She also wore a lacy cream linen cardigan that was a bit twee for anyone over thirty, and would have looked far better on Molly. Charlotte even glanced down to the side of the table, quickly taking in Bella's three-year-old heeled scarlet espadrilles with the age-bent flower on the front, shoes chosen for Tube-travel comfort rather than style. At least her toenail polish was perfect, although Charlotte's expression suggested the shade might be last year's pink.

'Probably because I need it? I think I just got lucky – if that's the word. Right place, right time. Anyway, if I write about it, are you likely to be able to use it? Because otherwise . . .'

'Sweetie, of *course* we can!' Charlotte assured her. 'Just make it funny and in-depth and go as all out on the unfilmed side as any contract will let you. *Gossip* is all. Like how much improvement is down to starving their victims for the duration, whether they let you have any say at all in the clothes or if there's a product-placement deal. You'll probably have to sign something, but the production will be *desperate* for the publicity. They'll give you carte blanche, I just know. Daisy and Dominic! Wow!'

'Maybe . . .' Bella said hesitantly. 'I was thinking . . . If I'm going to make a total tit of myself on national TV, I was wondering about getting ahead slightly, so that not every single bit of me gets ritual humiliation. I've already decided I'll absolutely refuse to be seen in my knickers, but I'll get myself a good haircut before the off, and I'll have my teeth brightened up.'

'Oh absolutely; good plan, darling – do everything you can not to look a total duffer. I'm *completely* amazed you haven't before,' Charlotte agreed with less than flattering alacrity. 'Now, shall we risk pudding?'

'It would help if the mirror was upright,' Jules complained, pouring a big shot of wine into her glass. She put the bottle (half empty already, how did that happen?) back on the chest of drawers. They were in Bella's bedroom, having decided over an early-evening drink in the kitchen that in order to prepare themselves for the inevitable scorn of these hyper-chic Dominic and Daisy people, they would give each other an honest once-over so they were already armed with proper knowledge of their problem body areas. They would be positive, be supportive and be ready to face the worst that any perfectly dressed, perfectly proportioned sadist could throw at them.

'I wouldn't want to be one of those poor women who cry when they get a good look at themselves,' Bella had mentioned nervously, wondering how stoic she would really feel when faced with herself in a 360-degree mirror and far too many cameras for comfort. Saul had promised it wouldn't be like that, but suppose they'd changed their minds? Suppose Daisy was a stroppy foot-stamper and got whatever she wanted? Were you allowed to say no?

'And think of someone hiking up your drooping tits. In their horrible critical hands,' Jules had added. Almost as one, they had raced up the stairs for the big-mirror moment.

'Sorry, the mirror's too heavy to move and it's kind of grown into the carpet. James managed to wangle it into place years ago with the help of two mates but even when the room was repainted, the decorator leaned it forward against a chair. He said he had a bad back and gave me that "I'll sue you" look, so I didn't dare push it.'

'Hmm. Well I suppose it will do. And anyway,' Jules smiled at Bella's reflection, 'we've got each other – for absolute truth! No holds barred! I'll go first.'

Bella looked at her reflection, seeing nothing but teeth that weren't quite white enough. Damn that foxy little Fliss – till her so-kind 'advice' she'd never given them a thought. Kept clean with a six-monthly scrub from the hygienist, they'd always looked OK. Now all she saw when she smiled in the mirror was middle-age beige.

Jules pulled her dress over her head and faced the mirror in her bra and knickers. The bra was pink and white girly gingham and her breasts seemed to be struggling to escape from it; her knickers were black and so plain, big and sensible they reminded Bella of games lessons at school.

'Oh Lord,' Jules said, closing her eyes against the sight of her own flesh, 'I'm so *not* doing this. Pass my dress back, quick. I don't have a spare tyre, I've got a whole new set of wheels. For a tractor.'

'No you haven't– you're not at all bad.'

'For a short, circular beachball. Thanks.'

'Look, stand up straight and it mostly flattens out. Don't you make your yoga class do that?'

Jules readjusted her posture.

'You see? Now you've got fabulous tits and there's a definable waist.'

'Only bloody just . . . I only get away with keeping my job because I'm still so bendy. Besides, they like a fat teacher – makes them feel better from the start.' Jules pushed her hands into the flesh each side of her body, inhaled hard and held her breath.

'You're fine. If you were wearing matching underwear it would help the overall look. It's just . . .' There was no other word for it, Bella had to come out with it. They'd promised each other honesty, hadn't they? A thirty-two-year friendship surely couldn't be killed stone dead by a bit of invited body-honesty?

'Go on, *what*? We did say honesty.' Jules's head nodded encouragingly, her spiky red hair flicking up and down.

'It's the saddlebags.'

'*What* saddlebags?' Jules leaned forward, peering at herself. 'That's not saddlebags, it's just . . . hip bones!' She prodded her thighs. 'See? Solid!'

'Then your pelvis has slipped!' Bella giggled. 'And hey, they're perfectly normal, just a bit . . . er . . . obvious. So whatever you wear on day one for the Big Appraisal, if that's what happens first, they'll need . . . well, to be *accommodated*. As will your tits. That bra is at least two cup sizes too small. If we invest in good underpinnings before we become victims, we'll be halfway there. OK, my turn.'

Jules topped up their glasses again. Bella peeled her skirt and top off, keeping her shoes on. A bit of heel elongated the calf, her mother had always said. Jules was small to start with and had kicked her shoes off, which, with the leaned-back mirror, had given an exaggerated impression of dumpiness. Maybe that was another 'before' trick they should watch out for. Bella was taller and leaner, but definitely pear-shaped. Both women, standing side by side, had a bit of stomach overhang, so Bella pulled in her muscles, which helped, and said, 'If we do this kind of contracting thing properly, we should end up well toned.'

Jules looked disbelieving. 'So how long do we have to keep it up for to get a result?'

'Er . . . for life, I think,' Bella laughed. 'Got a feeling it's the only way to make it work.'

'Chrissake, I've had two Caesareans, *and* one baby was a ten-pounder! No one can expect me to look like Kate Moss! So OK, smart-arse – any ideas how I can disguise the saddlebags and you can make your bum look like a neat little Cox's apple instead of a whopping great Bramley – all in a matter of days?'

Bella sat on the bed, took a big slug of wine and pulled her top back on, feeling suddenly dispirited. It wasn't just the teeth thing, it was the all-round exposure. What was she letting herself in for? Well, she'd seen similar programmes; she had some idea. She quite liked her privacy, contrary as that might seem in a journalist, but it was too late to pull out now – in her head she'd half spent the location fee.

'You know, I so wish I hadn't got us into this!' she confessed. 'I don't even *like* those programmes; they're just ritual humiliation. I've thought that ever since I saw one where Gok Wan held a woman's hand and ran her round a department store, showing her what would suit her. The camera followed, from behind and just below her.'

From the depths of her dress, which she was pulling on over her head, Jules said, 'Sounds all right; what was to object to? I like Gok, except when he rummages his face in women's tits. If he tried that on me, I'd slap him.'

'Oh, I like him too. But this victim hadn't got a skirt on. Boots, jacket, yes. And then just these big beige knickers and big white cellulite thighs. It just seemed so cruel. I was thinking, when she sees this later, she'll sob into the sofa cushions. Perfectly nice-looking woman, *why* couldn't she have been allowed a skirt? How did she let herself be cajoled into it? That's why we need to promise to back each other up, so we don't get persuaded to look like complete prats, however much they bleat on about what makes good television. We'll get classy underwear, Jules. Bras that fit, matching knickers that hold us in a bit. That's definitely all you need, all we *both* need. And me, I need to get my teeth whitened. If we're sorted with the basics, they can then do their worst. With luck, no one will be watching anyway.'

Molly could sense she was being watched. She and Giles were sitting, as they did on many a school afternoon, on the low wall outside the Cross Man's house, waiting for the bus. The Cross Man was there – a blurry dark shape behind his net curtains, waiting to find something to complain about so that he could rap hard on the window with his walking stick and glare at those who dared to pluck so much as a leaf from his privet, or carelessly drop a cigarette end or sweet wrapper on the pavement. Giles put his arm round Molly and pulled her close, kissing her. Rap rap went the stick, as they'd known it would. Laughing, they turned round and waved to the Cross Man, who had moved his curtain to glare at them through pale, glittery eyes.

'We've made him happy now,' Molly said. 'Something to grumble about makes his day.'

'He's not the only one watching us,' Giles murmured into her ear. 'Across the road, outside the shop. Aimee alert.'

'No surprise there – she's everywhere I look. It's like having a stalker.'

Aimee Lewiston was leaning against the window of the newsagents, drinking from a Coke can and staring across the road at Molly and Giles. Her skirt was a tiny frill of part-faded denim. Her bare legs vanished into black Uggs, even though the weather was still scorching.

'Do you fancy her? She's looking pretty hot.' When Aimee was about, Molly felt around twelve years old. Aimee practically shimmered with sexual experience and carnal knowledge.

'Well she would be hot, in those boots,' Giles teased. 'I'm thinking sweaty toes. Not good.'

Molly play-punched him. 'You know what I meant! She's been following us round like a hungry dog. And dog's a word I chose *on purpose*.'

Aimee's persistent staring was making Molly nervous. She had a way of pursuing boys she fancied, so ruthlessly that they were worn down by her fixation. She was living proof that you could get anyone you wanted by just sticking close and making sure that you were forever in their field of vision. Oh, plus by blatant sexual availability. Not many teenage boys had built-in resistance to that, not even when they were very happily going out with someone else. That her quarry was someone else's boyfriend always sharpened Aimee's competitive edge, and it was as clear as vodka that Giles was next on the trophy list. Molly glared across the road at her, wishing a plague of livid scarlet spots on her chubby yet pretty smooth-skinned moonface.

'I don't fancy her. God, I'd have to be desperate,' Giles said. His bus was coming. 'Gotta go, babes. Facebook later, text you, call you.' The bus pulled up and the doors shooshed open. A crowd of schoolkids surged forward and Giles waited till they had shoved each other past the driver before swiftly kissing Molly and leaping on. As the door began to close, Aimee suddenly hurtled on to the bus, falling against Giles as it lurched away from the pavement. Molly was on the receiving end of a hugely triumphant smirk as Aimee turned and rudely gave her the finger before pushing ahead of Giles up the bus stairs. He followed – he always sat upstairs. Molly looked away, wishing that for once he'd decided that the lower deck would be a good enough travelling place so he wouldn't be going up the stairs, copping a look up Aimee's skirt at an undersized thong that you could guarantee didn't even cover the basics. 'I'd have to be desperate,' he'd said. He was seventeen – so he probably was.

# SEVEN

It wasn't at all a dignified position. Although this didn't quite rate with having no knickers on and her legs splayed in gynaecologists' stirrups, Bella could think of few other situations where she'd have absolutely hated anyone she knew to walk in and watch. She lay almost horizontally with her hands clutching the arms of the chair in white-knuckle apprehension, her lips held wide open and away from gum contact by a hideous oversized plastic contraption that looked as if it had been designed for someone with a mouth as large as Mick Jagger's. Little rolls of cotton wool were wedged, hamster style, between her cheeks and her gums, and the inside of her mouth was agonizingly dry and uncomfortable.

A good twenty minutes in and Mr Ruben, the dentist, hadn't even started on the whitening process yet. Radio

Two was twittering in the background and the dental nurse was speculating across her as to whether Cyprus would be more fun than Ibiza, club-wise. Mr Ruben, who Bella would have guessed knew only about the kind of clubs that went into a golf bag, grunted uninterestedly. He didn't seem very interested in Bella either and, having agreed to fit her in at short notice for state-of-the-art instant tooth-brightening, appeared reluctant to have further verbal contact, though Bella would have put folding money on the likelihood that he'd jack up the charm when it came to bill-paying time.

As she'd walked into the surgery, he'd handed her a new shrink-wrapped toothbrush and ordered her brusquely to scrub her teeth right there and then at the rather scruffy and chipped sink, but once she was in the chair he wasn't going to waste energy with inevitably one-sided chat. 'Good morning' would have been nice. Still, Zoe had assured her he was *the* man for the job, so here she was; and it was too late to request that he explain each stage of what he was going to do . . . she could no longer speak. At all.

She couldn't see a lot, either, because there were big and not at all comfortable plastic safety glasses across her eyes, fixed to her face with elastic round the back of her head. The screens could do with a wipe; everything was blurry and distorted. The nurse applied cream to

Bella's lips and murmured 'Sunscreen' at her, for which communication Bella felt almost tearfully grateful. Next, she could just make out Mr Ruben approaching with equipment. He too was wearing a plastic visor and she could only hope he could see through his better than she could through hers. But then something was painted on all her front teeth with reassuring care – this man possibly had a sideline hobby in painting miniatures. Next, what felt like an entire harmonica was crammed inside her mouth, the room lights went out, and Bella was suddenly in the dark with a beam of ultraviolet aimed at her teeth.

She so wished she'd asked how long this would go on and if she should prepare for pain. It could mean hours of agony. But Radio Two jangled on, DJs joshed and babbled and the nurse, with nothing to do, flicked the pages of a magazine. The minutes staggered past, slow and lumbering, and Bella relaxed a little. Nothing was hurting, so far. She could safely (cross fingers) drift away and dream a bit. Then . . . zing! A weird tingle of something mildly electric coursed through one of her incisors.

'Was that pain?' Mr Ruben switched off the ultraviolet and removed the harmonica from Bella's mouth. She nodded – it had hurt in the same way that an unexpected piece of silver paper against a filling did. He smiled, which was unnerving.

'First phase is done now. And yes, you might get a few twinges, occasional trills of discomfort. And there'll be occasional darts of it now and then for a few days. It'll settle. Now – we do this all over again; twice. And another twenty minutes each time under the light.'

Now he tells me, Bella thought, still unable to speak. I'd have gone for a pee before we began, if I'd known.

'Look at this! They've put a run-over poodle on the front page!' Shirley complained, frowning into Bella's Mac on the kitchen table while Bella loaded Molly's abandoned breakfast plate and mug into the dishwasher. 'I've gone through the whole of the local paper online and there's nothing about me being arrested!'

'Maybe it was a busy week for hot news? Was Walton overwhelmed with parking wars and planning battles?' Bella asked.

'A *poodle*!' Shirley pushed the computer away in disgust. 'It wasn't even a hit-and-run. Dog ran into the road, van ran into it, everyone very upset but it's hardly *news*. And it's funny how there's always someone with their camera, ready to take a shot rather than being any use. This wouldn't have even made page seven if it hadn't been for some amateur snapper with a blurry camera; their phone presumably – I mean look!' She turned the computer for Bella to see. 'I can imagine getting to the pearly gates and having to wait around while the idiot ahead of me gets a shot of St Peter on his iPhone to email back to his family.'

'Was it dead?' Bella needed to know about the poodle. She briefly pictured it at a doggy version of heaven's entrance, surrounded by canine photographers. This shot of the dog showed it in its owner's arms, lying flat out and looking confused by all the fuss.

'No! Not even dead! "In shock" it says here. How on earth can they tell?'

'They tremble. And their ears and noses go all hot, like cats when they've got a fever.' This comment came from Nick, a young and amazingly quiet scenery carpenter Saul had sent to the house to measure up the kitchen for its on-screen look. He'd arrived just as Molly left for school and had slid noiselessly into the house and shimmied round the kitchen like a ghost while Bella had her porridge and a glass of milk, the only possible breakfast combination allowable for forty-eight hours following yesterday's tooth treatment. That was another little piece of information Mr Ruben had left till the whitening deal was a done one.

'Rubbish.' Shirley was dismissive. 'It's a poodle – they're just drama queens.'

'But Mum,' Bella interrupted, 'I thought the last thing you wanted was to have your crimes written up in the local paper. Isn't that why you're holed up here? Escaping the press and the paparazzi of Surrey? What happened to worrying about what Lois across the hall would think?'

'Crime. Not *crimes*,' Shirley corrected Bella. 'Only the one. I don't make a habit of it, you know.'

'My mum nearly got done for assault once,' Nick contributed as he lined up his tape against the back wall. 'Last year she walloped this big lad who'd chucked a chocolate wrapper on the ground. Told him to pick it up and when he wouldn't, she clouted him. Someone got the police but the kid said it was OK, he deserved it. So *his* mum hit my mum instead but not very hard, so they called it quits.'

'I assure you I haven't been *hitting* anyone,' Shirley told him firmly. 'There was simply a silly mistake over an item of clothing in a department store. They've offered me a caution. I've told them I'll think about it.'

Bella wanted to laugh. How had her mother turned the whole thing round so that it seemed the police were now doing their best to please her? She could imagine her surrounded by detectives who were pleading, 'Look, this is our best offer,' with Shirley wrapping herself protectively into her summer-weight, duck-egg-blue pashmina, wincing at gravy stains on shiny ties and despising their unpolished shoes.

Nick looked at her with what seemed like sympathy, and scratched his ear with his pencil. 'A caution? Really? Shame. Maybe you could tell them you'd like to upgrade to an ASBO . . .' He smiled broadly.

Shirley gave him a look. Bella held her breath. The mood her mother was in after trawling fruitlessly through the *Walton and Weybridge Herald* this morning, she wouldn't have been surprised if Shirley ended up doing something to Nick that would get her remanded for months in custody, all bail out of the question. But, to her surprise, Shirley was decidedly cheerful. 'You and your mother seem to have an excellent grasp of human foibles, young man. You see, it's a perfectly reasonable aim in life: if you can't be a good woman – be a *notorious* one.'

'Oh Mum!' Bella laughed. 'You *are* a good woman! It was only a lapse!'

Shirley smiled in a disconcertingly secretive way. 'A *good woman*! How much you don't know about me, Bella my darling! I do hope that your own life will perk up a bit soon. Perhaps this makeover thing will help and you'll meet someone lovely, who'll give you a happier, no, a *broader* outlook. Now, if you'll excuse me, I've got to get ready. I'm meeting a *friend*.'

'Are you? That's nice. Anyone I know? And where are you going?'

'No – er, no one you've met. We're just venturing into town for a bit of lunch, possibly. A little light shopping, you know.' Shirley was already moving towards the door. Escaping, Bella thought, a bit like Alex when he was being evasive about his plans for the evening.

'If you're going towards Piccadilly, we could take the train together,' she suggested. 'If you can wait half an hour?'

'No, no it's fine darling, honestly! I'm . . . er . . . being met!'

Nick turned and grinned at Bella as Shirley left the room fast in a haze of Arpège. 'She's OK, your mother, isn't she? She *knows* stuff.'

'She does, doesn't she? She always did,' Bella agreed, considering. Shirley was being . . . what was it? Got it, Bella decided, she was being *triumphantly mysterious*. She was up to something and it was just to be hoped it wouldn't lead to more trouble. But for now, any major mother discoveries would have to wait. Bella was going to meet Saul at the production office and be introduced to these Daisy and Dominic people. It was kind of him – the rest of the group were having to wait a few more days, till almost the start of the filming, but he'd told her that the fact that they were turning part of her house upside down meant she deserved a bit of privilege. She just hoped going out in the breeze wouldn't set her newly sensitive teeth jangling. Oh, and there was the small question about what to wear to meet a couple who spent their entire working lives putting together celebrity wardrobes. Presumably (if she took that Carole's advice) anything but black.

* * *

'So where's she gone this time?' James asked Alex. Alex shrugged and wandered ahead of his father through the kitchen and out to the garden. 'Dunno, give her a bell, Dad. Or text. Ask her?' he suggested, returning to the lounger under the cherry tree where he'd left Henry James's *The Turn of the Screw*.

James hovered around, looking twitchy and overheated in a suit and tie. The day had turned into yet another blazing one. 'And who are those people in the kitchen? Is this something to do with that film thing she mentioned? She hasn't been touching base as to what's going on.'

He perched on the edge of Alex's lounger and Alex sighed and moved his bare feet out of the way.

'Like I said, ask her,' Alex repeated. 'She's gone to a meeting. Work, maybe? I don't know. She goes out. Gran's out too. Moll's at school. I'm . . .' he indicated the book. 'I was just reading. Do you want some tea or something?'

'Oh . . . right, sorry. Getting ahead for next term, are you? Good, good. OK, you just carry on. I'll, er . . .' He stood up and started to back towards the house, deadheading a couple of antirrhinums on the way.

'Oh, are you going? Why don't you stay for a bit?' Alex called. 'You sure you don't want a drink or something?'

'No, no, don't disturb yourself. I know you're not yet

used to me being back in your life in this face-to-face way. I'll see myself out. I just had something to talk to Bella about, that's all. I'll see you in a day or two, next week maybe.'

Alex got up and followed him back in. 'Well actually no, you won't. I'm off to France in a couple of days, with Ben and Mick. Surfing for a while, then back to Oxford.'

'Ah – are you? You see,' James clicked his fingers, 'I told Bella you'd practically left home!'

Alex looked puzzled. 'Not quite. Uni's only thirty weeks in the year. And this'll only be my second year.'

'Yes, but it's not for long, in the scheme of things,' James argued. 'So who'll be here while you're away, keeping an eye on this lot?' He indicated the crew, who had joined Nick and were now taking the doors off the cupboards. 'Do you think I should move back in? They could do any amount of damage.'

Carpenter Nick frowned at him. 'We are here, you know,' he muttered.

James glared. 'I can see that. I can see very untidy evidence of your presence. There's dust everywhere. This is my . . .'

'Dad! Leave it, please. Mum's got it covered.'

'That's what I'm worried about,' James told him. 'All this *malarkey*. It's just all disruption and mess. Now come on Alex, be honest, wouldn't you rather move to somewhere a bit less *rambling*? Somewhere smart and clean and fresh?'

'Not really.' Alex looked vague. 'Hadn't thought about it. Why?'

'Bella hasn't said anything?'

'About?'

'Selling the house? Downsizing? Freeing up capital?'

'No. Should she've?'

'She could have raised the matter with you, yes. We've talked about it.' He ran his hands through his hair and sighed.

Alex shoved his hands in the pockets of his jeans and shrugged. 'Hasn't said a word not to me, anyway. Sorry.'

'OK, OK, I can't say I'm surprised, but I did hope she might have run it up the family flagpole by now. Never mind. Look, tell her I was here. And tell her . . . Actually, no don't. I'll connect ear to ear with her later. Enjoy the surf, Alex, and be careful.' He went to leave but having opened the front door, changed his mind and came back. 'Alex, while I'm here, do you know where there's a spare front-door key for here? I seem to have mislaid mine – left it in Scotland I expect.'

Alex hesitated. 'Er, well I don't know. I mean, I don't want to be funny, Dad, but you haven't had a key for here for years.'

'I know,' James laughed. 'But that's only because I wasn't in the area. It would save a lot of hassle, now I'm back.'

'Does Mum say it's OK?'

'Oh don't worry about Bella, it won't be a problem. We've got a few loose legal ends to tie up and it would be very handy. Most of the relevant paperwork is here, that's all. I know what she's like . . . it'll still be in the desk in the sitting room, where it's always been.'

Alex opened one of the few remaining kitchen drawers. 'OK, here you are, then. Don't lose this one or she'll blame me.'

James pocketed the key and made a swift exit, leaving Alex with the scenery crew. Nick looked at him and grinned. '*Connect ear to ear?*' he commented.

Soho again. Twice in one week. Bella swung along the hot and dusty pavement feeling cheerful and cosmopolitan. Her hair was freshly washed and glossy and it tickled warm and soft against her neck. Better yet, her seven-shades-whiter teeth gleamed their full money's worth and seemed to have stopped being attacked by random jangling electric sparks. She managed to get past the fabric shops of Berwick Street without going inside to drool over magically coloured silks and, side-stepping cabbage leaves blown down from the market stalls, turned up a cool shady alleyway to find the address Saul had given her.

The apprehension was mounting, as if this was an interview for a job she desperately needed. This was not the case at all – at the worst she could simply say, oh well that could have been fun, but didn't look like it was going to be, and walk away. But then there was Saul; she didn't want to let him down. Wasn't that always the way? When you thought you had all the choices on your side and that opting out was a real possibility, you ended up feeling responsible for someone else's project going right. She tried telling herself it was nothing to do with her, that if she didn't do it or lend them her house (though it was a bit late on that score – by tonight half her kitchen infrastructure would be on its way to a storage lock-up somewhere, not to mention that in her head the location fee had become an essential income component), then they'd find someone else. Never mind that Saul had such a friendly manner and such appealing grey-blue eyes. So, if you thought like that, did Jules's spaniel.

She found the pink door Saul had told her to look for, almost hidden under a thick tangle of honeysuckle that seemed far too rampant to be growing in a pot, and rang the bell.

'Come on up, Bella!' Saul called to her from an open window above. She was conscious for a second only of the scent of honeysuckle, lush and heady between his smile and hers; she quickly pushed the door open and climbed a broad wooden staircase that had been painted to look like a floral carpet runner, with the kind of design that you saw in unmodernized pubs. The practical side of her wondered why anyone would go to so much trouble when it would have been so much easier simply to put down real carpet, but she decided it must be an ironic design statement, the sort to be expected among visual media folk. Even with magazines she'd worked for, the art department had been very separate from where the copy was produced – a remote enclave with specialized computers and an exclusive and mysterious vocabulary. Those who worked in there dressed more wackily too: engagingly art-school.

'Bella! It's so good to see you.' Saul greeted her at his office door and kissed her lightly. The scent of the honeysuckle was still all around him. The room was the full depth of the building, very light with big windows and painted deep pink. The walls were hung with framed black and white photos of half-built structures. Some were famous – Brunel's Tamar bridge was there; so were Canary Wharf and the Empire State Building, but many were identifiably film sets – all works in progress. He must have a thing for scaffolding.

'Let me introduce you to Daisy and Dominic,' Saul said, indicating a couple across the room sitting at a blue glass circular table. 'This is Bella – one of your victims and in a way, our hostess – in terms of the set, anyway.'

Dominic stood up to greet her. He nodded at her in a friendly enough way but didn't actually speak. He was forty-something, tall and skinny to the point of possibly questionable health, wearing black from head to foot (apart from a silver leather belt), which set off hair that must have been modelled on Nicky Clarke's, being long, lion-blond and perfectly blow-dried to give an impression of far more volume than was actual. Bella could see little shines of pink scalp here and there, and found it endearing. His smile, which was so crooked you could almost call it diagonal, dazzled – more tooth-whitening, for sure – but his face was crazed with smoker's lines, which unfairly managed to make him look rugged rather than ragged.

'And this is Daisy.' Daisy remained seated but put out a thin, fragile-looking hand with perfectly oval nails painted deep dark red, just as Charlotte's had been a few days before.

Daisy was a dramatic and slightly alarming sight. She was wearing purple-framed sunglasses, the biggest Bella had ever seen, and her mid-length blue-black hair was scraped back into a ponytail and secured with a circlet of pink feathers and purple ribbons. But it was what she was wearing that confused Bella. It seemed to be an oversized orange towelling bathrobe, in which Daisy looked tiny and terribly frail for a woman who might not (and it was hard to tell when you couldn't see someone's eyes) be any more than late thirties. Bella smiled and said hello in the kind of softly sympathetic voice suitable for invalids, then looked at Saul, half expecting him to explain that Daisy wasn't feeling terribly well, perhaps had been staying overnight . . . where? Possibly an apartment upstairs? And that she hadn't got dressed because she was feeling a bit feverish and certain she was coming down with flu, so would be going straight back to bed after putting in a few aspirin-fuelled minutes at this meeting. But then if you had flu, you probably wouldn't wear that much near-black lipstick. It certainly wouldn't make you feel better if you accidentally looked in the mirror.

'Hello Bella, nice to meet you,' Daisy said in a rather flat voice. Only half a smile. Bella felt immediately that she'd disappointed, somewhat. Was it to do with her last-minute Jigsaw-sale dress? Was mauvey-grey silk (sprinkled with blue and cream flowers) all wrong? And the taupe gladiator-type sandals – they must be unforgivably last-summer to a woman who dressed the nation's style icons and probably possessed enough inside knowledge to predict exactly what the world would be wearing four years from now.

'OK, well now you're here, Bella, and it's so close to lunchtime,' Saul was saying, looking at his watch, 'I thought we might go out and have something to eat. There's a little bistro just round the corner, very relaxed.

We could get to know each other over some wine and a bit of lunch. Is that all right with you?'

Bella gulped. Ah . . . she hadn't thought of that. This could be tricky. But his smile looked almost boyishly hopeful and she wasn't going to be impolite by refusing. She would just have to do her best with whatever the menu offered and besides, she was quite hungry.

To her surprise, the wan-looking Daisy was coming too. Bella almost asked her if she wouldn't rather be going back to bed instead, feeling concerned for her as you would for a listless, over-pale child, but Daisy got up, briskly tightened her orange tie-belt and gathered up her huge floppy handbag, which, combined with the robe, only added to the impression that she was a little girl playing dressing-up in her mother's clothes.

'Oh great, let's go. I'm starving!' Daisy announced, trip-trapping swiftly towards the doorway on the highest heels Bella had ever seen. Bella wasn't a shoe expert, but even she recognized the signature scarlet sole of Louboutin. Daisy was quite a small woman – how she had feet long enough to cope with a six-inch heel was one of those questions that could keep a woman awake at night. Bella, following her down the clanky wooden stairs, could feel one of her 'I Really Don't Get . . .' columns coming on. More than that, she was also curious about the big orange coat-thing. From her vantage point close behind Daisy, she could now see it wasn't actually made of towelling but of something cleverly woven to look like it. It was presumably one of fashion's deep mysteries, to which she hoped soon to become privy.

The restaurant wasn't busy. The waiter led them through to a courtyard at the back where there were several sun-speckled tables under a vine-swathed pergola. Fat bunches of blue-black grapes hung over them, giving an impression of somewhere far more exotic than dusty central London. In a sunny corner, wide-open blue trumpets of morning glory twined up a trellis, and maroon nasturtiums tumbled from boxes halfway up the walls.

'Oh this is pretty! We could be in Italy,' Bella said. Saul looked pleased at her approval. 'Exactly – that's why I love it here,' he told her. 'It's like a tiny escape from London without the hassle of travel. No airports, no queues, no screamy children.'

'I know – by the time you get on the plane you wonder why you bothered,' Bella agreed. 'And . . . not really related to children, where's Fliss? Has she got a day off?'

'Having a duvet day,' Daisy snarled. 'Lazy infant. Says she's got a migraine but my money's on a hangover.'

'Come on now Daisy, she's put in the hours. Don't begrudge her a sickie for once,' Saul told her.

The waiter brought menus and offered drinks. Bella asked for a spritzer, feeling the need for something long and cool for the hot day.

'White wine for me,' Daisy requested. 'With a separate glass of ice, please.' She still hadn't taken off her sunglasses, and Bella was very curious about what lay behind them. It was hard to feel she could even begin to get to know someone who was resolutely hidden. And wasn't it rather rude, too, to be so determinedly keeping the eye contact this one-sided?

'Interesting coat,' Bella ventured. Well, it was a start.

'Oh, you like it? Dries. Next season's. This was a runway model, from the show.'

'She'd like you to think they practically paid her to wear it.' These were the first words Bella had heard from Dominic. She'd begun to wonder if he had a voice at all. 'Truth was,' he leaned closer, his sardonic smile reminding her of a pleased cat, 'a model threw up on it – God knows how, it's not as if the poor darlings eat anything, but only Daisy here wasn't too squeamish to take it off their hands and give it a wash.'

'Enough, Dom; it's worth thousands. What's a bit of puke at that price?' Daisy's smile was even more alarming than Dominic's. Pretty, Bella thought, admiring more gleaming teeth, but frightening in the same way as a vampire in a movie in the first revelation of fangs.

'Personally I think it looks like a bathrobe,' he sniffed. 'Don't you, Bella?'

Bella wasn't sure what to say. The honest answer would be yes, but she didn't yet know these people well enough to say so.

'But a *Dries Van Noten* bathrobe, darlings!' Daisy put him right. 'You'll see Cheryl in one before Christmas, trust me. But after that, it'll filter down.' She went back to studying the menu, leaving Bella with the certain knowledge that 'filtering down' spelled the end of all interest for any item of clothing.

The waiter approached and Bella studied the menu. Difficult. The others ordered but still Bella dithered.

'Tricky, this,' she began, 'The thing is . . .' She hesitated, then admitted, feeling utterly foolish, 'I know this sounds completely mad but right now I can only eat white food, so if you could just tell me . . .'

The young waiter, who was black, snapped in an intensely Caribbean accent, 'So it won't be rice and peas or goatwater stew for *you* then, honey. You want spaghetti bolognese or a pie? Safe and European?'

Dominic snickered. She caught Saul giving her a look of horrified disbelief. Oh God, Bella thought, they've all totally misunderstood.

'No, I mean . . . yes. It could be rice. White rice. But not the peas. I meant *literally* white food. As in chicken, or white bread or plain potatoes, pasta – though not wholemeal. Sorry.' Bella felt flustered and more than a bit idiotic.

The waiter shrugged, bored now, indicating that food-fad-wise, he'd just about seen it all. Now in an accent more Bermondsey than Barbados, he said 'Look, I can get you plain grilled chicken, a risotto . . .'

'Actually, that would be lovely, a plain, simple risotto.' She checked the menu. 'This one with chicken will be fine but no mushrooms in it, please.' She felt hot and bothered, knowing she'd have to explain herself and wondering why she hadn't earlier. Too silly of her, really, but then who didn't hope to keep their personal vanities private?

When the waiter went, Daisy suddenly removed her sunglasses and touched Bella's hand. 'Sensitivity?' she asked, surprisingly gently. And goodness, what huge blue eyes – why ever did she hide them? She realized Daisy was older than she'd originally thought too, possibly a similar age to herself. The quirkiness of her look had blurred that issue.

'Yes. In a way.' Ah – Daisy got it. Of course she did – even fresh snow would look a bit tawdry against her teeth.

'I understand, *totally*,' she sympathized, 'I only do wheat and dairy on alternate days. Tomatoes *never*. And every third week, no carbs for five days. Have you had the Kaz tests? Do you know your Bimelow Reaction

Rating? It makes *all* the difference once you know about that.'

'Er . . . no, sorry, I've never heard of those.' Bella glanced at Saul. He was looking at her in a strange way, as if he'd just discovered something about her that was a long, long way from pleasing. What had she done?

'I don't have any allergies or food sensitivities at all. It's just my teeth,' she explained, feeling she'd been caught out here. 'I had them whitened by this mad laser treatment a couple of days ago and the dentist warned me not to eat food with any colour in it for three days, because the laser has removed a protective layer and it needs that time to grow back. That's all. I did it because of this programme.'

Oh why did it sound like an idiotic confession? It was nothing, really, but she felt silly, vain and . . . caught out.

'Oh God, is that all?' Daisy looked disappointed. 'I thought you had some *really* interesting food issues! Of course, looking at you properly, I can see you probably haven't.'

'Daisy!' Saul warned. 'Back off now!' To Bella's surprise his hand quickly squeezed hers under the table. It was a very welcome reassurance and made her feel much better.

'OK, sorry, sweetie!' Daisy sighed. 'I'm just feeling a tad mid-season today. September is a difficult time in this business. You can't move anyone on to autumn/ winter while the sun's still blazing, and yet linen, for example, is so *over* once the August bank holiday has gone. Do you see?' This was aimed at Bella. It felt like a test. But in fact Bella did see, sort of. Her ever-stylish mother would see even better, she thought.

'I think so. Though surely it doesn't matter that much?' Daisy took a sharp intake of breath, as if Bella had committed some deep heresy. Perhaps she had. She tried to make amends. 'I suppose it's similar to how my mother always swears you absolutely *cannot* wear velvet after New Year, even though the winter has barely set in.'

'Oh she's absolutely right!' Daisy smiled. 'Gosh, what a star she must be. You don't take after her, then?' Bella experienced the same kind of nettle-sting moment that she'd had with Charlotte only days before. This one wasn't so uncomfortable though, for how could she take seriously any clothes-sniping from a woman in a coat that she could wear to a fancy-dress party as the Honey Monster? Oh, the curse of being habitually polite. If only she was the manners-free kind of bitch who could come right out and say it.

'So what are our other victims like?' Daisy asked as the food arrived. 'Because frankly you're a bit of a let-down, I don't mind telling you, Bella.'

'Daisy!' Saul protested. 'Play nicely, please.'

'I *do* quite mind being told it, actually,' Bella retorted.

'Good for you,' Saul muttered. 'Don't take any crap.'

Dominic leaned back against his chair, saying nothing. His silence was a bit unnerving, but maybe he knew better than to cross Daisy. Bella now felt thoroughly unfazed – *no way* did she any longer intend to go through this ridiculous charade. They could, she decided, use her house and the rest of the writers' group in it, but she wasn't going to be sneered at by bloody Daisy.

'Look – I'm sure you can do this without me . . . there are others . . .'

'No, really, don't go dropping out now.' Saul squeezed her hand again beneath the table.

'Hell no, don't do that!' Daisy smiled sweetly. 'It's just that this is the problem, isn't it? You don't look *too* bad as you are. I only meant, what's to change? We can tweak at the basics – your hair is desperate, frankly, but otherwise you already seem to have a teeny clue how to put an outfit together.' Bella softened, feeling slightly wrong-footed. Then Daisy got back on form with, 'For an amateur, that is, obviously! It's just that there won't be quite that *oh wow* factor at the end of the show that a *really* extreme change would make. Still, we can work on something, I'm sure. Frump you up a bit at the start, maybe. And sometimes it's the small things that make the difference. A good handbag would pull you together – and colour counselling. I mean, we're working on the whole person here, and realistic solutions. We're not doing a *Ten Years Younger* scenario.' She shuddered. 'Ugh – all those frizzy-haired people who've never looked after their teeth or even *exfoliated*. Imagine.'

'So what are the others like?' Saul asked. 'I know we get to meet them soon, but you could give Daisy and Dominic some handling tips. Do any of them bite?'

Bella pulled flat-leafed parsley out of her risotto, feeling like a picky child eater. She loved it normally, but worried about how rigidly she had to stick to Mr Ruben's instructions. If she accidentally ate it, would her teeth be stained dark green?

'Well . . .' Bella thought of Dina with her long, straggly, greying hair. Dina didn't approve of hair colourants, couldn't be bothered with make-up. And Phyl, whose skin was as smoke-ravaged as Dominic's. And Jules's saddlebags. But then there was Zoe, who was so Boden-cute and fresh-faced that it would be hard even to want to tweak her look.

'Er . . . I think one or two could be a challenge!' she assured them.

'Oh good! That's what I like to hear.' Daisy grinned. 'Something to get my teeth into.'

'Now that,' Saul leaned close and murmured to Bella, 'is exactly what I'm slightly afraid of.'

# EIGHT

There was just enough broadband signal for Molly to use the Internet on her laptop in the garden, so long as she stayed close to the kitchen and didn't go to the bench at the far end under the trees – her favourite sunny outdoor spot. Nick was in the kitchen, screwing handles shaped like big silver starfish on to the new kitchen units.

She scrolled through her Facebook updates and seethed (yet again) about Aimee's from the day before, which crowed: *I know something that you don't know.* The timing was all she needed to know exactly what Aimee was talking about. She'd made a play for Giles and was winding Molly up. Aimee must have raced up Station Road straight from pressing her fat dimply thighs against Giles on the bus and Molly could just see her hurtling into the house, straight to the computer to drop just enough of a clue that would be guaranteed to rile a rival. And it was working. Was it ever. Cow. Giles was away on a two-day field trip but she'd text him, see if he was contactable out there in the Welsh hills, and try very, very hard not to ask what foul suggestions Aimee had made to him. Oh, but they wouldn't be *suggestions*, would they? Nothing so subtle from a girl who'd been caught on camera giving a blow job to Carly's boyfriend (ex now, obviously) by the bins at the back of Pizza Express.

Molly felt depressed, as if she were the one who was all wrong and acting difficult. Giles might well casually add himself to Aimee's other-people's-boyfriends total, just because of her simple lack of complication. Aimee wouldn't be picky about a venue for sex. *She* wouldn't be holding out for a warm, romantic atmosphere and peace and low lights and the right music and only a *little* bit of alcohol and someone who'd say they loved her and make it something special. She just wanted another notch on her broomstick, and to be able to look at you with that sneering, smirking, 'OK follow *that*' expression.

'Oh isn't it lovely and quiet at the end of the day! Those men, I thought they'd never stop bashing the kitchen around.' Shirley came out and sat beside Molly, putting two mugs of tea on the table.

'Here you are darling, I thought you might like a

drink. Nick's moved the kettle into the utility room while he paints the walls, bless him, so we can still be human.'

'Thanks Gran, good thinking. Looking amazing in there, isn't it?'

'It is. And it all works. I thought we'd be left with pretend taps, no sink and a cardboard worktop painted to look like granite. But no, it's all genuine – they surely can't be expecting to break it down after and take it all away again. Bella would be mad to let them, whatever the cost. Why can't real workmen get it done that fast? You'd be talking about weeks normally. This is like those shops that get an entire refit over a Sunday. I did think your mother was a bit crazy, going in for all this just so someone can tell her a lot of rubbish about what to wear. I mean, if she doesn't know by now . . . but the house is getting the benefit, at least. So, Moll darling, what are you doing? Homework?' Shirley sneaked a quick look at the screen. 'Or socializing?'

Molly smiled. 'Bit of both! Just about to work on a Jane Austen essay but I thought I'd see who's on Facebook first.'

'Ah – Facebook. I'm going to give that a go some time soon. I've got so many people I've met when I'm travelling and I'm sure it would be easier to keep up with them this way. The whole world seems to be in there.'

'Not quite everyone does it,' Molly told her. 'We've got this girl at school, Olivia. Her parents don't approve of computers and they don't even have a television. Half the time Liv hasn't a clue what we're talking about.'

'Parents can be so thoughtless,' Shirley said. 'I can see they might not want to be slaves to the media, but it's terribly unfair to inflict your prejudices on your children if the result is social isolation.'

'Oh, Liv goes online at school. But she has to do all her homework in the library cos she can't do it on a computer at home. I think her folks would really like her to write with a quill pen and ink that you dunk into.'

'Well, so long as she knows how the technology works, I suppose she'll be all right. So are you Facebook friends with absolutely everyone you see every day anyway? Is there any point when you see them all the time?'

'You sort of have to be, really,' Molly laughed. 'If someone from school asks you to be their Facemate you don't say no. It's manners. Even if later you hate them, you still leave them on the list because *un*friending them is too drama-queen and . . . what's that lovely word you used to say I did?'

'You used to *flounce*,' Shirley reminded her. 'When you were about fourteen you made a point of being quarrelsome during meals. Rather than lose an argument you'd scrape your chair back and flounce out of the room. I remember worrying you were anorexic and were making an excuse to go and make yourself sick.'

'Yuck no!' Molly giggled. 'I was just being *teenage*.'

'You're still teenage!'

'Not like that.' It made her smile now to think about it, as if the fourteen-year-old Molly were half a lifetime away from the nearly-eighteen one. How much more would she have changed by the time she was twenty? Would she look back on this being possessive about Giles stage as something completely infantile? She tried the thought that they might still be together, then the possibility of them not being. So much could happen between now and then. So much could happen between now and Saturday, come to that.

'So who is he?' Shirley suddenly asked. 'This boy you're thinking about. Are you sleeping with him?'

Molly squealed. 'Gran, aaaagh! Mum was so right – she said you used to be really embarrassing when she was young.'

'Ah, but am I embarrassing *you*?'

'No. Um . . . yeah! Just a bit.'

'In that case I apologize. And it's all right, Molly darling, of course you don't have to answer the other question. That's your privilege and choice.'

'No, no it's OK.' She took a deep breath. 'I'll tell you. He's Giles and I love him madly, we've been going out together for a few months but been schoolmates for, like, ever? I haven't slept with him yet but I want to.' It all came rushing out in a near-garbled blast – she didn't particularly want to tell Shirley about the Mum-interrupted near miss.

'If you want to, what's stopping you? So long as you're careful . . .'

Molly laughed. 'That's what Mum said!'

'She *did*? Good heavens! She always used to close her eyes and put her hands over her ears if I ever mentioned the subject when she was your age! So what's the problem with Giles?'

Molly watched Keith the cat sliding down from the top of the fence. He'd got his eye on a bird – she could tell by the extra-slinky way he was moving. Even descending from eight feet high he managed to look as if he was being ultra-careful about being seen and heard. She could just see him now under the camellia, long low body tensed, head forward, eyes keen on his quarry. Then one more tiny move and the camellia leaves rustled. The bird flew off.

'It's just . . .' Molly put her hands over her face and giggled. 'I can't believe I'm having this conversation with you! You're my *gran*! But OK, it's just, like, Giles and me? I haven't . . . before, though we got close to it. So I want it to be special, you know? Somewhere nice, lovely music, no interruptions, just, you know . . . *special*.'

'Oh it will be,' Shirley assured her. 'It will be. But if it's going to be special, it can be at any time and anywhere. Making love isn't about decor and music. And it'll be special with the next one as well, don't forget that.' She smiled and patted Molly's hand. 'There's a first time with each of them, all through your life. But trust me, it's never as special as the *second* time with any of them. That's when you find out if it's really going to work. The first time is just the two of you saying, "I really want to do this with you" and bumbling your way through it. Trust me, darling. If you really, really like him, don't hold out for the right scenery – that way you might miss the moment.'

While Molly was still figuring this out, Shirley got up. 'I'll go and see if there's anything in the fridge for supper. I told your mother that if we still had anything to cook on then I'd organize something, but I've been out most of the day and only just got back.'

'Oh, no, it's OK – Mum texted,' Molly told her. 'She says we're all going out for supper as a farewell for Alex – he's off to France tomorrow. There's no need to cook anything. Even Dad's coming – I think Mum's hoping he'll pay.'

'Ha! James?' Shirley almost spluttered the words. 'I doubt it! He'll be totting up the bill, working out who's eaten what and then demanding an exact whip-round accordingly! Sorry, darling, I know he's your father but he could always be a bit *careful* when it came to cash.'

'Oh it's all right, I know what he's like! He offered to take us all out the other week, when he came back from Scotland. Perhaps he's different now he's on his own.'

'Leopards and spots . . . We'll see, shall we?' Shirley stood up and picked up their empty mugs. 'You and me, we could have a little bet if you like' she said. 'I'll put a pound on him not picking up the bill. And as I'm not cooking, maybe I'll have a little gin and tonic instead. Can I get one for you, darling?'

Molly looked up at her grandmother's face. It wasn't just the sun making it more than usually radiant. There was something about the expression, the gleam in her eyes.

'No, I'm fine thanks but, Gran? You asked me so can I ask you?'

'Hmm? What's that, sweetie?'

Shirley, halfway into the kitchen, looked back at her with eyes widened to an expression of exaggerated innocence, as if she could already guess the question.

'This man you're seeing – and don't say you're not because I know you are: you keep going out all the time and looking all glam. Who is he?' Molly asked. 'And . . .' Was she bold enough? Yes – it worked both ways. 'Are *you* sleeping with him?' Molly immediately wished she hadn't said anything. How rude was she? And what a ridiculous question. Just because Gran had a sparkly look about her, it didn't mean she *was* seeing someone. And even if she was, surely old people didn't do things like that, however wild they'd been in the past. If you were a grandmother, like Shirley, it must have all stopped years ago.

'He's called Dennis. And yes, since you're brave enough to ask, as a matter of fact I am!'

Bella, halfway down the stairs, could have sworn she heard a key rattling about in the lock just before the doorbell rang (the usual James three-ring speciality). She ran down to the hallway, opened the door and there he was on the step, looking late-summer elegant in a beige linen suit and a pale blue shirt. His face was very pink, plump and smooth, like a freshly bathed baby.

'Isn't Alex with you?' she asked him as he came in. 'I thought I heard a key.' James gave her a light hello kiss and she was slightly surprised he didn't smell of baby lotion.

'Er, no he's not . . . Isn't he here? I thought he was the point of us going out tonight.'

'Oh I expect he's upstairs somewhere, or maybe in the garden. He was around earlier. Funny about the key sound but it must have been something else.'

'You look nice!' James remarked brightly. 'Different, somehow. That light turquoise shade really suits you.'

'Heavens, thank you! Very sweet of you to say so!'

Bella was taken aback for a moment; James had never been much of a one for positive personal comments during their years together. She could honestly only recall him being complimentary on occasions such as when she'd got the bath clean enough to meet his exacting hygiene standards, or when he could see his face perfectly reflected in the smear-free oven door. A newly cleaned fridge, all contents perfectly ordered and every shelf wiped with Borax, could be guaranteed to make him feel more thrilled to the point of potential sexual arousal than if she'd paraded around modelling the rudest items from the Agent Provocateur catalogue. And, as their marriage trailed to its inevitable messy end, only the scent of Country Pine Flash could raise so much as a smile. Maybe it was her brighter teeth he'd noticed, though he wouldn't realize that was the difference. The dress itself wasn't that special, but it was one she'd describe as a reliable old friend and which she'd three times consigned to the charity-shop heap and then rescued a day later. Daisy would probably suggest she tore it up for dusters.

'Before we go out, come and have a drink and look at all the work that's been done,' she said, leading James to the kitchen, where Shirley was assembling another gin and tonic.

'Hello James – it's been a long time, hasn't it? How are you?' she said, flinching slightly as he went to kiss her.

'Fine – or I was till I saw this!' he said, gazing round the room in what looked like near panic. 'I thought it was *you* getting the makeover, Bella, not the house!' He ran a finger over the sparkly blue-speckled granite work-top, checking it was real. 'God! What have they *done*? Are you mad? It's not staying like this, is it? Please tell me it isn't. The walls are *orange*!'

Bella laughed. 'James, don't exaggerate! They are *not* orange. That's a very delicate coral and I love it.' She took a bottle of Sauvignon Blanc from the fridge and poured a generous glassful for James. Perhaps he would loosen up a bit after a few sips of wine.

'And all that turquoise glass on the wall behind the units . . . hardly in keeping with the house, is it? Where are the tiles?'

'The tiles are in a skip somewhere, and this whole room isn't in keeping with the house, James. It never has been. We knew that all those years ago when we had it extended. If we'd wanted it to stay all Edwardian, we could have stuck with the small gloomy rooms and put in some stained glass and fringed velvet curtains. In brown. Don't you even like the new cupboard doors?'

'Not bad, I suppose,' He admitted grudgingly. 'I mean you can't really go wrong with oak, can you, though that burr pattern is a bit fancy. And I'm glad to see they've made use of the same carcasses, because the original doors were perfectly good and they can go back on after these shenanigans are all finished.'

'Hmm. Well . . . I haven't decided yet, but probably not, actually.'

'Decided? What's to decide? This is just all props, isn't it? They have to take everything back at the end, surely?'

Funny how wound up James was about a kitchen he'd walked out on ten years before. Bella almost wished Nick and Co. had taken up half the floor and installed a plunge pool and feature fountain as well.

'Not necessarily. I can opt to pay for it apparently – they'll just take it off my location fee. It'll be rock-bottom price because not only do I get it all at cost, it also saves them the dismantling time and restoring the paint colour. Sounds like a deal to me. Instant house upgrade for minimal outlay.' Outlay she shouldn't really be spending, given the shaky work situation, but when would a chance like this come again?

'Gran and Alex and me all like it too.' Molly wafted into the room, catching the end of her mother's sentence. 'But Gran said you wouldn't.'

'Your gran doesn't live here.'

'Neither do you,' Shirley swiftly reminded him.

'I just think that it's not necessarily the best time to spend money on doing up this place.' James sounded near to defeat.

Bella hoped he wouldn't start on about selling the

house – this just wasn't the right moment – not till she'd talked it through with Molly and Alex. She tried her one potential trump card: 'Oh I don't know, I'd have thought a bit of sprucing up could only increase the value, wouldn't you?'

Ah, that got him. Bella could almost see the cogs of calculation turning in James's head.

'Hmm . . . maybe, maybe.' He was looking brighter already. 'So. Are we going to this restaurant, or what? Where's Alex? Is he upstairs making himself presentable?'

' 'm here. 'Lo Pa.' Alex ambled in, wearing faded blue board shorts and an old grey hoodie that might once have been black. Much of his long hair was still wet from the shower. He was wearing flip-flops. 'Ready when you are, dude.'

James, leaning back against the worktop, looked him up and down. 'Are you sure? Is that what you're wearing? I understand this is a restaurant that has *tablecloths*, not wipe-clean vinyl.'

'Yes he's sure. He looks scrubbed up enough to me. Come on, let's just go, shall we?' Bella said, feeling as if she was herding sheep. Oh, didn't it promise to be *such* a jolly evening?

'All right, all right – I just hope our venue of choice doesn't have a dress code. They'd need to lend you a lot more than just a tie,' James grouched.

'A tie! Who wears ties!' Alex laughed.

'Grown-ups do,' James sniffed. He moved away from the worktop and there was a loud ripping sound. The back pocket of his trousers had caught on the new starfish door handle.

'You see, Bella?' He turned to check the extent of the damage. 'I told you! This is *not* practical! Surely now you'll agree you *have* to change it all back to how it was?'

'Sorry – can't oblige! But I might rethink the starfish handles,' Bella replied, searching in her handbag for a safety pin. 'Here you are,' she said as she handed him a pin. 'Really, it's only a tiny rip, nothing serious.'

It was an Italian restaurant again, because it had the menu options where everyone could find something to like, but not the one just up the road this time. All the same, Bella was happy that this too was only a few minutes' walking distance from home. Her Mini wouldn't have been big enough for all five of them, and James would have fussed for ages over where to park his Lexus and told Alex off before he'd even been close to accidentally scuffing the leather seatback with his shoes.

How, Bella thought as they sorted out who was sitting where at the circular table, would she ever be able to afford another home this close to the centre of the town on only half the money from the house sale, if James ended up getting his own way? She tried not to think about it, using an old technique that Shirley had suggested to her when she'd been awake half the night in the middle of a teen crisis many years ago. This was to tell herself there was nothing she could do about it *right now*, so nothing could be achieved by worrying. Instead she concentrated on the menu. She could, she thought, safely introduce some non-white food to her newly sparkling teeth but she decided she'd give it one more day, to be safe. That meant no red wine, hard as that was going to be when having pasta. Pasta and red wine just *went*. How on earth did manic dieters find the discipline to forgo all their favourite foods for months on end, when she was finding it hard to do without a few inessentials for a mere three days?

'So – some idle weeks on a French beach, Alex,' James said as soon as they'd ordered. 'Can't be bad, can it? I hope you've found a decent place to stay.'

'Nah – we're sleeping in Ben's van,' Alex told him. 'Can't waste cash on accommodation.'

'In a *van*? With no facilities?' James shuddered.

'Well it's only like camping. I mean, it like *is* camping,' Molly said.

'But after August, low season, surely a clean little *pension* wouldn't be ruinous, cash-flow-wise?'

'Dad. It's sorted, OK? We'll be fine. Anyway, you don't want me to end up as the student with the biggest-ever debt, do you? Thought you'd approve of my *360-degree thinking*.'

'Alex . . .' Bella warned. Shirley was now grinning rather wildly into yet another gin and tonic, Molly had her head down and was quietly texting one of her mates, while Alex and James seemed to be spoiling for a full-scale battle. And all this still only at the antipasto stage. She looked at the couple on the next table. He was silent, tucking lustily into a huge mound of red-sauced pasta, while his date sat with her simple salad untouched, quietly (too quietly, alas) talking non-stop and intently at him. Relationships, she thought – who could fathom them? Had those two always been that way, she wondered, and did this conversational one-sidedness trouble either one or both?

'Well, I suppose if it saves money . . .' James was obviously torn on this one. 'Talking of which, how long is this TV fiasco going to take, Bella? Have you done a per-hour breakdown as to whether the fee is worth the aggro? And where will you stay while it's happening? Do you think it'll be safe to have the house empty overnight? You won't be giving these people house keys, will you?'

'Whoa – slow down! In order of asking – about a week, maybe ten days. Yes, it's worth it. And it turns out we don't have to move out after all,' Bella told him. 'Saul said that as they only really need to use the kitchen and the garden then we might as well stay put if we don't mind tripping over cables and lights a bit. The kitchen all works perfectly well and it's part of the show to have us doing usual stuff, making tea or toast or something and maybe having some lunch and so on. Anyway, at the end of each day we get it back to ourselves. There'll be a catering truck, so we won't starve.'

She glanced at the next table again. The man was still stolidly eating. The woman was still talking, but half her salad had gone. How had she managed that? She hadn't even picked up a fork last time Bella looked. Bella was almost tempted to drop her napkin so she could see if the food had been scooped under the table.

'Damage. You must watch for damage,' James warned. 'They're notoriously careless, film crews.'

'Carly's mum says it's anti-feminist to have people tell you what you should and shouldn't wear,' Molly chipped in as the food arrived. 'She says it's all a big plot by woman-hating fashion designers who make clothes that only look good on flat boy-shapes. Then they can laugh at the ridiculous dieting lengths that perfectly normal women go to trying to make themselves that shape too, so the clothes will look right.'

'When I look at some of the so-called "clothes" that turn up over the seasons, I can see Carly's mum might have a point,' Shirley agreed. 'Remember those veil things that completely obliterated the faces but left the models otherwise naked? I'm not sure pubic hair has any place on a fashion catwalk. How, exactly, was that supposed to be translated for the high street market?'

Molly giggled. 'Gran, you're like *so* upfront?'

'Appropriate choice of word there, Moll!' Alex laughed.

'Oh Molly, darling, don't go all prissy now!' Shirley poured some wine into Molly's glass.

'I'm not! But I think Carly's mum's right too.'

'Maybe she is . . . and at a very bizarre level,' Alex said, 'the extreme demands of high-end fashion could undermine the nature of the universe because instead of evolving by way of the survival of the fittest, you get survival of the flattest, thinnest and least likely to be able to breed. Converse of Darwin. Not so much evolution of the species but the potential end of it. Just for a size zero.'

'Good grief Alex, no wonder you got into Oxford. That's convoluted but so clever.' Shirley was admiring, but then turned to Bella. 'Darling, really, I know you're doing this so that you can write about it, but have you considered the danger of them making you look a bit of a fool? Isn't that how so-called reality TV works, by bullying perfectly nice people a little *too* much? Because really, there's nothing wrong with the way you put yourself together. Apart from under-accessorizing, of course. Statement jewellery – you can dramatize any plain outfit with that.' She looked around the restaurant for an example, finding a useful one two tables away, and pointed out her quarry to the others, raising her voice. 'You see? Like that outfit over there.' She was being loud, heads were turning. 'Dull in its own way, colour-wise, but look how she's added . . .'

The woman Shirley was indicating turned, sensing she was the one being discussed; she got up and immediately came over to their table. Shirley looked alarmed, as if afraid the woman had come to slap her and tell her to keep her opinions to herself.

'Bella! Gosh! Fancy running into you here!' Bella was thrown for a second, barely recognizing Dina, who had always expressed complete scorn for fancy clothes and make-up. Her long hair, a patchwork of greys and rust shades, was piled up in a tumbledown sexy way and clamped into place with a big tortoishell clip. She wore a simple dark emerald dress with a lacy jacket in the same colour – Ghost, Bella guessed. She had silver hoop earrings and a silver necklace set with big chunks of bronzy stone. She still wore no make-up but somehow this was fine. Her eyes were the colour of the necklace stones.

'Dina – you look fantastic! How are you?' Bella hoped she didn't sound too amazed – how insulting would that be? But it was a shock – Dina was normally a voluminous skirt and baggy top sort of woman, covering a substantial body mass with as much fabric as possible while claiming she really was above caring. Now she was looking positively glamorous and potentially another disappointment for Daisy and Dominic – Dina, of all people, seemed to have the what-to-wear thing sussed perfectly well, thank you.

'I'm fine!' Dina told her. 'Looking forward to our TV style-trial. I've quite come round to thinking it's a good thing. Are all of you going to be in it too?' she said to the table at large.

'Sorry Dina – no, this is the family. Son Alex, daughter Molly and my mother, Shirley, who was just pointing you out as an example of top accessorizing. And . . . er, this is James.' How to describe him? 'He is Molly and Alex's father.' Well, he was. 'And this is Dina – one of my writer friends. She's going to be one of the Fashion Victims with me next week.'

James was looking at Dina in quite an odd way, Bella thought. His eyes were wide and staring and his mouth was unattractively half open. Any moment now, he'd be dribbling. Was he all right?

'The wind will change and you'll be stuck like that,' she heard Shirley murmur to him.

'Hmm? What?' He jumped, startled back to earth.

'Well, it's really good to meet you all,' Dina said. 'I'm over there, with my brother, so I'd better get back to him. I'll see you next week, Bella. Oh, and . . .' She leaned close to James and picked up a fork. 'Couldn't help noticing, there's a small mark on that. You might want to send it back.'

'Thank you *so much*!' James beamed, taking the fork from her, using his napkin rather than touching it.

'Now that,' he said, when Dina had gone back to her seat, 'is what I call a woman.' He sighed, looking quite flushed. 'Does anyone want pudding? Molly? Don't hold back anyone, this is all on me.'

'Good grief,' Shirley whispered to Molly, 'to my enormous surprise, it looks like I owe you a pound.'

# NINE

Daisy was twirling round and round in Bella's kitchen, arms out like a child playing windmills. The sleeves of her yellow kimono top (over a purple satin tulip skirt, over orange lace leggings, scarlet killer heels, a combination which shouldn't have worked but just *did*) billowed and flapped. 'Oh now this is a *gorgeous* space! I've seen smaller village halls!' She abruptly stopped twirling, adding very quickly, 'As a child, I mean. Ballet class and Brownies, that sort of thing. Haven't been near a village hall in years. Obviously.' She shivered slightly, as if the very idea of being more than five miles beyond Notting Hill was too hideous to contemplate.

Bella tried to imagine Daisy at a ballet class: she'd have been sure to have perfectly colour-co-ordinated ribbons rather than the usual random what's-available ones sewn on the hem of her character skirt, and to have been the one girl in the class whose wrapover cardigan was cashmere.

'So – this room will be just the thing, with a bit more gussying up!' Daisy continued. 'And how clever of you, Bella, to resist having an island unit in here! Most people would have, wouldn't they? And you'd have lost some of that wonderful open feeling!' Bella didn't tell her that the lack of an island crammed with artfully hidden kitchen gadgets was down to her and James running out of renovation money at the time it was all built. But Daisy was right – it would have spoiled the space.

Daisy strutted around, touching surfaces, peering into cupboards, pulling back even further the already open folding doors to the garden. Bella didn't mind at all – the kitchen no longer felt entirely hers; with Daisy, Dominic, Saul and Fliss here, this had become a workplace, their set. The more comfortable and at home they all felt in it, the more relaxed they would be and the easier this palaver would be for everyone. And it did look good. Saul had taken Bella's huge naive Caribbean painting of a market in Grenada from its usual place in the hallway and hung it on the coral wall. With the turquoise sea in the painting's background reflecting the glass on the opposite wall, it somehow pulled the room's new look together. She knew it would never return to its original position.

'There's usually a sofa in here too, and dangerously overfilled bookshelves and a couple of tables for magazines and stuff over there . . .' She pointed to the wall opposite the long row of units. 'They've all been taken away. Saul thought we should keep the dining table, though.' Saul was now in the garden, talking to Fliss about bringing in more plants to obscure the fence and the neighbours' washing line.

'Yes . . . possibly move it to the wall, though, when we actually start . . . it's very big. And so *many* chairs,' Dominic drawled. Bella felt immediately defensive about her chairs, as if she were a woman herding her very large family on to a crowded bus and sensing a vibe that she should have been more careful not to conceive so frequently. But these were only chairs. Twelve simple upholstered Ikea dining chairs, each covered in either cream or turquoise fabric. She told herself firmly that if she were to start being sentimental about those, she might as well give up on this makeover malarkey right now. She was going to need a very thick skin.

'Well I don't provide seating for twelve on an everyday basis, Dominic, but there'll be a lot of us here this morning; your other victims – or should I call them "clients" – are all coming,' Bella told him, feeling she was explaining herself to a hyper-critical ten-year-old. 'I pulled out both extension leaves on the table and brought extra chairs from the cellar so we can use this like a boardroom table. Is this OK? Or did you want something less formal? Maybe use the garden more? What's the plan?'

She'd already been through some of this the day before, when the director and the lighting crew had arrived to do some measurements and some mysterious technical murmurings about light values. Her role then had been easy – point them at the kettle, put out the blueberry muffins she'd made, show them where the tea and coffee were and keep out of the way.

'It's fine.' Saul came back in and reassured her. 'Today is about the programme content, not the scenery. Fliss will measure everyone, Daisy will talk generally about the overall programme structure and then to each of you one at a time about personal style preferences and how what you wear has to fit into your lives and then . . . Bella, if Daisy and Fliss do you first, I was wondering – would you like to come with me to the prop house to pick out a whopping great sofa? I thought that seeing as it's your house you should at least get a say in what we have in here. Owner's privilege? And you already heard most of what Daisy and Dominic have lined up format-wise when you met them before. I'm thinking something like a horseshoe shape, something as off the wall as possible.'

'Puce,' Fliss said. 'I like puce. You should get that.' She was looking very organized today, very tidy in a black pencil skirt and her hair up in a topknot, as if she was taking her PA look direct from a 1940s film. Bella watched her carefully unpacking a stylish scarlet satchel and lining up pens, a tape measure and a heap of notebooks in different colours on the table.

'She has a thing for stationery,' Saul murmured to Bella. Bella was instantly reminded of her own schooldays, that first day of term with a new pencil case, sharp pencils, a scuff-free eraser. Even now, on her desk in her little upstairs office, she had most of the contents of Paperchase, bought on many a whim and the certainty that she might need them some time. All the same, not many grown women have a need for a box full of coloured pencils.

'So what do you think about coming to the prop house? Have you got time?' Saul asked her quietly. 'I could do with your input, frankly.'

'You're talking about me, aren't you?' Fliss suddenly said, glaring at Saul. 'It's about the sofa thing, isn't it?'

'I'm talking about *a* sofa, yes. But not about you.'

'You're going to tell her, aren't you? Go on, I know you're dying to. Humiliate me if you want, I don't care.'

'Fliss, Fliss, I wouldn't do that.'

'It's OK – I know I'm only the *work experience*. What do I know?' She stalked out of the room and Bella heard the door of the downstairs loo being slammed hard.

'Wow – what was that about?'

'Ah . . . well it was quite funny really – though it seems not so to Fliss.' Saul led Bella out to the garden and they sat together on the bench. 'Fliss had a run-in with me over props. I should have known better; she's already made it clear that clothes are her only real interest. I told her she could go on her own to look at sofas and she came back all excited and said she'd hired two. She then showed me the photos on her phone . . . they were lime green and inflatable. I tried to be positive and pointed out these would be a brilliant choice if no one was actually going to sit on them. But plastic squeaks with every move – it would be like putting everyone on whoopee cushions. Her second choice was cane, which would have been OK if we were doing the show in the garden, so I had to turn that down too, though I told her I might just hire them anyway, put them out on the terrace, depending on how much room the guy from *Green Piece* leaves us after he's brought the plants to tart up the garden. She said I didn't have to, there was no need to patronize her.'

Bella said, 'But you weren't, were you? You liked the cane ones!'

'Ah yes, but it was all too late. I'd made the mistake of laughing when I saw the blow-up sofas she'd chosen and she went right off on one, immediately.'

Bella laughed. 'Oh, I can see she would. Molly would

be exactly the same. You hurt her feelings and her pride!'

Saul scratched his head. 'Well, I don't have much experience of girls like her. Mostly the twenty-something pointy-shoed girlies in this business are all hyper-efficient and terrifyingly grown-up. But with Fliss, one minute she's wanting to be taken *really seriously* because she's an *adult* and the next she's sulking like a fourteen-year-old.'

Privately, Bella considered this might be something to do with the stepfather/stepdaughter situation. She was longing to ask about his home life, but this wasn't the moment. Faintly in the background, she could hear the doorbell. The rest of the troops had arrived.

'And it's yes,' she said to him quickly before they both got caught up with the others. 'Yes, I'd love to come and look at sofas with you.'

'I don't suppose you've had a chance to tell your family about us yet?' Dennis asked Shirley as they left Tate Modern and walked hand in hand along the riverbank towards the Globe theatre.

'Not yet. I keep hoping to get Bella on her own in a quiet moment, but there hasn't been one. Her house is in chaos just now with this TV thing going on. There are people in and out of the place all the time. How about you? Have you said anything to yours?'

Dennis laughed. 'I tried to! I was dying to – and trying to – over Sunday lunch at Harriet's, but every time I thought there was a chance to talk properly to her, one of the children would play up and she'd be distracted. Her gormless lump of a husband doesn't seem to have any input with the domestic routine so there she was, organizing the entire meal and dealing with the twins at the same time. I think his only contribution was to point out rather sardonically that five seemed to be a "difficult age". I told him to wait till they were fifteen, but Harriet gave me a look. I don't think she wants her husband to see nothing but years of trouble ahead in case he does a runner. No great loss that would be, if you ask me. He only cares about golf and Formula One and his God-awful estate agency. *Exclusive and superior properties.* Ye gods – you can really only say it in a Hyacinth Bucket accent.'

Shirley could hear a distant busker, playing 'Like A Rolling Stone'. In her opinion not an easy number to do if you weren't actually Bob Dylan himself.

'Do you remember,' she said, momentarily diverted from their conversation, 'way back when Dylan was known as Bobby Dylan, rather than Bob? Of course that didn't last. I remember when he was such a new phenomenon; down at *Les Cousins* we used to argue over our pints of Guinness about whether he was a genuine poet or an upstart pretender.'

'He was so very young, wasn't he?' Dennis said. 'That was about when I worked out I'd never change the world with my own written words, when someone ten years younger could write with so little seeming effort. Harriet's keen on him, surprisingly. But then I suppose he's one of the few who've accumulated fans through the generations. Leonard Cohen's another one.'

'Maybe that's how we tell our families,' Shirley laughed. 'We wait for one of those two to come over here again, get a load of tickets and let Bella, Harriet and your Toby bond in the O2.'

'Or we just *tell* them. Next time we see them. Just come out with "by the way, I'm seeing someone." ' He squeezed her hand tighter and smiled at her. 'Someone very, very special.'

'It should be so easy, shouldn't it? After all, we're single adults who don't have to answer to anyone. And you're right, Dennis, this is *so* special. I feel like a young girl again – and it's showing. I might not have had the chance to tell Bella, but Molly knows. She could tell just by looking that there was something going on in my life. She even asked if I was sleeping with you!'

Dennis stopped mid-pavement and looked at her, astonished. 'Good heavens! Did you tell her you were?'

'Of course I did. Why lie? I'm not embarrassed about it!'

'No, but I bet she was. Wasn't she horrified at the very

idea? She must think people our age shut up shop years ago, if they'd allow that we ever discovered sex at all, that is. As we said before, how little they know, bless them.'

'She didn't seem to be surprised or shocked or anything. If she was, she had the good manners not to show it, but at seventeen if their reaction is "yuck" they usually come straight out with it!'

They'd reached the Globe theatre. Outside were posters advertising the forthcoming season of plays.

'We could go to something here, if you like,' Dennis said, as they scanned through the list. 'Is there anything you fancy?'

'I'd quite like to see *Doctor Faustus*,' Shirley told him, 'but . . . it's not on till late November. Won't it be cold in there, having no roof? I'm imagining a frosty night – or a chill damp fog; fingers and toes going numb even with furry boots and the warmth of the audience.'

'We could go well prepared, with picnic blankets and a flask of hot tea?'

Shirley thought for a moment, then said, 'Hmm. I'm not sure. I think . . . I much prefer doing that kind of outdoor thing in warmer weather. I wouldn't be able to concentrate on the stage if I'm thinking about my freezing toes. Do you mind?'

Dennis put his arm round her. 'Of course I don't. We'll come here and see something in midsummer instead. For now, though . . . do you fancy retiring to the hotel for a nice little afternoon nap?'

'With eclairs?' Shirley giggled.

'Eclairs and a glass or two of bubbles, definitely.'

'Oh then I do, I do . . .'

'Colour, shape, accessories and make-up. And of course the make-up aspect includes hair,' Daisy said, fixing her gaze on the hectic shambles that was Dina's crowning glory. 'Colour comes first because without knowing how to make the best choices there, nothing else can fall into place. You can wear the most gorgeous little Prada number, absolutely right for your body, showing you off to perfection but if it's the wrong colour for you, you will look merely ill. So to start with, you will all be colour-analysed. Filming will of course be going on throughout the process and I promise,' she showed her gleaming teeth but Bella wouldn't have quite defined it as a smile, 'it won't be at all traumatic. We are not here to make you look idiots.'

'Well that's a relief,' Jules said, helping herself to another chocolate brownie. Dominic leaned across the table and, without a word, slid it out of her hand and returned it to the plate. Jules gave him a defiant look, picked up the brownie again and took a deliberately oversize bite. Bella tried not to giggle. Oh, this was going to be such a hoot to write about.

'Next we move on to *shape*. Possibly the most important aspect of this whole venture. Now the shape for next season is *egg*,' Daisy stated with profound solemnity, as if she were the Chancellor of the Exchequer making a life-changing budget announcement. Bella watched as Fliss wrote down 'EGG!' on her pink notepad and then embellished the word with three different-coloured felt-tips.

Phyl spluttered into her coffee. '*Egg?* What in the name of buggery do you mean by *egg*?'

Dominic turned in his seat and stared at her. Phyl shifted slightly, waiting for him to speak, but he merely continued his gaze.

Daisy frowned, not at all pleased to be laughed at. She took a deep breath. 'I realize *egg* isn't the easiest shape to work with but, believe me, I've dressed some tricky figures in my time and honestly, hand on heart, I can say that any season's must-have shape can, with a bit of give and take, be made to work for anyone.'

'I don't doubt it,' Phyl said, 'but why do we have to "work" with a "season's shape" at all? What's wrong with *just clothes*, for heaven's sake?'

'Phyllis, darling,' Daisy cut in, 'first let me say, I *love* your chick-biker look but without being tricksy, I don't think you've quite grasped what we're here to achieve . . .'

Phyl pushed back her chair and stood up. 'It's

Phyllida, actually. And I'm dressed as a "chick biker" because I ride a great big bike – practical clothes for practical reasons, you see? And no, I think you might be right. I don't think I've quite grasped it at all. You said you weren't going to make us look like idiots and then calmly announce that we're going to be dressed as Humpty Dumpty? Right. I'll go outside now, if you don't mind, and have a smoke. And while I'm out there I promise I'll do my best to come to terms with this *grasping the concept of egg*. Lovely brownies, Bella my darling, you must give me the recipe.' She gave Dominic a final glare as she left the room.

'And then there were four . . .' Daisy sighed, because Phyl had gone out via the front door and soon after there was the unmistakable sound of her Harley-Davidson revving up and pulling out of the driveway. 'I have a feeling we won't be seeing the return of Phyll*ida* any time soon. Anyone else want to quit while we're about it? We can *just* afford to lose one more but if anyone else bunks off, then that's it. Show over unless we go out on the street and round up a few more. But the whole point of this is not random strangers, but people who know and support each other.' Dominic, beside her, patted her gently on her feather-clad shoulder.

'Um . . .' Zoe ventured, half putting up her hand like a nervous child in school. 'Actually the nanny walked out this morning. And I'm a little bit pregnant and feeling awful. And Calypso is coming up for her SATs and needs all my help. Time-wise, I thought I'd manage, but now I'm here and I've heard what this will involve, I'm wondering about it.'

'Just a tip, sweetie.' Daisy smiled at her. 'When making excuses, only use one. Anything more is gilding an already dazzling lily.'

'So I can go?' Zoe sounded as if she were asking to be allowed off games.

'Of *course*, darling! You're not under house arrest! And good luck with the nanny and the SATs thing. I promise, I *do* so totally understand! Our children come first, always.'

Bella felt confused – this sweet, understanding side of Daisy was quite unexpected. Why did people do this? Or was their very unpredictability what made the human race so fascinating? All the same, on balance she thought she preferred to know where she stood with people. Anything else (and that cheating lust-rat Rick came to mind) was too wearying.

After Zoe had gone, Daisy's smile looked genuine for the first time. 'Now *that* one I really didn't need!' she said. 'I'd already got Bella down as the token borderline reasonable-looking one. Zoe was frankly superfluous to requirements. *Very* cute in that wholesome Fulham sort of way, if a tad Stepford Wife meets Pollyanna. That one will never dress in anything but virtuous Boden and Brora and yet *still* manage to make everyone think she's stylish.' She shook her head and her ponytail swung against her ears. 'Quite an achievement, that. So very few can pull it off. I had very little idea quite what to do with her. OK, on to accessories now. Dominic? Over to you, or shall I?'

'Armour,' he stated, the unaccustomed sound of his voice rather surprising everyone. 'It is important to think of accessories as armour . . .'

'Oh it's good to escape!' Bella said, settling into the passenger seat of Saul's little Mercedes. 'I was close to quitting along with Zoe and Phyl!'

'No! Please, Bella, you can't back out now – I'm counting on you as an ally.'

'Against Daisy? But I'm terrified of her.'

'Oh that's normal, everyone is,' he laughed. 'I think probably the kindest way to sum her up is "mercurial".'

'Hmm. Sometimes she's just plain rude, if you don't mind me saying. I mean, I assume she's a friend of yours so this is me being tactful, but to be honest I prefer people who are easier to know. I just don't have a clue where I am with her. One minute she's being quite vile and I think, that's *it* – I don't need to put up with this, and then the next minute she's all sweet and rather lovely.'

'Part of her never-ending charm. She throws you to the sharks then chucks a lifebelt out after.'

'If you're trying to say she's got a soft centre, then I'd say it was very deeply buried. And what's with Dominic? How can he put up with her?' Bella asked.

'By being silent, I think, and letting her do the talking for both of them. As a team, that seems to be how it works. And by him being completely devoted to her. She inspires a massive amount of loyalty, does Daisy, once she's let people get through that shell,' Saul said quietly, turning off the road and in through huge metal gates covered in warning signs about alarm systems. Bella wondered if she was being slightly told off. Well, she wasn't going to apologize, because Daisy had come across, so far, as about eighty per cent vixen. How was Bella supposed to presume there was a Nice Side if Daisy wasn't going to show it?

'OK, we're here,' Saul said. 'It's not exactly West London's most attractive building but, as Daisy definitely *wouldn't* say, it's what's on the inside that counts.'

Saul was right – the vast blue corrugated shed, placed unromantically among industrial ugliness between railway lines on the edge of Willesden, wasn't where anyone would normally expect to find the most extensive selection of contemporary furnishings, including those of the most prestigious designers. Once on the inside, Bella and Saul were faced with acres and acres of all kinds of furniture. The first section they passed through looked like a series of office-reception areas, each being a grouping of sofas and tables and desks from differing periods. A few people were actually working at some of them, admin staff making practical use of the kit till someone needed to hire it.

'So what do they do if someone suddenly wants to rent it?' Bella asked, watching a girl munching a sandwich while working on an Apple Mac at an incongruously manky desk that wouldn't have looked out of place in the prison governor's office in *Porridge*.

'Move all their stuff to the next unit, I expect,' Saul told her, waving to one of the staff further up the warehouse. 'It must be quite fun, wondering where to set your work up each day, but a pain if it disappears suddenly when you'd just got comfortable. But here, up these stairs – come and look at this lot.'

He pushed open a swing door and led Bella up two flights of stairs. The stairwell walls were densely covered in framed pictures: sundry seaside scenes, landscapes, a collection of child portraits, Hogarthesque etchings, abstracts. Then they went through another door. 'This isn't where we need to be, but I thought you might like to see some of the oddities of this place,' Saul said. 'It's a complete museum of ephemera in here.'

It was, Bella thought, laid out like a supermarket full of madness. Instead of food on the near-endless rows of shelves, the place was crammed with *things* – everything anyone could possibly need to dress a drama from early twentieth century onwards.

'This place doesn't do the antique stuff. All the prop houses have their specialities,' Saul explained as Bella walked around, exploring. On one shelf was a row of bubble-gum vending machines, maybe fifty different sorts. Old radios, kitchen blenders, Barbie dolls, shop tills, kettles, lamps (standard and table), were lined up. There was an island with at least a hundred vacuum cleaners of varying vintage and, behind a selection of early sixties Formica-topped tables, a corner floor area bizarrely populated with stuffed animals.

'Ugh, genuine!' Bella squeaked, stroking the back of a growling cheetah.

'All genuine,' Saul told her. 'Amazing, isn't it? Imagine working here and it being just an everyday thing to be asked for a dozen stuffed penguins. But anyway – on to what we're here for. We need to go back down these stairs . . .'

The floor below was stocked almost entirely with chairs and sofas, rows and rows of them. High on a shelf were stacks of every shape and shade of Philippe Starck's transparent Ghost chairs. Along a wall were leather Barcelona chairs in every available colour and Bella recognized iconic designs of Arad, Eames, van de Rohe and so many others.

'Wow . . . this is . . .'

'This is *not* your average permanent-sale furniture warehouse!' Saul laughed, finishing her sentence for her.

'Understatement! It's more like being in a fantastic museum of contemporary design. And hey, look!' A bit overexcited, she got hold of Saul's hand and pulled him across to a scarlet sofa shaped like a pout. 'Here's that famous lips sofa – Kiss, is it called?'

They sat on it side by side and she suddenly felt rather silly and shy and horribly conscious not only of the name of the sofa, but that she'd grabbed his hand and practically forced him on to it with her, a bit like dragging a reluctant victim under the mistletoe at an office party. She so hoped he hadn't assumed she wanted to test the sofa out as a literal kissing venue, because she didn't. Absolutely not. Admittedly Saul was attractive, but post-Rick the very idea of becoming romantically entangled with someone again was miles from her mind. It must be like getting a cold, she thought suddenly – for quite a while after, you have absolute immunity from reinfection. Long might it last – being content to be single was very restful.

'Er, sorry – just got a bit carried away there,' she said, getting up again. 'I just so love it that this place has such unexpectedly amazing stuff in it. I mean, DFS it *isn't*.'

'They've got a lot of ordinary household items as well, but with the really rock-bottom-end furnishings it's often as cheap just to buy it as to rent. There's always someone on the crew who'll take it off your hands. Seen anything you fancy?'

Was he teasing her? Possibly. His blue eyes were quite glinty. Staying resolutely businesslike, Bella looked along the length of the warehouse. 'I quite like that pink one, but I think I've seen it somewhere before.' She pointed out a rather elegant low velvet button-back sofa, simple and sleek.

'Jonathan Ross's show, two seasons ago,' Saul told her. 'This place is a retirement home for chat-show sofas.'

'Ah, of course it must be. And look, there are the Designers Guild chairs from the interview area at Live 8 a few years back! I remember because I liked them so much at the time – love the madly vivid fabrics.'

'Sadly we need to keep it plain so as not to distract from the clothes, otherwise I'd go for something from Squint, all crazy bright patchwork on fairly traditional framing. A couple of mad overpatterned chesterfields would look great in your place.'

'They would, wouldn't they?' she agreed. 'But shouldn't we look for something puce? To cheer up Fliss?'

Saul shook his head. 'Bless her, but *not* puce. Sorry Fliss!'

A deep lavender shade turned out to be a good compromise, though – the two of them agreed on a sofa that resembled a long curved row of tyres, if such a thing were possible in light-purple velvet. Saul made Bella sit on it for a while to check it was low enough so that Jules (the smallest of them) would not be left with her feet dangling in mid-air, and that it wasn't so deep that they couldn't actually lean back on it without falling awkwardly against the cushions. It worked – Saul made arrangements with the Apple Mac girl, and the business side of the outing was over.

'I hope Fliss approves,' Bella teased Saul as they got back into the car.

'Oh she probably won't. And Daisy will have a moan about it as well, no doubt.' He switched on the engine and pulled away from the building, turning to smile at her. 'Everyone thinks they can have a pop at the art choices,' he said. 'It's such a broad target. The clients never have a go at the heavy-duty technical stuff, they don't know enough to say, "Are you sure about tungsten lighting? We'd prefer HMI's" or "Do you think a 9/8 lens is really appropriate for this shot?" or "Why don't you use a Western dolly?" because they wouldn't have a clue. But when it comes to choosing from paint charts, or whether to have blinds or curtains, they've all got an opinion! Next time you look at a contemporary TV show or even just an ad, see how much beige there is, because when everyone's taken a shot at the art director, that's what you're left with. Bland, murky, boring. Hey,' he suddenly perked up, 'it's gone one, shall we go to a pub for a bit of lunch? You must be starving by now.'

'Hmm, I am rather,' she admitted. 'I didn't dare eat one of the chocolate brownies in case Dominic slapped my wrist.'

'Oh he wouldn't tell you off,' Saul told her. 'He likes you.'

'Really? He should let his friendly side out a bit more often. Mind you, as we said, it must be tough, working with Daisy.'

'Oh, tough hardly begins to cover it, believe me.'

There was an unexpectedly free parking space outside the London Apprentice by the river. The day was so warm and bright that most of the outside tables were still occupied, even though it was almost 2 p.m. Saul sent Bella to bag a table that was just being vacated by a group of suited young men and went inside to get drinks and see what was available, food-wise.

Bella gazed out over the sluggish Thames. The tide was low – if you weren't afraid of mud, at the lowest tide you could probably just about walk to the little midstream island.

'Spritzer for you and I hope you don't mind, but I ordered us a couple of prawn-salad sandwiches in case they're about to shut down the food service. I can change that to something else if you want me to?'

'No – it's fine! Sounds perfect. Cheers!'

'Here's to the programme.' Saul chinked his glass against hers. 'May you not hate the whole lot of us by the time it's over.' Bella laughed, but Saul didn't.

'No really,' he said, looking serious, 'it can get very tense, all this media rubbish. At its worst, everyone gets so wound up you'd think there was no other world outside the fizzing fishbowl of the shoot. I'd so hate it if you and I didn't end up as still friends.'

Bella felt her heart rate notching up. He shouldn't look at her like that. She was immune, or supposed to be, and besides – she would never again get caught in a married-man situation. She took herself back to the picture she'd had once before of his so-perfect home life, the gorgeous wife (mother of cute Fliss), the stylish house, none of which she knew about in reality. All the same, it was a useful device to keep her grounded. As would be what she was about to ask him; surely it came next in the being-chatty, being-friendly thing. And once it was out of the way she could get on to why Fliss claimed she *didn't* know her stepfather.

'So – your wife . . . is she in the business too?'

'Er . . . actually, no . . .' Saul was quiet, staring out

towards the island. He hesitated for a moment. Bella heard a duck squawking on the river, a sound like crazy old-lady laughter. Then Saul said, 'No, she isn't in the business. She died.'

# TEN

Another half-dozen ducks joined in with the first one's cackling. Bella wanted to tell them to shut up – this wasn't the time for their frivolity.

'Oh. Saul, I'm . . .'

'Sorry.' Saul supplied the word for her. 'Yes, I know. Everyone is.' His smile was a sad, half-sized one; he was doing that gentle, reassuring thing that people do when they've sprung the shock of death, as if it's their responsibility to make the unaffected one feel better, rather than the other way round. 'There's nothing else you can say really, is there? We British don't do death very well. It's an embarrassment. So I'll quickly tell you all the things that I'll assume you'd want to ask, and get it over with.'

He took a deep breath. 'It was a long time ago – coming up to six years. It's just a depressingly ordinary and sadly too-frequent tale. Lucy found a lump; after a lot of to-ing and fro-ing for tests and everyone saying how extremely unlikely it was to be serious, it turned out to be breast cancer. She had a mastectomy, chemo, plenty of state-of-the-art treatment and even more assurance that it would all be all right. Except . . . it wasn't; when you're young, if it takes hold it really does gallop through your body. So that's it really. She was thirty-nine when she died. Back at the beginning of her illness she'd joked about whether it was true that life began at forty, and if so, that could be very handy for her – Lucy always did have a terrific sense of irony!'

'So young.' Bella hated herself for stating the obvious, but as Saul had pointed out, there just wasn't a right phrase.

'Too young,' Saul agreed. 'And too awful a way to go, at any age.'

'So now you're . . . ?'

'On my own, yes. I live over that office you came to in Soho. I've managed to buy the whole building, bit by bit, over the years, and I like being in the busy, noisy centre of things. There's a roof garden to escape to when I feel too city-bound, and I love it up there with my plants and the birds. I found after a while, and after some not-great attempts at thinking I should settle with someone else, that I'm quite good at living by myself. I like the space, the peace, the being able to shut off from a job that's mostly waffling on about trivial and inconsequential things. Perhaps if I worked in news or current affairs I'd feel different, but often I'm faced with the certainty that the kind of programmes I'm making aren't anything to do with a grown-up life. But, hey, OK I've told you about me, what about you?' he asked her as the sandwiches arrived. 'What happened to Mr Bella, or is he just away somewhere? Ah . . . was he the guy who'd upset you that first time we met?' Something about the spark in Saul's eyes told her that his opinion of James was somewhere on the 'he's a twat' scale.

'Yes – that was James. But we're long divorced. *Very* long,' Bella told him. 'He went off to live in Edinburgh with someone who matched his manic standards of domestic hygiene but, well, recently he's come back to the area – or "relocated", as he'd put it – and is sticking his oar into the murky waters of my life wherever he can. If it were down to him, I'd be moving into sheltered accommodation any day soon, and eking out my remaining years in a sterile wipe-clean cage. He . . .' she hesitated. Would Saul want to know any more? Did he need to? Probably not, but as he'd shared something so personal it seemed only fair.

'He wants to . . . what he calls "realize the liquidity in our joint property".' She tried out James's phrase, finding it no less ludicrous this second time she'd heard it.

Saul looked both puzzled and amused. 'And in English that is . . .?'

'He wants to sell the house and take half the cash. He hasn't lived there for ten years. Oh . . . !' She put her hands over her face, feeling deep and sudden gloom. 'Look, I'm sorry. You don't need to hear this. It's so superficial compared with what you've just told me.'

'No, go on . . . you can tell me. I'm always interested in how crazily humans tick. But you said he left, and that you're long divorced. Surely that means he can't just . . .'

'Ah, well we left it all a bit muddy when it came to the house, because it was where the children were growing up and we didn't want them to lose their home as well as their father,' she told him. 'And now they're older he's back to cash in his share, a bit like the bad fairy coming to put her evil long-ago spell into action. You know, honestly, I've loved getting involved in all this TV stuff, because just for a little while I don't have to think about my crap life.' She laughed. 'Just lately far too much has gone a bit wrong.' Appalled, she felt her eyes fill with tears. So much for thinking the worries about money, her quarter of a job, her shaky future and (grrr) bloody James were on hold. Scratch the surface . . . And this was the second time Saul had seen her all weepy – it was where they'd come in. He must think she was like a leaky tap.

'Come out with me,' Saul suddenly said, reaching across and taking her hand. 'For dinner, I mean. One night soon, later this week?'

Bella smudged the back of her spare hand across her eyes. The wobbly moment evaporated quickly. She'd have to watch that – she'd never been one for over-emotional episodes. It was to be hoped that was a one-off, and surely not unconnected with what Saul had told her about his wife. It certainly put the ridiculous defection of New York Rick into perspective.

'I'm sorry, that was a bit unexpected! I'm really not the instant-tears sort.' Her voice was shaky and she felt slightly silly. How sweet of him though, to take pity on her so quickly and ask her out. But what to say now? If she said no, he'd think she didn't like him enough even to go on a no-strings date, when of course she did. After all, she was out with him now, wasn't she? But if she said yes, he'd be stuck with his very kind spur-of-the-moment impulse and have to spend an evening being close and social with her. Did he *really* want that?

'Look, you don't have to . . .'

'I know. Hey, it's not a mercy date I'm offering, just two unattached people having a friendly evening together. I'd like to spend some time with you, without the prickly presence of Daisy, Dominic and everyone else,' he said simply. 'So it would be a pleasure. If *you'd* like to, that is. Oh – and if you *are* unattached . . . ?' He looked serious, questioning. 'Ah . . . my mistake, is it? You're seeing someone. After all, why wouldn't you be?'

Bella laughed. 'Hell no. Quite the opposite, honestly. I've had a recent scalding in that department, so I think you could safely say I'm firmly out of the date market right now. So yes, yes I would love to have dinner with you. Thank you for asking me.'

It couldn't have got round the sixth form faster if Aimee had stalked the corridors with a loudhailer or sprayed it in paint across the football pitch.

'What did she do? Stick a poster up by the reception area? Write it in lippy on all the loo mirrors?' Carly said to Molly as she drove the two of them home. 'I mean, you'd think she'd want to keep it quiet, wouldn't you, the mad, sad cow. *Everyone* knows. You can't go past an open doorway without hearing "Ohmigod! Have you heard . . . ?" '

Molly gripped the car door handle hard as Carly stood on the brakes to let a Volvo out of a side turning. It was great to have the occasional lift home like this, and the heavy school-run traffic meant it was bordering on comfortable to be stuck in a traffic jam, so Carly couldn't whizz along chatting and half oblivious, giggling 'whoops' every time she missed a gear change. All the same, Carly still managed to do a lot of sudden things. Like tell her Aimee was pregnant, confirmed by a wee-on-stick test that very morning, in school and between, apparently, Maths and Design Tech. This was the first Molly had heard of it, even though everyone else seemed to be in on the news. But then she had been in the library for hours working on *Hamlet* (a very tedious and self-obsessed bloke, in her opinion).

'Maybe she thinks it makes her some kind of big deal,' Molly speculated. 'You know what she's like for being a drama queen. She's keeping the baby, then? Is she going to be pram-pushing like Lisa Page? Shame really, because although Aimee's a pain and a really mean slapper, she's pretty clever. She was supposed to be applying for Cambridge.' There was a sneaky bit of pleasure to be had from this news, Molly worked out. If Aimee really was pregnant, it might make her feel sick enough to be put off chasing other people's boyfriends. It could, as her grandmother would say, clip her wings a bit. Also, did boys fancy pregnant girls? Or would they think that they might cop for the blame – or at least the responsibility if they started sleeping with her, even after the event? And what about if she got clingy with one and asked him to be her birth partner, or something? No – they'd mostly keep a safe distance now. Ha!

'Um . . . don't think she's said about keeping it. It's anyone's guess. I'd have thought that if she *wasn't*, then she'd have kept quiet and just slid off to some, like, clinic place, wouldn't you?'

'I think it's a bit lame that she's told the whole school before she tells her folks. Or maybe she sent her mum a text, soon as she got the result. Can you imagine that? "Hey mum am PG. L8ers". Mine would have an epi.'

'Mine too. Ballistic isn't the word.'

'So. Who's the daddy, you think?' Molly giggled. 'Or is there a list?'

'That's another thing that's anyone's guess.' Carly grinned. 'I can't imagine there are many who *aren't* in the frame for this one, can you?'

'Well, apart from Giles, no. I suppose not. But it's probably not someone from school. Isn't Aimee always showing off that she's out clubbing at places up town where she can pull something a bit more sophisticated than teenage boys? I think she was just practising on the boys at school, like learning on the nursery slopes in skiing.'

'Maybe it's one of those older ones, then. Perhaps she's got some rich old git on the go.' Carly slammed on the brakes at the lights, having decided quite late that amber was very close to red and not really good for a gamble.

'Rich, yes. But rich and careless!' Molly laughed. 'Pregnant! Wow, what an idiot!'

There seemed to be people everywhere. Saul dropped Bella off at her gate and left to go to a meeting at the

Soho office. Bella had plans to go out later to do some much-needed food-shopping, but she'd have to get the two trucks blocking in her Mini to move out of the way first. The front door was wide open and cables trailed through the house. As she went into the kitchen she could see a couple of hefty young men manhandling a huge palm tree into place halfway along the side flower bed, supervised by Keith the cat, sitting on the fence looking furious at his territory being so invaded. Bella sympathized. The kitchen worktop was covered in coffee mugs and scattered with sugar, and she had a heart-sinking certainty that when she looked in the fridge there might still be a bottle of milk but it wouldn't contain enough even for that one cup of tea that she craved.

Of Shirley and Molly there was no sign at all, which meant the house could have been open for hours for this crew of total strangers. Much as she liked Saul, just at this moment she could cheerfully have abandoned this whole mad project, thrown the lot of them out and slammed the door after them. So this was Saul's idea of minimal disruption, was it? They'd be able to carry on living in the house, no problem? Right. Who was in charge here? Nick must be somewhere about – she wanted a word with him.

'Sorry love, could you just move to your left a bit? I need to get to the kettle.' A big bearded man in a sweat-stained T-shirt was suddenly blocking her view of the garden work.

'"*Love?*"' she snapped at him. 'And who are you, if you don't mind me asking, to be making free with my kitchen appliances?'

Ugh . . . she so wished she hadn't said that. How snooty she sounded. She could imagine them all later, down at the riverside pub with pints of Wifebeater beer, laughing about her and her 'eew lah-di-dah *kitchen appliances*!' She wouldn't blame them. For now, though, this poor man simply looked puzzled. 'Um . . . I'm from *Green Piece Garden Company* . . . dressing in some plant life for the shoot? And you are . . . ?'

'I'm Bella. I live here. It's my house. What happened to film catering? I didn't expect to be feeding the five thousand.'

Nick came in from the hallway carrying a saw and a big screwdriver. 'Hi Bella – sorry about this. It'll all be clear in an hour, I promise. The catering only turns up for the actual shoot. But . . . we've come equipped!'

With a *ta-da* flourish, he opened the fridge and there were several bottles of milk, from full cream to organic skimmed. He then showed her new boxes of tea, bags of coffee and a tin of biscuits near the kettle.

'All tastes catered for, from Dominic's camomile tea to the sparks's Nescafé,' he said.

For the second time that day, Bella felt a bit tearful.

What's the matter with me, she wondered. Maybe it was just about the way the house was being taken over. The upheaval was giving her a taste of how it would feel to be moving out. Half her kitchen furniture had gone, there were packing cases and strangers everywhere and she no longer felt there was a place in it – certainly not downstairs – for her. All she needed now was for James to come swanning in, hand her a cheque for a very slender amount and demand the house keys from her, and her day would be complete.

The burly garden bloke had, while she'd been pondering this, rinsed out half a dozen mugs and made tea.

'I did one for you too, love,' he said kindly. 'You look like you need it.'

'Thanks, I definitely do,' she said, accepting a cup so strong that it looked as if, as James's late mother used to say, you could 'trot a mouse over it'. She accepted his offer of a couple of chocolate HobNobs too, feeling the need for the comfort of something sweet.

She took the tea upstairs to her study, shut the door and switched on her computer to look at emails and play a bit of Spider. Peace. At least up here all was as normal, even if she could still hear some shouts and bangs from below. What on earth were they still finding to do? Presumably something madly technical, though this morning it had all looked like a perfectly normal house to her and she'd thought they'd seemed happy enough with that. And why were they forever in and out of the downstairs loo? It was almost constantly flushing (which, given they were all men, was something, she supposed). She'd have to buy an industrial-size pack of loo roll at this rate, and charge it to the shoot.

Ideally she'd now go and have a calming bath and then lie on her bed, clothed in only body lotion and her silky robe, and watch something soothing like *Escape to the Country*, ogling beautiful houses in remote areas she would never want to live in, though she'd find herself a teeny bit tempted. But somehow, she would feel peculiarly vulnerable – shy, even – about indulging in such intimate pampering with a horde of unknown blokes crashing about downstairs. How could she possibly relax? Any second one of them could trail up the stairs and knock apologetically on the door to ask about the location of a fuse box or the garden tap.

'Bella? Are you in there? They said you were up here somewhere.'

Well, at least this was a familiar and welcome voice. Jules tapped on the door and opened it a few cautious inches.

'Hi Jules – come on in. Are you OK? Please don't tell me you're giving up on this as well. I couldn't bear it to be just me and Dina. And Daisy would go into orbit.'

'No, no it's fine, I'm still resigned to crushing

victimhood. I just came to see if you fancied coming over to mine for supper. My menfolk are all out at a footie match and I'll be on my lonesome otherwise. And bring Shirley and Molly as well, of course. It would get you out of all this. It must be hell; though I have to admit I quite like that wifebeater vest and toolbelt look on those tech boys, myself.'

Jules came in and sat on the old wicker chair beside Bella's desk and started making a tiny paper aeroplane out of a Post-it note.

'You're right, it's not wonderful, not right now,' Bella told her. 'But I've only just got home and I'm feeling grouchy and tired. They say they'll be gone soon, but the thought of cooking . . . and I haven't been to the shops for any food, either. Oh God, I'm so chaotic. So, thanks, Jules – I'd love to take you up on that.'

'Seems to me,' Jules said, 'that you've taken on a bit too much here. But hey, look, I'll go now, leave you in peace. I only popped in to invite you – I was just on my way back from walking the dog. So – have a shower or something and then . . .'

'Aaagh! Are you saying I'm all smelly and vile?' She thought about Saul, how she'd been sharing his intimate car space less than an hour ago. He'd leaned across and kissed her goodbye, just briefly. How terrific to have had deodorant failure even before their date. How off-putting must that be? Not that she was thinking of it as a date. Definitely not – she'd said as much when he'd asked her. But all the same . . .

'No of course not – I only meant it would de-stress you!'

'Oh, right. OK – as soon as I hear that front door slam and the last of them going, I'll get in the bath for a lovely soak. I don't know where Molly or my mother are, but I expect they'll turn up when they're getting hungry. Family – they're just like cats, aren't they?' She yawned and ran her hands through her hair. It felt slightly sticky and in need of a thorough wash. She wondered what Dominic had in mind for it, makeover-wise. She quite liked it as it was – floppy mid-blonde, a bit layered and hanging soft against her neck. The worst-case possibility was that he'd decide she needed a cute little urchin cut. Unless you had a neck as skinny as Audrey Hepburn's and a face as elfin as Mia Farrow in her heyday (and who, past forty, did?), that was absolutely *not* a great look. She only hoped she'd have the strength to put up a fight if he got over-insistent.

'I'll leave you to it.' Jules got up, flying her little paper plane down to the gardeners below. 'See you later. It's only chilli and stuff, nothing fancy, so come whenever you like.'

'OK, thanks so much Jules, I will. And I'll bring wine.'

* * *

It was amazing what twenty minutes lying in warm, scented water could do. Bella felt so much better as she towel-dried her hair and pulled some of her best underwear (Elle Macpherson, black lace on blue satin) out of the drawer. Then, only half conscious of what she was doing, she put it away again and pulled out some rather plainer – though still pretty (cream with pink dots) – Marks & Spencer kit.

'Oh God, what am I thinking?' She sat down abruptly on the bed, feeling shocked at herself. Whizzing uninvited through her head had been the idea of keeping the Elle Macpherson for the date with Saul. No! She didn't *do* dates any more, and certainly not the sort where her underwear was likely to be on view. Going out with Saul didn't mean she was *going out* with Saul. I must, she told herself, keep control over my inner slut. All the same, she decided that the cream and pink would work better under her pale blue and white spotty Banana Republic dress. If you were thinking slutty, she reasoned as she fastened her bra, there was nothing more tarty than having dark underwear showing through pale fabric, now was there?

'Oh the peace and the bliss of a normal household!' Bella said as Jules poured glasses of cold Pinot Grigio for the four of them. 'I must have been mad to let them take over the house. There are cables and lighting stuff and big silver box things everywhere. The things we do for money.'

'Well, if you call my place normal . . .' Jules commented, stirring a huge vat of chilli con carne on the stove. Her glance swept across the big family kitchen-dining room. 'This part seems to be a holding area for everything the male contingent lose interest in but might just want to pick up again when passing through.' A guitar leaned against a sofa. A heap of scuffed trainers lay in hazard-formation by the doorway. On the dresser were computer cables, a Wii, a pile of CDs. But just in front of the table the doors to the garden were open and the sweet rich scent of night phlox out on the terrace was wafting in. At that end of the room all was order and the table was prettily laid with candles and pink napkins.

Jules's husband and her teenage sons were out – gone to watch Chelsea play Manchester United at home, and not expected back till much later. Some early scoring looked promising for Chelsea's victory, and a victory meant post-match celebration and a slow homecoming.

'I thought we'd have it with jacket potatoes and sour cream – or crème fraiche if we're supposed to be thinking about how the camera puts on ten pounds,' Jules said, pulling a big bowl of salad out of the fridge and handing it to Bella to put on the table.

'You've gone to a lot of trouble,' Shirley said.

'No I haven't. I made at least treble what we need, so I can freeze some for another night. So really, it's nothing, honestly. Anyway I'm glad to see you all. I'd have had a lonely old evening, trawling the channels for makeover programmes and getting all nervous about how we're going to be treated. I swear, if that Daisy woman insists that citrus brights really work with my red hair, I will walk out. I hope she isn't going to turn us all into clones of her. We'll look like a cageful of mad parrots.'

'She's pretty scary, isn't she?' Bella said. 'If what you wear is about saying what sort of person you are, then no wonder Dominic hardly dares open his mouth.'

'He's madly in love with her,' Shirley remarked. 'Any fool can see that.'

'*What?* Is he?' Jules said.

'I hadn't noticed – what makes you say that?' Bella asked.

'I only saw them briefly when I was on my way out the other day, but it's obvious. He watches her all the time. And wherever she is, he's only a couple of steps away. You check, next time. I think she scares him as well, though.'

'She walks all over him,' Bella commented. 'But we're not going to let her do that to us, are we?' She felt anxious, having another wave of certainty that this was a silly, time-wasting mistake, and would result in them all looking like a bunch of noodles on primetime TV.

'No, we're not.' Jules backed her up. 'I'm not wearing an egg cosy for anyone, even if it's got a Prada label, and if she insists you wear a puffball skirt that makes your arse the size of a planet, I'll slice it off you with a bread knife if I have to.'

'Honestly,' Shirley looked puzzled, 'I don't know why you two are getting so steamed up about it. First of all you could have just said no, but as you didn't, then don't fuss. After all, it's only *clothes*. None of it really matters.'

'It's all right for you to say,' Bella told her. 'You are so confident about what you buy that even Daisy couldn't make you wavery.'

'Gran's the one in the family who's got total *style*,' Molly said. 'Everything you wear looks amazing, like *designer*?'

'Well, I've learned to shop *very* carefully,' Shirley replied. 'And thank you darling, how sweet of you. I shall leave you all my money when I die.'

'Yes, thanks Molly,' Bella teased, 'for making me feel like a no-hope frump.'

'Oh you're not. You're OK. Just!'

'Well, I've been to Rigby and Peller.' Jules went to the fridge and took out a tomato salad. 'And I've mortgaged my soul for underwear that hauls me in and flattens me down to the point where I won't be able to eat a single thing because my digestive tract will be huddled in a teeny corner of my torso, completely unable to function. So, let Daisy and Dominic do their worst. Come on, let's eat.'

'I've got a free afternoon tomorrow,' Molly told Bella as they sat down. 'So do you mind if I hang out and watch them do the first bits of filming? Didn't you say that's when it starts? I won't get in the way, I promise.'

'You'll make me nervous, watching me screw up and look silly,' Bella joked. 'Can't you take your computer down to the library and do some work there instead? Or just stay up in your room? Though it might be noisy, I suppose.'

'Oh let her join in. It'll be educational.' Shirley pleaded Molly's case. 'Don't all young ones want to be in *media* these days? With any luck, seeing how it's really done will put her off.'

'I am *here*, you know,' Molly said, spooning crème fraiche into her potato. 'Oh yum, this smells so good.'

'Well maybe you could watch, I suppose, if you don't get in the way. Ask Saul. We're on colour tomorrow; Daisy's bringing someone in to tell us what suits us. Humiliation number one – we have to wear no make-up at all and have our hair shoved under a white hairband.'

'I think it's a really good idea,' Shirley said. 'At least when you know a bit more about colour, it'll get you out of wearing black, Bella. If someone else tells you it makes you look washed out, perhaps you'll believe them.'

'Someone already did, thanks Mum.' Bella laughed, thinking of the Carole-in-New-York moment. 'Don't worry, I've already got that message in my head.'

'We mustn't drink too much,' Jules said, as she topped up Shirley and Bella's glasses and then her own. It was just the three of them now; Molly had gone home to watch a must-see science fiction drama on TV. 'It's going to be bad enough being filmed all bare-skinned. A hangover face in the mix would make it even worse.'

'Oh, a good dose of moisturizer will sort you out,' Shirley advised. 'And a dollop of that wonderful Clarins Beauty Flash Balm. That doesn't count as make-up and it'll tighten your skin up nicely. I swear by it.'

'Thanks for the tip,' Bella said, feeling suddenly dispirited at the thought of what lay ahead. 'We're mad. I hate the whole idea now. Though I did have a great day today at the props place with Saul.'

'Ah – so, yes how did it go? He *likes* you!' Jules teased, prodding her arm.

'I like him; but not in that way.'

'I think he likes *you* in *that way*,' Jules giggled. 'He doesn't look at me or Dina the way he looks at you!'

'You're imagining it,' Bella laughed, 'and besides . . .' She stopped. Their conversation at the pub seemed a long time ago, but the intimacy of the subject matter was still close in her mind.

'Besides what? Is he married? Oh not another one,' Jules groaned.

'Another one?' Shirley queried.

'Don't ask, Mum. It was yet another of my hopeless mistakes. No, Saul's not married; well, he was . . . but she died. Years ago.'

'And he hasn't remarried? Wasn't he happy?' Shirley persisted.

'Er . . . Well actually, I don't think I should be talking about him like this. It feels wrong. He's on his own, he says. Unattached. That's all I know. He sounded like they were very happy, though.'

'Hmm.' Shirley was pensive. 'It's funny, you know, but over the years I've found that the ones who've been widowed but were really happily married tend to marry again, or at least settle with someone else, pretty soon after the loss of the first wife. If marriage has been a happy state, they're keen to repeat it. Too many then rush into it with the first person who gets to them.'

'But what if they have that feeling that no one could possibly match up to the first one? Wouldn't that make them go the other way, to avoid getting involved because they're so sure it's going to be second best? And what about that feeling that they couldn't bear to lose someone all over again?' Bella asked.

'Ah, but,' Shirley said, 'after the initial mourning and grief, the truly happy ones find it's the actual *marriage* they miss as much as the person. The sharing and the laughs and the companionship . . .'

'And the cooking and the laundry services and so on!' Bella laughed.

'And the sex,' Jules contributed.

'Oh, sex; well yes. An attractive man can get all the sex he wants, but to have the kind of sex where you don't want to be on your own immediately after and wish that the partner could stay, rather than go home . . . that's just worth so much.'

'Well . . .' Bella finished her wine. 'I've no idea really, about Saul. All I know is . . . um . . . I'm having dinner with him on Thursday night but . . . *What?* Why are you looking at me like that?'

Silence. Two pairs of eyes were wide and staring across the table at her.

'What is it? I'm just saying . . . it's just friendly. To talk about the programme and stuff . . .'

'You're waffling, Bella!' her mother said.

'Wow, you're a secretive one, aren't you? Why didn't you say something before? See how right I was?' Jules was triumphant. 'I *told* you he likes you!'

# ELEVEN

What *was* Shirley up to? The thought had crossed Bella's mind the night before, during dinner at Jules's house. As Shirley was giving them the benefit of her widow-position wisdom, it had vaguely occurred to Bella that her mother was finding it very comfortable and convenient living away from her own home. It felt a bit mean, well *very* mean really, but Bella had had one of those detached moments and had thought, 'How come you're still here?' Now she had woken up trying to work out why Shirley had not only not yet gone home, she hadn't even mentioned that she ever intended to.

She got up quickly and went down to the kitchen to make a cup of tea, took it upstairs and pulled the curtains back (another stunning day; was a drab, miserable winter on its way to punish them for such glorious late-summer luck?) She climbed back into bed to think while gazing out into the avenue's chestnut trees, which were starting to change colour. They were late turning: fat conker cases were already dropping the first of their fruit, but the leaves had clung to their green as if unwilling to let the autumn begin. Now the edges of the leaves were becoming multi-toned, through the subtle yellows and heading for the scarlet and bone-dry browns.

Twice now, in the time she'd been staying at Bella's, Shirley had slipped back to her own flat to bring over some essential wardrobe item. Why hadn't she moved back home? When the shoplifting story hadn't been in her local paper she could easily have returned to Walton, but instead, in spite of the chaos in Bella's house, she was happily settled in and showed no sign of returning. Hmm. It was working all right so far . . . but was Shirley secretly planning to move in permanently with Bella, infiltrating by the subtle means of *not going home*? But oh . . . was there something wrong with her mother that meant she preferred not to be living alone right now, but to be enjoying the company of her family *while she could*?

She didn't look ill, that was for sure. In fact Shirley was looking pretty radiant these days. Her hair – a sleek, silver bob – was always perfectly styled, her clothes were enviably well put together (eat your heart out, Daisy) and she was forever . . . going out. Ah, maybe that was it. Bella's proximity to a Tube station – that must be the attraction. It was so easy for Shirley to get into town from here, to go to the endless exhibitions and galleries that she so enjoyed. Meeting friends, she'd said the other day. You didn't do that if you were ill . . . or did you?

Bella finished her tea, went into the bathroom and switched on the shower. In one way James had a point, she thought. In a few years, with both Alex and Molly grown up, she would be more or less living alone; unless of course they both finished university and came back to the nest, unable to afford to buy somewhere to live. But if they didn't . . . did she really want to spend the potential years of freedom (even at risk of loneliness) with her mother? It would be like being sent back to childhood. Her childhood hadn't been too bad, once her alcoholic father was off the scene. All the same, she didn't want to have to do it all again. She let the water cascade over her hair and decided: Shirley would have to be tackled, if only to see what was going on.

'Panic, panic, PANIC!' Daisy squealed as she raced into Bella's house, followed by Dominic. Fliss trailed behind, looking sulky. 'We really *do* need one more victim! I mean, *subject*. Obviously. Yes. *Subject*. Three just *won't* work! Saul! One more!' Saul was in the garden, directing the placement of some last-minute tubs of Japanese anemones. He took his time coming into the house, possibly, Bella thought, building up some inner strength to face Daisy in full wrath mode. She wondered if he'd mentioned their forthcoming dinner date to Daisy. Something told her he probably hadn't. Anyway, it wasn't anyone else's business but hers and Saul's, so why would he?

Daisy was ranting to whoever was within range, not really focusing on anyone in particular. Today she was wearing open-toed cream canvas boots and a dress made from vintage teal and indigo Hermès horse-head scarves. Over this she had a little aubergine bolero of what looked like long, overstraightened hair. Bella tried not to think it might be human. Whatever it was, it made her think of shrunken heads in museums and the stuffed animals in the prop house she'd visited the other day. *Please,* she thought, don't let this be a look Daisy might insist they all went for. Dominic was looking alarmed, keeping his distance and loitering by the doorway. This certainly wasn't a moment when any adoration for Daisy was apparent in him.

'Ideally, yes, four would have been perfect, but we've talked about this and we decided it would work far better than bringing in someone who is unconnected with the others.' Saul was talking to Daisy quietly, as if hoping she too would lower her volume. A lost cause – if anything, Daisy got louder.

'But I've changed my mind! It's just not *symmetrical*! And besides, it's supposed to be a group of supportive friends – that was the whole point. Three is *never* supportive! Everyone knows that. With three, ganging up happens. Threesomes never work!'

'This one might . . .' Dominic dared to venture. Daisy glared at him. He put his hands up in surrender and backed away.

'But couldn't having just three make it dramatically tense?' Bella suggested, wishing immediately that she hadn't said anything, and half looking for something to hide behind in case of flung missiles from Daisy.

'*Dramatically tense?* I don't need *dramatically tense*!' Daisy hissed. 'I need bodies to dress! I've got a truckful of clothes on their way from designers and stores who are *lending* me all their top tat on the understanding that it will get *highly valuable* airtime! I'm short of that skinny cute one and I need another!'

Saul laughed. 'Ah – I get it!' he said. 'You didn't cancel the Zoe factor from the wardrobe angle, did you? You'd ordered it all in even before you met her and then when she quit, you forgot! And now you've got a whopping great rail of size 8s coming, haven't you?'

Daisy flung herself on to a chair, put her arms out along the table and her head down on them. Silver bracelets clanked as she drummed her small fists up and down in frustration. Her blue-black hair, with today's weavings of peony-pink silk threads, spread across her shoulders like a magpie wing, mingling slightly horrifically with the shiny tresses of the bolero. Dominic, meanwhile, had sloped off into the garden. Bella could see him at the far end, keeping well away from the furore and having a sly cigarette break under the plum tree.

'Have you got her number? The Zoe one?' Daisy's head came up again and her startlingly wide blue eyes were fixed on Bella.

'Sorry – she's gone to stay with her mother,' Bella told her. 'She's feeling terribly morning-sicknessy all the time.'

'Oh God. Terrific,' Daisy sighed. 'OK – we'll work with what there is. It'll be fine. After all,' she rallied and her frightening vampire smile appeared, 'those suppliers need me more than I need them. I *mustn't* lose sight of that. *Mustn't*.'

'Mum?' Molly walked into the kitchen and opened the fridge. 'Mum, are there any like, bananas? I'm hungry?'

'I shoved them into the bread bin in the utility room,' Bella told her, 'and aren't you supposed to be at school till lunchtime? Saul says you can come and watch this afternoon if you like, but you're . . .'

'Oh! You must be Molly! Bella's talked about you!' Daisy leapt across the room to Molly and started tweaking at her hair, which clearly hadn't yet seen a brush this morning. 'And aren't you pretty! You'll do *perfectly*! And you have a lovely youthful shape too!' Daisy went on, pulling Molly's floppy T-shirt back so she could see the contours of her body better.

'Gerroff!' Molly pushed Daisy's hands away and shrank back, cornered against the fridge, 'Do for *what*?' But Bella could see, then, the mists of Molly's morning brain clearing. 'Oh you're Daisy, aren't you!' she suddenly squealed. 'I've seen stuff about you in *heat*. I loved what you made Colleen wear for the Grammies!'

'Molly – *how* divine to meet you! So darling, how would you like to be on my programme?' Daisy sounded as if she were illicitly offering sweets to a child. Then she turned to Saul. 'Perfect for Fashion Victim number four. Oh thank you God.'

'Oh wow, can I really? Like, makeover clothes and hair and stuff? Thanks!' Molly flicked her hair back and pouted, instantly in model mode, 'I thought I was only going to watch. Wait till I tell Carly. And Giles, wow!' Out came her phone, the banana quest all forgotten.

'Er, no. No, Molly, you can't!' Bella stepped in, feeling she was going to have to physically pull her daughter away from this madwoman. She turned to Daisy. 'She's got A levels soon and too much schoolwork to get through. And right now *she's got to get to school*.'

'Oh but *Mum*! That's *soo* not fair! No school this morning, so *nerrrr*, because French is cancelled. Got a text. I've got ages till the exams and this won't take long . . .' She looked at Daisy and Saul anxiously. 'Will it?'

'No! Hardly any time at all! I promise.' Daisy was almost purring at Bella. 'Really, we can just do the minimum with her, and besides, it's *educational*, surely? Don't you agree, Dominic, darling?'

Dominic smiled at her, looking delighted to be consulted but saying nothing, just nodding.

'Taking clothes on and off and having your hair ponced up isn't what I'd call educational.' Bella felt like a prim old party-pooper, but Molly's university chances were surely too important to jeopardize.

'Well, there I disagree,' Daisy said, holding Molly's hand and stroking it. Bella felt cross, as if Daisy were claiming her daughter and putting a spell on her. From the rapt look on Molly's face, that was exactly the case.

'Learning what looks good on you, how to apply make-up so you don't look like a clown, slut or idiot, these are *life skills*. In the end, what Molly learns at these sessions could have a huge effect on her future. Imagine.' Daisy now took hold of Bella's hand too, standing between mother and daughter as if she were about to join them in holy matrimony, 'Imagine, a few years down the line. Molly's at an interview for a job she really, really wants. Say it's between several applicants who have almost identical qualifications. How she presents herself, armed with what Dominic and I can teach her and the confidence she'll get from looking good, could make all the difference in beating the competition. It's a tough, dog-eat-cat world out there when it comes to work; a girl needs all the weapons available to get where she wants to be.'

'OK Daisy, lecture over. This is between Bella and Molly, nothing to do with us.' Saul intervened.

'But Daisy's right, Mum!' Molly seemed to have decided for herself. 'And I can put doing this programme on my personal statement for university. Everything helps.'

'I'm beaten.' Bella felt exhausted, worn down by both Molly and Daisy. She felt Saul squeeze her shoulder, sensed his sympathy in the face of this unstoppable Daisy/Molly juggernaut. And she could, in spite of her objections, see that Daisy had a point – she just wished this could all be done for Molly over a few hours on a weekend instead of intruding into school time. And if this was a hint of what was to come, she could see herself in a week from now: her toffee-coloured hair hacked off to an inch short and hennaed scarlet, killer heels she constantly fell from, ankle-length pencil skirts that she couldn't walk in, cinched-in patent leather belts that stopped her breathing, satin, black, everything she didn't want. And worse, she saw herself staring into a full-length mirror, brainwashed into smiling at her absurd reflection and really believing she loved what she saw. Aaaaagh! Perhaps having Molly onside could even help.

'Thanks Mum! I'm way up with the schoolwork so *please* don't worry! It'll be *ace*!'

'Darling, I know today is going to be difficult . . . but . . .' Shirley found Bella outside the kitchen, watching Nick and the burly one plus two rather feeble-looking boys manhandling the huge lavender sofa in through the garden doors. It wouldn't fit through the front door, and she and Saul had had one of those mutual 'Oh no!' moments when they saw it being unloaded from the truck. It really was one big piece of furniture. Luckily it had fitted through the double gates at the side of the house, and the men had huffed and puffed their way round to the back garden with it.

'Too big, do you think?' she asked Saul as it was plonked on to the walnut floor.

'It'll be fine,' he assured her. 'Just wait till the protective wrapping is off it. It'll look fantastic, trust me. We made a good choice together here.'

'Bella, I really do want to ask you . . .' Shirley persisted.

'OK, OK, I'm all yours. Difficult day, you said? Understatement. So what's with the "but"?' They were surrounded by men. Bella moved her mother further down the garden, away from flapping ears. 'What is it? Are you all right?'

Shirley was looking anxious. Ah, this is it, Bella thought, her heart sinking fast, she's had terrible health news and is about to tell me. But Shirley shook her off and started walking back towards the house where Saul was talking to Nick.

'I just need a lift, late this afternoon, that's all,' she said. 'But I can see it's not the best time. No, in fact, don't worry at all – I'll go on the bus. On my own. I'll be fine. Honestly.'

Bella followed her and sighed, recognizing a certain amount of subtle emotional blackmail. Every mother's speciality, she thought ruefully. She'd done it to Molly, one day Molly would certainly do it to her children. If Shirley was being devious enough to resort to this, she must be pretty much all right. If it was something serious, she'd be more straightforward.

'Now Bella,' her mother lowered her voice, 'I just had a call from the police. Later today would, it seems, be a good time for me to go and get my little piece of trouble dealt with.'

'Your caution? I was going to ask you about that. I was surprised you hadn't heard anything about it by now.'

'Shh! I realize Nick knows, but I don't want the whole crew calling me ASBO Gran or something, thank you.'

'Telling you today is a bit short notice, isn't it? I thought they'd send you an appointment.'

'Um . . . they did,' Shirley admitted. 'They sent a letter to Walton. Lois has redirected my mail and it's only just arrived. I have to go later this afternoon or early evening, and I'd quite like you to come with me. If it's not too much trouble.'

'Yes, of course I'll take you,' Bella said. 'Saul said we should be done for today before five, if that's not too late. Are you feeling a bit wobbly about this police thing?'

Shirley hesitated. 'Er . . . no, I don't think so. It all seems relatively straightforward, though I have to say . . .'

'Are you changing your mind about saying you're guilty? Because you can, you know, I'm sure. No one could blame you for deciding you don't want a criminal record after all.'

'No, it's not that. I'll live with it. No, I was just going to say it'll be nice to have you there with me. I mean, apart from at Jules's last night, we don't really see a lot of each other at the moment, do we?'

Bella looked at her, wondering what on earth to say to that. 'Um, well actually, isn't it mostly *you* who is always on the way out of the house?'

'Ah yes, but . . .' Shirley smiled in a disconcertingly dreamy way. 'Yes, OK you're right, I am. But later, we'll have a proper catch-up, all right? There are one or two things I need to talk to you about.'

'You don't sound very pleased for me. I thought you'd be really excited about it, like I am. What's wrong with you?'

Giles was being a disappointment. Molly sat on the bench under the plum tree, talking to him on her mobile. She'd thought he'd be really happy for her, really up for seeing her on telly all kitted up with gorgeous make-up and amazing hair and shoes to kill for, but he was being all grunty and moody.

'Sorry,' he muttered. She waited. Nothing else. No reason why he couldn't communicate more than one word at a time to her. So far there'd been about three: 'Hello', 'Great' and now 'Sorry'. The 'Great' hadn't sounded genuine, either, when she'd babbled on about the programme.

'Are you jealous – is that it? Because I'll be getting lots of attention?' Molly suggested. She could see the silent Dominic man watching her. For someone who was supposed to be a style guru, she was surprised he didn't do something with his own hair. It wasn't quite a comb-over, but it looked like he backcombed it to boost volume. In a high wind it would all move sideways like a dislodged bird's nest. He was sitting on the doorstep up by the kitchen, staring down the garden at her and making her want to go and hide behind the camellia. But that would look obvious and rude. And she didn't want to get on the wrong side of the man who was going to restyle her hair and who'd be organizing her make-up and all the pretty accessories for whatever mad stuff Daisy dressed her up in. Ooh, she couldn't wait! All she needed was someone to tell who'd be almost as excited as she was.

'Are you still there?' Molly said to Giles. 'You're all quiet. What's wrong with you?' What had changed since lunchtime yesterday? He'd been all over her when they'd been lying on the school field over by the trees and he'd been pinning her to the grass, tickling her. She'd loved that, all the closeness and the sexiness of it. If they'd only been alone and not surrounded by half the stupid school and a rounders match just yards away. He'd gone home soon after though, having a free study afternoon.

'Hey – did you hear about Aimee?' she asked him. Maybe some gossip-sharing would change his mood.

'Yep,' he grunted. Nothing more.

'Look – are you like *really* busy or something? Am I interrupting some essential Wii game or wha'ever? Because you're so totally not into talking to me right now, are you?'

'Sorry,' he said again, sounding even more distant. 'Laters, maybe, yeah?'

And he'd gone. It wasn't a lot by way of a goodbye. None of the usual 'love you babe', no down-the-phone kisses or reluctance to end the call. Molly looked at her mobile as if expecting it to tell her what the real problem was. She got up and went back to the house. As she walked through the kitchen, heading for the stairs and her own room, she looked back. Dominic had got up and was still watching her as he, too, went towards the kitchen. Get used to it, she told herself. Millions are going to be watching you. Millions minus, if his mood was anything to go by, Giles.

If this was supposed to be a way of easing them all into the whole makeover thing, it was pretty unnerving. The four fashion victims sat in a row on the lavender sofa facing Daisy. Fliss skipped around somewhere in the background, making notes on a clipboard with a lilac Barbie pen. The guest colour consultant was a bony woman in her mid-fifties called Esme. She wore a startlingly vivid azure and black wrapover dress which could find very few curves to cling to, and her hip bones, when she walked, seemed to travel several inches ahead of the rest of her.

By contrast with Esme and the ever-spectacular Daisy, Bella felt that she and her three co-victims were at a terrible disadvantage, having had their faces scrubbed of all hint of colour by Simone the make-up artist. Psychologically, if they wanted the victims to be in a position of useful vulnerability for maximum acquiescence, the plan was highly effective. Bella's plea to Simone for some Clarins Flash Balm to tighten up her skin had met with the incomprehension she'd have expected from someone too young to know how useful it could be. Bella had had to slide up to her room and sneak down a tube of it, which she, Jules and Dina had applied secretly and hastily in the downstairs loo, in the hope it would give them an instant magical facelift effect.

In addition to the starkly naked skin, they were now wearing white hairdresser-style gowns from neck to knee and had their hair hidden under white towelling bands. 'I'm trying to think this moment has to be the *nadir*,' Dina muttered to Bella, as Simone raced across the room to give Daisy's already perfect maquillage a brisk brush-over.

'Oh please, let's hope so. Surely it can only get better?' Bella murmured back.

'It's OK to talk; in fact we really want you to, to make it natural,' Saul reassured them as he moved the young cameraman sideways a foot or two. 'Preferably not all at once, if you can manage that for the sake of sound clarity, but we can always edit.'

And then, suddenly, they were under way. Daisy did a confident and word-perfect short introduction, explaining how colour was going to be the starting point rather than the usual makeover-show finishing one.

'It's the difference between someone saying, "Oh I like your dress," and them saying, "Oh you're looking great!"' she concluded. 'With the first, it isn't the wearer they're noticing, but the clothes. However stunning they may be, your clothes are there to reflect *you*, not the other way round. Esme is our colour expert – she'll explain what she's doing as she goes along. Esme?'

'Thank you, Daisy! Now, here we have our four blank canvases . . . I can see we have our work cut out here, ladies. Daisy showed me some "before" shots of you in your usual clothing choices.' Her tinkly little laugh struck a snidely patronizing note.

Bella immediately felt aggrieved. She glanced sideways at Jules and realized she was feeling exactly the same. *Not*, surely, the most tactful start.

'What I'd like to do,' Esme continued brightly, 'is begin by asking you all to say which colours you already think really suit each other, and which you think don't do you any favours. Bella, would you like to start? As Molly's mother, you must have an opinion on what looks good on her.'

Molly's huge eyes were challenging her mother to *dare* criticize her clothes choices.

'Well, she's seventeen,' Bella said. 'What *doesn't* look good?' Molly beamed at her. 'But . . . well, I always think she does look very washed out in grey. It's a very *old* colour for her. And baby pink too, actually – she almost vanishes in it . . .'

'Thanks Mum!' Molly glowered. 'I've got like *loads* of grey?'

'And what about Dina? Is there a colour you've ever thought you'd like to see her in more often?' Esme asked.

Bella thought of Dina in the restaurant the other night. It seemed like months ago but was barely a week. James had twice since asked after 'your beautiful friend'.

'Dark green,' she said immediately. 'She looks wonderful in it. It does something to her eyes.'

Bella glanced across at Saul. He was leaning against the worktop by the sink, smiling at her. Laughing, she assumed. Now he'd seen her face stripped back to nature and her hair wrapped away out of sight, would he still want to have dinner with her? Even waking up first thing in the morning, she could look better than this. Not that he was ever likely to see her in that context. Definitely not.

It was hot under the lights. Simone kept coming over with tissues to wipe dewy beads from foreheads, as Esme explained about the colours being coded down to four 'seasons'. She draped metre-square silky swatches of subtly shaded colour across their shoulders, and while watching each other by way of a big mirror, they were supposed to discover which tones made them look alive and bright and which made their skin tones look muddy and unwell.

'And when Esme has finished with you, you'll all get your personal colour swatches,' Daisy said, dancing around with a heap of scarves, and then producing a little folder of fabric scraps to show the camera. 'We all need to carry them whenever we go clothes shopping, isn't that right, Esme? I *never* go anywhere without mine!' she gushed. 'I'm a *summer*.'

'Exactly.' Esme simpered at Daisy. 'You are *such* a summer; always cool, soft and light!'

'Yeah, right,' Saul whispered in Bella's direction, giving her a terrible urge to giggle.

'This is really a load of bollocks, isn't it?' Dina, her shoulders heaped to chin-level with shiny fabric squares, suddenly said to Esme by way of the mirror. Then she turned to Saul. 'Am I allowed to say "bollocks"? I'm not, am I? Sorry.'

'Could you maybe do that bit again but say "rubbish", this time?' he suggested, nodding to the cameraman to keep going.

Esme stood wide-eyed and shocked by the sudden rebellion, holding up a piece of maroon cloth like a flag and glaring at Dina's reflection. Daisy smirked in the background, looking delighted. Bella, Molly and Jules sat silent, waiting for Esme to fire some verbal shrapnel.

'But it *is* mad,' Dina persisted. 'I mean, honestly, I'm sitting here pretending I can see that petrol blue looks better on Bella than the royal blue and really, it's not so different. And no, I'm *not* colour-blind.'

'And we've got no make-up on. And we're under all these mad lights,' Jules joined in. 'No one sees us like this, not in real life. So this could be all wrong.'

'And I feel really happy wearing grey,' Molly chipped in moodily, chewing a nail.

'You're far too young for grey. Try purple,' Esme snapped. She looked furious, as if she'd like to slap them all.

'Purple's *goths*,' Molly scoffed.

'And if Jules keeps buying blue like she said she usually does, maybe it's because she's old enough to know which colours suit her by now?' Bella added to the fray.

'Don't you *want* to improve your colour sense? You're being terribly negative!'

Bella caught sight of Esme's left foot, slightly raised. She was clearly *that* close to having a stampy tantrum.

'That dress doesn't actually suit you, you know.' Dina looked Esme up and down. 'That vivid blue is far too harsh. Something softer would work much better.'

'But I'm a *winter*,' Esme hissed. 'Always have been. This shade is in my spectrum.'

'Children! *Please*, can we get back to why we're here?' Daisy clapped her hands together like a teacher rounding up infants from the sand table.

'Children? *Children?*' Jules glared at her, pulled off both her white gown and her hairband and flung them on the sofa. 'You see, that's the thing with all this! Being told *this is right, this is wrong*. We *aren't* children, Daisy!'

Jules was looking frankly menacing. Saul stepped forward, nervous that she would strangle Daisy with one of Esme's fabric samples.

'We'll take a break there, I think. OK, everybody? Back in ten . . .'

'So apparently I'm a "spring".' Bella was keeping the chat level light and bright as she drove Shirley to the police station. Her mother seemed not quite herself, and Bella assumed this was because she felt apprehensive about the coming interview.

'Yes. I could have told you that,' Shirley commented sharply.

'Yes – I'm sure you could,.' Bella agreed. 'We weren't very kind to poor Esme. She was only doing her job but we gave her a hard time. Saul and Daisy decided that us being stroppy made better footage than having us all meekly accepting our colour lot, so Esme had to cut quickly to the chase and leave us bickering about whether cerise was possible on anyone at all, *ever*. And I can't ever see me in the shade of mustard that she raved about. How can you trust a woman in orange eyeshadow?'

'Hmm.' Shirley seemed miles away. As well she might, thought Bella, realizing she'd overdone the distracting technique.

'Look . . . are you feeling nervous about this? If they'll allow it, do you want me to come in with you?'

'No, no, I'll be all right.' Shirley was breezy again. 'I mean, what can they say? That I've been a naughty girl and not to do it again? I'll just agree with everything they say and get it over with as fast as possible.'

'You didn't do it though, did you. That's what's bugging you.'

'I did it. But not on purpose,' Shirley said. 'I'm not changing my mind about admitting it, so please don't try to make me.'

'Wouldn't dream of it,' Bella muttered to herself, making a turn into the town's car park.

The duty sergeant looked from one to the other of them when Bella told him they'd turned up for a caution, then went off to find someone to deal with them.

'He can't decide which of us looks guilty,' Bella giggled.

'It's obviously me,' Shirley whispered back. 'You're in old jeans and I'm dressed up for the occasion.'

A uniformed girl who looked barely older than Molly led Shirley away. Shirley glanced back and smiled at Bella, who then sat down to wait in the reception area, wishing the place was supplied, like a dentist's waiting room, with magazines. Once they were out of here, she planned to take her mother to a tea room or to a pub and get her to talk about her future plans. Just possibly she was simply waiting till this little ordeal was over before getting on with her life as normal. However blasé Shirley seemed to be, having this near-conviction hanging over her must have been a worry.

Shirley was back in under ten minutes, smiling broadly as if she'd been told the root-canal work she'd dreaded wasn't going to be necessary after all.

'So it was OK then, was it? No horrible surprises?' Bella asked as they left the police station. She felt glad to be out in the open. Being in that place with its posters picturing wanted suspects and warnings about gun crime, knife amnesties and the dangers of drugs was enough to unnerve even the most innocent visitor.

'It was fine. They didn't treat me like a demented idiot, which was a plus, but of course they had to underline how serious my crime was. I've promised I'll never do it again. I just hope I don't.'

Shirley was striding back towards the car park at a

furious pace, impressing Bella with her balance on what must have been four-inch heels. Shirley's mid-blue footless tights impressed her too. Not many women past seventy could get away with that look, but combined with a simple slate-grey shift dress (*not* egg-shaped) and a lot of chunky silver bangles, on Shirley it was a sheer head-turner.

'Look – shall we go and have a quick early drink somewhere?' Bella suggested, starting to feel breathless at the pace. 'We could talk . . .'

'Oh no, darling. I haven't got time! I have to meet someone and I don't want to be late! We can talk in the car though, now I've got that over.'

They'd reached the car park and Bella quickly glanced at the Mini's windscreen, half-expecting a parking fine even though she knew she had time left on her ticket. It would be Sod's Law that it had fallen off the dashboard or that she'd put it there upside down. Once inside the car, with her mother suitably captive and willing to chat, she began with, 'You seem very settled at our place.'

'Oh, it's very comfortable,' Shirley agreed. 'It's lovely to see so much of Molly and with all this television hoo-ha going on, we aren't short of entertainment, are we?'

'But . . . I just wondered, is there anything . . . er . . . wrong? I mean, have you decided you don't want to live at your flat any more? Are you . . . I mean are you *well*?'

Shirley looked at her, amazed. 'Of course I'm well! Why ever would you think I wasn't? I wouldn't be going out so much if I wasn't, would I?'

'Ah. Good point. Yes, you are forever sliding out to "meet friends". Anyone in particular?' It had briefly crossed Bella's mind that Shirley might be consulting doctors, but her mother did have a glow and energy that illness would surely have wiped out. Maybe the most stylish woman in Walton was simply having a lot more fun strutting her Betty Jackson and DKNY stuff in a more central arena.

'Has anyone ever told you, Bella, that you're something of a control freak? You should be pleased I'm having a busy social life. I'm a long way from being ready for a slow existence of slippers and cats.'

'Oh I am happy for you, honestly. It's just that you're not being very communicative about it, that's all.'

'You really want to ask me when I'm going home, don't you?' Shirley was way ahead. She could easily have pleaded not guilty in court, Bella thought, there'd have been no danger of a medical report finding anything blunt about her faculties.

'Well I did wonder if you'd gone off living in your flat, if you maybe didn't want to go back there for some reason. If you feel like moving, I can help you organize it all.'

'When I move out of there it won't be to live with you,

Bella, don't worry. Being a house guest is fine, but if we lived together permanently we'd be like two cats in a box,' Shirley said. 'And yes, in answer to your earlier question, there is someone special I've been meeting, and I'm afraid I must confess I've been using your premises simply because getting to where this friend is based when in London is far easier from there. I probably should have told you sooner but . . . well a woman likes a bit of privacy, even from her own family. There's a lot I don't know about you too, isn't there? Such as you no longer mention that married chap you were seeing, the "mistake" you mentioned over supper. I take it he's now off the scene.'

'All over, a while back. Nothing to tell. He ended up not worth talking about, trust me. But don't change the subject; what about this friend? Is it a man?'

'Of course it's a man! He's called Dennis and we met on the cruise back in July. We're seeing a *lot* of each other and having a wonderful time.'

Bella suddenly realized that since she'd got back in the car she hadn't been breathing properly. Oh the relief that her mother wasn't hiding some deep, dark illness that she'd been struggling to deal with by herself but had simply been having fun, swanning around with a man friend.

'Oh now this *is* exciting!' She couldn't have been more delighted for her mother – Shirley had been solitary for many years now, since she too had given up on 'mistakes'. 'So you two have been seeing each other for months? How lovely for you! Do we get to meet him? Where does he live? Does he have a family as well? What's he like?'

'Slow down! He lives in Dorset, he has grown-up children and a couple of grandchildren and I'd love you to meet him very soon. We just wanted some non-family time for a while, just as a couple with no ties – the way you can be when you're young and free. And then last week over tea at the Ritz, he asked me to marry him.'

Shirley had come out with that one as casually as if Dennis had asked her for the next dance, and it took a second or two for the words to sink into Bella's brain as she pulled out abruptly into the roundabout traffic and almost collided with a BMW. She was aware of waving fists and several blasts from more than one car horn.

'Holy f—! Er . . . good grief! What did you tell him?'

'I said yes, of course!'

# TWELVE

Oh, a day of peace – if you didn't count the chaos of film kit all over the ground floor or getting used to the idea of your mother suddenly deciding to marry someone you'd not yet met. All the same, Bella stretched out in bed and savoured the luxury of having twenty-four hours of quiet and calm in the house. Daisy and Dominic had a long-scheduled appointment with a visiting American film star who needed the kind of fast and thorough wardrobe update that you could, frankly, only get in Europe, so they were off to Selfridges way before opening time to check through their selection of clothes, shoes and accessories to take to her hotel. 'A piece of piss,' Daisy had confessed as soon as the rather defeated Esme had been soothed and packed off. 'She's a skinny, big-gobbed sort with perfect posture and years of red-carpet practice. She'd look good in a binbag.'

Dominic had nodded slowly, watching Daisy to make sure, Bella now thought, in the light of Shirley's view of his attachment, that she'd noticed him agreeing with her.

'And career-wise, she couldn't act her way out of one,' Daisy then bitched through her scary smile. 'She couldn't do sincerity if her pet puppy died right there on the set.'

'And thus you completely shred the hard-won professional rep of a three-times Oscar nominee!' Saul had commented wryly. 'Way to go, Daisy!'

Keith the cat was stretched out across the end of Bella's bed. James would have had a fit if he'd seen that. No pets, had been his adamant rule when he'd lived at the house, convinced that they were put on the planet solely for the carriage of germs and disease from the outside world into his near-sterile sanctuary. Bella wondered if Molly remembered that her instant reaction on being so very gently told that Daddy wouldn't be living at home any more was a hugely excited, 'So can we get a puppy?' Bella had been tempted to go along with the idea, having in mind something big and protective and friendly, along the lines of Nana in *Peter Pan*, but the thought of taking care of two young children alone, as well as having to clear up after a whopping great dog, had been just too much. They'd settled on the spoilt and lazy kitten that was now the big, sprawling Keith. She reached down and stroked his ears. He twitched slightly and stretched out a broad paw, claws showing, browny-pink pads flexing.

What an idle life cats have, she thought; how blissful to know that all your needs are catered for by one devoted person. Not that she'd have wanted her own life to be like that, but having had almost total lone responsibility for the home and children made her pretty fierce about James wanting to stroll in and cash in half the house. But today, Bella resolved that James, the filming and all hassles would be firmly off the radar. She would concentrate on catching up on some work, if partly to keep tonight's dinner with Saul out of her mind and her adrenalin level under control. She didn't want – or intend – to feel all fluttery about a man again. It took ludicrous amounts of energy and brain space. It led to trouble and let-down, and the recovery-time from Rick wasn't, she felt, quite over yet: she was sticking with the no-involvement rule. Not that getting involved with a man who wasn't really over the loss of an adored wife was anywhere close to an option.

There was plenty to do with this spare day; Charlotte had emailed, wanting an update on the progress of the shoot, and nudging for a few gossip snippets to keep her interest going. And Bella's publisher was wanting her to check over the cover copy for the next Orchard Girls book.

And there was her mother . . . since she'd come out with her 'I'm getting married' bombshell, she had, maddeningly, not been around to talk about it. On her return from the police station she had had a shower, packed an overnight bag and raced eagerly off into the evening to meet Dennis, assuring Bella she'd be back the following afternoon. She and Dennis were off to break their good news to his son Toby in Oxford, and planned to stay overnight at the Randolph hotel. Bella had about a hundred questions, if she could only pin Shirley down for a proper conversation. She tried the term 'stepfather', and found it rather strange and slightly wrong, as if it turned her into a little girl again. Maybe this Dennis too would find the idea a bit flinch-making, and they could happily agree it was never to be uttered. But most of all, she hoped he was a Nice Man. He must be. Shirley had had a few suitors over the years and had always, in the end, decreed them 'not enough fun'. How lovely that she must have found one who was. Never too late, was the message there.

From downstairs, Bella could hear the sounds of Molly crashing around in the kitchen. Strange how quite a delicately built girl could manage to make so much noise and be so heavy-handed while doing nothing more physically demanding than sliding bread into a toaster and taking butter and marmalade out of the fridge. Bella hoped she wasn't scratching the new worktop or splodging marmalade on the glass splashback. A little part of her was feeling this wasn't quite her kitchen just now but belonged to Saul's production company, which meant they should all treat it as if they were house guests. Ridiculous, but unshakeable; after all, it was possible that at the end of the filming, in a moment of fervent site-clearing, some of the crew would simply unbolt all the new doors, lift the worktop and load it all into a truck while she was down at Waitrose. As with so many things in life, it was probably best not to get too attached to it too soon.

Bella climbed out of bed, put on her cosy old towelling bathrobe and padded down the stairs. Keith followed, miaowing for breakfast and plaiting himself dangerously around her feet.

'You OK, Moll?' Bella asked, going to switch the kettle on. 'School early today?'

'Mmm.' Molly, over at the table and flicking through a magazine, mumbled through a mouthful of toast. 'Carly's pickin' m'yup.'

'That's lucky. Oh and you're not wearing grey! You look lovely – that vanilla top is perfect. You've been checking through your colour swatches, haven't you? Maybe there's something in it after all.'

'Er, like *nooo*?' Molly stared at her as if she'd suggested she'd stolen every item she was wearing. 'This old top was just like *in the drawer*?'

Bella laughed, not believing her. 'Funny how you and I were both spring . . . though in my case no spring chicken, of course.'

Molly smiled, her mood softening. 'Oh Mum, don't say that. You look great. For . . .'

'For my age. Thanks.'

'No, I didn't mean . . . I meant that you look really good ~ for any age. Or you can do. When you try, like going out and that. I was so right about you and black though, wasn't I?'

'Yes, yes, I know. I just wish I'd known years ago – I still think it's the useful lazy-woman's option. Listen Molly, as it happens, I'm going out tonight. Will you be all right, just you and your gran? I'm going out for a quick dinner with . . . er . . . Saul.'

'Ooh! I knew it! He fancies you! And of course I'll be all right; I'm nearly eighteen, not *eight*, Mum.'

'OK, OK, sorry! And as for fancying me, he *like so* doesn't, as you'd say. It's just a friendly thing, a sort of thank you for letting them use this place at such short notice. Though as I've got pretty much a new kitchen out of it I should really have invited him out, I suppose.'

' "Just friendly". Yeah right! So where are you going and what are you going to wear?'

'Er . . . oh a restaurant in Covent Garden . . . and I haven't thought what to wear yet. I'd wear my lovely black dress but . . . I don't know, I try not to believe in all that colour stuff, but I can't feel the same about that frock now.' She sighed, thinking of her shiny Joseph dress. That could have been so perfect, but apparently only if she'd bought it in purple. And possibly if she didn't still associate it with the Rick disaster. Oh well. Not that it mattered what she wore, really. As she'd said, this was just a friendly thing. She really wasn't going to race into the town just for a very quick look-see at the shops in case the absolutely perfect pull-it-all-together little frock was on the first rail she looked at, begging her to take it home and make her evening perfect. No.

The kettle was boiling. Decaffeinated tea now, she decided as she felt the adrenalin zapping again. She chose a tea bag from one of the crew's selection of boxes, something that might minimize the risk of blood-pressure overload.

'You should ask Gran. She always looks great. She could do that Daisy's job *so* easily – she'll tell you what to wear.'

'If she were here,' Bella said. 'She's . . .'

'Out with Dennis. Yes I know.' Molly took her plate and mug to the sink and hesitated for a moment.

'The dishwasher's on the left,' Bella reminded her. 'Where it's always been. So you know about Dennis?'

'Oh ha ha,' Molly said. 'Did she tell *you* about Dennis?'

'Well . . . yes.' Bella was wary. It was down to Shirley to do the marriage announcement. It wouldn't be fair to break the news to Molly without her say-so – or did she know about it already and was thinking the same? 'Why, what's she said to you?'

Molly looked guiltily breezy and replied, 'Oh nothing much! Only that she's *seeing* him!'

'OK – well I don't know much about him either. I'm sure she'll say a lot more about him soon.'

'Yeah, maybe. Gotta go. Just going to brush my teeth. And Mum?'

'What is it? Are you sure you're OK about tonight? If Gran's off out again, you could have Carly round or someone else; I'll leave you some fancy instant food in the fridge if you want.'

'Giles. Can he come over tonight?' Molly looked at the ground, suddenly finding something fascinating about the walnut floor.

'Yes, of course he can. So long as . . .'

'Eeuw, Mum, don't say it! I promise! And just to make sure, you could lock your bedroom door!' And she was gone – a flash of messy wheat-coloured hair, her vanilla top and skinny jeans and she was up the stairs, the cat (now full and needing yet more sleep) bounding up after her.

'I only meant . . . don't let him get in the way of your schoolwork!' Bella went to the doorway and called rather lamely after her.

'No you didn't, Mum!' Molly yelled back over the banisters. 'You meant "Make sure you don't get pregnant!" Maybe I'll remind *you* about that when you go out with that Saul bloke tonight!'

Good grief, Bella thought, laughing as she went back to her tea and put a croissant into the microwave, when did it become OK for daughters to talk to their mothers like that?

Bella had dealt with emails, written a few taster paragraphs about the programme for Charlotte and wasted half an hour looking through the estate agent details of the dismal rabbit-hutch premises that James thought would suit her so perfectly. Now she had, strewn across her bed, just about every outfit that she'd bought over the past decade. For the first time, she rather wished Daisy had insisted on trawling through each of the fashion victims' own wardrobes. In a bossy instant she would have been able to give Bella an idea of what 'mid-season' was about, and how to dress for going out with a man who was Just a Friend on an autumn night that might turn chilly. 'Layers are *key*,' she could almost hear Daisy insisting vehemently into her ear, completely disregarding the fact that layers, however thin the fabric of each, do tend to bulk out anyone who is over a size 8. *That* much, Bella didn't need Daisy to tell her.

In a decisive moment, Bella picked out skirts, trousers, a couple of dresses and three jackets, none of which she'd worn for ages, and stuffed them into a binbag. Wow, that felt good. She looked around the room and, still intent on purging, added a heap of no-longer-used make-up items.

'There!' she said, feeling satisfied as she started hanging her diminished collection back in the wardrobe. 'That's so much better.'

'Talking to yourself?'

Bella heard herself shriek and her heart rated doubled. James was standing in the bedroom doorway, smirking at her.

'How the hell did you get in? And what are you doing up *here*?'

'You'd left the garden doors open,' he said, not shifting from the doorway. She moved closer, brandishing a metal coat hanger, and he backed away.

'I opened them to let fresh air in, not stale husbands,' Bella snapped. 'You can't just sneak up the stairs like that.'

'Sorry. I didn't mean to scare you,' he said, 'I only meant . . .'

'Look, James, I don't care what you meant. You can't

make free with the premises after all this time, no matter what it says on the deeds.'

'Deeds. Yes, that's what I've come about.'

'Then you should have called me. Right now, I'm busy. I'm sorting.'

'So I see. Ready for a relocation situation?' he asked eagerly, eyeing the remaining clothes on the bed. She pushed past him, going down the stairs with her bulging binbag.

'No, not for moving. Just to get rid of too much stuff. Come on James, out of my house. I've got things to do. We can catch up another time, just give me a call.'

She heard him mutter '*Our* house' not quite under his breath, but let it go.

'Oh but while I'm here . . . er . . . your friend Dina?' James lingered in the hallway. 'Is she, you know . . . spoken for?'

Bella smiled, feeling almost fond of him for a moment. 'Oh James, in spite of all your corporate-speak nonsense that sounds really quite sweet and old-fashioned!'

He shrugged. 'Just a small but apposite paradigm shift in terminology,' he said. 'It seemed to fit. Anyway, is she? I'm just curious.'

'No, she's not with anyone just now, is the answer to your question. Dina's husband died suddenly after an episode with . . .' Bella hesitated; this was Dina's private territory. 'He had a heart attack, several years ago. Overdid it in sport, all very unexpected.'

'Sport' was broad enough. No need to mention the prostitute or the school-style cane.

'And she hasn't found someone since?' James looked quite excited. 'Has the world gone mad? A beautiful woman like that on her own? One who cares about soiled cutlery? She seems the sort to keep Dettol wipes in her car.' Bella thought he looked more thrilled at this possibility than he would have if Dina had kept an extensive array of pleasure-enhancing lubricants in her Fiesta's glove box.

'Do you know, I think she probably does. Her car always smells extremely pine-bleachy, that's for sure; like a freshly cleaned public loo. And she keeps special driving shoes too, and takes off her street ones before she gets in.' James closed his eyes in bliss; he looked close to swooning. One brief meeting in the restaurant and it was the dental nurse thing all over again: instant infatuation.

'Dina is part of our *Fashion Victims* programme, so she's here most days just now,' Bella went on. 'Tell you what, why don't you give me a call some time tomorrow and I'll see if I can fix a meeting for the two of you?'

Well, she thought, as he bounced happily back to his car, at least it might distract him from selling the house.

* * *

'You mean you don't want to come over? Empty house?'

What do I have to do, beg? Why has he gone remote all of a sudden? Molly sat on the stairs wondering this as she listened to Giles breathing into the phone. Breathing, saying nothing. What was that about? Usually he never stopped talking. And where had he *been* in the last few days? He hadn't turned up in school. She'd texted him four times today – not one reply.

'You know, empty house as in *nobody home*? Giles? Are you still there?'

'Yup. Am here. I just, I like can't come tonight. Got stuff on. Late with coursework. Sorry babe. Another time, yeah?'

'Are you blowing me out here, Giles? Totally, as in for good? Because that's what it sounds like to me.' Molly chewed her thumbnail, dreading the answer 'Yes'.

'No! Not at all! Still love you Molly.' He was muttering it, as if someone were close by and listening. Perhaps they were. Probably it was Giles's mother, who was one of those energetic gym mums who whizzed around the house and seemed to be everywhere, always smiling and big-eyed and pleased to see everyone and wanting Molly to talk hair and clothes with her because, she complained, she was outnumbered by men in the house and in need of girly chat. Nice and friendly as she was, no wonder Giles preferred to see Molly when he was safely off the premises. The last time they'd been in his room (just watching *Doctor Who*, luckily), his mother had bounced in clutching a copy of *Marie Claire* to ask for an opinion on a cropped studded-leather jacket. Did Molly think she was too old to wear it? Yes was the clear answer, but 'No' had to be said, yet in a tactful, 'deep down I really mean yes' way.

Molly had come to the end of her patience. To her it was a clear case of 'Still love you, BUT . . .' Too cowardly to face her and come right out with the truth, was he? Her heart was thumping painfully and she felt choking tears on their way. Something had changed since he'd rolled her on the grass under the trees on the school field, and she had no idea what. And it looked like she wasn't going to find out in a hurry, as there was nothing coming down the phone but faint and distant breathing. Not very even breathing come to that, though not uneven in a *good* way.

'Yeah right. OK. You love me. Like you're giving me reason to believe it. Let me know when you're ready for a conversation. Bye.'

She clicked her phone shut and went into the kitchen. There was no Mum to hang out with – she'd got a date. No Gran – so had she. Everyone was out having man-friend fun and she was left at home with Keith the cat, who was asleep, shedding fur all over the ridiculous purple velvet sofa. Fliss would be cross in the morning; it would be her job to brush it all off.

She had a look in the fridge, took out the remains of last night's shepherd's pie and shoved it into the microwave. When the *ping* went she looked at it, felt slightly ill and left it on the worktop, unable to face eating it because all her insides were already filled up with a solid lump of sheer misery. She went and lay on the sofa alongside the cat, looking out to the tall tobacco flowers in the garden, almost luminous white in the deepening dusk. Carly – she'd talk to Carly. She might come up with what was wrong with Giles. And even if she couldn't, she'd do her best to cheer her up. That's what best mates were for.

Mon Plaisir, on the cusp of Soho and Covent Garden, was a restaurant that Bella had been to before, though that time it had been a bit of a rush as she'd been there for an early pre-theatre supper with a bunch of women friends. She remembered it for the speedy service, friendly French staff and pretty, slightly quirky decor. She arrived early, but not by so much as to look embarrassingly eager, and as the cab dropped her off in the crowded narrow street, she could see Saul crossing the road to meet her.

'Bella!' he said, kissing her. 'You're looking gorgeous!' So the simple fallback – yet non-black – choices were the best in the long run: a three-year-old silky ginger dress with tiny cream spots (Jigsaw), cinched in with a chocolate obi-style belt (Toast), cream crêpey jacket (Handwritten).

'Oh . . . thanks! So are you!' Well, he was – why shouldn't she say so? So simple for men: an unstructured blue-grey jacket plus white linen shirt equalled casually instant style. It was funny, it struck her now, that men wore such a limited range of items: basic shirts, jackets – they didn't vary *that* much in design and yet some men had the knack of looking wonderfully comfortable and effortless, whereas others seemed always stiff and awkward and as if they'd been forced reluctantly into their outfits by bossy uniformed nannies. Saul was one of the former sorts, James, regrettably, one of the latter; when he wasn't wearing a tie, he kept touching his neck as if worried that something vital was missing and that he was bordering on embarrassing exposure. Saul looked as if he didn't actually possess a tie. She tried not to think of him owning a black one for funerals, one that was stashed away in a corner of a drawer since the day he'd buried his adored wife. Now wasn't the time to be morbid.

They were given a corner table, at the L of the padded banquette seating. 'Oh good,' Bella said as they sat down. 'I really don't much like sitting opposite people, do you? It always seems a bit remote and formal, like a job interview. I much prefer this right-angle thing.'

'Me too, and I also think the side-by-side thing is a bit

odd too,' he agreed. 'As if you're on a bus. And if it's with someone you don't know well, there's that leg-touching thing that you can't avoid and you're wondering if they think it's deliberate. And maybe it is, but then you wonder the same about them . . . Oh, sorry, Bella, I'm waffling!'

'You are a bit!' she told him, amused that he too seemed a bit nervous. 'But it's OK. And I'm glad that so far we agree we're happy with the seating arrangements.'

'Yes. It's an excellent start,' he said, all pretend serious. 'Always good to begin *without* a disagreement, I think.'

The waitress handed them menus and asked about drinks.

'Champagne, yes?' Saul suggested.

'Mmm, thanks, that would be . . .'

'Another plus on the non-disagreement side. I'll stop counting now, I promise. So – do you have any colour restrictions on food today? Green only? Or are you going to be really tricky to feed and insist on blue?' he teased.

'Not green; it's Thursday so . . . ooh let me see, it's red – I'll have to have red mullet and tomatoes. I can eat nothing else today.' Bella scanned over the menu quickly. She was quite hungry, but the mildly anxious sort of hungry where she knew that if she were suddenly faced with a large plate of something, she'd only be able to eat a quarter of it before the butterflies inside her crowded out her appetite. Ridiculous really, to feel all teenage like this. Saul was such a warm friendly sort, so easy to be with, she really should simply relax and enjoy herself. Instead, behind the butterflies, she had a feeling of mild dread, as if this evening really mattered and that if it all went wrong, nothing in her life would ever go right again.

The champagne arrived, Saul raised his glass and smiled at her. 'Here's to . . . er, what shall we drink to? You choose.'

'I suppose it should be to the success of *Fashion Victims*,' Bella said, clinking her glass against his.

'And I suppose you're right, because, being a woman, your lot always are . . . but . . . tonight's *not* about the programme, don't you think?'

'OK, if *not* the programme, then . . . ?'

'To us? Or is that presumptuous?'

Bella hesitated, wondering quite what he meant. To presume he meant it in a start-of-a-romance kind of way would be . . . well . . . *presumptuous*. But the thought of it caused a surge of those inner butterflies. Unexpectedly big ones, almost hawkmoth size. At this rate, she was going to have to swallow a vat of insect repellent to keep them under control. To be safe, she took the humour route. 'OK then, here's to us still being on speaking terms this time tomorrow.'

'Excellent – that's a good one. But I can't think why

we wouldn't be. All is well at the moment,' he looked at his watch, 'a whole fifteen minutes in.'

'Exactly – it's looking good so far,' she agreed, sipping her drink and feeling a sudden elated rush of the bliss of being out, single, free and in the company of a sweet, attractive, friendly man with whom she had no intention of getting involved.

'Wow, that's one hell of a smile!' he commented. 'What brought that on?'

'Um . . . oh I don't know! Just feeling happy to be here, right now, that for a few hours everything's OK and home and the hectic stuff and all dull reality can be left behind?'

He was looking at her, saying nothing but smiling, happy with what he saw. She went on, nervously feeling she should fill the silence gap, 'Now you think I'm nuts, don't you? That I sound like some tragic escapee from suburbia who so rarely gets out that I'm going to behave as if I'm on . . . oh I don't know . . . an overexcited *hen night* or something, and get ludicrously giddy.'

'I don't think that at all. I think you had a rare recognition of a truly happy moment. *Carpe diem* is all very well as a motto, but it only works if you realize the day has been seized. Usually we never notice till it's whizzed past. And don't put yourself down, Bella. I know about your non-suburban work life: you're a successful journalist, a top-class writer and you have a job anyone would envy. But I also know more about *you* than you'd think – remember I've turned a big part of your home upside down. Seen how you are in it, how your family co-exist. I know your tastes in paintings, colours, plants, what's in your fridge, what's on your bookshelves, some of the things that people usually don't get to know till way down the line in a relationship.'

'All a bit one-sided so far, isn't it? Slightly unfair. I don't know anything like that much about you. Only . . .' She hesitated.

'. . . only about how I work and about Lucy. I could have – probably should have – mentioned I'd also had another very brief marriage that didn't last. It was never meant to.'

Bella thought about what her mother had said about those who've been happy rushing to repeat the experience. She didn't want to probe into the mistake it had obviously turned out to be.

'Oh, that's . . . well, sad, I suppose.'

'But Lucy was very much a "life-goes-on" woman,' he continued. 'And she made me promise not to go in for shrines and eternal grieving, and I haven't. She's a great memory, but a long-distant one now. Even so, however much you live in the present, when you lose someone like that, eventually they turn into – oh I don't know – some weird information barrier that has to be got over when you meet someone new. Bit of an elephant-in-the-room thing, really. That's why I told you about her – because if I'd left it much longer and *then* said something, you'd think I was still completely hung up on the past.'

'So you've been single for a while, then?'

Saul laughed. 'Not devoutly so. I'm not a natural at the casual stuff, though. How about you? What's the "after James" story?'

'After James . . . well . . . OK, I'll give you a brief history of my non-love life in one short paragraph,' Bella began.

And it was during the grilled tuna with fennel (both had chosen the same) that Bella realized the old saying really was true after all: looking back now, recounting the Rick-in-New-York episode *did* make her laugh, and Saul too. It came under the heading of fun and self-deprecating anecdotes. She told Saul of her flight from the hotel ('a bit overdramatic, now I come to think of it. I should have just stayed on and enjoyed the city on my own,') and her venomous cursing of the innocent guest, after choosing the wrong bedroom door.

'I was so furious and let down at the time, the last thing I ever expected was that it would become something to giggle about,' she said.

'Maybe it's who you're telling it to,' he suggested.

'OK then, or maybe it's just the way I tell 'em.'

'Pudding?' he asked as the menus were handed out.

'I couldn't, honestly. This has been wonderful, but I really couldn't eat another thing.'

'Coffee, though? Either here, or we could go to the Bar Italia, or . . .'

'Or?' she asked, all mock-innocence.

'Well I've seen yours, maybe you'd like to see mine. Er . . . place of residence, that is!' he clarified, as Bella was overcome with a giggle attack.

'OK – yours. I'd love to. I've seen the office, now show me your rooftop garden.'

Out on the pavement the street was buzzing with crowds let loose from theatres. Every cab had its light out. Saul took Bella's hand and steered her through the throng at Cambridge Circus. 'We could walk there, but . . .' He looked at Bella's shoes, which were strappy, high-ish sandals. 'Those look like car-to-bar shoes only, not really for pavement use, am I wrong?'

'A bit wrong – I'd never wear shoes I couldn't run for a bus in, but it would have to be a not very fast-approaching bus. By Daisy's standards, they are practically flats.'

'By Daisy's standards, everything short of completely perpendicular counts as flats. OK – this is what we'll do, then,' he said, raising an arm towards the traffic. A bicycle rickshaw, driven by a smiling boy, stopped beside them and Saul gave the address. 'Hey, you two romantics,' the boy said in what sounded like an appropriately Italian accent, 'you be warm under blanket and you can snog.'

Bella climbed in, slightly wary of how vulnerable the fragile vehicle would be to the surging buses, cars and taxis. Saul tucked the blanket across them both and put his arm around her. She snuggled close, glad of even this small gesture of protection from the brutal traffic surrounding them. 'Have you ever been in one of these before?' he asked.

'No, never!' she laughed. 'I suppose I think of them as just for the tourists. But tonight I do feel a bit like a tourist myself, seeing this part of the city with you. It must be the unfamiliarity of being in this mad contraption that gives it a whole new angle.'

In truth, it was the excitement of being with Saul, she realized. It was that fragile elation of being with a man whom she was really, really beginning to like and who was quite possibly feeling the same about her. It made the city seem newly radiant; every Soho building looked like an architectural masterpiece, every overspilling ordinary bar seemed gilded and exotic. This was dangerous, heady stuff, she thought, as the enthusiastic and skilled rickshaw driver pedalled madly and wove in and out of the near-static traffic with terrifying verve.

'The driver will be cross with us,' Saul said, pulling her closer towards him.

'Why is that?' she asked.

'Because we're not doing what he told us to do. He said we have to kiss. So I think we should. It's our duty.' His mouth brushed the edge of hers.

'I think we should too . . .' she murmured. 'It would be so wrong to disappoint him.'

# THIRTEEN

This immediate post-coital moment was, Bella recognized, when she might possibly have been thinking, 'Oh-oh, I shouldn't have done this.' 'First date?' she heard long-ago agony aunts raging at her from her teenage years. 'You slept with him on the *first date*?' She half agreed with them; what sort of woman does that? Mmmm, *this* sort, and with no regrets whatsoever, she thought happily from beneath Saul's naked body, the most intimate part of which was still inside her. There wasn't anywhere else she'd rather be.

'Oh God, that was . . . just . . .' Saul murmured, his mouth a millimetre from her left ear.

'Shh, don't say anything.' She was afraid the ecstatic spell would break. Her heart was still thumping frantically, her breath was hard to catch and when she shifted slightly she felt yet another tiny orgasmic ripple, feeble now after the cataclysmic main event, but as if her body was reluctant to let it all stop.

'Earthquakes,' he whispered. She could feel his heart thumping too, a counter-rhythm to hers.

'Earthquakes and aftershocks,' she whispered back.

'You are such bliss,' he told her, kissing her neck softly.

'Or am I just a wicked slut?' she giggled. 'I didn't exactly play hard to get.'

'Well, neither did I,' he said, still holding her tight as he rolled his weight off her. 'In the interests of sexual equality I insist on claiming as much easiness of virtue as you.'

'OK, we'll share it then,' Bella agreed.

'You know what else just occurred to me?' Saul pulled the duvet over them and snuggled down close to her. 'We met because of a programme about what to wear. How to look good in clothes. And here we are, I've got you looking the most fabulous ever, in absolutely nothing. The viewing public is missing out. No one else gets to see you like this. Well, not tonight anyway. Of course, I can't speak for tomorrow or yesterday.'

She thumped his arm. 'Hey, no one else at any time. I'm not *that* much of a loose woman!'

The butterflies from earlier in the evening had all settled now. This was what had caused them to flit about for all that time: anticipation of the inevitable, as for the whole evening the erotic charge had been zinging and building between Saul and Bella. In the restaurant it must have been obvious to their smiley waitress, who had clocked them inching closer together as the meal progressed, noticed their fingers so firmly intertwined by the end that they had only separated with reluctance for mere seconds so Bella could put her jacket on as they left. And she'd wished them a *very* happy rest of the evening with a knowing glint in her eye. And the rickshaw driver: he'd recognized a newly loved-up couple when he saw one.

Now, as the two of them lay in exhausted peace, the sounds of midnight Soho crept in from the street below. Bella could hear a distant police car, the whirr-clunk of a bin lorry, an angry drunk shouting, a bottle bank being emptied, the distinctive throb of a Harley-Davidson. Urban sounds, much the same in cities the world over.

'I didn't get to see your roof garden.' She reminded Saul that this was what he'd promised her. 'Isn't that how you lured me up here? To admire the rooftop views and the plants?' Scents of night stocks and tobacco plants wafted in through the open window. Apart from the city night sounds, they could be miles away in a country garden.

'At the time there seemed to be matters more urgent than a house tour,' Saul teased. 'If you remember . . .'

How true, Bella thought contentedly, how wonderfully

unseemly and hectic their haste as they'd hurtled up the two flights of painted stairs. Saul had led her into the bedroom as if both were scared there was a fast-approaching deadline on this moment of passion.

'Oh, I remember. I'm hardly likely to forget this, am I?' she smiled. 'But . . . I hate to say it, and it's with more regret than I can bear to think about: I'm going to have to go home.'

Saul tightened his arms round her. 'Are you sure you can't stay the night? The garden is at its best in the early morning. Coffee on the terrace out there? All the cute little cockney sparrows lined up on the railings for crumbs of toast? And if pushed, I'll admit the thought of letting you go is unbearable.'

'I'd so love to stay, but I just can't. I really do have to be back. There's Molly . . . I know she's pretty much grown up and she's got my mother there too, but I don't want her to catch me creeping in at breakfast time in last night's clothes. Daughters don't like to be faced with that kind of thing, trust me. It rates very highly on the – "Eeeuuw!" – scale.'

'Hmm, fair point . . . plus I'd be driving you home and then staying for the day's shoot. It's "Shape" tomorrow. Real clothes for real women, according to Daisy. I try not to think what the alternative to that would be.'

'Does Daisy know anything about "real women"?'

Bella giggled, wriggling free to the edge of the bed to look for her abandoned underwear. 'I'm amazed she deigns to deal with the likes of anyone over a size 10, when her work life is all about people with no apparent space for internal organs.'

'Oh, Daisy's no fool. She knows where the money is, and the recession is kicking even the top earners. High end or high street, she doesn't mind who she's working with so long as someone pays her. Her job is as fragile as anyone else's these days. She'll make you all look great, no worries, because that's what's in her interests. Like I said, she's no fool.'

'In that case, I'll look forward to it; I just hope I won't look too knackered.'

'If you look the way you do now,' Saul said, pulling her back towards him and kissing her softly, 'you'll be stunning. You've got the most fabulous glow about you.'

It was only a lot later in the minicab home (on Saul's company account) that Bella – half asleep – started wondering about Fliss. Since that one mention when he'd first brought the girl to the house (and oh, how long ago it seemed) that Fliss was – or had been – Saul's stepdaughter, and the rather sad comment about not really knowing her very well, he hadn't said anything about his connection with her. He and Fliss got on generally OK on a work level, but didn't seem close otherwise, which was possibly, Bella conjectured as the cab went across the Hammersmith flyover, because Fliss had been raised not by Lucy. Or had she been with Lucy till Lucy became too ill to cope and then gone to be brought up by her natural father and, possibly, a new partner of his? That could have meant a double agony for Saul – losing not only his wife but also the daughter he'd been helping her to raise. Or not. Fliss would have been seventeen when Lucy died; if Saul didn't, as he said, know her that well, perhaps she'd grown up with her father from long before that, or even with grandparents. The situation was open to a huge range of speculation. Bella could wait, though curiosity could only hold out for so long. If this relationship were going to run, (and it was off to a promising, if speedy, start), all would become clear soon enough.

No one at home was still up, and all inside the house was darkness and silence. Either Shirley or Molly had left the outside light on for Bella, and, dog-tired but still elated, she set the burglar alarm and then went straight upstairs and took off her clothes for the second time that night, although this time they came off in a rather slower and less urgent manner. She should have showered, really, but she was too exhausted to do more than quickly brush her teeth and give her make-up a cursory wipe-off with some cleanser. Then she collapsed into bed and set the alarm for seven the next morning.

Sleep was unexpectedly elusive: behind her closed eyelids the whole evening raced past in delicious cinematic flashback, and she felt tinglingly tense and unable to relax.

Rick had never made her feel like this. Although they'd only had a few nights together, she'd soon realized he was a man who couldn't make love without first arranging all the necessary accoutrements on the bedside table. She could almost laugh now, thinking of how, when they'd spent a night in a gloriously lush hotel in Devon, he'd carefully and very tidily lined up condoms, a box of tissues, his watch, glass of water and his mobile phone. The arrangement hadn't included, she'd noted at the time with some disappointment, the frangipani massage oil she'd bought from the spa shop that afternoon, and when she'd suggested it could be fun to give it a try, he'd looked at her as if she'd suggested some outrageous perversion and rather starchily said something about not wanting to get oil all over the sheets. How like James, she now thought in retrospect, and, once again, what a lucky escape. She rolled over in the bed and hugged the duvet round her, still scenting a deliciously evocative trace of Saul on her body. Sleep, she willed herself, sleep; and then when she woke it would be such a short time till she saw him again.

* * *

Molly opened one eye and peeked at the greyish daylight sneaking in through the pencil-thin gap she always left between her curtains. She closed the eye again and pulled the duvet over her head. Last night's awfulness hadn't gone away in her sleep. She'd slightly hoped it would be like a tooth when the fairy came, leaving a pound under the pillow in place of a manky molar. Anything would do to replace yesterday's news; it didn't have to be a present, just so long as it was anything but the thing Carly had told her. But it was still there, at the front of her brain, crowding everything else out.

She longed to stay in bed all day, see if just a bit more time would do the trick. If she kept out of sight, lay still, breathed evenly and calmly and didn't see anyone . . . no, it wouldn't change anything. You couldn't un-know stuff you'd been told. And you couldn't un-know the thing your gutless boyfriend (*ex*-boyfriend) hadn't had the nerve to tell you himself. 'I'll have to tell you, because I'm your best friend. And everyone except you knows, and that's not fair,' Carly had said, sitting on the mad purple sofa in the kitchen. Had there been a bit of excitement about her? A bit of wallowing in the drama of it all? You couldn't deny it, in all honesty. And Molly accepted that. She'd probably have felt the same.

There were sounds of life downstairs. The crew would be coming in soon after nine and she'd have to be up and looking ready to rock, like a professional. Daisy was going to dress them all up in real clothes at last, and much as Molly would rather slob out on her bed for the whole day watching brain-dead TV, she wasn't going to let her utter misery get in the way of the chance to be made to look *totally* fantastic and show all the smirking, gossipy school bastards that Giles had made more than just the one massive mistake in his stupid, stupid life.

Bella was not only last to bed but she was first up, too. As she lay in the bath and saw through the window the weak daylight taking its time to appear, she was reminded that autumn really was on its way, in spite of the day promising to be another hot one. And there was something else about autumn – the near-spooky early quiet outside. The birdsong of spring and early summer was missing, as if they were all conserving energy and avoiding excess and frivolous activity to maintain body strength against the cold to come. And some, of course, had gone. In spite of the continuing warmth, the house martins that made their muddy annual nests under Bella's gable eaves had already migrated with their fledglings, knowing from the day length that they only had a certain time in which to escape to safety for the winter.

The butterflies inside Bella, though, they were back with a vengeance. As she quickly dried her hair and pulled on her most flattering jeans (Daisy had asked for them all to be in denim for the start today) and a loose, pale-turquoise linen jumper, she could hardly keep her hands from trembling. Saul would be along in about ninety minutes for the day's shoot. How would they be with each other in front of all the others? If they tried to be cool and suitably businesslike would everyone (or anyone) still twig that something major had changed between them? Surely they couldn't *not* notice the erotic sparks?

And . . . halfway down the stairs (not first down, she could smell toast and coffee wafting up from the kitchen) she actually stopped still and clutched the banister rail at the horror of an alternative possibility: suppose Saul had had qualms and second thoughts in the night? The last thing he'd said as she got into the cab was that he was falling in love with her. Oh, please, she prayed silently, feeling like a schoolgirl with a huge and thrillingly reciprocated crush, don't let him have woken up with a whole opposite mindset. She shook the idea out of her head – it did no good to second-guess people and drive yourself to nervous wreckage. Instead she focused on the day's immediate basics. Tea, breakfast, making sure Molly actually woke up on the right side of midday.

'You missed all the drama last night.' Shirley was there ahead of her, leaning on the worktop reading the paper and waiting for the toaster to deliver.

'Did I?' Bella rather thought she'd had plenty of drama of her own but wasn't about to tell that to her mother, however much Shirley would relish a full-scale, detailed fess-up. 'Why, what happened?'

'You haven't seen Molly yet?'

'No? Why? Oh God, has something happened to her?' She felt cold, suddenly. What kind of cruel cosmic pay-back would it be, that something dreadful happened to Molly while her feckless, selfish mother was out having raunchy, rampant fun? Maybe even the mothers of near-adults weren't allowed by the cruel gods to do that, even when they'd put in the full number of caring years and deserved occasional time off. 'Tell me, quick! Is she all right?'

'She's sort of all right. She will be, she's young and tough and eventually she'll get over it, even if just now she thinks she never will,' Shirley said. 'But her silly arse of a boyfriend, he'll be stuck with what he's done for a long, long time. He's got one of the girls at school into trouble.'

What a quaint old phrase that was. Bella had first heard the term when she was a very small girl of four or five, said about her own babysitter Louise who'd become pregnant at seventeen. Shirley and Louise's mother had been talking over tea and cake, saying that Louise had *got into trouble* and that in the old days it would have meant she'd have had to get married but that times were different now. Bella remembered it clearly, because for a few years after that she had thought of married women as people who'd done something very wrong, for which they were condemned to punishment-by-wedding. It was quite a game, trying to guess their crimes, but it had also puzzled her enormously because when people announced they were going to get married, it always seemed to be such good news.

'Giles has got someone *pregnant*? Bloody 'ell, what an idiot! Who?' Bella was rather ashamed that her immediate secret reaction was relief that it wasn't Molly. 'Is the girl keeping the baby?'

'Apparently.' Shirley shrugged. 'What a silly thing she is. Why would a girl choose to be encumbered with a child at her age? She'll never get that time again, and nobody of seventeen has yet learned enough to be much use to a younger one. Girls today . . .' she sighed. 'They talk about babies as if the baby stage is all there is, and they'll be forever cuddly little things that they can carry about like dollies. If instead you said to a teenager who was thinking it was a cute notion, "Would you like to have a snotty, tantrum-crazed three-year-old who's being slow with the potty-training?" I wonder how many of them would say yes?'

'None, I imagine, when you put it like that. Perhaps that kind of reality should be part of school sex-education classes. Did Molly say who the girl was? Did Giles come round and tell her? She said she was asking him over. Poor Molly. Poor everyone, really.'

'No he didn't!' Shirley was spreading butter on her toast in a manner that conveyed outraged fury on her granddaughter's behalf. 'Her friend Carly told her. She was here with her when I came in from seeing Dennis. Molly was pretty much inconsolable. She sobbed her heart out all over me after Carly had gone home.'

'My poor Molly! I should have been here.' Bella made tea for herself and another one to take up to Molly. The elation from the night before fizzled away. Dead butterflies, she thought, her body and brain now feeling leaden with sadness for her daughter.

'No, Bella, it wasn't down to you. It wouldn't have made any difference and besides, you're her mother. Girls don't always want to confide in their mothers – sometimes the distance of another generation is useful.'

Bella smiled at this, remembering how often Shirley had so unsubtly tried to wheedle personal information out of her in her youth. As there really hadn't been a lot to tell, she'd been constantly disappointed. She probably had a point about the generation thing, too.

'Well I'm glad you were here for her, Mum. Thanks. Did you tell her you were marrying Dennis?'

'No. It wasn't the moment, was it? I'll tell her soon.'

'OK – I just wondered if she'd already known. That's all.'

Bella felt furious with Giles for not having had the nerve to tell Molly about the baby himself, though at the same time she had to admit to herself that it wouldn't have been easy for him. But what kind of boy simply puts his head in the sand and waits for the school gossip machine to let his girlfriend know that he's been so spectacularly, disastrously unfaithful? And why had all those school sex-education classes been so ineffective? How difficult was the use of a simple condom? Saul had managed it perfectly well. But then he was a grown-up, with possibly many years of practice – something she didn't really want to think about. Maybe Giles hadn't quite, in a manner of speaking, got to grips with that particular skill.

She put a couple of croissants in the microwave and set the timer, then took Molly's tea up to her, expecting her to be half asleep and exhausted from a disturbed night. But Molly, instead of languishing in bed as Bella had imagined, was actually up and on the landing on her way to have a shower.

'Tea for you, Moll. And I just spoke to Gran. Are you . . . ?'

'I'm fine,' Molly interrupted abruptly. 'I'm just angry now. I'm not going to school today, either,' she said, giving Bella a don't-make-me challenging look. 'I'm going to stay here and do the clothes thing with you all. I know Daisy said we could do mine later in the day when I get back but I *really* don't want to go and see anyone at school today, OK?'

'All right . . . it's your work schedule so you know what you can afford to miss and what you can't. Are you sure you feel up for all this filming malarkey, though?'

Molly glowered. 'I'm not *ill*, Mum. Just . . . pissed off! That Aimee, she's such a slag. And how could Giles? He'd said he didn't fancy her, that he'd "have to be desperate". Turns out he already *had* been desperate when he told me that.'

Her eyes had gone glittery with tears. Bella moved to hug her, but Molly backed away and said, 'Don't be nice to me, please! If I cry I'll have a fat red nose.' She gave Bella a small, sad smile and vanished into the bathroom.

Saul hadn't changed his mind. Half an hour before he was due to arrive at the house, Bella's phone buzzed with a text message.

*'Can't wait to see you again. Ten minutes x'*

Jules, just arriving, caught Bella grinning at the message and pounced on her.

'Well? Tell me . . . how was it? Did you . . . ?'

Bella looked at her and tried to control her smile.

'Oh God, you *did*! Oh you lucky, lucky slut!'

'Shh! Someone might hear!' Bella hissed. 'It's early

days and we've got to keep it quiet while all this lot's going on. I don't want Daisy deciding she's going to fit me up with some piss-take goth wedding outfit or something.'

'*Wedding?*' Jules exclaimed. 'Already?'

'No! Don't be daft, that was just . . . oh you know. Just keep the last-night thing to yourself, OK Jules? Please? Look – Simone's calling us for make-up. Catch up later?'

'We'd better. I need info. I have a dull married life and need vicarious thrills where I can get them.'

Bella was in the sitting room with Simone the make-up artist when Saul's car pulled up on the gravel. Daisy had arrived early, been made up and had just finished having her nail varnish retouched. She'd gone to check that Fliss wasn't skiving in the mobile canteen out on the roadside. Bella watched her from the window, crunching delicately across the stones in her skyscraper platform sandals and stopping to talk to Saul after he'd parked his Mercedes in the driveway beside Bella's Mini. To Bella's newly hyped-up state of mind, the cars parked together seemed significant, portentous, like another confirmation that what had happened last night was . . . all right. More than all right.

Must get a grip, she thought, moving away from the window. This was ridiculous – she was feeling as hyped up as a teenager. And it was a feeling that she was mildly sad to acknowledge as new to her. How had she married

James when she'd never felt quite like that about him, not even at the beginning? She'd loved him, certainly, in a warm and tender sort of way, but mostly it had been more of a feeling of comfort and safety that she'd had with him, something to do with being cared for, having someone to care about. Home-making, nesting, children. She had no regrets that all these had been with James, in spite of how he'd come to drive her half insane in the end, but this madness that she now felt towards Saul . . . Was it a basis for a proper relationship or just a whopping great piece of truly physical lust that would vanish as fast as it had arrived?

She could feel her heart picking up speed as Saul approached the open front door, and she went out to meet him, wanting to see him alone for a moment before having to share him on a purely businesslike level with the rest of the crew.

'Good morning!' he said, smiling, taking her hand and leading her to the privacy of the leafy passageway at the side of the house. 'Sleep well?' He put his arm round her, pulling her close, stroking her.

'Not too bad, considering!' she said. 'And you?'

'Kept waking up and wishing you were still with me. And then I wondered if you'd have decided by this morning that it was all a horrid mistake.'

Bella laughed. 'I thought exactly the same about you! *Do* you think that?'

He kissed her, softly. 'What do you think?' he whispered. 'I haven't had you out of my mind for a single second.'

'OK, point taken! And same goes for me. But . . . Molly had a horrible boyfriend episode last night, and I don't think she'd take too well being faced with her mother looking all loved-up and silly. So we really must stick to the professional-distance stuff that we agreed on last night.'

'I know. It would change the whole work dynamic, so if I snap at you or boss you around in there, just think of it as a gesture of affection.'

'It's a deal.' Reluctantly, Bella managed to take a tiny step away from Saul. 'Look, we'd better go in,' she told him. 'I can hear Fliss shouting at someone in the garden, and the other victims will be here any minute.'

'OK, after one more kiss . . .' he said. 'You're just looking too irresistible.'

'That'll be the make-up. Simone is making us look "natural". You wouldn't believe how long that takes.'

Molly, Dina and Bella were on the purple sofa watching Jules being filmed coming in to join them from the garden, cheerfully unaware that the camera outside had been focused on her behind for the past five minutes while she walked across the lawn with Daisy. Daisy was today wearing a near-demure yellow flower-sprigged mini tea dress – 'Topshop!' she'd announced in a triumphant squeal – with gold and grey herringbone leggings that had cost about twenty-seven times as much as the frock. And 'No, not leggings, they're *treggings*,' she'd corrected a mystified Dina, who had said that leggings looked rather on the hot side for the weather. Dina had turned to Bella and mouthed '*treggings?*' at her, still none the wiser. Back in the kitchen, Daisy addressed the camera and the three on the sofa at the same time, standing next to Jules (who was reaching into the cupboard for biscuits) and patting at bits of her clothing now and then. 'Every style guru, every fashion magazine in the nation will, at some point, tell you there are jeans to suit every woman,' she began, tweaking Jules's back pocket. 'This is actually a big, fat, lie.' (Three sharp prods to her derrière – Jules dropped a HobNob into the sink.) 'They will try to tempt you with skinny, boot-cut, flares, low-rise, high-waist and other little gimmicky tricks to convince you that there is no butt shape that can't be enhanced by the right tight denim. But there are many, many women out there who shouldn't be seen in the stuff, *ever*. And Jules here is one of them!' She stopped for a moment to take a breath and to explain that at this point, the shots of Jules's bum would fill the screen.

'Oh thanks for that!' Jules laughed. 'I thought you said you weren't going to make total twats of us all?'

'Please don't say "twat" on camera, Jules,' Saul reminded her, grinning. 'We'll put an edit in there. OK, carry on.'

'I'm not making you look bad, I promise.' Daisy beamed. 'Just wait . . . you'll thank me in the end, sweetie, trust me.'

'If you say so!' Jules surrendered, and Daisy continued to the camera, 'Of course if Jules had a job on a remote hill farm where no one could see her arse – oops, sorry darling!' she smirked at Saul, 'bottom – as she bent to get the eggs out of a chicken coop, or could watch her walking across the moorland with a bucket of oats for a pony, then fine. Here in urban Britain, anyone whose bum is this close to the ground should avoid – no – run *very very* fast from the time-honoured rodeo look. And don't, as Jules has done here, think you can get away with wearing a long and baggy top to cover the sins beneath.' She made as if to raise the hem of Jules's long, pale-blue and white Empire-line top, but backed away with professional speed when Jules gave her a don't-you-dare look. Instead, Daisy pulled the fabric tighter, gathering it up in a handful behind Jules's back to make her point: 'Because, as you can see here, the waistband, the fly and the belt loops on all jeans are really pretty bulky. They *add*. Jules looks just about passable if she keeps completely still, sucks in her flesh and stands up permanently straight like a soldier on parade, but whoever does? The minute she moves, all the cluttery fabric trims beneath just bulk out more.'

'Well thanks for that, Daisy!' Jules responded remarkably cheerfully. 'So what do I wear instead? *Everyone* wears jeans!'

'Not me, darling,' Daisy told her. 'In spite of being slim and with far longer legs for my height than you'd expect, I *eschew* denim for its inflexibility, not to mention the fact that it's cold in winter and too hot in summer and it can smell nasty when damp. Jules, you need smooth and sleek if you're going to wear trousers; side fastenings, not front; and no pockets, though I'd maybe allow some flattish side ones, just big enough to slide a credit card in. No other details whatsoever. Trust me. In a moment, when you're trying things on, you'll see exactly what I mean. Inches will fall off.'

'Right, cut there!' Saul said. 'That's pretty good, Daisy. If typically rude . . .'

'Honest, thank you very much, I prefer to call it honest. It's what I'm being paid for,' Daisy cut in swiftly.

'OK, honest if you must, yet deep down helpful. That was an excellent piece of cutting to the chase.'

'Thank you, darling. Just doing my job.' She smirked at him, blowing him a kiss.

Bella was apparently allowed to wear jeans, but only boot-cut and in darkest blue or black. Molly, who had cheered up enormously, was pleased (but surely not surprised) to be told she could wear the skinniest and skimpiest with impunity, but Dina was, like Jules, considered the Wrong Shape. This didn't faze her at all for, as she put it, she 'wouldn't be seen dead in jeans' and had turned up that day in a long stiff denim skirt which Daisy had said looked like an awning on the front of an old ironmongers. Dina hadn't seemed to mind this, either. 'It's all right, I don't possess any denim. I picked it up at a charity shop just for today. It can go straight back again now. I washed it before wearing it, of course.'

'When are we going shopping?' Jules asked, as Daisy and Fliss led them out to the wardrobe wagon. Saul, Dominic and the camera crew weren't needed at this point while Daisy took them through clothes selection and some essential trying-on. Bella locked the front door after them all, just in case some sneaky burglar saw an opportunity for a quick thieve while she and the others were being zipped into their new looks. As an excuse for the house being open, she didn't think this would go down well on an insurance claim for theft.

'We're not going shopping,' Daisy told Jules. 'The viewing audience all know what a shop looks like. The other programmes like this have those pointless scenes of women looking pathetically confused in high street stores, flicking through rails of ghastly cheap things. There's no need for that. Dominic and I have done the choosing for you – that is what I'm here for and what I do for a living. And besides,' she added, 'much of what we have here isn't yet high-street available. The viewers will love that. *You'll* love it.'

'Sounds like an order,' Dina whispered to Jules as they boarded the wardrobe wagon. This was a massive truck parked out in the road. Inside, four long rails of clothes were arranged, one for each of them. The interior resembled a theatre dressing room and was surprisingly large, having a pink velvet chaise longue and a bulb-lit mirror the length of one wall, which made it all horribly hot.

'How did the A-lister go yesterday, by the way?' Bella asked Daisy as she had a first wary look at the contents of her rail. 'Did she like what you'd collected for her?' She pictured the bemused actress, even now wandering London in a skirt made out of long, purple, polyester hair, and wondering if she should comb it, plait it or just stroke it a bit.

Daisy grimaced. 'Nightmare! The bitch had *put on weight*! Deliberately! It seems it's not good in the current economic climate to look too thin. Apparently it smacks of not being able to afford food, so well-fed is the new size zero and if the world doesn't recover sharpish, everyone will be desperately showing off that they can stuff themselves to the size of the residents of Tonga. Nothing fitted her. Selfridges had to courier round a whole repeat batch in a bigger size.' She closed her eyes as if to wipe out the memory. 'Apart from handbags, of course; thank the Lord for extreme handbags. Dominic was in heaven there.'

Daisy turned her attention back to the truck's clothes stock.

'OK – bearing in mind the principle of *egg*,' she said, 'I'd like you each first of all to pick out one dress, a skirt, two tops and what you consider the perfect trousers. I'm going to see how you all do on your own first.'

Bella, pulling her own jumper off in order to try on a silk top, became aware of a ringing sound somewhere beyond the truck. An alarm, fire or burglar. She was vaguely hoping for the sake of the sound man that it would have been sorted before the afternoon's session, when Fliss opened the truck's back door and the noise became a lot louder.

'Mum?' she said to Daisy. 'There's an alarm going off. I think it might be . . .'

'Not "Mum" at work, Fliss!' Daisy snapped. 'I've told you before.'

'It's my alarm, isn't it?' Bella dropped the silk top and pushed past them all, running down the steps and across the gravel to her open front door. Bloody hell, how had that happened? Who was in there? But more important – had she heard that right? 'Mum'. *Daisy* was Fliss's *mother*? Bella's heart thumped hard and her brain was a confused whirr. Putting a very obvious two and two together, she came up with . . . Saul and Daisy as a couple. As the other marriage. Why *the hell* hadn't Saul told her?

'Wait! Bella, we'll do this together, it could be dangerous!' Jules caught up with her by the front door. The two of them ran into the hallway and there was James, prodding hopelessly at the burglar-alarm keypad and looking flustered.

'Bella, you're only half dressed!' he said. 'Have you been out in the street like that in just your bra? That could be a sign of . . .'

'No of course I haven't!' Bella almost spat the words, more furious with Saul than with James. Damn. Now she was at a disadvantage, facing James in just her jeans and her pale blue polka-dot M&S satin special. 'But I'm hardly likely to expect a burglar to hang about while I get dressed, now am I?'

'But I'm not a burglar! And you've changed the code! That's why the alarm went off,' he told Bella and the collection of hyped-up onlookers who'd gathered behind her. 'Now the police will come and you'll have to pay for a false call-out. *Not* 360-degree thinking, that, now is it? Oh – hello Dina! How nice to see you again!' James had spotted Dina and was smiling at her in a disturbingly eager way.

'James, what the hell are you doing here? And how come you have a key?' Bella demanded furiously. She wanted to hit him, clout his stupid, over-pink face with its 'I'm always right' expression. Not so much because he was there, invading her territory like this for whatever reasons of his own, but almost entirely because a whole Connect Four-style grid's worth of puzzle tiles were tumbling uncontrollably into places in her brain that she didn't want them to reach. They'd started to tumble the second Fliss had so casually called Daisy 'Mum'.

# FOURTEEN

'Look, at the end of the day, there's nothing to stress about. I only popped in to pick up a few documents that need checking over. You know? Those deeds we talked about the other day?' James had eventually stopped smirking at Dina and confessed readily to Bella, the moment she'd dragged him away so they could talk alone. First she had reset the alarm and cancelled the police. Thank goodness the others had some sense of tact and had gone to check out the lunch menu in the catering truck.

Bella grabbed a hoodie of Molly's from where it was abandoned over the banister rail. Big and comfortingly baggy on Molly, it fitted Bella fairly snugly. She and James went through the kitchen and out into the garden, where they sat on the bench to talk. Bella felt determinedly inhospitable, as if she were entertaining a stalker, and was not at all inclined to offer James a drink, even though he'd looked meaningfully at the kettle as they passed through the kitchen. Then she felt bad – he was, after all, the father of her beloved children – and she dashed back inside and quickly made him a cup of his favourite camomile tea.

'Thanks. I didn't want to disturb you, Bella, that's all, that's why I let myself in. And besides, I thought you weren't here.'

'Right. Isn't that a bit contradictory? Where does "not disturbing" me come in, if you actually thought I was out? How many other times have you sneaked into the house when I've been off the premises?' She had a vision of him skulking behind the privet next to the front gates and felt slightly ill at the thought of being spied on, even by someone she used to know so well. Had he been in her bedroom, apart from that time she'd been there? Surely she'd have sensed if someone had been in, especially as James was so heavy on the aftershave. He probably thought it had disinfecting properties.

'I haven't been in before. Honestly.'

'Apart from sneaking up on me in *my own bedroom*,' she reminded him.

'I wasn't *sneaking*. Just looking for you. You could even see it as a heads-up about locking doors.'

'Oh, I did. Which is why the front door was locked

just now. Did you wheedle a key out of Molly or Alex?'

'I wouldn't say "wheedle",' James protested feebly. 'I simply asked Alex and he found one for me.'

'That was pretty underhand, wasn't it? You knew I didn't want you to have one. And don't pull the old "this is half my house" number. *You don't live here,* James. I could probably get a restraining order, you know.'

'Well that would be overreacting somewhat, don't you think? Surely common sense can come to the party here, if we're going to move the issue forward in this space?' He'd got his pompous face on now. She could almost see his chest puffing out, like a bumptious pigeon. The reversion to jargon matched his stance perfectly.

Bella laughed. 'You know, if I had a clue what you were talking about, there's a chance I could agree with you. Look . . . give me back the key and go away, will you please James? If we're going to have an "issue" over the house, then I really will need to consult someone about it. All the same, I won't be obstructive. Just the house deeds, was it?'

'House deeds, mortgage details, all that. I somehow lost track of it all and I wanted to take a look under the bonnet, so to speak . . .' He sounded more hopeful than a few minutes ago, possibly thinking she was caving in.

'Yes, I've got them and believe it or not, I even know

where they are. You know, you could have just asked me – I'm perfectly willing to photocopy them all for you. But I've been thinking about this. Remember I've been paying the mortgage here for the past ten years, on my own. We only lived here together for three years before that after we left the rented place, and the deposit for this house was entirely from my grandfather's legacy, if you recall. I have a feeling that if I owe you anything financially, it won't be an awful lot. Sorry if that's a bit of a blow, but it can't be as big a one as being made to think you're going to be instantly evicted and banished to live in a box, believe me.'

'Aha! We shall see. And as I said before, it's mostly you I'm thinking about. This place is going to be far too big for you when you're on your own.'

Oh, and she *would* be on her own. She could see that looming worst-case scenario so clearly: a chill, lonely, lover-free future, punctuated by hectic, over-optimistic short-term forays with a series of men who were badly acquainted with truth. Grim. *Another* bloody mistake. How many times in her life was she going to have to go through the 'never again' disappointment with men? This is *it*, she decided, never again would mean just that. She really could do without people who only gave her half the story.

'You don't need to think about me, James, thanks all the same. If you didn't spare me a thought when I was running myself ragged looking after two infants and trying to get my career going, then it's a bit pointless, not to say unconvincing, trying to make up for it now, isn't it?'

'OK, OK. Sorry. Look, I'll leave the document-sourcing with you and we'll touch base again soon.' James got up and stretched, his shirt pulling tight across his corpulent middle. Bella suddenly felt rather sorry for him. He used to be very fit, very active when younger. He'd played in a Sunday football team and been quite careful with his health (which was where the over-concern with hygiene had begun). Now he looked as if he'd given up on keeping himself in good physical condition, and was undeniably heart-attack shape. Washing his hands and sponging down every surface he came into contact with wasn't going to save him from that.

She was about to say something about taking care of himself, wishing him well, but he cut in first. 'I really don't like that purple monstrosity you've got in there.' James pointed to the sofa. Bella felt a pang of sadness, thinking back to the so-lovely day when she and Saul had chosen it at the prop store. 'The sofa isn't staying long,' she told him. 'Just till all this lot go. Which will be very soon, I hope.'

She meant it. Depression washed over her as, looking into the kitchen from the garden, it suddenly felt like a completely false room and nothing to do with her. Just another empty film set. She could almost wish her manky broken pink tiles were back again. And her creaky old cupboard doors with their dated ironware. The coral wall would have to be repainted – if Saul was just another lying and devious bastard, then she didn't want any reminders hanging about to taunt her that she'd been taken for a mug by a man. Again. Would she ever learn? Was Saul really another Rick? When had he been intending to come up with the missing information that he was, or had been, married to Daisy?

Over dinner, when she'd told him about the Rick-in-New York episode, even though she'd turned it into very much a funny story, she'd made it pretty clear that the one thing she valued and desired in a relationship was absolute honesty. And here they were: Daisy was Fliss's mother. Daisy was Saul's ex-wife. If she *was* actually ex. If this was the case, then why was there any problem about saying so? She felt weary at the thought of having to prise some deep truth out of him. In spite of her accepting that most information about a new partner tended to come out gradually over time, this was one major omission he'd made here. OK, it was early in the relationship and everyone was entitled to privacy about their past . . . but this particular bombshell was right here in the present, right here on her premises. Best to quit now – might as well get used to that worst-case future she'd briefly foreseen a few minutes before.

'And look, James, you were asking about Dina the other day. She's over by the catering truck. Why don't you go and have a word with her?'

Well, someone else might as well be lucky in love, even if she couldn't, she thought. Bella walked him out of the door. 'Just a tip: Dina likes horror films but on DVD on her own sofa, not at the cinema.'

'Quite right too.' James looked as eager as a puppy whose owner was teaching it to play fetch. 'Cinemas are full of filthy fools eating and slurping and spreading their germs . . . I'll just go and say hello to her, see how she is.'

'Good luck!' Bella genuinely wished him well, pocketing the door key he'd handed over. He was looking very happy now, like a small boy diverted from a tantrum by the promise of a treat.

'OK, now I've got you on your own!' No sooner had James strode off in pursuit of Dina than Jules seemed to pop out from behind the hibiscus.

'So? Are you going to tell me any more? Where did you go after the dinner? Did he leap on you suddenly or did you seduce him subtly till he couldn't resist or . . .'

'Ooh Jules! You made me jump!' In truth Bella had thought for a millisecond it *was* Saul, back and keen to pounce when she was apart from the others. The internal butterflies kicked off again.

'Are you going to tell me, or was it so magically wonderful in a disgracefully private way that you can't say a single word about it in case the spell evaporates?'

Bella thought for a moment. Really, she didn't want to say anything at all to anyone, but if she didn't, Jules would be hurt and puzzled and would look at her in a Concerned Way all afternoon. She couldn't face that. It would be bad enough facing Saul later, let alone coping with someone else doing too much wondering.

'OK, look come through to the garden; I'll give you the bones of it before the others come back.'

'Ha ha! Bones! Did he jump on yours?' Jules was nothing if not upfront.

'Jules! So subtle, not! Hey, it's lunchtime; do you fancy a sandwich in here rather than out in the truck with the others?' Bella opened the fridge. 'I've got a load of chicken and some salad stuff, though what about Molly . . . she's out there . . .' Bella thought about how Molly had been feeling earlier. So that would be two in the house that evening having man-misery. She only hoped her mother was having better luck out with hers (wherever they were . . . did all older people gad about as much as Shirley and her new beloved did?) or it would be all-round tears and a takeaway later. Not a jolly prospect.

'Don't worry about Molly; last seen flirting with that nice boy who plays with the big fluffy sound thingy.'

Bella's heart upped its pace. 'Are they all back? Is . . .' her voice faded out. She couldn't quite say his name. Ridiculous – whatever she was speculating about in terms of the Saul-and-Daisy scenario, she had to work with both of them this afternoon. And tomorrow and the next day. Of course, she could just see him alone later and ask him to explain. But if she did, she wouldn't know if he'd ever intended to come out with the truth. This was a case of setting a test for him, and she didn't like herself very much for it.

'No, no one else is here. It's all clear for you to tell me all,' Jules said.

Bella and Jules assembled a couple of doorstep-sized chicken salad sandwiches, deliciously spread with cranberry sauce but no butter, 'as a gesture towards the diet', Jules claimed, and splodged with mayonnaise as a bonus, then took them outside to the garden with generous glasses of Sauvignon Blanc.

'Not enough to make us pissed,' Jules assured Bella as they settled at the terrace table, 'but enough to loosen us up and make us sparkle on camera later. I hope. OK, now I'm sitting comfortably, you can begin.'

'We went out for dinner at Mon Plaisir,' Bella told her, 'That's . . . er . . . about it really.' It sounded a flat, dull event when put like that. Thinking of how it had really been gave Bella a delicious reminiscent tingle, followed by a surge of sadness.

'Oh come on! I didn't forgo Mandy's crispy bacon and avocado salad just to hear you say you had a Quite Nice time, thank you, and with no details!' Jules studied her intently. 'I've seen the way you two look at each other. There's definitely a buzz between you. Or was. Did it all go horribly wrong? It didn't look that way this morning. You had that glow-of-shame. I was *so* envious.'

Bella felt ridiculously close to tears. This wasn't allowed or Simone would have to redo all the so-natural make-up, right back to basics.

'No.' She sighed and pushed the second half of her sandwich away, suddenly without any appetite. 'No, it all went horribly right. It was fantastic, brilliant. But – maybe I'm just not cut out for being good at relationships. There's always some great big furry fly in the ointment. Sorry, Jules, I can't really talk about it right now. I know that sounds a bit up-myself-ish but I promise I'll explain some time after all this stupid *Fashion Victims* palaver is over. It's just a bit too close to home with this going on. I can't wait to be back to normal, if I'm honest. And,' she laughed rather shakily, 'I don't care what Daisy says, I *don't* want to wear the skirt on my rail that's got a waist like a gathered-up paper bag! I had one of those years ago, a suede Maxfield Parrish one which I thought was gorgeous, but it made me look like a big tree trunk with a frill round its middle.' She felt she was waffling, anything to distract Jules from talking about Saul.

'You should tell Daisy about the old skirt – she'll be desperate to know if you've still got it. She'd go, "Oh but *darling,* how *perfectly* vintage." '

'Perfectly vintage if you want to look like that elephant in a ballet skirt. Babar, wasn't it? I used to read those books to Alex and then later Molly.'

That was all back in the days of James. James had been a good and rather sweet father, till he decided that cleanliness might be the closest thing to godliness but was also next to impossible for a household with small, messy humans and an ordinary, imperfect, mortal woman in it. Bella felt sad for the swift passing of time, the even swifter passing of love. She felt rather silly, too. After last night, she'd really thought she and Saul had something special going. Now she could see it was just plain old geed-up lust with little depth to it. That, she thought as she cleared the remains of the sandwich away into the bin and finished the last of her wine, *that* would teach her to hear one tiny, insubstantial bit of information and blithely assume there was no more to the story.

'Oh it's hard to beat *Breakfast at Tiffany's,* even if the film is a bit tame compared with the book. In the book she was *definitely* a tart and he was a kept man. In the film it's only lightly implied.'

'Or possibly a case of *politely* implied,' Dennis suggested. 'The Americans are a bit prissy about that sort of thing. Not quite done, openly embracing an immoral woman as a heroine.'

'A flawed one, though; in many ways Holly Golightly is hard to like.' Shirley felt utter contentment as she and Dennis emerged into the rush-hour crowds and sunlight from the Prince Charles cinema near Leicester Square. 'All the same, it's one of those films that's such a perfect old friend. Like *The Great Escape* at Christmas; you have to watch it even though you've seen it a good dozen times before and probably know most of the lines, just to make sure it's still there.'

'And next week they've got *Some Like It Hot*. I know we could see all these on DVD but I think there's something special and a bit naughty about sliding off to the cinema in the afternoon,' Dennis said. 'At one time it would have been an unthinkable indulgence, wasting daytime in frivolous entertainment, especially a sunny afternoon, cooped up in a cinema *in the dark*. Now, we have all the leisure time we want and can do what we like. *And* at concession rates! We're *supposed* to do this!'

Dennis was holding Shirley's hand, guiding her through the five o'clock crush and making her feel thoroughly cherished. It was a long time since she'd felt like this with anyone. And the cinema had reminded her of her own teen years; plush, small and with such snuggly double seats.

'Where shall we go now?' she asked as they walked down Wardour Street. 'Do you fancy tea at Patisserie Valerie?'

'I've got something else in mind,' he told her, hailing a taxi. 'Just a little item that I need to pick up somewhere not too far away. It's for you, actually. I think you'll like it. At least, I hope so – is there a woman born who doesn't like a spot of luxury shopping?'

He must have thought this through, Shirley realized as she climbed into the back of the cab, because their mystery destination was a secret written on a piece of paper and passed between the driver and Dennis. The driver was smiling, his eyes twinkling at Shirley by way of the mirror as he pulled out into the traffic and headed towards Regent Street, then turned off into the small back roads.

'I won't ask where we're going,' she said to Dennis, 'because I can see you're enjoying the mystery. Are you sure I'm going to like it? Luxury shopping sounds fun but if it involves something completely mad like . . . oh like a parrot from the Harrods pet department, then I have to tell you now, I don't like birds very much.'

'Oh no! That's it then!' Dennis laughed. 'If I'd known you wouldn't want to share our life with a big sweary cockatoo I'd never have asked you to marry me! No, I promise it's not a parrot. And we're here.'

Shirley looked out of the cab window: Tiffany's. Of course it was. First the film, now the real thing. How perfectly sweet of Dennis! 'We should have our noses to the window and be having pastries and coffee!' she laughed. 'Except of course our generation does *not* eat on the street!'

'Certainly not,' Dennis agreed. 'Though I've been known to indulge in an ice cream on Brighton seafront.'

'Oh, I think that's allowed,' she conceded. 'In fact it borders on compulsory.'

Shirley had never been inside Tiffany's Bond Street shop. One Christmas she had bought silver Elsa Peretti earrings for Bella from the Tiffany concession in Harrods – the same Christmas that Bella had co-incidentally bought Shirley her broad silver bangle. However, she had never had reason to visit the big flag-ship store and for a woman who was well used to quite upmarket shopping, she was surprised to find she felt mildly intimidated as the doorman opened the door and she and Dennis stepped inside.

The display counters in front of her glimmered with diamonds. Shirley hung back a bit, unsure. She wasn't unsure about marrying Dennis, not in the slightest, but was ambivalent about the formal engagement-ring thing and hadn't anticipated that they'd be doing that particular ritual. Her late husband had given her his mother's sapphire and pearl ring when they'd got engaged, purely because it was apparently a family tradition to hand this ring down through the generations. It had never really fitted and she'd thought it rather old-fashioned but had kept it carefully in its little velvet box, feeling she was keeping it safe for her mother-in-law, should she ever feel the need to pawn it or even just to look at it. She never had. Perhaps she hadn't much liked it either.

'Oh good grief. All those diamonds! I really don't like diamonds!' It felt like a heretic thing to blurt out, here in this temple of jewels. She hoped none of the assistants had heard – she really didn't mean to insult their stock.

'Oh!' Dennis laughed. 'Just as well I didn't go ahead and buy one and plonk it in a cake or something then, isn't it? Or . . . Are you having second thoughts? I do hope not.'

'Not about marrying you; of course I'm not. But engagement rings – I've never been that keen on those. I don't see the point of them, really.'

'Yes, I completely agree with you! That's why we're not buying one!' He chuckled and pressed the lift-call button.

'Oh!' She felt flustered now, sure she'd made a horribly embarrassing mistake. 'Of course, sorry! I'm being disgracefully presumptuous. Maybe you've come to buy yourself some cufflinks.'

'And maybe I haven't,' he told her, pushing her gently into the lift. He pressed the button for the top floor: Repairs and Engravings.

How little they really knew each other, she thought. And how little it mattered. At last she could trust that the all-important thing was how they felt about each other. They were fully formed, as evolved in their lives as they were going to be, and could absolutely accept each other as they were. Dennis was someone she loved being with and who loved being with her. As Molly would no doubt say, 'End of'.

Shirley waited by the lift while Dennis went to talk to the assistant. Out of the window, across the street, was the Salvatore Ferragamo store. It was, from ground level, just a plain, rather dull building, gilded here and there with the kind of ordinary olive-wreath design that decorated so many London shops. But from up here, not far from roof level, she had a perfect view of a stunningly ornate plaque depicting Caspar, Melchior and Balthazar. She studied it, feeling privileged to be getting this sight of it that no one below could see.

'I should probably give you this when we're in bed, or in a restaurant or something.' Dennis reappeared, clutching a small box. 'But I can't wait. I'm just dying to know if you like it. I'm now thinking maybe *I* was being presumptuous – I'm afraid I skipped straight to the wedding ring. Do you think that's something to do with not wanting to waste time?'

It was, if you could think of it that way, an unassuming little ring. Platinum. Plain platinum with one simple rose sapphire set into the metal.

'Dennis, I love it. It's absolutely perfect.'

'Here, let me put it on.' He slipped the ring on to her wedding finger. 'It's not unlucky, is it? I mean you have to see if it fits . . .'

'Oh it fits, all right! How did you know the size?'

'Ah – when we went to the Byzantine exhibition, you slipped a ring on your finger in the gift shop and it fitted, but you said you didn't like it that much and put it back in the display . . . so I nabbed it and secretly bought it.'

'Devious!' Shirley looked at the ring in the window's light. 'The stone, it's pink but it's a sunset pink. The rays of the sun just as they're going.' One of them would almost certainly die, she suddenly thought, die in the next five, ten years, if they were lucky enough to have that long. She felt a stab of future pain; this really was a sunset romance. If only young people, and she was thinking more of Bella than Molly here, if only they realized how fast the time goes. Please make the best of love that you can, don't waste time holding out for something 'more' perfect; she sent a silent prayer up for her daughter.

'And – I'm so glad you like it, because I can't return it. It's engraved,' Dennis told her. 'Have a look.'

Shirley removed the ring and peered at the inscription.

'It's to commemorate that day we first really *knew*,' he said. 'It just says "Barcelona", and the date.'

Fliss and Nick had strung four brightly coloured washing lines up in the garden. The day had a hot, dull haze to it and the plum tree was looking as weary as the humans were feeling, dropping overripe fruit on the lawn down by the back wall. The cat lay stretched out in the shade of the camellia, fast asleep. Bella could see his pale tummy rising and falling evenly as he breathed. Every now and then his feet twitched, then his mouth and whiskers flicked as if he were trying to miaow in his dreams. If cats *had* dreams, she thought, watching Keith snoozing, oblivious to the activity around him. Perhaps he fantasized about the next mouse – the big one that kept getting away – or catching something bigger, more of a trophy than a mere pigeon, his current favourites.

Bella felt hot in the custard-coloured cashmere sweater that Daisy was making her wear. Beautiful as it was – and it certainly suited her – it was definitely one for a far more wintry day, plus it had silly puffy mid-length sleeves and was tight around her arm just below the elbow. The silky caramel tulip skirt was too big and for the sake of the shot had been held together at the back with tiny bulldog clips. Pins would have marked the fabric. 'Don't sit down, whatever you do,' Daisy ordered. 'The skirt will crease across the front and you'll have latitude marks over your thighs. *Not* attractive.' All very well, Bella considered, feeling lucky she didn't want to go to the loo: she'd have had to take a helper and the whole lot would have had to come off. She leaned against the door frame, hoping that was allowed, and shifted her weight from foot to uncomfortable foot. Five-inch-heeled shoes that each had four lots of buckles to be fastened were 'not practical', as Dina had daringly put it, when Daisy had said that this was a 'perfect everyday look'. Jules backed up Dina. 'Exactly; imagine you're a mum trying to get your kids off to school. Are you really going to have time to do up eight buckles on your own shoes when you've just battled to get your four-year-old to put hers on the right feet and fastened?'

'But you don't have a four-year-old, do you?' Daisy looked blank.

'But the viewers might have!' Dina snapped back. Revolution brewing again, just as with Esmé the colour expert, Bella thought, wishing she felt more enthusiastic.

'The shoes are well cool,' Molly said. 'I'd love them.'

'You see?' Daisy counted this as an all-out win and strode off to talk to Saul.

Bella kept her distance, but watched how the two of them interacted. There was nothing to suggest any intimacy, past or present, nothing beyond a professionally easy manner of working. They seemed to be very much in tune about how this programme should go – that was what their job demanded, though. That must have all been worked out way back at the pre-production stage. But then Saul and Daisy laughed together about something and Daisy gave Saul a brief hug before coming back to join the others. Saul caught Bella looking at him and gave her the kind of smile he'd had in bed the night before, after sex. She smiled back, turned away and went into the house, where Daisy told her to stand up straight and not slouch about and crease the skirt. Thanks, Daisy, she thought.

Apart from the choices they were each now wearing to start the afternoon's session, the clothes that each of them had selected from the wardrobe wagon were on hangers, strung out on the brightly coloured washing lines.

'It reminds me of my old mum's back garden on a Monday,' Daisy murmured, looking a bit faraway. She gazed at the clothes for a moment, then snapped back into the present and strode out across the lawn to alter the arrangement of clothes on the line that contained Molly's selection.

'Are you all right?' Saul was suddenly by Bella's side. 'I've been dying to talk to you, touch you,' he whispered. 'It's agony trying to keep this professional-distance thing going.'

Bella moved a step away from him, partly to stop herself wrapping her arms round him and nestling against his body. Just physical, she told herself. It's just lust; get over it.

'I'm OK,' she said, wishing she felt as cool as she sounded. 'This is just something to be got through. Only a couple of days, then it's over.'

'And then we can . . .' She felt his hand stroke her back, slide under her top on to her bare skin.

'No, wait . . .' She pulled away further.

'Sorry!' he laughed. 'I know, I know. I mustn't touch the clothes in case we completely muck up the whole look and Daisy puts us in detention.'

Bella felt herself freeze a bit at his casual mention of Daisy. So easy. So normal. So – some time, possibly even now – married to her.

'And we don't want to confuse the issue either,' he went on, as if nothing could possibly be wrong. 'Pleasure and business and all that. Can I see you tonight, though? Stay on after they've all gone and maybe take you out for a drink or something? That pub by the river?'

'Look . . . I just . . .' Oh hell, this was difficult. 'Thing is, I really need to spend some time with Molly later. She's had a boyfriend disaster. And maybe . . . maybe we've gone a bit fast into this?'

Saul frowned, looked intently at her. His eyes were full of disappointment and she felt terrible. But couldn't he see that her eyes might be expressing the same? Why couldn't he *read* her need for honesty?

'OK – I get it,' he told her. 'What's that saying? "If it seems too good to be true, then it probably is." You want a bit of distance, space. I can give it to you, really I can. I'm ridiculously in love with you – I really want you to know that, but you can have anything you want. Just . . . ouch.'

He moved away from her and turned to the crew. 'Right you lot, five minutes! Places, everyone!'

# FIFTEEN

After a day of being kitted out and zipped in and out of clothes and shoes and draped with necklaces and bracelets till she felt she'd almost rather spend the rest of her life stitched into one big snuggly Babygro, Molly would have preferred to visit any other shop than a clothes store, but Shirley had texted and told her to get on a bus and whizz into town to meet her as soon as she'd finished being a fashion victim for the day. It felt like an order, but quite a nice one. What could be bad about spending time with her gran? She was like an extra mum but with an element of safe distance. Molly could tell her things knowing they wouldn't be dragged up and used in evidence against her at some future time, which she and her friends found usually happened with mothers.

Molly found Shirley waiting for her at the entrance to

the shopping mall, where she was watching a quintet of exuberant violinists busking in the middle of the pedestrianized street and getting in the way of the shoppers.

'Are you all right, Gran? And oh . . . isn't this the place where you got . . .' Molly dropped her voice to a whisper, '. . . *arrested* and that? Is this the first time you've been back?'

So that was what it was about, she thought. Shirley had lost confidence and needed her support. She felt both privileged (after all, Shirley could have asked Bella) and a bit sad. She didn't want her gran to be feeling shaky about something as simple as mall-visiting. That would be mad. No one was going to be pointing at her and hissing *'Shoplifter'*.

'It is where I had that *mix-up*, yes. But don't worry, Moll darling, I haven't asked you along because I can't trust myself not to nick several fancy hats and a cashmere coat. I just thought you might need a bit of cheering up, so I decided I'd take you out and treat you to something lovely. So . . . let's see what you've learned from these *Fashion Victims* people,' Shirley told her as they went through the doors and felt the cool, welcome draught of air-conditioning. 'And I'd like the company of my beautiful granddaughter for a while. Are you all right, darling? How is it going with the boyfriend situation?'

'*Ex*-boyfriend,' Molly reminded her, sidestepping a group of shrieky pre-teen girls sprinting suspiciously fast out of Claire's Accessories. 'Carly says Giles hasn't been in school. I think he's keeping out of Aimee's way. He's sent me about twenty texts today. All too much too late. And *texts*. He couldn't like, just *call*? Why can't boys talk?' On cue, Molly's phone beeped again. She glanced at the caller ID and switched the phone right off.

'You could reply to him. Let him lead up to the talking part,' Shirley suggested. 'If you don't encourage him to talk to you, you'll never get past this pointless stalemate.'

'Yeah, but Gran, he can't undo what he did. So what's he going to say? That it's twins? That Aimee gave him a nasty disease as well? Last week, when I was thinking it was me that had done something wrong, I couldn't get a *word* out of him. Couldn't he even begin to imagine how that felt, after how we've been to each other for the past five months? I thought he'd decided to dump me just because I'm a bit picky as to where I have sex with him. Obviously he's *not* so picky, as it turns out. Not even about who he has it with. *And* it had to be Carly who told me about the stupid *baby*, not him. Sorry. You don't need to hear all this really, do you?' It would probably be an odd conversation to have with anyone who wasn't Shirley. Her mother would be too sympathetic and soppy, trying to hug her and reassure her. She didn't want that. Right now she wanted to rant. Shirley, thank goodness, was looking completely unfazed.

Molly felt slightly sick now she'd mentioned the child out loud. This made it a human. A person. A real live small child that didn't just lie in a frilly cot, waving its limbs randomly and looking cute, but a real growing little girl or boy that in no time would be off to school, have play dates, birthday parties with mad cartoon cakes and believe in Father Christmas. She wished now she'd said 'pregnancy'. It seemed less real. Certainly less permanent. What was Aimee thinking of? Did she really want a baby? And if so, did she really want to share it with *Giles*? He didn't even like her. She probably didn't like him much, either. He was just another tick on the to-do list.

'I don't mind what I hear, darling. I have no shock gene at all, as your poor mother remembers all too well from her own teen years. But I do want you to be happy again. I hate to see you so miserable over a boy. And you won't be happy till you at least talk to him, see what can be salvaged, if anything. And even if nothing can be, at least you won't be in this miserable limbo any more.'

'You know, I can see he'd want to do *all that* with Aimee,' Molly went on. 'I mean, like, well everybody else has, and she probably does it . . . like . . . er, really well?' She could feel her face going pink and hot. 'But why would she want to keep *his* baby? If she really wanted one, why not take the morning-after pill this time and then pick out someone who actually quite likes her and get pregnant with him?'

'She sounds a poor little mixed-up thing to me,' Shirley told her. 'I'm inclined to feel a bit sorry for her, to be honest.'

'I used to be, too,' Molly admitted. 'Till it was my boyfriend she sha— stole.'

Shirley stepped on to the escalator and Molly followed. On the first floor, Shirley led her towards a branch of Zara and stopped in front of the shop's window display. 'I like this place . . . there's always something good and a bit quirky in here. Let's go in and have a quick look.'

Molly indicated a mannequin sporting a floral micro smock-style dress, cinched in with a wide, obi-style belt in black leather.

'Carly likes that belt.' Molly pointed to it. 'But . . . well, she's not nine inches wide like the model. I think it would look all wrong on her. And that dress, she likes that too, but it would bunch up over her bum and make her look fatter than she is. Not that she *is*, not really.'

'You did pay attention, didn't you, darling? That Daisy knows her stuff. And I don't care what your mother says – learning how to make the best of yourself *is* useful. However low your mood, wearing something that delights you can lift you just that bit from the depths.'

'You always look cool but you never had lessons, did you?'

'No – but when I was younger we didn't have the choices that you have. And clothes had to last, so you learned to choose carefully. Now – whatever Daisy's taught you about what *suits* you, there's another game with clothes . . . dressing to have the impact you want on the people you're aiming at. Let me show you . . .'

The last shoes, the last bracelet had been packed away for the night in the wardrobe truck, and most of the crew had already left. Only the brightly coloured washing lines remained, strung across the garden like leftover party decorations. At just after six o'clock it was still warm enough to sit outside, and Daisy, Saul, Fliss, Jules and Bella were in the garden having a well-deserved glass of wine and some olives and nuts kindly left for them by the caterers. Dominic had rushed off to a handbag launch party, leaving Daisy looking a bit crestfallen at not having been invited along. She'd been moping for much of the afternoon, ratty with Fliss and abrupt with the victims. Twice Saul had had to stop the filming to tell her she had a face like a slapped arse and would she please smile occasionally for the camera.

'I can't,' she'd whined, flicking her blue-black hair

about. 'I'm pissed off. I want Dom to take me with him tonight and he says no.'

'Think of your pay cheque,' Saul snapped. 'That should make you smile.'

Molly had vanished somewhere into the teenage unknown and Dina had gone home the minute they'd finished filming, saying something about needing to feed her cat but looking far more glittery and excited than the prospect of opening a sachet of Whiskas merited. Bella knew it was something to do with James, and was glad. Someone had to have a go at the day's happy rations, and anything that distracted James from trying to move Bella into a beige bungalow had to be welcomed.

Bella was aware of Jules's eyes flicking in flagrant curiosity between her and Saul, looking for signs of, presumably, love's crackling flame. She wasn't going to find any. Saul was being friendly enough, but even allowing for the pact on being cool and professional, he was being far more remote than she could have ever wanted. In spite of her misgivings about him, she didn't want 'remote' at all, deep down. She wanted uncomplicated, honest passion. And if the unalloyed euphoria of the night before was now damaged, she still longed for him to grab her hand and race out of this house with her, drive her in the little Merc to Soho, then take her up to his roof garden where they could lean on the railings side by side, bodies tantalizingly touching, watching London life drift past below them, and he could tell her about . . . oh yes . . . being married to Daisy. Pop went the wild-fantasy bubble. Bella, so uncomfortably close to Daisy on the bench that every now and then a foot or a thigh would come into accidental contact, felt sickeningly conscious that she was sitting beside the wife (current or otherwise, oh *surely* not current – by how vast a margin would that make him the world's biggest cheating bastard?) of the man she'd slept with – and had felt herself falling in love with – the night before.

Saul didn't wear a wedding ring, but with Daisy it was hard to tell. She habitually had several rings on two or three fingers of each hand, all flamboyant and chosen to tone with whatever she was wearing. Bella tried not to stare too blatantly to see if a plain gold band nestled among the tourmaline and opals on her left hand, but she caught herself, on the rare moments that Daisy's expressive gold-nailed hands were still, eyeing her left ring finger, just in case.

'We need to have a party when all this is finished.' Daisy's mood lifted as she gulped down wine rather quickly, 'Can we do that here, Bella? Just the victims and the crew and so on? The catering people can rustle up a bit of nosh – maybe a barbecue. We're right in the absolute suburbs, aren't we, here? Isn't a barbecue what people have in places like this? Such fun!'

Bella, who wasn't at all in party mood and was trying to ignore Daisy's customary little stings, nevertheless didn't want to be a downer on the others. 'If you like,' she agreed – with Mandy the cook in charge, plus all the kit from the truck, it would hardly be a hassle. 'I've got some outdoor lights in the cellar. Perhaps Nick could rig them up in the trees.'

'Settled, then.' Daisy nibbled the edges of an olive. 'You were all *wonderful* today, by the way. Sorry I've been a bit vile. I've loved this gig – you've all been *stars*.'

'You mean we've been good girls and done what you've told us, don't you!' Jules said.

Daisy, beaming her scary Transylvanian smile, was being unusually generous with her praise. 'Jules, admit it, I know what I'm doing – those straight-leg linen trousers were perfect on you, weren't they?'

Jules laughed. 'They were, and thanks for that. I'd never even have looked at them on a shop hanger. I can't hundred per cent promise I won't still sometimes wear jeans, but I'll make sure it's when nobody's looking. I wouldn't want to inflict my vast behind on the outside world for fear of an outbreak of mass fainting.'

'Well, in the privacy of your own home, I suppose that's *just* about acceptable,' Daisy conceded. 'I mean,

I'm sure we all – though not me, obviously, because I know you can't go wrong with essential cashmere lounging items – have secret slobbing-about outfits that we couldn't be seen in, not even to open the front door to the postman. This one here,' she waved her glass in the direction of Fliss and wine slopped over the side on to the table, '*she's* got some Paddington Bear winceyette PJs, haven't you darling?' She continued in a loud pretend-whisper, 'She wears them when she's watching reruns of *ER* or if she's feeling a bit peaky.'

'Mum, please!' Fliss mumbled, embarrassed to be picked on. 'You're pissed!' It was true that Daisy had downed her first glass in record speed. She was now close to finishing the next one.

Daisy cut in, loud and emphatic, banging her glass down dangerously on the table. 'Ah – now that's what I meant to say earlier after the burglar-alarm thingummy happened!' she slurred. 'Remember when we're at work, Fliss darling, it's an absolute rule: you call me *Daisy*, not Mum. Otherwise looks very neposh, er . . . nepo-thing.'

'Nepotism,' Bella supplied for her, wishing they'd all just go home so she could lie on her bed and drift into sleep.

Bella saw Saul flash a look at Daisy. 'Ah, now I get it . . .' he murmured to no-one in particular, then he leaned forward and quietly asked, 'Bella, could we just go inside and talk?'

'When they've all gone,' Bella murmured back.

'I'm not pissed!' Daisy snapped suddenly. 'I just haven't eaten much today and this *hugely* acceptable vino is going straight to my head.'

'Sweetie, you don't eat much *any* day,' Saul sniped back. 'The moment you allow a carbohydrate past your lips, it'll be breaking news on CNN.'

Jules winked at Bella. 'Been a long day,' she commented briskly, quickly finishing her drink. 'And it's possibly getting to the tears-before-bedtime stage.' She nodded almost imperceptibly in Daisy's direction. 'I think I'll go home and see if any of the other inmates of my asylum have thought about supper.' Jules stood up, ready to leave. 'Come with me a sec, Bella, I need to ask you about *Molly's exams*.'

Bella took the hint and followed her, but as she went, she heard Saul saying, 'Fliss, can you take Daisy home? I think it's time . . .'

'Sorry Saul, I didn't bring my car. I'm meeting someone in Richmond.'

'OK . . . down to me then, I suppose. Come on Daisy, I'd better drive you home before you make a complete idiot of yourself.'

Bella glanced back at him. He looked weary, hauling a rather wobbly Daisy off the bench. So much for the chance to explain. Was he really being kind to his ex-wife, or just copping out?

'What's going on?' Jules stage-whispered to Bella as soon as they got to the hallway. 'Did you and Saul have a sudden spectacular falling-out? I mean call me old-fashioned, but usually between secretly loved-up couples there's at least a bit of sly eye contact . . .'

'It's unexpectedly complicated. Possibly, *probably*, dead in the water,' Bella told her, feeling glum. She'd only had half a glass of wine, and decided that was enough for the night. Any more and the miseries would set in even further. Saul couldn't have failed to twig that she knew now who the mother of his stepdaughter was.

'Oh darling, I'm sorry! You really don't have much man luck, do you?'

'No!' Bella gave a shaky laugh. 'But there you go: my own fault. I just rushed straight in there, didn't I? Again! I must be one of those stupid people who really does keep on making the same old mistakes.'

And as she watched Jules pacing away across the gravel to the gate, there were Saul and Daisy behind her, about to leave. Daisy was lurching slightly sideways, tottering on her sky-high heels.

'Till tomorrow, then!' Daisy put her skinny arms round Bella and hugged her. 'You are *quite a nice woman* you know, Bells.' She smelled faintly of hyacinths. Through the tumbling flat dark curtain of Daisy's hair Bella glanced at Saul, who was looking a bit frantic – as well he might, she thought. 'I'm amazed you haven't got some man who *totally* adores you.'

'Me too, Daisy. Me too,' Bella told her, feeling nastily caustic.

'But you have,' Saul murmured to her.

'One of my own, I meant,' Bella snapped back. Please just *go*, she willed them. Never mind drifting to sleep, she really just wanted to lie down and weep for a while.

'Daisy, come *on*.' Saul was impatient now.

'I'm being taken home! Come on, husband!' Daisy demanded, abruptly letting go of Bella and snuggling up to Saul. 'Help me get across that lethal gravel.' She turned back to Bella. 'Terrible stuff, gravel, you know. You could break an ankle on it in heels, easy peasy. And it is *vilely* provincial.'

'Yes, it is,' Bella agreed, all bright and brittle. 'But I recommend it highly for pre-warning you when unwanted visitors are approaching. You get an extra few minutes before some scumbag breaks your locks and nicks the telly. It was James's idea, way back. He was in his security-mad phase.'

'I really must talk to you, Bella,' Saul said. He moved towards her as if to kiss her, but this coincided with her stepping back inside the doorway. Damn, the moment missed. Now she'd looked openly hostile and she hadn't meant to at all.

'OK,' he said, his face clouding. 'Look, I'm really sorry

that there's a bit of confusion. But I can explain . . . we really need to . . .'

'. . . go home! We need to go home!' Daisy interrupted before he could finish. She clutched Saul's hand and tottered across the gravel, pulling him with her. Saul looked back at Bella, briefly and with what could have been an apologetic appeal for clemency. Whether for being economical with the truth or for Daisy being drunk (which was hardly his fault), Bella couldn't tell. As she watched Daisy gigglingly pick her way across to his car, she thought about what it was they said in theatres for good luck. Bella trawled her brain to remember; oh yes, that was it – *break a leg*. While she would never go quite that far with malice towards Daisy, just now it was hard not to wish on her a lightly turned ankle.

Bella lay on the purple sofa and tried some yoga relaxation techniques with a bit of restorative deep breathing. She was now alone in the house and instead of finding the solitude peaceful and calming as she'd hoped, she felt restless and agitated and more than a little cross with herself for having leapt into yet another man mistake. Taking clothes on and off all day (as opposed to flinging them off in a rush of passion the night before) was surprisingly tiring, and her arms ached lightly from hauling things over her head. Her thigh muscles ached too, but that, she realized with a flash of delicious recall, was nothing to do with the day. That was from making love with Saul, and heavens, it had been so fantastic. It seemed close to tragic that it would possibly never happen again. Oh well, she tried telling herself rather bitterly, *some you lose*. The phrase sounded so hard and cynical.

She closed her eyes and tried to put Saul out of her head, thinking of something else: where *was* Molly? She'd rushed off as soon as Saul said that was it for the day, and she hadn't so much as sent a text to say where she was. Bella thought of her own teenage years, of being accused by her mother, as every adolescent had surely been since Moses was a boy, of 'treating this place like a hotel'. It had seemed a peculiar expression, as she and her mother weren't at all familiar with the kind of grand hotels that weren't run on far tighter rules and regulations than the average family home.

Holidays had been mostly in rented seaside cottages, but on the occasions she and Shirley had stayed in small hotels – for a family funeral, weddings, big anniversary parties – the proprietors had been very strict about mealtimes, about late-night comings and goings and general behaviour. It was now way past seven and still no Molly. If this *were* a hotel, and if she'd cooked, she could almost justifiably refuse if Molly came strolling in and attempted a late booking for dinner. Still, so long as whatever the girl was doing cheered her up and helped her get over the Giles thing, Bella could only wish her luck with it.

In spite of (or possibly because of) spending the day chatting about the superficialities of who looked good in what and churning out sound-bite opinions to order, Bella had a sudden urge to distract herself by getting some work done. Gradually, as she lay idly on the sofa thinking about – of all things – *accessories*, a magazine piece was becoming almost fully formed in her head. It had to be got down in writing immediately – at least in note form – or it would vanish, so she brought the Mac downstairs from her office, put it on the kitchen table and started on the piece while what she wanted to say was fresh in her mind.

'I really don't get . . . Statement Handbags' she began typing, determined to get Saul out of her brain, at least for an hour or so. Daisy and Dominic had accessorized every outfit they'd all worn over the past few days with items they kept referring to as 'important pieces'. How, she wrote, can a handbag ever be described as 'important'? The contents, for sure – money, credit cards, driving licence, diary, phone, photos of friends and family – but the bag *itself*? Many of the bags Daisy mentioned, in a tone close to that of a fervent worshipper, were priced at well over a thousand pounds. And they were never of a practical size – that was another thing. Either they were large enough to transport a well-grown three-year-old (and whatever did you put in a bag that size to pad it out and stop it looking as pathetically empty as a just-milked udder? And could you even reach to the bottom corner when you were scavenging for loose change to make up the amount for a parking meter?), or they were teeny, dolly-sized evening bags which weren't long enough to hold an essential Tampax, and which bulged and wouldn't fasten if you dared add a tissue and a lipstick.

Who, exactly, at the average party/office/restaurant, she continued, would recognize the 'importance' of this trophy accessory that cost as much as a sofa? And how mortifying was it to those who *were* in this elite circle to have to downgrade to a chain-store shame item in times of credit stress? Who would want to be the sort of person who needed to impress a tiny teeny band of total strangers who would know the retail price of the sack-thing you were carrying your wallet and Oyster card around in? It was a weird exclusive little club she couldn't ever imagine wanting to join and, fired up by pent-up fury about the mess that she'd laughingly call her love life, she speedily bashed out seven hundred satisfying words that lashed the bones out of these perfectly innocent and possibly beautifully crafted fashion items.

There, she thought, as she ended with the virtues of

the unpretentious canvas tote, *that* felt better. Much.

She went back to the beginning of the piece, tidied up the prose and emailed it to Charlotte at the *Sunday Review* before she had time to change her mind about it, then made herself a cup of tea. While she was texting Molly to ask when she'd be back, her phone rang.

'It's me, darling. Charlotte. Lovely piece you've just sent me, very pacy and furious. You sound as cross as a trodden-on snake. I take it the makeover thing is pissing you off, big-time?'

'Hi Charlotte, oh it's not so bad . . . just tiring. But it's nearly finished. How's the *Review*?'

'Oh fine. Listen, we're looking for someone to cover skincare. I was wondering if you might be interested?'

'Well yes I would, absolutely!' Oh joy, Bella thought, crossing her fingers, at least one thing might turn out all right today.

'The only thing is,' Charlotte sounded a bit hesitant, 'it's all very *high end*. You'll need to go to a lot of product launches and so on. We really need to feel that when you're out at events, you'd be representing the image of the . . . well you know . . . sort of a bit cutting edge, kind of thing. '

'Er, image? The readers don't need to see me, Charlotte, surely? Or do they?'

'Well there'll be your byline shot, but really it's not

just about that . . . it's more about the PR people and so on. I know they need us onside more than we need them, but it's a glamour business, obviously. We'd need you not to be . . . oh I don't know how to put this without sounding vile. If I just say, *tea dresses* and the word *never*, will you be offended, darling?'

Bella looked down at her old jeans and softened linen comfort shirt. Image. Right. So she might not fit the gig on frock grounds. She'd see about that. She had an idea.

'I promise I'll never so much as look at ditsy florals ever again, Charlotte. After this week, I am now style incarnate. But look – we're wrapping up the *Fashion Victims* thing tomorrow and having a gathering here at my house. Why don't you come along? See what we've been doing? And you can meet Daisy and Dominic . . .' That should do it, she thought, recalling Charlotte's squeal of delight in Quo Vadis when she'd mentioned their names.

'Oh, yes! I'd be delighted to! It'll be *lovely* to see you!'

Only if I'm not wearing a flowery matron-frock and cropped cute ballet wrap, Bella thought ruefully as she hung up and returned to her computer to close it down. *Tea dress*, she thought, I'll bloody show Charlotte.

There were several new emails in her inbox and she began opening them, quickly consigning to the junk the usual ones offering to enlarge bits of body that she didn't possess, and deleting others that promised online shopping bargains from rather safe catalogues that she was normally quite fond of but now felt more picky about. She was, she was amused to find, all clothed out for the moment. It was quite a liberating feeling. Now if she could only manage to feel the same about Saul, love and relationships, life could be just hunky-dory.

A new message flashed up as she was about to shut down the Mac. Saul. Stupidly and infuriatingly she went instantly trembly and tense. What on earth would he say to her in an email? She hoped, prayed, that he had more class than to reveal his married status via something as impersonal as the Internet. That would put him even below the level of Rick, who, she now thought, might well have almost deliberately – even at a subliminal level – let his wife do it for him. However else would she have known he was going to be at that New York hotel, unless he'd somehow told her? If he really had used Carole as a means of dumping a mistress, it showed quite a resourceful – if cowardly – streak in him.

Nervous at what she would read, Bella clicked the email open. It was short, only a couple of lines. She couldn't decide if this was a disappointment or not. Much as she wanted detail and information, reams of rambling explanation in an email would mean that talking face to face about this was something Saul intended to avoid.

*'We need to talk – in person, not by phone. Tomorrow, please, on our own. Everything is a stupid tangle of misunderstanding and I'm so sorry. I do love you, Bella, please don't doubt it.'*

*Not* to doubt it was her instinct, she was surprised to find. She was also surprised at how touched she felt by the straightforward, uncomplicated message. It had simple sincerity in it. She pictured Saul at home in Soho, possibly in the big scarlet office surrounded by all those photos of half-built structures. All that work in progress. She saw him at the big table, tapping out the message to her in the fading evening light, trying to find the right words, maybe writing too many, discarding them till he'd whittled it down to those few bare-bones sentences. Below in the street would be other rickshaw cyclists, ferrying other romantically entwined couples; there would be so many people in the restaurants and bars, holding hands and trusting each other's love. Well lucky them, she thought sadly, may it all work out the way they dreamed.

If Molly wanted someone to blame for ending up in Giles's bed that night, she'd have had to pick Shirley, who had simply taken her by taxi straight from the town centre to his house, leaned across to open Molly's door and more or less hurled her out on to the pavement.

'All right Molly, I looked up Giles's address in the

phone book. You agreed you'd talk to him but you have to do it *now*. It's the perfect moment for you. Can't hang about for you though, I'm off to meet Dennis. Bye, darling, and good luck!' she called, throwing Molly's bag out after her, slamming the door shut and telling the driver to pull away immediately so Molly couldn't change her mind.

The cab sped away, did a swift U-turn and Shirley waved goodbye. Molly waved back, ruefully realizing that the entire shopping trip was a con. Here she was in the new black skinny jeans Shirley had bought her (exactly the shape Daisy had told her to go for), and a coral-coloured long top (colour from the spring palette), too-hot high black strappy shoes and with a speedy but effective make-up makeover from a girl on the Bobbi Brown cosmetic counter ('Just for fun, darling,' Shirley had persuaded her, 'let's see what the professionals can do,') who had gone to a lot of trouble with three shades of eyeshadow and too much mascara. As a finishing touch she'd mussed up Molly's hair and clipped it up loosely with a butterfly slide.

'Perfect,' Shirley had decreed, inspecting the finished version of Molly. 'You look a bit less pink and scrubbed, more along the lines of Sandy from *Grease* when she's in the leather outfit. Though nowhere near as *obvious*, of course.'

'Do you mean I look a bit slutty?' Molly frowned at

her reflection. 'I'll try it out on my next conquest, if I ever get one. I suppose boys like this sort of thing.' She thought of Aimee and her tops cut so low that most of her bra showed. Was that all it took?

'No, you don't look at all slutty. Just a little sexier than usual but also *in charge*. It suits you. It is,' Shirley added rather mysteriously, 'perfect for the purpose.'

What she had meant, Molly now realized, was that it suited *this* purpose. The one she'd had in mind all the time. Talk about devious. Her own gran had completely set her up. Could you trust *anybody*? Slowly, she went towards Giles's garden gate. The space where Giles's mother kept her car was empty; it would be just the two of them. It would be a long walk home, so she might as well get this discussion with him over with. If he was in.

She rang the doorbell, feeling quaky and yet strangely in control, as Shirley had assured her she would. It really was something to do with this not-quite-her new look. It was as if she'd put on a costume to play a particular role. A sexy, confident one – not hiding her body under baggy hoodies. None of the cute-and-cosy hiding of hands up her sleeves. She waited a while, getting no answer and hearing no sign of life from inside. This was mad – she should have texted or phoned first. Perhaps Giles was on a trip to Mothercare picking out prams with Aimee. But just as she turned away, the door opened and there, rubbing his wet hair with a towel, was Giles.

'Molly! Er, wow! I was so not expecting you – sorry, was in the shower. Got dressed dead quick when I heard the bell. You're looking very . . . er . . . different, very . . . er, come in.' He looked embarrassed suddenly and she realized the word he'd been thinking was 'sexy'. Good. Serve him right – now he'd see what he was missing. She stalked in past him, enjoying the unusual sensation of being those few powerful inches taller on the mad shoes. Ah yes . . . perhaps her gran had a point.

'Yeah. Well I just felt like a change.' She shrugged. Although she knew she looked stunning, she actually felt slightly uncomfortable. Her mouth felt all sticky with hyper-shiny lip gloss. Her hair was escaping its clip and the jeans might possibly be just that bit too tight.

'Is it what they made you wear on that programme?' he asked, looking her up and down. Although she felt very *contrived,* she could tell he liked what he was seeing. She could see how the what-you-wear thing could collect results.

'No. It's my choice. I like it.' She shut up then. He was the one who was supposed to be doing the talking. It crossed her mind, suddenly, that possibly he wasn't alone in the house. Suppose he'd got Aimee with him? Perhaps (eeuw!) they'd been having soaped-up porno shower action? She started to back away towards the door, appalled at her imaginings, her confidence shrinking.

'Maybe this was a mistake . . .' she said.

'No don't go! Come in, *please* – I really wanted to see you.' He looked like a pleading puppy, she thought, so sad and desperate. She relented and followed him into the kitchen. Music was coming from upstairs but she sensed the house was otherwise empty.

'Drink?' he offered, opening the fridge.

'No thanks. Oh, well yeah, maybe some water.'

He poured them both some chilled water from the fridge tap, and the coldness of it almost froze Molly's fingers to the glass.

'She's not pregnant,' Giles said. 'Aimee, I mean.'

'Yes I know you mean Aimee,' Molly snapped. 'Unless she's just one on a list.' This was such a mistake. She and Giles were almost circling each other in the kitchen, nervous and unsure what to say.

'She made it up, just to get at you. She's jealous. Mad, bonkers and jealous,' he told her.

'Why didn't you say, then?' Molly asked. 'Why did you go all silent on me and not want to see me? If there was nothing in what she'd said, you could have just laughed it off and told her to get lost, and we could all have moved on.'

'Can't we get past this now? I'm sorry I was such a flake. I got scared.'

Molly could almost feel her brain cells stretching and flexing in an effort to make sense of this. Why would he be scared if there was nothing to be scared about? Because there was, that's why.

'Right. But . . . although she's not pregnant, you had sex with her, didn't you?' Well obviously. The brain cells relaxed, job done. *'That's* why you were scared. You thought she might really be pregnant.' She felt detached now, having sorted the truth. She could almost feel sorry for Giles; he looked close to tearful, so penitent.

'Why?' she asked him. 'Was it because we hadn't? I mean, you know I would have . . .'

'It wasn't about you.' He wouldn't look at her. 'It was about me. I wanted it to be so right for us, just like you did. But . . . well . . .' He laughed, nervously. 'You aren't the only one who hadn't done it before, OK?' He laughed again. 'You don't know how much of a big-deal admission that is for a bloke, Molly! I expect you'll want to go home now.'

'So why Aimee?' She was still puzzled; was he saying he had sex with Aimee so Molly would somehow get the benefit? How so?

'She's done it all. With everyone.' He shrugged. 'It was like . . . I don't know, going to a class or something. Just a . . .'

'Learning curve?' How harsh, she thought. Poor Aimee, functioning as nothing more than an all-comers' sex manual. How could they treat her like that? Why would she want them to?

'Molly, I'm *really* sorry. I know you're going to say we're totally over, but I do still love you and I wish I hadn't done it. Truly, I feel gutted on every possible level. I mean, how unfair was it not just to you, but to Aimee? She's a human with feelings and I treated her like some hooker. I hate myself for that.'

Turning point. Molly took a step closer to him, put her hand on his face, stroked him gently. If he'd only been sorry about *her* and had dismissed Aimee as no more than the school bike as so many others did, she'd have turned and left the house and never come back. But he hadn't. With some people, she thought as he pulled her close to him, it was worth looking past their mistakes.

# SIXTEEN

The dawn was arriving much later now the year was so close to the autumn equinox. At seven thirty it was only just light and in spite of the continuing heat, there was no more pretending that the year wasn't fast heading towards the cold season. Bella was up early and ready for the day after a restless night in which she'd flipped about in her sleep, first feeling too hot, then thirsty, then too cold. She'd wandered around, thinking and brooding, staring out of the window at the empty avenue below and startling herself with her own reflection in the big mirror.

Her eventual 2 a.m. reply to Saul's email was short; she'd simply written that she hoped they'd get a few minutes together some time today during the filming. His instant response (had he kept his iPhone next to the pillow, anxious to hear from her? The part of her brain that didn't want to give up on him rather liked to think so) was that he really hoped they could do much better than that. She felt the same – if he was going to come out with some terminal let-down truth, she would obviously prefer it not to be in front of friends, family and film crew.

Does all this relationship agonizing ever stop, she wondered as she made her way round the terrace with the garden hose, watering the plants in their pots. Did her mother get moments like this with Dennis, or did a time come when everything was straightforward, grown-up and complication-free? It didn't seem much to ask, once in a lifetime, to hook up with a man who had no tricksy little secrets, but Bella hadn't come across one of those in years, so perhaps they were heading for extinction.

The garden was still lush and leafy, partly thanks to the slotted-in extra plants from *Green Piece*. She gave those an especially large drink, feeling she was their babysitter and that she was responsible for making sure they were returned to their home thriving and well. Her own flowers hung on from high summer, still blooming prolifically but with seedheads forming now; new flower heads were smaller, as if the plants were flagging, and petals were dropping.

Nasturtiums tumbled untidily, trailing from their pots across the paving; the deep-pink cosmos – thanks to regular deadheading – still had many buds ready to open, but the nicotiana were setting seed and their leaves were starting to look a bit yellow. She thought about the ones whose heady scent had wafted in from Saul's roof garden as she lay in his bed – they too would be turning, dying down and producing smaller, less showy blooms on ever weaker little offshoot stems. Her nicotiana had bits of twig and grass cuttings and grit clinging to their sticky, resinous leaves. Saul's would have the oil-slick-coloured feathers from rooftop pigeons on them.

'It's a bit chillier out here these mornings, isn't it?' Shirley appeared at the kitchen door, watching Bella. She was wearing a dark-blue velvet dressing gown, managing to look elegant even straight from bed. How did she do that? Bella's hair never seemed to be as sleek as her mother's, which fell straight into place at the first touch of a comb. On nights such as the previous unsettled one, Bella's hair went sweatily damp, then fixed itself into mad random angles so that by the time she woke up it was sticking up all anyhow. Today her fringe had a crazy sideways kink in it and some of the back was matted like an old doormat, but it didn't matter – this was make-up and hair day. They were all to be whizzed up to a film-set salon near Waterloo so they'd be glammed up when they returned to the house for a final dress-up and the end of the show. This time tomorrow, she told herself, this chaos would all be over and they could all get back to some kind of normal life and no-one would be hanging around like the fashion police, sneering at the Wrong Cardigan.

'Sorry, do shut the door if you want to,' Bella told Shirley. 'Are you cold in there?'

'No, it's OK, I'm fine. Coffee? I'm just making some.'

'Oh tea for me, I think. I'll come in now; I've finished the watering.'

She switched off the outside tap, wound the hose back on to the reel, then came back into the house and washed her hands. The terrace was shinily drenched and all the plants dripped, but the heat-promise steaminess of early May and June mornings was no longer there. It simply looked as if there'd been rain.

'There are millions of spiderwebs but not so many snails,' Bella commented to Shirley. 'Is it the time of year or the dryness?'

'Probably both. They're a mystery, slugs and snails. I expect you can look up on Google where they go in winter. Off on cruises, like affluent pensioners, I expect.'

'On which note, when do we get to meet Dennis?' Bella asked. 'Don't you want him to meet us? I know Alex isn't here so it's not the full turnout, but I'm dying to check him out myself.'

Shirley raised one perfectly groomed eyebrow. 'Do

you want to see if he's suitable? If his intentions are properly honourable?'

'I didn't doubt that they are. It's wonderful that you've found someone at last, for . . .' Her voice trailed off. Well, it had to be for love, didn't it? What else could it be?

'I hope you weren't going to say "companionship", Bella,' Shirley teased her. 'Because how wrong can you be! Do you think there's a cut-off point at which everything shuts down and that magic attraction turns into something dulled and non-physical, non-emotional, so that you express how you feel by, I don't know, visiting National Trust houses? Making cakes?'

'Well it might explain a few things about the WI,' Bella quipped. Shirley didn't look amused.

'OK, sorry. Keep ignorant mouth shut, Bella,' she told herself. 'But I suppose I did assume something kind of declined with the menopause. Is that not what happens? Doesn't it all feel more . . . *restful*? I'm really beginning to see the point of the word "contentment".'

'If anything *does* expire with the menopause,' Shirley said tartly, 'then you haven't got that much mileage left in you either, my girl. I bet you hadn't thought of it that way, had you? You and Saul – I could see from your face you were up in the air about him early yesterday, then pacing about half the night, and now you look like someone's slapped you with a herring. Why can't you just get on with it? Stop waiting for everything to be so damn *perfect*. Nothing starts that way; you have to want it, make it happen.'

'Right. Compromise, then. Yes, that would work. Let me see, I'm a woman who serially picks men with background baggage, I can only get a job if I learn how to dress better, my ex-husband is telling me I have to move house . . .' Bella switched the kettle on again. Endless tea – the British way of coping with everything from a grazed knee to massacre.

'Oh Bella, do stop sounding so defeated!' Shirley sounded exasperated. 'Not compromise *at all*; the opposite. Go with your instincts and stop *analysing*. You don't seem to get it yet that time is the most precious and finite thing. Stop *wasting* it.'

'But . . .'

'No buts. You like Saul, don't you? He likes you. So what are you looking so fraught about?'

'The fact that he's married – or has been married, to *Daisy*? And didn't actually get round to mentioning it, even though they've both been here in the house for the past however many days it is now? I've just made yet another of my man mistakes. I give up.'

Shirley shrugged. 'Not necessarily a mistake. I bet you haven't asked him about her, have you? And besides – Daisy and Dominic. I already told you, any fool can see they're besotted with each other, even if neither of them have quite fathomed it out yet. Why else would he put up with her? Why else would she trail him around with her when she can quite obviously do the whole job perfectly well on her own?'

'Of course I'm going to ask him. I was giving myself some time to . . .' Bella began.

'. . . to fume and steam and get yourself into a stew imagining the worst,' Shirley interrupted. 'That's what I mean about wasting time. Even Molly's got the hang of this bit about men. She needed a push, but she's gone and sorted things out with her boyfriend. You can learn a thing or two from her.'

'Ah now, Molly – have you told her about you and Dennis getting married? I didn't say anything to her because I thought you'd probably want it to come from you.'

'No, I haven't told her yet. I didn't think it was tactful till she was a bit happier. Later today, I will. I'll bring Dennis over as well.'

'Oh good – but I hope he won't mind all the upheaval here. Daisy's decided we've got to have a party in the garden later, so we can be filmed being "natural" in our lovely made-over looks.'

'Excellent – we'll gatecrash. It'll be fun. And Bella?'

'Hmm?'

'Don't let them cut your hair too short. And don't go any blonder either. You'd look terribly harsh. Now – I know you're all wound up and probably feel as if you've swallowed a clay boulder, but you're looking peaky and I'm starving. Let's have a bacon sandwich to go with this tea.'

Yes, let's, Bella thought, switching on the grill and feeling a bit more cheerful at the thought of comfort food. And later, if it came to a tussle at the salon about her hair, she'd get the hairdresser to give Shirley a call. Even Nicky Clarke wouldn't dare cross *her*.

'And we get a cab back as well? I could get used to this!' Molly said to Bella as they went into the hairdressing salon tucked away behind the South Bank complex. Molly had been very chatty in the car, completely revived after the previous misery. She'd come flying into the house looking radiant and glossy late the previous evening, as Bella was about to go to bed.

'All on again, is it?' Bella had guessed as Molly almost skipped across the kitchen to forage in the fridge.

'Mmm. Yum. Yes – me and Giles. It's all cool. And Aimee's not pregnant. Stupid cow. She was just being jealous. You've got to feel sorry for her.'

'Have you? That's very generous.'

'Yeah, well, sad, desperate people will do anything to get what they want. But then it can all go wrong for them.'

'I think that's called karma, Moll,' Bella told her.

'Not nice, whoever you are,' Molly decided.

Molly, in her revived mood, was now loving the luxury of being driven to an area she'd normally get to by train. 'It makes me feel all celebrityish,' she said, bouncing around a bit. Well, here was one whose mood had changed overnight, Bella thought, pleased for her daughter. Lucky her, and long may her beautiful glow of happiness last.

As she went through the polished steel door into the building, Bella's butterflies returned at the thought of facing Saul and whatever it was he would be telling her about the him-and-Daisy set-up. She tried to calm her thudding heart, thinking how much she now wished that she and Saul had had a simple, explanatory phone conversation the night before instead. What was the worst he could have said? 'Daisy and I are together but . . .' But what? They had an 'open marriage'? Did people still have those? Or he could have said that they *weren't* together – in which case why had he left it till now to tell her they'd ever had a connection? If they'd talked it through hours ago, she would have had a chance of feeling calm by now. How silly of her to have put the moment off – how ridiculously *flouncy*, to use a favourite word of her mother's.

The door was still swinging shut as Saul – who must have been waiting to pounce – grabbed Bella's arm and pulled her outside to the street again. She caught sight of Molly's face smiling at her through the steel door's porthole window. Her grin was positively impish.

'You're abducting me,' Bella protested to Saul. 'I'm supposed to be having my hair and face all made over. And don't they need you in there too?'

'Yes, I'm abducting you,' he agreed, holding her hand firmly and walking fast away from the building, towards the river. 'They can start work on someone else and do you later. Not that you need it. And no, they don't need me either for an hour. I've sorted it. Come on, let's get away from here.'

Tourists thronged the South Bank; the queue for the London Eye was as long as in the holiday months of July and August, and everyone, to Bella's eyes, looked as if they were having the most enviable stress-free time, cameras clicking, the line of people moving amiably and without impatience or complaint.

'I wouldn't get to talk to you alone in there with all the others around, so this was the only solution,' Saul continued, still walking so fast Bella almost had to break into a trot to keep up. He was squeezing her hand tight, as if scared she'd run off.

A group of chattering Japanese tourists, each one pecking at a phone and oblivious to anyone in their path, separated them for a moment.

'Not that in this crowd you could really count it as "alone". Whoever said you can be more alone in a city than anywhere else had never done the South Bank on a warm autumn day. OK, come on,' he said, setting off again towards the landing stage, towing her along with him. 'I've had an idea.'

They were just in time. The safety barrier was about to go up before the ferry left. Saul quickly sidestepped the operator and he and Bella jumped on board.

'Where is this thing going?' Bella giggled as they raced through the cabin where the more cautious trippers were sitting with their guidebooks and their maps, past the bar and to a row of empty seats out in the open in the stern, like schoolchildren bagging the back seats on a bus.

'I haven't a clue,' Saul told her. 'I don't care if it's going all the way to the Thames Barrier and across to bloody France. I just wanted to get you to myself without you sliding out of range.'

'Before you start,' she interrupted, 'can I just ask the only thing I really need to know?'

He hesitated. 'I can't stop you. But I'd prefer to get everything in the right order.'

They were passing Tate Modern and then the Globe Theatre – the latter looking tiny by comparison, like something cute built for dolls. 'Wait, first I just want to know . . . are you and Daisy still married?'

'No,' he replied immediately. 'Not for a long, long time. And it wasn't really what you'd call a marriage.'

Bella bit back a very tart 'And what *would* you call it then?' and instead said carefully, 'Look, I do understand some of it, in a way. It was something my mother said about after a partner you really, truly loved has died. About how you'd want to try to have that experience again, because it had been so wonderful and you want it back. It even sort of explains Paul McCartney and Heather Mills, a bit.'

'Well, a *little* bit!' Saul laughed, and then looked more serious. 'But it wasn't like that, not even slightly. That's why I wanted you just to listen and not have me tell it all out of sequence. Daisy and I weren't married after Lucy. That's the thing. Daisy was *before* Lucy. About a hundred years ago – or that's how it feels.'

The boat, having gone under Tower Bridge and out of the Pool of London regulations, suddenly picked up speed. Jets of water, spritzed up from the engine, blew back over Bella's hair. She took no notice but felt slightly shivery from the cold spray. Saul put his arm round her and she relaxed against him, snuggling close. Because, as her mother had reminded her, *why not*?

'*Before* Lucy?' She was seriously confused now. 'How come before? And I know you don't want me interrupting, but why on earth didn't you tell me all this before? You knew from what I said about Rick that I really can't be doing with secrets and lies. An ex-wife, honestly explained, I'd have been fine with. Even Daisy.'

'*Even* Daisy?' Saul looked disbelieving.

'Yes of course, even Daisy. But go on, why didn't you tell me?'

'I didn't say anything because Daisy asked me not to. It's as simple as that. I'd promised her I wouldn't mention it to anyone on the show, way before we started the *Fashion Victims* filming.'

'But why? That's a pretty unfair demand in this case, isn't it?'

'As it turned out, yes. But then I'm not in the habit of falling for people when I'm working. Or at all. Ever. Thing is – Daisy's incredibly ambitious and clawed her way up from nowhere to get where she is now. She absolutely loathes the idea that anyone would think she was getting work on the who-you-know basis, and this is a very small industry. Everybody knows each other. Nobody trusts husband-and-wife teams – even long-divorced ones – there's always that suspicion that one of the two isn't as up to the job as a carefully chosen outsider would be. She's also incredibly private about her personal life. I mean, how much have you actually learned about her during this programme? Absolutely nothing, that's what. She keeps it all inside. I bet she gave Fliss hell when she let it slip that Daisy was her mother.'

Bella smiled. 'She wasn't exactly thrilled, that's true.' True? Daisy had looked as if she could have slapped poor Fliss at the time. 'Though if *you* hadn't already mentioned that Fliss was your stepdaughter, I still wouldn't have been any the wiser.'

'I know. Stupid of me. Fliss told me off about that later, said if Daisy knew she'd kill me. And I would have told you all this stuff after the show was finished. Of course I would – I really thought it could wait two more days. Honestly, I just went along with Daisy because that's what she and I had agreed before the start. It was stupid of me, but if I make a promise I keep it. And Daisy's not usually so communicative. By last night she was loosened up enough with everyone – and there were no crew around.'

'She was as loosened up as a newt by the time she left. And I assumed she was warning me off you. It certainly felt like it, the way she sort of *claimed* you to take her home.'

Bella watched a mother trying to restrain a pair of small boys from leaning too far over the boat's side. She and James had once spent a fraught couple of hours on a channel ferry during a rough crossing, trying to keep the overexcited Alex and Molly under control. James, ever-squeamish, had refused to go on the deck where the seasick hordes had gathered.

'So you and Daisy . . . you must have been incredibly young?' The cement block that had seemed to be lodged just above Bella's heart was now dissolving fast.

Maybe, just maybe, this could be all right. She'd see . . .

Saul took hold of her hand, twining his fingers through hers.

'Daisy and I were at school together, just friends, never dated or anything. Her background isn't anything like you'd imagine. Her mother brought her up alone after her father left. Very impoverished, devoutly Catholic and proudly keen to be seen as "respectable". A generation or two earlier, she'd have been one of those women who scrub the front steps every day so the neighbours don't accuse her of letting herself go.'

'So Daisy wasn't born to the high life of style and top-end fashion then?' Wow, Bella thought, how very much you can't tell about people. Daisy came across as pure Sloane Square, born and bred.

'Daisy? God no! She's a complete self-invention. She was always mad about clothes, always making really original ones for herself because she had no money to buy them, looking that bit different and edgy with charity-shop things she'd altered and weird furnishing fabrics off the market.'

A vision of Daisy dressed in a frock made from maroon Dralon and faded floral chintz crossed Bella's mind. She'd bet even that would have been enviably chic, damn her. A couple wearing matching cagoules, and with maps round their necks as if they were walking the Pennines, came out on to the deck and hesitated, looking at Bella and Saul. The man nodded apologetically at Bella and turned away, heading for a seat out of earshot.

'After school,' Saul continued, 'we didn't see each other for a few years. But then when I was in Los Angeles on a rock video, Daisy was there on the next lot, working as a stylist.'

'So you fell in love with the girl from back home and got married. Sweet,' Bella cut in, feeling slightly queasy, and not from the boat's movement.

'No, no, Bella.' Saul shifted so he could face her properly. 'It was nothing like that. She'd already had Fliss by then, but had split with the father after only a few months. She was about to fly back to the UK because her mother was dying. Her mother hadn't even seen the baby and she wanted to take her home, let her mum meet Fliss. But there was something else . . . her mother wasn't about to die happy if Daisy came home as a single mother. It would count as a disgrace and a huge disappointment. An on-the-spot husband wasn't really needed – the absence could be explained away somehow, but Daisy really wanted to be able to assure her she was married, give her the comfort of thinking her daughter hadn't gone completely to the bad.'

'Ah. Oh that's so sad. But why *you*? Didn't she have a boyfriend she could . . .' What was the right word here?

'Use' had been what she'd wanted to say. '. . . Persuade?'

'No – Fliss and work took all her time. It was because I was there, at the time; old friends, no emotional ties and complications – I wasn't seeing anyone. We did the ceremony a bit drunkenly at a wedding-chapel shack thing in Vegas, couple of the crew from the video were witnesses. Wham bam, certificate in hand. Job done and off she goes, back home.'

'That's one hell of a favour for a friend.' And it was. It was kind, spur-of-the-moment generous. You'd didn't, Bella reckoned, get many men like that to the kilo.

Saul said simply, 'I felt sorry for her. She was very young, very alone out there with her baby, trying to get her career off the ground in a horrible cat-eat-dog business. And besides,' he smiled rather ruefully and looked at Bella, 'Daisy has a knack of getting what she wants. It was only after the deed was done I realized how cleverly she'd let me think the solution to her dilemma was actually my idea.'

'Ha! I've noticed that. She made me try on a skirt with something called a *paper-bag waist.* And very nearly convinced me that not only did it look great but that I'd picked it out myself.'

'There is one thing she's making no headway with, though . . .'

'Dominic?' Bella guessed.

'That's the one. They've been circling each other for

months. Somehow they just can't quite cross that gap.'

'Maybe . . .' Bella began tentatively, 'maybe it's to do with Dominic knowing she keeps work separate from the personal?'

'Partly. But I also think that besotted as he is, he's also pretty damn scared of her.'

'Wise man,' Bella agreed, as the boat pulled up at the O2 arena and all passengers except the two of them queued to get off. 'We *Victims* know exactly how he feels.'

'So where've *you* been?' Back at the salon Jules was waiting to grab Bella the moment Saul left her side to talk to the director. 'Daisy's not here either, just Dominic. He and Henri the hair man are going *mad*!'

'Were we that long?' Bella asked, running her fingers through the still-wet ends of her hair. She must look a complete fright. If Charlotte had seen her right now there was no way she'd have given her any kind of job where she'd have to go out in public. 'Surely not everyone's been done yet, have they?'

'No they haven't, just Molly and me so far. You didn't even notice my new look, did you? World of your own . . .' Jules shook her newly cut hair, which had been given an even wilder array of scarlet and pink streaks. 'Don't you think I look like Zandra Rhodes?'

'It looks fantastic, Jules – love the pink bits. I hope I

get something that's as good. If Henri's cross, he might take it out on me.'

'Ha!' Jules snorted. 'By the look of you, you won't care if he shaves off every last bit. I take it,' her voice went down to loud-whisper level, *'all is well?'*

'All is *very* well, thanks.' Bella's smile was uncontrollable. She was going to look manic on camera, all teeth and wildly glittery eyes.

'Ugh!' Jules wrinkled her nose in disgust. 'There's nothing worse than being shut in a room with the newly loved-up. Come on, you can tell me all later – let's see what they're doing with Dina. I hear *raised voices*.'

Dina was putting up resistance. The words 'crowning glory' were uttered (by her), countered by 'frizzy horror-show bird's nest' from Henri the stylist. Dominic glared silently at the pair of them and the camera rolled.

'Really long hair is a symbol of clinging to your youthful glory days,' Henri was saying. 'The youth and the glory are long gone and frankly, past the age of thirty-five, hair this long simply smacks of desperation and immaturity.'

'I like Dina's hair long,' Bella challenged him, feeling Dina was being unfairly picked on here. 'It's part of who she is. She's not representing "a woman of her age", she's just *her*. That's her style.'

A salon junior approached Bella with a gown,

wrapped her in it and led her away to the basins. Bella hung back, wanting to hear the argument, but was pushed firmly down into a squashy leather chair and her head was painfully rammed against the sink's edge.

'Something feathered, short, almost *gamine* . . .' was being said as Henri ignored Dina's opinion and, out of the corner of her eye, Bella could see him running a finger and thumb over Dina's tresses, checking the texture.

*'Gamine?'* Dina's voice covered at least two octaves. 'I'm pushing fifty, for heaven's sake! I thought you said I wasn't to cling to my youth? Just chop a few inches off the stuff and stop thinking Audrey Hepburn!'

Henri gave in, but on one condition. 'In that case we'll be giving you an up-do,' he told her in a tone that made it clear he would stand for no argument on this. 'I want you to see how you look with the bulk of your hair above your shoulders rather than below. Deal?'

'Deal.' Dina grinned at him through the mirror. 'I win!' she called across to Bella, then her eyes in the mirror widened with horror. 'Sheesh, will you look at Daisy!'

Daisy crept into the salon, sliding through the barely open door like a cat that had been missing for days. She looked . . . well, the word *scarecrow* came to mind. How many chunky beaded bangles, Bella wondered, as the girl vigorously scrubbed shampoo into her scalp, could a pair of skinny arms take? How many multicoloured, beaded, gilded and feathered layers could even a thin little waif like Daisy pile on before looking as if they were forced to wear their entire wardrobe because they were about to go and live on the streets? She had the big sunglasses on again and the high, cream open-toed boots over turquoise tights. Bella, craning her head as far as she could, saw Dominic take one look at her and actually step back till he crashed into the wall mirror and knocked over a banana plant. Saul halted the filming and told Fliss to get Daisy some strong coffee.

'He looks terrified.' Molly tiptoed up and sat beside her mother.

'I'm not surprised,' Bella whispered. 'She looks awful. All wild. Ill, even.' The girl slip-slapped conditioner over her head and started the slow scalp massage she'd been taught. 'So, have you got any plans for Christmas?' she asked.

'What's wrong with you? You look like shit.' Possibly only someone who'd once been your husband, however brief and unconsummated the marriage, could have got away with talking to a woman like that.

Saul and Bella – her wet hair wrapped in a towel – took Daisy and her coffee outside to a little palm-planted courtyard at the back of the salon, so that filming could continue with her well out of sight.

'Hangover,' Daisy muttered. Her eyes were still hidden behind the glasses. Bella guessed that the words 'piss-holes' and 'snow' wouldn't have been inappropriate if they were on view.

'But you didn't have that much, did you? You weren't *that* bad,' Saul said.

'Not then. Later – at home. My life's *crap*.' From under the sunglasses, fat crystal tears ran down Daisy's pale face and dropped on to her furry orange shrug.

'Er . . . shall I, um, more coffee . . .' Saul was getting up, making an escape.

'Coward!' Bella whispered to him; Daisy, after all, was *his* friend, not really hers.

'It's just . . . she might talk to you. Woman stuff?' he murmured back, his mouth tinglingly close to her ear. She watched him walk away, back to work, looking back at her from the doorway, smiling.

Bella unwrapped the towel from her head and handed it to Daisy. 'Sorry, I haven't got any tissues. This will have to do,' she said, smoothing down her damp, mussed-up hair and feeling thankful the warm sun was shining on her. A cold winter day, and Daisy would have been out here alone, no question.

'Thanks,' Daisy said, dabbing at her face and poking the towel ends under her glasses to mop new tears. 'You should go inside; your hair's all wet – you'll catch your death.'

'My mum used to say that.' Shirley probably still did, now she thought about it.

'Mine too,' Daisy sobbed into the towel. 'Oh I'm sorry Bella, I'm not really like this.'

'I know. What started it off?'

The door opened and Molly brought two more cups of coffee and some ginger biscuits, then swiftly went back inside. She had the distinctly nervy look of someone who'd picked the short straw for this little mission.

Daisy gave a big sniff and took off her sunglasses, fixing Bella with a watery stare through eyes that had been too thoroughly made up with shades of green and purple shadow, most of which was now halfway down her face. She looked like an advert designed to shock, offering refuge from domestic violence.

'*You* started it off, actually,' Daisy said. 'You and bloody Saul. So obviously so *bloody* . . . happy.'

Bella thought back to the day before, most of which had been taken up with the two of them *not* being happy.

'But . . . we . . . weren't. Then.' She couldn't deny it about *now*, though.

'Oh I knew, the moment I got to your place in the morning.'

'Right. And you mind that . . . because?'

'Because I'm *not*!' Daisy's voice was a childlike, petulant squeak.

'You're in love with *Saul*?' Bella was confused now.

'No! Don't be ridiculous. With . . . someone else. Who doesn't give a flying one about me.'

'Dominic,' Bella said.

'Did I say Dominic?' Daisy was defensive. 'I did *not* say that name.' Her huge eyes started overflowing again. 'He wouldn't take me to the launch last night. I think he thought I'd look all out of place or something. I mean, *me*! I *am* style!'

'Hmm, sometimes you are. But maybe sometimes you're just a bit too . . .' Bella struggled for words.

'Too *what*? Too distracting? Too stunning? Too . . .'

'Theatrical?' Bella supplied for her.

'And what's wrong with that? How else does someone of five foot three and a small frame get themselves *noticed*?'

'Nothing's wrong . . . except, well do you need to be centre stage the *whole time*? But hey, what do I know. You're the stylist, you tell me.' Bella looked at her, taking in the strange collection of flung-on clothing that Daisy was wearing.

'Yes . . . I think I do need to be central.' Daisy sounded subdued now. 'I know he likes me. Usually we do everything together. It's just . . . we never get any *further*. And now I think we never will. It's like he just can't let himself get nearer. It's like, however obvious I am, he doesn't seem to *see* me.'

'Hey, I've just thought of something.' Bella could feel a small plan forming. 'You won't like it but you have to promise to go along with it when we get back to the house after this. OK?'

Daisy sighed and dunked a biscuit into her coffee, not seeming to notice that drips of it fell on to her silver skirt.

'All right. I promise,' she said sulkily. 'Whatever it takes, so long as you don't go running to Dom and telling him all this.'

'Of course I won't,' Bella assured her. 'Just go home for a couple of hours, get some sleep.'

'I will, or I'll look crap later for the wrap party. But it won't make a difference, you know, whatever you've got in mind.' Daisy mopped the last of her tears, blew her nose noisily and handed the towel back to Bella.

'Oh thanks,' Bella said, feeling an unusual moment of empathy with James as she held the towel by one far corner. 'And Daisy, just – don't be so *defeatist*.'

Ye gods, she thought, I've turned into my mother.

# SEVENTEEN

'Softer. I think that's the key. What do you lot reckon to this one? When we've got the dress right we can add accessories, but not too many. Keep it minimal.' In the wardrobe truck, Bella held up a dress that was the same lavender shade as the huge, mad sofa in her kitchen. It wouldn't matter – Daisy wouldn't vanish into the scenery, colour-wise, as they'd all be in the garden when the cameras were on her. The dress was Vivienne Westwood, all sharp tailoring and unexpected fabric twists, but it was plain. Chic. Grown-up but edgy just the same.

'*One* colour? And *minimal*?' Jules commented. 'This *is* Daisy we're kitting out, isn't it? She's not going to want something as classily plain as that.'

'But this time it's not about what she wants,' Dina told her. 'It's about what will make her look good enough for

Dominic not to be so terrified of her and all that clutter she decks herself in. Bella's right – she's been dressing herself in a kind of barricade. I love this dress, Bella. Well, who wouldn't?' she sighed, holding the dress against her and looking at herself in the mirror. Quite a lot of Dina could still be seen each side of the garment.

'She's so *petite*,' she went on, 'I bet Daisy will never go on a date that turns into a real promise and then spend twenty minutes in the loo, biting the label out of her knickers so he doesn't get to see they're size XL.'

Bella, Jules and Molly turned to look at her. 'Dina?' Bella spluttered. '*You've* done that?' Oh Lordy, she thought . . . surely not . . . James?

Dina smiled and blushed. 'I have. And I wish I hadn't said it now. It's this sodding programme – taking your clothes on and off in front of people makes you go all *revelatory*. I can't wait to get back to normal because I don't do that sort of thing. I like to keep the edges of my life clean and neat, like my flat. Telling is messy.'

'Never mind messy!' Jules squeaked. 'Who was the man? Was it . . . ?' She glanced at Molly, who was now flicking through a rack of belts. 'No . . .' Jules shook her pink-streaked head. 'Don't tell us. Scrub that.'

'It wasn't . . . who you're thinking of.' Dina's blush deepened. 'It was ages ago. Er . . . shall we find Daisy some shoes?' She laughed wickedly. 'Nice sensible flat ones? Lace-ups?'

* * *

While the four victims were being given a make-up retouch and zipped into their favourite clothes choices, Mandy and her assistant from the catering truck whizzed together plenty of party food in record time. Nick hung Bella's fairy lights in the trees and magically conjured up plenty of champagne, all the bottles crammed in ice in big plastic storage boxes borrowed from Wardrobe.

'Now, I don't know if Saul's told you, but we're absolutely *not* rounding off with one of those embarrassing scenes where the new versions of *you* are suddenly revealed to your gob-smacked, weeping families,' Daisy told them in a kind of end-of-term talk. 'That's just too cheesy and excruciating and nobody knows quite what to do or how to behave. Not to mention it's rarely done in one take, and even the most gifted amateurs can't keep faking the frankly insulting level of awe and amazement that seems to be required. So,' she said, 'you lot will be wearing your final choices and simply all mingle around being party-chatty, keeping it low key and normal and natural as if the cameras weren't here. You've all done brilliantly so far, so I can't see this being a problem.'

'I never would have thought this could work on me. I really did think I'd look all vast and chunky but I don't,' Bella said to Jules, as Daisy tweaked at the paper-bag-waisted skirt she was now wearing. 'I love it.' And so, later, would Charlotte. If this outfit didn't impress her into giving Bella the skincare job, then nothing would.

'Fess up now, Bella; you didn't trust me from day one, did you?' Daisy said, rejecting a gold bangle and replacing it with a silver one – broad links, interspersed with filigree hearts.

'No I didn't, to be honest. Not since the big orange coat,' Bella admitted. 'But you really know what you're doing. And I *love* these shoes. They remind me of dance classes when I was young.'

'They're by Tracey Neuls, darling. Canadian designer. Two-tone with a spotted heel and sole isn't for everyone, but you can carry it off,' Daisy said approvingly. 'Because with shoes like these, you need to wear bold-coloured tights, to draw attention down to floor level. That means confidence about your lower leg. Yours are reasonable.'

'Ha! Damned with Daisy's typically faint praise!' Jules said, flicking at the chiffon sleeve of her drifty ginger-coloured top, a choice that not many would immediately pick for a woman with pink and red hair, but which somehow worked. 'Now, do we look OK? Are we about to join the throng? I'm desperate for a glass of bubbles.'

'Soon.' Bella looked at her. 'We've got the *other thing* to do first . . .'

'You look fantastic.' Daisy stood back and surveyed her charges. 'And all thanks to amazing me!'

'And Dominic,' Dina reminded her, stroking the silky velvet pile of her drapy crimson Lilith dress.

'And us?' Molly ventured. 'Weren't we pretty good too?'

'Stars, darlings, absolute stars,' Daisy conceded, for once managing to smile in a very non-vampire way.

'OK then, Daisy,' Bella said. 'Before we get any further . . . you've got to come with us.'

The victims surrounded her before she could protest and almost frogmarched her out to the wardrobe truck.

'Bella has a plan for you,' Dina told her. 'And it will work. You've had it all your own way with us . . . now it's our turn.'

It was like needing to keep touching a special favour for luck. Bella and Saul obviously couldn't do what their perfect personal choice would have been and either stay inextricably entwined together for the evening or vanish entirely to be alone somewhere, but as the early-evening celebration went by, they kept drifting back to each other just to hold hands for a few seconds, to kiss in the hallway out of sight of the cameras, to exchange smiles over groups of people. Jules's husband and one of her sons had turned up along with Carly, and Molly and Giles had to be asked more than once not to be so thoroughly draped over each other that the camera couldn't get a view of Molly's gorgeous pink and purple Barbara Hulanicki frock. Charlotte arrived and greeted Bella with slightly insulting incredulity. 'Darling! You *have* scrubbed up gorgeously! Whoever would have imagined it!'

'Thanks Charlotte, and yes – who would imagine I could actually look almost passable?'

'Absolutely!' Charlotte agreed, leaving Bella almost breathless at her lack of tact. The job as skincare correspondent, though, that was now hers. That was the important bit. Ordeal by egg-shaped clothes and pegtop trousers and jeggings and paper bags had been worth it, career-wise.

'You have binned your ballet-wrap cardigans, haven't you?' Charlotte had one last moment of anxiety as she confirmed the job was Bella's.

'All in the charity bag,' Bella lied, for – after all – off duty she would wear what she damn well wanted, thank you.

'Thank *you*,' Daisy, in the Vivienne Westwood, pink lacy tights and only one simple necklace, whispered to Bella. 'Dom's asked me out for dinner after this. He keeps touching my hair. Does it look as if it's unreal or something?' Looking slightly bemused, she ran her fingers through the softly curled ends.

'No – it just looks . . . touchable.' Bella assured her.

Simone had also – under Bella's instructions – done Daisy's make-up with unaccustomed subtlety. One squeak of protest from Daisy and Bella had reminded her that it wasn't about *her*. It was about looking approachable, a bit vulnerable. It seemed to be working.

James left Dina's side for a quiet word with Bella by the plum tree. 'Found the perfect woman,' he told her. 'You should see the inside of her fridge.'

Bella, on the far side of a couple of glasses of champagne, giggled. 'James, that sounds like a filthy euphemism!' she spluttered.

'Filthy?' James laughed. 'Dina and I would never entertain *filth*!'

'No of course not, only joking! Look, I've got all those documents sorted for you in the house if you want to take them away with you later.'

'Right . . . er, thanks, Bella. Kind of you. But, well maybe I was rowing the boat a bit too fast here. Shall we . . . um, just forget about it for now? I've rather got other things on my mind. Don't want mental clutter, frankly, one only has so much mental bandwidth. No rush.'

'Oh – well all right then. Another time, I guess.'

'Quite. When we're both a bit less . . . preoccupied, we can talk, diarize a meet.'

'*Diarize?*' Oh James – you really are a whole language away from the rest of us!'

And maybe the time was approaching, she suddenly

thought as she looked back at the brightly lit massive kitchen, all open to the garden, when she really could be thinking of moving on from here. In some ways he'd been right; not about the bungalow thing or living somewhere with space for a stairlift, but this place really would be far too big when Alex and Molly weren't in it. And besides . . . something more central had an enormous appeal. The owner of the 'something more central' was watching her from beside the house. How hard was it not to run (in her funny spotty-heeled shoes) across the lawn to hug him once again?

'Gran's here!' Molly called. 'Come and see who she's brought! She's getting *married*!'

'Oh my God – who is *this*?' Daisy's voice rang out over the party chatter. She was gazing at Shirley, who had just arrived with Dennis.

'That lady,' Bella told her as she went to greet Shirley, 'is my mother.'

'Your *mother*? You two have the same *genes*?'

'Oh Daisy! You are such a perfect bitch!' Saul laughed.

Daisy took no notice but almost fell on Shirley before Bella could get near her.

'You look *amazing*!' she told Shirley. 'Burberry Prorsum, am I right? Yes I am. That collar line with the over-pleats: *so* distinctive. Do you always dress so brilliantly? And that skirt – vintage Chanel?'

'New Look, actually. About twenty-five pounds,' Shirley told her, trying to sidestep her and get to Bella.

'Genius!' Daisy sighed happily. 'At last, another woman who can combine designer with high street. Oh, if they all could . . .'

'If they all could do that, you'd be out of a job, sweetie. Never forget that,' Saul reminded her.

'Mum, I'm so glad you could get here.' Bella hugged Shirley and handed her and Dennis a glass of champagne each.

'Bella, Molly, darlings,' Shirley was looking slightly nervous, 'this is Dennis.'

'So lovely to meet you at last,' Dennis said, kissing Bella first, then Molly.

'Dennis – welcome!' Bella said. 'And congratulations! I just know Mum is going to be so happy with you.'

'I think it's great too,' Molly said. 'But *please* don't make me be a pink satin bridesmaid, will you?'

'Oh gosh, are you two getting married?' Daisy's eyes became suspiciously glittery. Possibly only Bella was not surprised by this.

'How wonderful!' Daisy went on. 'Now tell me, because there is surely no more important aspect: *what are you going to wear?*'

# Just for the Summer

## Judy Astley

'Oh, what a find! A lovely, funny book'
Sarah Harrison

Every July, the lucky owners of Cornish holiday homes set off for their annual break. Loading their estate cars with dogs, cats, casefuls of wine, difficult adolescents and rebellious toddlers, they close up their desirable semis in smartish London suburbs – having turned off the Aga and turned on the burglar alarm – and look forward to a carefree, restful, somehow more fulfilling summer.

Clare is, this year, more than usually ready for her holiday. Her teenage daughter, Miranda, has been behaving strangely; her husband, Jack, is harbouring unsettling thoughts of a change in lifestyle; her small children are being particularly tiresome; and she herself is contemplating a bit of extra-marital adventure, possibly with Eliot, the successful – although undeniably heavy-drinking and overweight – author in the adjoining holiday property. Meanwhile Andrew, the only son of elderly parents, is determined that this will be the summer when he will seduce Jessica, Eliot's nubile daughter. But Jessica spends her time in girl-talk with Miranda, while Milo, her handsome brother with whom Andrew longs to be friends, seems more interested in going sailing with the young blonde son of the club commodore.

Unexpected disasters occur, revelations are made and, as the summer ends, real life will never be quite the same again.

'A sharp social comedy . . . sails along very nicely and fulfils its early promise'
John Mortimer, *Mail on Sunday*

'Wickedly funny . . . a thoroughly entertaining romp'
Val Hennessy, *Daily Mail*

9780552995641

## Size Matters

### Judy Astley

---

Big and beautiful? Or thin and miserable?

Jay has always envied her cousin Delphine. While Jay was brought up in a large, noisy and chaotic family, Delphine was indulged, perfectly dressed with a co-ordinated bedroom, an immaculate wardrobe, dancing lessons and monogrammed silver-backed hairbrushes. Now Jay lives happily with her architect husband and their three teenage children, running a successful cleaning company and trying to keep some kind of order on her disorderly household, while Delphine has long since disappeared to Australia with her second husband. But Jay does sometimes wonder whether she should be more like her cousin – utterly well-organized and with a size ten figure.

So Jay decides to diet. But what should it be? High carb, no protein? High protein, no carb? High fibre? Wheat free? Fat free? Food free? She tries them all, with a variety of successes and failures. But then Delphine reappears, with a third husband in prospect and the same old air of apparently effortless superiority. Jay never considers that perhaps Delphine is the envious one . . .

'As irresistible as triple choc fudge cake – with extra cream'
*Mail on Sunday*

9780552771856

## Blowing It

### Judy Astley

---

**Sorrel** is about to go off on her Gap Year. She *sooo* wants a home to come home to.

**Ilex**, her brother, is trying to upgrade his flat and marry his smart girlfriend Manda. He'd like some immediate equity.

**Clover**, the elder sister, has plans that involve a bijou second home in France. And she wants it *now*.

If only their parents would be *sensible*. If only they would sell their large, rather grand but somewhat dilapidated home and hand over their inheritance. But parents aren't always as sensible as their children. They are planning on blowing the lot . . .

9780552773201

## Laying the Ghost

### Judy Astley

---

Have you ever wondered what your ex is up to?

When Nell was a student, she and Patrick were a serious item. Nell really thought Patrick was The One, despite their often tempestuous relationship. But then Alex came along. He seemed the safer, more restful option, and thanks to her over-controlling mother she opted for him instead.

Now nothing is going right. Alex has left her to live in New York with a younger, blonder woman. Escaping to the Caribbean for a recuperative holiday, she is mugged at Gatwick and her bag is stolen. It's crisis time – and she makes two decisions:

First – she will take lessons in self-defence.
Second – she will try and find Patrick again.

Is she trying to put the past behind her – or setting out to ruin her future?

'Warm, funny and unnervingly true to life'
Katie Fforde

9780552773218

## Other People's Husbands

### Judy Astley

---

When Sara, as an art student, first met Conrad he seemed like the most glamorous man in the world. Already a famous painter, he was the sexiest thing she'd ever met. Her mother told her that she shouldn't marry him – that the twenty-five-year age gap would tell in the end – and the end is now (apparently) approaching fast. Conrad has decided that it would be good to die before he gets seriously old, and has started behaving very strangely.

Sara, meanwhile, teaching art at a local college, is not short of younger male company – other people's husbands, ones she tells Conrad all about, who are just good friends. But there's one she somehow doesn't get round to mentioning . . .

9780552774642